The Corleone Christ

To John, with thanks
Many thanks for
reading for me.
GJMann

The Corleone Christ

G J MANN

Copyright © 2025 G J Mann

The moral right of the author has been asserted.

Apart from any fair dealing for the purposes of research or private study, or criticism or review, as permitted under the Copyright, Designs and Patents Act 1988, this publication may only be reproduced, stored or transmitted, in any form or by any means, with the prior permission in writing of the publishers, or in the case of reprographic reproduction in accordance with the terms of licences issued by the Copyright Licensing Agency. Enquiries concerning reproduction outside those terms should be sent to the publishers.

The manufacturer's authorised representative in the EU for product safety is Authorised Rep Compliance Ltd, 71 Lower Baggot Street, Dublin D02 P593 Ireland (www.arccompliance.com)

This is a work of fiction. All characters, organisations, and events in this publication, other than those clearly in the public domain, are fictitious and any resemblance to real persons, living or dead, is purely coincidental.

Copyright: Book cover and inner sleeve images are created and owned by Freda Rose.

Troubador Publishing Ltd
Unit E2 Airfield Business Park,
Harrison Road, Market Harborough,
Leicestershire LE16 7UL
Tel: 0116 279 2299
Email: books@troubador.co.uk
Web: www.troubador.co.uk

ISBN 978 1836281 207

British Library Cataloguing in Publication Data.
A catalogue record for this book is available from the British Library.

Printed and bound by CPI Group (UK) Ltd, Croydon, CR0 4YY
Typeset in 11pt Minion Pro by Troubador Publishing Ltd, Leicester, UK

This book is dedicated to my family. Firstly, my wife, who has supported my trying to learn the craft of writing, with love and sound sense. Secondly, our three children who provided various kinds of support. Lastly, to my grandchildren. I hope they might one day see that Pops gave some thought to who we have been in the past and, the kind of humans we need to evolve to become, taking urgent action together to safeguard ourselves and our children: plus, all other species and our habitats, to cool and sustain our magical planet.

THANKS, AND ACKNOWLEDGMENTS

I want to thank Thea at Jericho Writers who took on the task of matching 'The Corleone Christ' manuscript with a superb editor. Dexter Petley, a published author, took on the task of assessing and editing. Dexter's very candid and professional work on this book taught me so much, providing me with some of the tools and advice I needed to bring the work to a conclusion.

I would also thank two other authors, John Lynch and A.A Abbott. Both, kindly undertook the task of reading what I thought was a final draft. They delivered helpful, no-nonsense, suggestions which helped a great deal, to go another extra mile.

I must also thank a group of friends and contacts who agreed to read for me. Oftentimes they have offered key perspectives and feedback that brought about significant changes.

AUTHOR'S NOTE

Along the way there have been those who have asked me, 'Why this book, focussing on this particular subject!?' Others asked, 'Is this really a story for you to tell?'

My answer is that this story originally came to my attention, as a British born citizen in 2008. Two Prime Ministers, one in Australia and the other in Canada, gave apologies to their Parliaments and First Nation peoples for their governmental Policies of compulsory removal of indigenous children from their parents, families, and their own nations. Independent Reports investigating these systems of compulsory child removal into destructive assimilation, were described as cultural genocides. New Zealand has recently come through a detailed investigation process into their own State and non-State Faith based systems of destructive child removal, incarceration, sexual and physical abuse of indigenous children. The facts and the narratives have been established through a Royal Commission Report, July 24. In this report the story of New Zealand's treatment of indigenous children, includes children being found in unmarked graves. ('Abuse In Care' Royal Comission Inquiry Executive Summary; Para: 7.)

During these reported investigations, these three territories were, and still remain, British Constitutional Monarchies. Queen Elizabeth 11 had been one of the Heads of State during this time, until her death. King Charles 111 has now taken over this role.

In my own professional background, I worked on behalf of children who had experienced family break down and often found themselves in care; most of these children were not only disturbed, unhappy, and broken by what had happened in their family lives; also, they had been damaged and abused within their relationships in the Residential Care Home institutions themselves.

So, I was shocked to learn that Canada, Australia and New Zealand had been purposefully enacting Nationally agreed policies and laws, to intentionally dominate, subjugate, discriminate, and destroy First Nation children's memories, their families, their cultural histories, and their relationships to their own discovered lands.

In 2021 a second Canadian, Prime Ministerial apology came after unmarked graves of children were found in Catholic run, Residential Boarding Schools; children had died during long, forced separation from their families in a Policy of assimilation

After Pope Francis and the Archbishop of Canterbury, Justin Welby had visited Canada, the Vatican announced a 'repudiation' of the evil, Catholic, 'Doctrine of Discovery,' March 30, 2023. The 'repudiation' made it clear that the Catholic Church was formally withdrawing itself from being a party to the use of the 'Doctrine', in the continued abuse of First Nation peoples, human rights.

Further research told me that the USA also had also adopted a national policy of domination, subjugation, and assimilation of many thousands of First Nation children between 1860 – 1978 under the motto, 'Kill the Indian, Save the man'. Recently, a first stage National investigation into their own Residential Boarding Schools system, conducted by the U.S. Federal Government, concluded identifying similar outcomes of gross child abuses, including children who died in the schools, having been buried in unmarked and marked graves.

I was struck by the common themes, policies, and practices of abuse in all four ex British Empire and colonial territories: these policies were operational before, and right throughout, the modern post Second World War era. It is hard to believe that these almost identical policies, laws and practices including, child theft, child abuse, child assimilation, and cultural genocides, were not known about at the highest echelons of British society.

Having undertaken the research, I therefore decided to try and take responsibility, as a British citizen,' in authoring this novel.

I have set this story in the USA because amongst the four ex colonial territories mentioned above, the USA has been the one nation which historically drafted and adopted a legal, Christian/theological justification for denying its First Nation people's ownership and governance over the land they themselves discovered, thousands of years ago. At the heart of this law, still in place today, sits the Catholic Doctrine of Discovery; in some of the academic literature, it is referred to as the 'American Doctrine of Discovery'. President Biden's recent apology, Arizona, October 25, 2024, neither gives reference to, nor addresses, the source of the repudiated and historic Christian ideology that fuelled the Federal Governments and the faith-based Boarding School culture of domination, subjugation, and brutality to Indian Nations and their children.

The withdrawal of Papal approval by the Catholic Church, to support any theological, legal precedence written into the 'American Doctrine of Discovery', must surely, now have profound legal consequences. These ex-colonial territories, who have all justified their historic domination, subjugation and brutality of First Nation peoples on the supremacy of Christian theology, no longer have any legal basis through which they can continue to do so. Surely, these ex-colonial Nations, their politicians and their Church leaderships must be called upon to accept the fact that there never was any basis for believing that the teachings of Jesus Christ would, in any way, have approved of the Catholic 'Doctrine of Discovery', or their worldwide domination and subjugation of First Nation peoples who had, like them, discovered and owned their own land.

GJ Mann

When Jesus Christ came upon the Earth, you killed Him. The Son of your own God. And only when He was dead did you worship Him and start killing those who would not.'
Tecumseh. Shawnee Chief and Warrior. 1768 – 1813[1]

We grant you by these present documents, with our Apostolic Authority, full and free permission to invade, search out, capture, and subjugate the Saracens and pagans and any other unbelievers and enemies of Christ wherever they may be, as well as their kingdoms, duchies, counties, principalities and other property . and to reduce their persons into perpetual servitude.'
Dum Diversus, Papal Bull, 1452. Pope Nicholas V.[2]

Day 1

The Festival of the Earth Day
Washington DC

Saturday
November 2

One Mother, One Father

'We've spoken to your shaman
On the winds and grassy plains
In the outback sounds of walkabout,
On the crowded streets and trains.
We've spoken in your synagogues,
In your temples and your church
We've spoken in your ashrams,
On the seas and in your mosque.
We've spoken to your homeless,
To your broken and bereaved,
To your Presidents and Prime Ministers
Their promise out of reach.
Yet still you want to possess us,
Own your path to God as might,
Arm yourselves with weapons,
Then kill and maim and fight.

You all came out of Africa,
Single creature, single habit,
Forget your tribal scriptures,
Unite for your Mother Planet!!'
Crossing the Red Sea
A Creation Anthology.

                                       Isaac Lightfoot, 1997

John Green's habit was to arrive at his office at 935 Pennsylvania Avenue early each day. But on this particular morning it was 7.00 a.m. and he had been delayed.

He looked very different in these troubled times. Like some reptiles, who regularly shed their skins, John had revealed the next shiny layer of his evolution. He had left his old 'skin' behind, shrivelled and abandoned beside a desert rock, sizzling in the midday sun.

So, today, John's 'skin' looked sharp and businesslike. His hair was well-trimmed, and his face was close-shaven. He wore a grey suit, black shoes, a white shirt with a blue tie. The icing on this image was a briefcase swinging from his right hand.

In a previous lifetime John had worked as an undercover cop. Then, he had been disguised in the role of a blind beggar on the streets of Chicago. He had worn unwashed torn jeans and leather walking boots. A grey hooded jacket kept the winter weather out, while 'begging' on the streets. John's hair was thick, brown and shoulder length. He was unshaven and wore dark glasses. In his lefthand he carried a white stick as he tapped his way carefully along the street.

In those days, there was little, long arm support from the City Police Department. Others taking on this role had either been outed, beaten or shot at. Some had died in the line of duty, while John still lived to tell the tale.

During all his periods of metamorphosis, the bedrock of John's personality was one of ruthless ambition. Today, just thirty-five years of age, he was a nationwide Executive Officer within the FBI.

2

Today was a big day in Washington DC history. The city was hosting an American Continental Climate Change event, led by the International Festival of the Earth; thousands of people would process toward the Lincoln Memorial, pressing governments for more urgent action to cool the planet.

Making his way to the office, John was thinking back a few days to a high-level citywide briefing for senior leaders of public services.

John remembered a conversation with the Deputy Leader of the U.S. Fire Administration in a coffee break; this private moment filled gaps of John's ignorance about what this new international climate organisation was all about.

He started by asking his colleague a few simple questions.

"Who are the 'International Festival of the Earth' anyway?"

The senior firefighter squinted at John's profile against the autumnal sunlight, as it shone into the walled garden of the Conference Centre they were attending. He took out an old-fashioned silver cigarette lighter with one hand, while placing a cigarette into his mouth with the other. Then, cupping his palm to shelter the flame from the breeze, he lit the tip.

"Well, John they have raced onto the scene by creating one global voice on climate change. The way I heard it, the small, individual organisations all voted to create the power they considered they needed; the lack of worldwide progress to reduce emissions had taught them a step change was needed."

"So, what do they do?"

"I'm told they live day in, day out, telling politicians, the press and human communities all over the world about what has, and hasn't, been achieved to 'heal the planet.'"

"So, that's a big job, right? How do they do that?"

"They have a Festival Board, one on each Continent. They're monitoring the global temperatures; still needs to be held steady at 1.5 degrees. Right now, it ain't happening; some say we could be heading for double that; so now the International Festival Board and the United Nations are determined, that every continent must leave their carbon in the ground and under the sea floor. A lot of people ain't happy about that, John."

John found himself just soaking up information.

"So, what are they saying right now?"

"If you listen to them right now, we're all on the road to Hell in a handcart, and pretty damn soon. You must know, John, people are dying all over the world; it's *fire and flood*; already it looks more and more like a Biblical catastrophe."

John responded, showing the very little he knew.

"Well, all I'm interested in is getting through this day of protest with high level of security, taking down any psycho's and hoping we'll get through it all without too many body bags."

The Deputy Leader looked John in the eye; he took half a step back, looked down at the ground, then diplomatically shook his head.

"John, I've professionally mopped up after these ancient enemies of *'fire' and 'flood'*, all my professional life; I've seen images you wouldn't believe; I've felt the grief of people losing their folks to drowning or burning. Even now I wake up, screaming and sweating on the nightmares. So, believe me, my heart and soul has listened, I've heard what the 'Festival' are saying. They're speaking truth to power, John."

The Deputy Leader stubbed out his cigarette under foot, then expelled what little smoke was left in his lungs.

"I'm sorry, John. You asked the question. I suggest you do some simple research, take time out. I suggest you start with YouTube. Look at some video footage of recorded climate change events this year. I'd say, don't just think about people; think about all the critters out there, their habitats, their families, all of them getting destroyed. Watching those video's will get your mind, body and soul to first base; afterwards, you and me, we can meet up, discuss some more questions."

As they were called back to their briefing, John thanked the Deputy Leader for his thoughts.

"Thank you for taking time with me. I owe you. I just needed to get the basics under my belt."

3

Arriving at his Pennsylvania Avenue office, John Green was heading into a meeting he had insisted on. He wanted to assure himself that the citywide, joint arrangements for security during the International Festival of the Earth Day, would do a good job. The main question he had was, did they understand their task?

Passing through the office doors, John made his way to a glass-fronted breakout room. He was meeting Phoenix Shultz, his Deputy, and her three Team Leaders, Jim Coogan, Charlotte Linklater and Jason Colbeck.

John's purpose was to eyeball everyone in the same room. He needed to be certain they'd all been hearing the same message.

On his appointment two years ago, John had insisted that he choose his own Deputy. Together with HR, he appointed Phoenix Shultz. She was young, strong, and dynamic; she was an African American woman with a huge potential. Not only was Phoenix a powerful, intelligent investigator, she backed up her instinctive practice with academic learning.

Since that time, they'd both been joined at the hip.

Both had put their shoulders to the wheel and restructured the service. They had cut out pretty much all of the dead wood. The branches they pruned were mostly those men, who were too long in the tooth; people who needed to pick up their pensions, rather than draw down their pay checks.

Together, both new brooms had decided the shape of service they wanted to create. Finally, they'd made it fit for purpose.

In their close working relationship, John had come to appreciate how important Phoenix's family was to her. She and her husband, Trent; they made an interesting combination. She was an extremely ambitious law enforcement officer and Trent was becoming a well-known, controversial portrait artist.

John, however, had only shared the minimum. He'd talked briefly about his wife Kay, who was a practising family psychotherapist; he mentioned they had two children, Theo, ten and Ava, eight.

Going forward, John made sure no one could put a cigarette skin between him and his deputy. Any differences they came across, he insisted had to be dealt with 'in camera'. John didn't want the prying ears and eyes of neurotic staff and senior management opening the doors of corporate manipulation.

4

Beginning his meeting, John hit the bottom line hard.

He immediately put them on the spot and asked if the team leaders understood their roles. What would they be doing for the day? How would they manage an outbreak of violence? Who would they be working with? Had they read the City Police and FBI joint procedures?

Phoenix found herself reacting to John's basic questions.

"Look, John, you're gonna have to understand we've been over this now so oft…"

The team leaders remained silent.

John looked at Phoenix, then looked over to the three team leaders, standing in a line.

"Listen, Phoenix, I just want to hear it from them, that's all."

"OK, Let's just get on…"

John looked over to the team leaders and told them to get a coffee.

"Take five."

After they'd gone, John and Phoenix began to straighten things out.

"Listen, Phoenix, we've been working together for a couple of years now. Leading this service, still sometimes feels to me like I shouldn't have to continue to spoon-feed your team leaders.

These guys are senior staff, they don't need you to protect them; they need to come prepared to answer my questions.

"We agreed a data set and disciplines with the director and her board. Question is, do these guys know what they are doing or not, Phoenix? That's the first question. The second question is, are they gonna deliver? Then they must tell me *how* they will complete the task."

Phoenix looked at John and tried to respond.

"Phoenix, listen. Ninety per cent of the time you and I understand one another perfectly. We've still got another ten per cent to go before we have one hundred per cent telepathy. Today is a big operational day; everyone will be watching, especially in the White House. They're expecting a secure, well-supported event."

"John, I'm trying to tell you, your questions are too basic, you must trust me to have prepared them. That's my job; we've already done this work."

John sensed Phoenix move in her chair to make another intervention.

"You're gonna have to humour me on this one Phoenix, okay? If I can't scrutinise and be reassured by my team leaders, goddam it, I wouldn't be doing my job. God knows Anna McKenna is always in *my* face about the attorney general and what he thinks I'm doing. So, if you and I can't agree right now, I'll brief another deputy someone who'll act up for you at short notice!"

John turned his eyes away from his deputy and gazed at the wall. A silence settled in the room; for a while both continued to eyeball one another.

Then, Phoenix smiled and shrugged

"Let's go through this then, John. I agree? I can see you're needing assurance that this operation is not only safe and efficient but will deliver."

Phoenix chuckled through a bubble of tension.

"Truly, I ain't makin' this up, John, I get it! But there are times when I'd prefer robotic telepathy with you rather than this negative tension. It might just make my life at work a little less stressful. You understand me?

"The fact is we ain't robots. This is not the way I want things to work between us! By now we should be working on trust. We're better than robots, we're humans. If you asked me, John, I don't think I want you banging on in my head, one hundred per cent, twenty-four-seven! I can tell you, you wouldn't want *me* in your head on that basis!"

John broke the silence this time, laughing aloud.

"Okay! Shall we call 'em back in then?"

As all three team leaders returned, John invited them to sit at his meeting table. Sitting down with them, John reset the meeting.

"Okay, Phoenix, give us your own thoughts on the citywide joint operation for the American Continental Festival of the Earth Day, then I'll ask these guys what they know about…"

Day 1　　　　　　　　　　　　5

Thurmond
West Virginia

Saturday
November 2

Frank Denman was a 72-year-old retired man who had worked in the coal-mining industry since 1972, aged sixteen.

He was up early, breakfasted and was cleaning down his kitchen. Frank was one of just three residents left in the town of Thurmond, which had become the coal ghost town of West Virginia.

Today, Frank was expecting a visitor at around 11.00 a.m. With his breakfast detritus cleared away, he took his daily walk to a derelict railway property he had discovered some twelve months ago.

This railway property had been the yardmaster's office, once owned by the Chesapeake and Ohio Railroad empire. Twelve months earlier, climbing up the staircase, he had found a small office with a rectangular, bare brick window space; it had once been the operational hub of Thurmonds coal industry; but now, it was exposed to all weathers.

Over time, Frank had taken it upon himself to renovate the room. Amidst the dust and decay there was still a robust, wheel-backed, wooden chair, standing beside an open, roll top desk.

A wood-burning stove stood in the corner, still connected to its flue. Frank had taken it upon himself to clean out the ash and clagg, then swept the flue. Afterwards, when he tested it, he was pleased that the stove still functioned well. Next, he had a new sash window made and installed; he also bought a couple of comfortable cushions for the wheel-backs seat and a back rest.

Now, when he visited the room during these chill fall and winter months, he lit the fire. Only then, did he sit by his window. On warmer, sunny days, Frank would grasp the windows brass pull hooks in his thumbs and forefingers to lift the bottom pane open; he loved the sound of the windows lead weights, strung inside its frame, as they joggled and settled, holding the window securely open and in its place.

Then, he would sit in comfort watching the trains pulling through Thurmond without stopping. Frank loved the metallic sounds of the trains as the wagons slowed and shunted. Then, amidst the train sounds of rail clank and deep throated whistles blowing, he would watch them disappear along their journey, returning Thurmond to its deathly silence.

There were times now, in the warmth of his room, Frank imagined the yardmaster himself resting on his desk; maybe he'd have been smoking a pipe, maybe labouring over his staff schedules.

Sometimes, when looking down into 'town', Frank fancied he saw the restless souls of bankers and shopkeepers, amongst their townsfolk. Occasionally, he might imagine the yardmaster himself, with his yardworkers, waiting on the platform. When a train arrived, they would quickly decouple for the train to take on water; then recoupling, the train would pull alongside the coaling tower, to take on its next load of 'black diamonds'.

Frank imagined all of them to be living in perfect harmony.

Each day, Frank increasingly found his room a thoughtful space; one in which he slid into reviewing his past. It was there, in the hollow silence, he finally understood the industry he loved must not be allowed to die. With the deep pain of that 'truth' resonating in his soul, with tears streaming down, he began to think through how to recreate a purpose for himself. How could he defend what was left of the coal-mining industry?

Frank often reflected on the fact that he was alone. His wife had died five years previously from breast cancer; both of his daughters had long since married and moved to the West Coast; slowly but surely Frank saw and heard less and less of them. They were both busy mothers and not so much concerned with him and their own family of origins.

They had stopped attending the Springfield mining disaster memorial service with him. On the days when his daughters spoke to him on the phone, they would both try convincing him coal mining was the past.

"Look, Dad, the whole world knows the truth, coal is filthy stuff! It's had its day. Science tells us it's choking the planet. Now Mum's not here, you've got to look forward. You've got your house, your pensions and your investments. We want you to make a new life; maybe find a new wife; go on holiday, anything you want! But, for God's sake, give up coal!"

Putting the phone down he'd often return to his audial and visual memories of being sixteen. He would return to the day his father and elder brother had walked out one morning together and never returned. He could hear his mother's guttural sobbing in the kitchen. By the evening fifty-five men had died in what became known as the Springfield mining disaster; the explosion had been felt all around a twelve-mile radius.

It was a momentous, defining day in his life; it forced him out of education. Frank's father had planned for him to do something other than mining; even then he had read the 'writing on the wall' of the industry; he wanted his son to have a different future. But this disaster forced him to change direction and enter the pit as a young tool nipper, beginning what became a lifetime career.

On the day the miners went back into Springfield Mine, young Frank became the workforce talisman. He led the men back to the pit from the front and was carried in on the shoulders of a smiling miner. The *Spirit of Jefferson* newspaper made the pit reopening front-page news, with a photograph and headlined story, '*A proud day for Dave Denman's boy!*'.

From then onwards the story had stuck to him. Frank had remained a living golden symbol of hope; remembered by his community applauding and watching the mine workers return to the Springfield Mine.

At the same time, he also became the 'man' of the house. It was him who earnt the money, supporting his mother for many years, until she passed.

Now, sitting in his wheel-back chair, Frank often found himself thinking forward from Springfield Mine; in his last job he had risen through line management, to CEO of the Natural Coal Mine organisation. Yet, eventually, the owner had forced him to close. In doing so, the owner had handed Frank a rust bucket full to the brim with all the slag and slops of closure. Professional to the end though, he had drunk down that foul stench, but never threw it up. Now, in retirement, that ferment of corrosion left him full of pain and guilt. He had destroyed the lives of miners and their families.

Later, in his attempts to reinvent himself, Frank was woken from the deep gaze of his thoughts. There were times when he found himself looking over the edge of a dark abyss inside himself; oftentimes he saw there was no future. He felt he must bring an end to time itself.

Deep down in his heart, Frank saw Thurmond for what it was; a town with its back broken; the only future for the town was to be devoured by the voracious appetite of nature itself.

Frank was determined to find a mission. It was do or die.

In summary, his decision was to fight tooth and nail for mining and drilling industries; he wanted to surround himself in the warmth, love and loyalty of the communities of people he loved.

First, he tried to become a politician, but the MAGA wing of the Republican Party had rejected him as a man from the distant past; they saw a man tilting at windmills instead of grabbing for the real levers of power for the future. The politics of these modern men and women, only believed in the Republican Party's new brand. So, they fed Frank a brutal message saying, 'Your overriding political interest in mining is never going to 'Make America Great Again.'

Stretching and awakening to stand, Frank knew that this day, November 2, was the first day of a new journey on a very different path. A day when the first results of many months of planning would breathe real life into his final campaign to deliver his legacy; he was determined to protect the way of life he and his people loved.

Anybody who knew Frank well, watching him on that day, locking up the yardmaster's house, would have seen a new man, a man with a new purpose in his step.

Frank was looking forward to welcoming his visitor, arriving at 11.00 a.m.

Day 1   6

Oklahoma City

Saturday
November 2

It was 7.30 a.m. Isaac Lightfoot sat on a wooden bench amongst the many trees, shrubs, and flowers he had collected and planted. The garden had been designed to attract as many birds, insects, and animals as possible.

Every day, Isaac tried to spend time with his garden. He loved to listen to its early morning chorus before the sounds of the city kicked off for the rest of the day.

A mug of strong coffee sat beside him on the widest end of a wooden armrest.

Isaac was 84 years of age. He was a registered Cherokee Indian.

Sitting on his bench, Isaac seemed comfortable in his blue jeans and moccasins. Looking down the garden, his brown weathered face was framed by a silver head of hair. Two long, white-grey braids rested on either side of his dark-blue shirt front.

On his wrists he wore two matching, turquoise bead bracelets; on his neck he wore a necklace fashioned from the same stone.

Isaac could feel the power of the sun's rays were already on the wane. He was thinking about his son Wohali, who would be leading the Festival of the Earth procession to the Lincoln Memorial.

Beside Isaac, on the bench, lay a back copy of a Sunday edition of *The Washington Post*; it was an edition he had stopped himself from throwing into the trash a while back. The headlines spoke of events in both Ukraine and China.

As he drank his coffee, Isaac was remembering an even older story he'd read somewhere about Russian soldiers who had been filmed escorting nine Ukrainian, blindfolded male captives, tied together, across a road in Bucha. It turned out these men were being led to their summary executions. Isaac had watched the online video of the event. He remembered that he had listened to a *'Predator'* Russian soldier ordering one of the victims, saying, *'Walk to the right, bitch!'*

Thumbing the pages of the copy of the *Post* he had saved, Isaac revisited an article about a big leak, of documentary and photographic evidence of China's detention and compulsory assimilation of some 22,000, First Nation, Uyghur people.

As Isaac re-read the article; he was reminded that Uyghur families and children had been separated and were subjected to living in camps. There was evidence of repressed birth rates, and a shoot to kill policy for escapees. There were growing concerns that Chinese authorities were destroying whole communities.

Other reading Isaac had done gave him well founded concern that this Chinese policy was aimed at detaching whole communities of First Nation, Uyghur people from their ancestral lands. The magazine pages reported on the propaganda spoken by the Chinese leadership, who informed American journalists and readers that these 'camps' were just places of 'education'.[3]

Isaac remembered he had read a while back a White House Press Release from the President, accusing China of committing genocide on the Uyghur people. These stories and leaked photographs from China showed Isaac pictures of yet more human *'Predator'* activity. As he put the magazine down beside him on the bench, he became consumed by his own thoughts and feelings.

Suddenly, Isaac quickly turned to look behind him.

Lately, he had begun to feel spooked in his garden; he could hear the sound of digging. Some days he heard a male voice humming a tune and the squeaking sound of a single wheelbarrow wheel. Other days there was just an aroma of tobacco smoke passing close by him.

At these times Isaac felt anxious; his breathing became laboured; privately, he was worried about his health and his state of mind.

Even though Isaac knew from long experience he'd heard these sounds in the past, the sounds and smells never failed to take him by surprise. He knew these tricks of the mind belonged in his childhood. But knowing this made little difference; Isaac had an increasing sense that his childhood was coming back to haunt him with a greater frequency.

As the dawn lightened, Isaac returned to thinking about the U.S. President's repeated statements, challenging the Chinese Government that they were committing a genocide against the Uyghur people; to Isaac these statements were nothing more than a childlike hypocrisy. Isaac thought to himself, *'The President must've forgotten his U.S. history. The Federal Government spent well over a century stealing Indian Nation children from their families from all over North America. I was one of them.'*

Sitting quietly, Isaac began to feel and hear his intruding memories, arriving at the Dakota boarding school. Try though he might, safe as he knew he was in his garden, he could not block out these images of himself as a four-year-old, held down on a hard floor. Images flashed through his mind, lit by night lights, transporting him to a bland, humourless, boot room.

Dark figures of men and women towered over him and surrounded the child inside him. This was a recurring pattern where Isaac found himself looking on, watching the scene over and over again; 'White Man' staff wrestling him to the floor. They cut his his braids and stripped him of the clothes his mother and grandmother had made for him.

As Isaac looked down the garden, he watched his adult daughter Woya, making her way up the garden. He finished his coffee, knowing she was coming to announce breakfast.

As Woya arrived, she rescued him from drowning beneath the waves of his dark ruminations.

"Isaac, our breakfast is ready! I'm sure you haven't forgotten, it's November the second. The day of the International Festival of the Earth in Washington DC. The day is finally upon us!"

Isaac looked up, shading his eyes against the early morning sunrise, just peeping over his daughter's shoulder.

"No, of course not. How could I forget? Today is a day for great celebration; two long years in the planning."

As they made their way inside their house, Isaac thanked Woya.

"You know, Wohali and I couldn't have got this far without you. You've shown us such loyalty; you gave us honesty, food and love; you kept our feet rooted in the soil. We could never have got to this point without you, Woya.

"Today though, it's just you and me together. We'll be watching your brother, Wohali, carrying the spirit of our greatest leader, Tecumseh."

Day 1   7

Washington DC

Saturday
November 2

The Festival of the Earth procession was officially due to start at midday. So, John, Phoenix and their officers were out on the street establishing their roles and street positions by 8.30 a.m.

As planned, John was stationed with all the citywide service leaders in a control room. The only professional John hadn't anticipated was a citywide medical director. He would advise law enforcement professionals about any significant public health matters, should medical treatment need to be administered.

Looking round the control room, John familiarised himself with banks of screens. A row of six police operators wearing headphones were observing all the pathways into the procession. In this way the citywide leadership team could, at any time, view and advise on any part of the whole procession and decide on any action needed.

Next door, and soundproofed, was the accommodation for all the TV hacks for all the main U.S. national TV networks. They also had their own bank of screens for twenty-twenty vision all along the Mall.

As the procession slowly got into gear John acknowledged to himself that the sheer numbers moving forward represented one of the most powerful forces of public opinion he'd ever seen.

The control room leader and chief of police for the day echoed John's thoughts entirely.

"Well, John, from where I'm standing tensions are rising. There are fundamental chasms opening up between our peoples about the climate. Let's put it this way, our job of providing security, law and order, it ain't gonna get any easier. What do you say?"

"Yeah, I can see what you mean. Personally, I just want this event over though. I ain't got an axe to grind here in any direction, Chief. My people are objectively briefed, they will deliver control unflinchingly, pure and simple."

The chief interjected.

"Whatever the human cost?"

"Yeah! Whatever the human cost!"

Right in the very front of the procession there was a young man, in his thirties, riding a white stallion; he was bare-chested and riding bareback. The burbling media narrative told all those people looking in on screens, across the wider world, that this guy was a Cherokee nation shaman.

The young shaman carried an ancient Cherokee lance in one hand and waved to the crowds with the other; close-up, on-screen footage showed John that the lance was genuine. Beautiful symbolic carvings had been etched into the bone shaft; eagle feathers fluttered from the heel of the spearhead.

Listening in on his headphones, John heard a TV narrator telling listeners that these ancient weapons had easily punctured sixteenth-century English and Spanish invaders, armoured chest plates.

In the yellowing autumnal sunlight, John squinted at the sepia image of rider and stallion, as they made their way toward the memorial. The stallion was traditionally dressed and decorated as a North American Indian 'paint horse'. The stallion's eyes were circled in bright red and blue paint; his nostrils were also painted in these same circular patterns and colours. Symbolically he was painted for 'war;' the war to heal the planet; even the planets of our galaxy, our Sun and Moon were painted on his flanks

The stallion himself seemed to respond to the cheering crowds and their music. Sometimes, he side-passed, first to the left and then, right. At other times he proudly high-stepped, alert, with his ears pricked. As his head nodded toward the crowds, he snorted loudly through his nostrils; some people stepped back, unsure of the power of this proud animal.

Standing together, John and the chief looked on; they sensed the increasing weight and density of the human traffic. Turning to the screens in the control room, they tracked the many different tributaries of people as they merged into a single, relentless human river flowing to its destination.

Listening with his headphones, John heard one buoyant live TV commentary feed, dominating the airspace of the Press Room next door.

'Where else in all our great nation should these voices for our planet be heard? For our nation, the Lincoln Memorial is the iconic, symbolic, seat of justice...'

Coming up behind a group of two hundred First Nation peoples, were a group of larger than life caricature puppets paradying national and international politicians. Following them, the sounds of several bands burst through with their carnival notes; good humour, and the vibrant rhythms of African American jazz filled the air.

8

Phoenix had been delegated into a leadership role of her street team covering the final destination to the Memorial itself. Her other officers and staff had been allocated to different teams all along the procession.

Phoenix's awareness was very highly tuned. She maintained close contact with her officers and relayed any messages coming directly down the line from the chief of police. Some of her teams were stationed on the first platform at the top of the Memorial steps.

As an African American woman, Phoenix was keenly aware that this was the same platform Martin Luther King had spoken his 'I have a Dream' speech way back in '63.

As Phoenix looked further back up the Mall, she could hear many thousands of voices and the distant hammering of drumbeats punctuating the syllables of chanted slogans.

'Our houses! Our farms! Our forests and our seas!
The failure of our President, bring us to our knees!!'

'Show us progress, cut the crap!
Sack the President, he's a prat!'

*'Smell the air, we choke on fumes,
Give us renewables, to heat our homes.'*

*'Shut down oil, coal and gas!
India and China must ban them fast!'*
*'Melting ice makes rising seas,
Landless nations make refugees.'*

*'First Nation peoples love their lands,
Gonna take control into our hands.'*

On the 'stage' for the finale of the proceedings, at the top of the steps, stood three podiums all hooked up to a sound system, so the crowds could hear the important speeches.

Phoenix spoke to her officers across the airwaves, keeping them alert, asking them to remain vigilant.

'Stay in the moment, scan the arriving crowds very closely.'

Finally, Phoenix watched the procession come to a halt. At the head of the procession was the beautifully decorated, blue and red 'paint horse' and the Cherokee shaman; both stood alone, separated from the pageantry of two hundred representatives of Indian nations, behind them.

A silence settled over the gathering crowds.

Then, a lone drum began beating. A man and three women from their different nations sang an ancient song of the Mi'kmaq Nation, called the 'Honor Song'.[4] The message of the song called on all peoples everywhere to help one another, as the Creator had first intended.

As the song concluded, the procession itself remained stationary, entering another period of disciplined and unified silence. The podiums on the 'stage' remained empty, they awaited the arrival of the two senior executives of the International Festival of the Earth and the U.S. Presidential Envoy for Climate Change.

In the silence, Phoenix looked on as the young Cherokee shaman began a silent drama of choreographed mime while staying on horseback; his arms were outstretched as if maintaining his balance. As she watched, Phoenix saw the shaman change his arm positions, holding the lance by his side. He raised his left arm and with a single finger, pointing and looking to the skies. Then, the stallion, without any visible command, suddenly reared onto his hind legs and held position; the shaman and stallion were pivoted, as a living statue, in perfect balance.

As the stallion and rider remained, there were waves of applause; cheers, whistles and chants rolled around the crowds, all the way back down the Mall, until the stallion stood back on all fours.

Then, all Phoenix could hear was the sounds of the silver jangling bells attached to the stallion's halter; they rang out as his head naturally rose and fell.

Phoenix stood, for a moment, mesmerised.

The crowd waited in silence, as the two most senior representatives of the International Festival of the Earth, Indira Anand and Grogan Small, took up their podium positions; finally, the U.S. Presidential Envoy for Climate Change took his place; their heads remained bowed as they arrived; then, lifting their eyes, they were seen to be humbled, taking in the awesome size of the crowds.

The images on the screens, in the control room focussed solely on the shaman and the stallion. The stallion… the shaman… the stallion… the shaman… the st

Day 1   **9**

Thurmond
West Virginia

Saturday
November 2

Having returned from his walk, Frank switched on his TV screen in the kitchen; then the doorbell rang; his visitor had arrived. Opening the door, Frank welcomed an older gentleman with a greying head of hair and a well-trimmed beard; he was wearing blue jeans, a checked shirt and a short leather jacket.

His name was Seth Soul. Frank had first heard about the plight of the Soul family, through his right-wing political networks in Oklahoma. From working together for the last two years, Frank realised they shared the same ambitions, but maybe for different reasons.

Frank warmly welcomed him into the house.

"Hi, Seth, good to see you. Hope you had a fair journey down? Look, I have fixed us a sandwich and a beer and you're just in time to see the Cherokee Indian on horseback; see, they're just standing there, at the Memorial."

"Good to see you again, Frank. Let's hope it goes well. I have left my bags in the car for now, I guess you'll show me the billet where I'll be resting up with the boys. You sure are snuck away here, Frank. Very well hidden. I've never been to Thurmond before, heard about it though. Sure, is a dead place ain't it?"

Frank chuckled. "That's true. Yeah, I'll show you the workshop and living quarters later. There's no need to worry. The three of you will be very comfortable while you're working here."

"We both know there is a lot riding on this; our whole credibility, our funding and our ability to do more business across the continent. Everything is hanging in the balance. The future of our campaign is resting in the hands of your two boys now."

Seth nodded and seemed relaxed.

"No worries, Frank, just believe; John and Charles have taken a lot of responsibility for making this happen today."

Taking Seth's jacket, Frank couldn't help but notice a forearm tattoo of a cockerel standing on a weathervane below his rolled up shirtsleeve.

They both settled down to watch.

Then it happened!

Day 1 — 10

Washington DC

Saturday
2 November

As if from nowhere, two rapid-fire rifle shots rang out close together.

To Phoenix's well-trained ear, it sounded more like a single shot cutting across from the shrubbery and trees to the right side of the Memorial façade. The shots had torn through the woven tapestry of the 'Festivals' prayerful finale; the carefully constructed choreography of messages from the dignitaries on the 'stage', to the faithful protesters, the joyful atmosphere of jazz bands; all had been destroyed in a simple trigger pull.

Phoenix, and many others had physically recoiled from the violent crack of rifle fire.

Looking behind her, the shaman's body was lying motionless on the ground. She could see the back of his skull had been blown out. The velocity of the rifle shot striking the shaman's head had lifted him off the stallion. Now, his body lay on the paved surface of the Mall, lifeless; the stallion had been felled where he stood, split seconds later. What seemed like one bullet, had been two; tragically, the stallion was hopelessly struggling, whinnying, trying to stand, while a fine spray of blood blew from his nose.

In the madness of the moment, Phoenix looked around her and she realised that her visor and jacket had picked up blood spatter from the shaman's bullet wound. People all around had gone to ground, crying and screaming; those who had brought children lay on the ground, covering them. A few in shock, simply stood and wept; others, strangely, took video footage and photographs of the scene on their iPhones.

Some people, trampled, lay injured or dead; one young woman had hidden herself behind the body of the struggling white stallion still trying to stand.

Time itself felt broken; in what was a few seconds, it felt to Phoenix to have been an extended lifetime; in shock, she heard the chief of police calling for immediate implementation of agreed planned responses to secure the scene. Waking, as if from a momentary time warp, Phoenix at once ordered her officers to protect the dignitaries, to shepherd them off the stage and into their waiting cars.

In her headphones, Phoenix had heard the chief calmly call for all the teams of officers further back in the procession to provide instruction.

"*Tell them to turn around, go on home now; tell them there will be another day; tell them if they've got information we need to hear, to approach us. Tell them if they have taken photographs or video footage, we want them to share it with us.*"

Almost at once the chief came down the wire instructing Phoenix through her headphones.

"Hi, Phoenix. Listen to me now! Are you listening?"

Phoenix looked toward the control room and nodded.

"I need you to assume the role of 'incident commander' out there. You need to gather your officers together. We'll need some of them clearing the area, searching for those who might be suspects still remaining on-site."

"Okay, Chief, understood!"

"You will also need to lead a detailed search; first priority is to figure out if there is anyone left inside the Memorial Undercroft; second priority, secure any sign of evidence that the shooters were based inside. CSI forensics are arriving as we speak.

"John and I agree the shooters must have used the Undercroft to hide out, then positioned themselves much earlier in the morning in the shrubbery cover on the side of the Memorial; that area needs cordoning off and careful searching by forensic officers. We feel their predetermined target was the assassination of both the horse and rider together.

"Listen, I know John wants to get a message into your head. John, you want to tell Phoenix."

"Hi, Phoenix, it's clear to me that the shooters didn't assassinate a powerful political figure like the Presidential Envoy. Their plan was to destroy the heart and soul of the 'Festivals' iconic 'messenger'."

"Okay, John, understood."

Phoenix immediately gathered her search force who were soon poised to enter the huge underground Memorial vaults below the Abraham Lincoln statue.

"Okay, Chief, we're just on the threshold of getting in. Speak later."

Leading her team through the high-security heavy iron door to the Undercroft, Phoenix followed instructions to switch on the wall lights which would illuminate the flights of stairs down into the first of three massive chambers. When the lights flickered on, a huge, eerie first chamber came into view. It was fifty feet deep from the bedrock of the Potomac River to the Undercroft ceiling; weight bearing columns rose up from the floor, securing the weight of the Memorial building and Abraham Lincoln's statue above.

Phoenix ordered her team to draw their weapons. She led from the front down the first flight of stairs.

It wasn't until they came to the second chamber where,

directly under the Lincoln statue, they found a pile of rubbish, presumably left behind by the shooters; there were food packets, blankets and toilet arrangements; all evidence of the shooters having been hiding out in advance of the assassination. Examining the number of materials, Phoenix hunch was they'd maybe been there for a couple of days.

The team cordoned off the crime scene and, eventually, after the search of the third chamber, Phoenix brought them back to the surface.

Returning into the daylight through the Undercroft doorway, Phoenix looked along an emptying Mall. The crime scene was secure; Phoenix quickly found out from her officers they had failed to locate the shooters.

The chief, seeing the search team emerge, quickly spoke to Phoenix.

"That's fine work Phoenix."

Day 1   11

Thurmond
West Virginia

Saturday
November 2

After the shots rang out it was clear that the assassination was delivered.

Frank looked across at Seth. They both stood up from their barstools and punched the air.

"Yes! Yes! Yes!! My boys have delivered for us both! For me, I can't tell you what it means, Frank. It means the world to me! To see that fuckin' Cherokee Indian, dead. At last, I can take my daughter back home."

He reached across the kitchen top and both men shook hands and laughed loudly together.

They looked back at the TV screen. The live footage showed the chaos before the crime scene was secured. For Frank the sight of Wohali Lightfoot, with the back of his skull blown out, lying in a pool of blood, congealing on the Mall paving, was shocking. He got up and made his way into the nearest bathroom.

Frank looked at himself in the mirror and saw his pale, sickly face. Suddenly, his eyes looked dark and sunken; Frank felt an unstoppable pressure building in his gut, he felt that warning twinge of nauseousness at the back of his cheeks.

Then, carefully lowering himself toward the pan, he knelt down, doing everything he could to throw up into the toilet bowl, as quietly as possible.

Afterwards, looking back in the mirror, Frank mopped the corners of his mouth with damp tissue. For the first time he truly realised this campaign wasn't just an idea anymore. For the first time he looked back at his reflection and gave himself some tough love: '*Get used to this, Frank, you've become a killer for justice!*'

Finally, he washed his face in a washbasin of warm soapy water. He smacked and pinched his cheeks, doing everything he could to bring back colour and a mask of normality.

Frank was determined to front out what should have been a shared pleasure between the two men. They had, after all, just literally fired the first shots across the bows of the International Festival of the Earth and their partnership with the U.S. Federal Government.

Coming back into the kitchen Frank clapped Seth on the back.

"Okay! Let's go see your accommodation and workspace for the next few days."

On the way across the yard Frank could feel Seth checking him out. In reality he guessed that he had probably heard him throwing up his lunch into the pan.

"You okay, Frank? I gotta say you're looking a little pale."

"Yeah, I'm fine. I've had a bug for a couple of days. You know how it is; these bugs hit your gut, then come and go for twenty-four to forty-eight hours. It's nothin'. I'm delighted at the success your boys have brought us both. I can tell you our network of people I've built across the whole continent, they will know now; I mean what I say. Now we're gonna destroy this International Festival of the Earth; drive them out of our continent.

"Then, Seth, we'll start drilling, mining and logging for real! The money people are gonna start making from harvesting the simple soya bean, raising beef and mining gold instead of preserving an ancient tree museum, will be phenomenal. They'll also be investing much more money into our campaign account; mark my words, there'll be new work for us."

Frank unlocked the barn and showed Seth the ground floor.

The first thing Seth saw was that the materials he'd requested had been delivered. A large stock of bur oak hardwood beams stood in a corner. Seth was a professional wood craftsman, walking around he stroked the work benches with the tips of his fingers. He picked up items of interest. Looking at Frank, Seth whistled through his teeth and smiled.

"Well, Seth, I can see just by looking at you, you've got what you wanted. Let me show you something you can't see."

Seth scoured the rafters, walls and flooring, but gave up.

Frank bent down and picked a small, integrated wooden rectangle with a fingernail. Then, he lifted a hidden brass ring embedded in the under-flooring; pulling on it, a section of floor tilted back with ease, lifted by an internal balancing weight. Seth, open-mouthed, saw a small staircase appear under the floor. Frank switched the light on, signalling to Seth to go down and look around.

"Well, Frank, you've certainly pushed the boat out here. You've ordered exactly what we need to progress to the next task when we're ready; this storeroom, with all the materials and tools, is a great resource. Never seen or smelt such a stock of different kinds of wood."

After Seth had looked all the way through the contents of the workshop Frank waved him upstairs to view the living accommodation.

"There's three bedrooms, a lounge and a kitchen up here, Seth. There's a well-stocked fridge and a bathroom along the corridor. If there is anything more you and your boys need then you've only to let me know. I'll leave you now to collect your gear and settle in."

Frank handed Seth three sets of keys and went to step downstairs and back to the house.

"Before you go, Frank, can I ask who else you have working with our team?"

Frank stopped, looked down and thought carefully before answering.

"Fair question, Seth. Are you and the boys looking to go on earning a living with me as my hitmen?"

Seth smiled and tweaked his grey moustache.

"Well, we could be. My family and other folk we know, right now, we want our USA to be in the best hands, if you know what I mean? I know for sure there are folks in other parts of the USA where they sense our 'roots' are under threat. There'll be people like us, people who the good Lord, Jesus Christ gave this 'Promised Land' to; people who still believe in our European ancestors and founders.

"You and I know He handed it to us through God's rules of 'discovery;' rules written by the Popes of the sixteenth century; in those days of enlightenment, if you were a Christian, the land was yours; if you were a heathen you had to give it up. It's our land Frank so, keep on with drilling deep, and digging cheap. I'm sure there's enough work for you and me to do till the day we die.

"So, now this Cherokee, Wohali Lightfoot, is eliminated, I reckon we could be up for joining your outfit for a while longer, Frank. That's if you'll have us. When we've done with the other members of the Lightfoot family we've agreed on, I reckon we could make another hit list! Yep, that's for definite!"

Frank reached inside his jacket pocket for his iPhone; he stopped Seth talking for a moment.

His phone had pinged notice of an incoming text.

"So, I've just received a text message from my driver, he's

picked up your boys in Washington DC where we planned and he's bringing them home!"

Seth put a hand on Frank's shoulder and laughed an excited laugh.

"Yeah, Frank!! The plan's gone like clockwork! Thanks so much, I'm proud and so grateful to you, keeping my boys safe."

In the midst of Seth's excitement, Frank looked him straight in the eye.

"The message is, Seth, you want to join me and go on the payroll, you need to be prepared to give up everything you know. Sure, as hell, you and I know, the cops and the FBI are gonna be crawling all over this today, tomorrow and every next day. You, my team and your boys, even me, we could in time become nomads with no roots at all; we could all be wanted men and women."

"In your work scouting the Lincoln Memorial, I know you worked with Suzanne Woodman. Well, Suzanne's the one who organised your FBI ID to scope the Lincoln Memorial Undercroft. She is on my payroll. I've known and worked with her for a long time now. She was my PA when I was CEO at Natural Coal. She is a good, reliable woman who understands my needs and I look after her. She works for me full time. There have been times when she and I had to take decisions to silence people. Financially, she's doing well on two good incomes.

"There are others working for me inside the FBI itself. One guy is the son of a mining family I knew way back at Springfield Mine; his father recruited his son to work with me in support of their mining community. That's the strength and love in the mining family for you, Seth; this young guy doesn't even remember meeting me as a child, but he trusts me because his father tells him to; that's loyalty for you.

"Then, there are U.S. senators and other politicians on the ground in Brazil and South America; all people who wouldn't want me to name them. They've helped me find some high-level public servants and some not so high; people we can put over a barrel because they are corrupt. I can ask them nicely; tell them, maybe not so nicely, what I want!"

Frank smiled.

"I'm a very reasonable man, Seth."

"There are also wealthy friends you'll never hear about who donate because they know I'm a man of my word. I'll help them clear land, get permits to mine and drill where governments don't want any drilling. You understand? This is a new dawn; an end to everything that's woke on this continent! We're taking back control, Seth; control over everything we love and everything that's rightfully ours as owners of these lands."

Seth nodded.

"Listen, Seth, if you're comin' on board with your boys long-term, we'll need to talk. Set down some understandings between you, me and them. Right?"

Seth smiled nervously.

"Yeah? Well, that sounds a bit serious, Frank."

"I'll tell you now, I've given up everything for this battle, Seth. I saw the truth over two years ago on a journey to Brazil. I was sitting in a bar in Manaus. The drink was strong, but the talk was sober. It was all about the International Festival of the Earth; I learnt they were forcing governments all over the world to leave all the carbon in the ground."

"Now my plan has cracked off today, way down in that bar in Manaus, I know they'll be celebrating.

"I'm taking this to the wire, Seth. It's time for a parting of the ways; time to separate the sheep from the goats. It's time to protect our own human rights and supremacy to survive, the best we know how. You and I, we both know this from two different perspectives. Yeah?

"Right now, you and I, we're the fittest creatures on the planet. Well, Darwin said, the fittest survive, didn't he? If we don't act, the 'Festival' people, with all their wokery, will be turning our tables in favour of the savages and the animals; they'll be handing our land back to them, Seth; animal habitats, and all! That's their plan.

"The talk in Manaus was, they want to fund armies of Rangers to protect the trees, the animals and their indigenous people; protect them from our people, the loggers, the miners, and the drillers. That's what they believe; they say the 'heathens' know best about this land of ours; they say they have what they call, 'traditional knowledge'.

"The 'Festival' man, they're the Kings and Queens of woke! If we don't act now, we European Christian descendants, we'll all be dispossessed; the funded pagan armies will take over; it'll be too late for us then Seth."

Frank was suddenly silent. He looked at Seth straight-faced, deep into his eyes.

"The truth is though, Seth, in my gut, I'm gettin' the feeling you think I'm a fucking lightweight..."

Seth drew a sharp intake of breath to speak. Frank put a hand up and quietened him.

"Listen, Seth, if I *ever*, and I mean *ever*, get to know you're disrespecting me, or you've become a risk to me in any way, I'll make sure you, your wife, your daughter and your sons, will all be punished. You'll never know when it's gonna happen, but as our God is my witness, I'll take you and your family down, Seth!"

Seth looked shocked; he listened and held his silence. But Frank was cool and silent; where he stood, he hardly seemed to breathe.

Then looking at Seth, deep into his cold blue eyes, Frank held his gaze.

"Am I clear, Seth? If you're hearing me now, you'll know the depth of loyalty I demand. It's either that or you'll be gone by the morning. You still want to join me, don't think you're gonna fuck me over, Seth!"

Seth opened his mouth to speak, but no sound came out of his mouth.

"Well, then we'll talk more later. But, let me say, if you and your boys don't want to join, that could be a problem too. Now we've worked together, you know a lot about me. You understand me, Seth? You're in midstream now. You even know where I live; so, I'd have to take all that into consideration, should you want to break your loyalty to me; well, even now maybe you know too much…"

Seth suddenly found himself gulping for words. He was trying to work out why the wind had just left his sails. Yet still he found himself trying to rally, gabbling at great speed.

"Frank, we got more in common than you think. My history and roots are with the people who sailed on the *Mayflower*. I'm even a descendent from one of that crew…

"Yeah, I've researched all that about you, Seth. I've gotta say, I never found a single person who sailed on the *Mayflower* with a name spelt 'Soul'. But my contacts tell me your grandfather and your father were there in Tulsa, at the burning of Greenwood. So, I guess that's okay then."[5]

Seth continued burbling on.

"Frank, this nation, it's just dried-up 'tinder'. I ain't talking wildfires, I'm talking about our way of life, it ain't got no backbone anymore. The time's coming, believe me, it'll burst into the cleansing flames of dieback; maybe it'll be another bloody civil war. There's a lot of talk of that right now! You and me, Frank, we're both sides of the very same silver dollar…"

Frank smiled warmly, nodded and put an arm round Seth's shoulder. He started walking, taking Seth with him, reassuring and calming him.

"I understand, Seth. You and me, we're fighting as a 'coalition' for the same One Nation and the Old Planet. The politicians used to call it, 'America First'. But I tell you now Seth, ain't one of those politicians who'd really flip that silver dollar spinning for a real civil war. You and I, we both know they're gutless wonders. Weak as mothers suckling their babies. All they can do is just string all those words together, but they'll never be able to do what your boys have done today. That my friend is the true strength of men. The politicians, while they fear us, they think they control us; truth is though they'll always have to rely on us to get this fuckin' thing done.

"One more practical thing, Seth, I have to be up early in the morning. I'm flying to Washington DC tomorrow morning. You're well set up here. I know that your boys, John and Charles, are arriving back here tomorrow. I'm sure you can give them a key, help them feel at home; but keep them in order. I'll keep in touch with you by telephone. I know you've got my number."

Frank placed one hand on Seth's shoulder as they shook hands.

"Good to talk to you, Seth. I'll see you for that other conversation we've mentioned; don't worry, we'll be just fine."

Frank smiled.

"Believe me, Seth, you and your boys, you've done me proud today."

Day 1   **12**

Washington DC

Saturday
November 2

When the shots had rang out, John and the chief had, like everyone else, instinctively and physically ducked toward the floor, inside the control room.

The chief had begun to enact the emergency procedures calmly and precisely while on his hands and knees. The crucial elements of the crime scene, like the shaman's body, the stallion and the Undercroft were quickly secured.

In time, John watched as the emergency veterinary surgeon arrived and dipped her head inside the tent. Quickly, quietly and humanely, the stallion's struggle for life was calmed and ended through lethal injection.

John heard the media coverage coming through on-screen and the hubbub in the background of the voices in the control room.

'*Is this then the death of the International Festival of the Earth and, inevitably, the end of the international hopes for agreements...*'

The commentary wittered on, filling in airtime while citywide services continued their work of securing the scene.

'*Then there's the hopes of millions of people whose properties, futures and livelihoods are being wrecked by the long-term changes in climate. North America and others in the Western Alliance believe in locking up all fossil fuels but China and India...'*

Listening, John heard the broadcasts end with a statement that he knew law enforcement would be wanting urgent answers for over the next few days and maybe for months ahead.

'Only God Himself knows who is behind this bloody assassination...'

13

In the midst of the chaos at the Festival of the Earth, John's iPhone rang. Momentarily he left the hubbub of the control room through its back door.

It was George Stanhope, Executive Lead for Homeland Security and Terrorism. George was John's opposite number. Both of them reported to the FBI Director, Anna McKenna; today George was acting for her, she was away for the day.

"Hi, John. I know you're there on the ground. Just give me your initial reaction off the top of your head. What do you think has occurred out there on the Mall?"

"Well, George, firstly, looking at the scene, I hope we can agree, here and now, this ain't no lone wolf operation. Behind the simplicity of this scene this was clearly an expert and well-planned assassination. George, this was a public execution. Unless you tell me different, I'm assuming we had no wind or word of this from anywhere; you'd have briefed me, right?"

George agreed. Then he asked John to continue.

"Okay. Well, secondly, I would say it was a political attack, of course. Could be climate terrorists? But do we have proscribed groups of those? I guess it could have been a racial attack. Whichever way, I would be badging this as far-right, 'home-grown terrorism' at this stage.

"Lastly, George, on the shooting itself, there had to be two simultaneous shooters involved. They took the horse and rider down at the same instant. The gunfire sounded like one shot. Could have just taken the shaman, couldn't they? My guess, though, is they'd planned to destroy the whole image and message of indigenous leadership. Could even call it a practical decapitation of the International Festival of the Earth's strategic aims?

"If you close your eyes, George, then think back to the silence before the shooting, you can almost hear one of the two shooters calmly counting in the trigger pulls together, 'one, two, three – squeeze!'"

George agreed, then chuckled down the phone.

"John, that's very graphic. What I've always admired about you, is you strip a process down to its most basic, separate moving parts."

"George, we must face facts, there could be other assassinations in the planning. This is your bag, though, George, 'terrorism.' Yeah?"

"Okay, John, never mind all that, right now it's all mere speculation anyway. Gets us nowhere. What I can tell you is, Anna McKenna and I have badged this as a serious 'critical incident'; it's of national and international importance. So, I've gotta tell you that since we rated the incident, Anna as director, and the attorney general have asked for you personally to undertake the investigation down south.

"I'm sorry, John. I'm phoning to direct you to connect with a 9 p.m. flight from the Ronald Reagan Washington National Airport to Oklahoma. From there, you'll interview the victim's family, take all the evidence, and follow up to investigate."

John felt he had just sleepwalked his way through the *Looking Glass* and then tumbled down a rabbit hole.

George continued.

"So, while Jim, Jason and Charlotte are out there on the

street and operational, I've already asked Phoenix to act up into the citywide control room on your behalf today. I've briefed the chief of police directly.

"Then, while you're away and matters at the Memorial are concluded, Phoenix will also take on active leadership and accountability for your service operations here in Washington DC. She'll be acting up into your executive lead role; she'll carry Anna's, and my own, full support and authority; this will free you until you conclude your own investigation in Oklahoma."

John was in shock.

"C'mon, George, you're kidding me. You and Anna are sending *me* to Oklahoma?"

"John, this stuff happens. You're listening, right!? We've got a name for the victim lying dead out there on the Mall. It's Wohali Lightfoot. He has a father, Isaac and a sister, Woya. They're all three of them registered Cherokee Indians. Wohali has a caucasian wife, Cary Lightfoot, she's living just round the corner from Isaac. They have a three-year-old boy, Danuwoa.

"To support your work, I've already commissioned a local emeritus professor of Native American Indian culture and politics based at Oklahoma University. She'll act as an advisor for you. The professor is also a member of the Cherokee Nation and will meet you as you arrive on the tarmac in Oklahoma at around 11.30 p.m. tonight.

"Also, I've taken the liberty of directing a couple of your interns, who are bright new graduate staff to help you out. Names are, Esteban Jackson, an African American guy from New York, and then Drake Collins, a caucasian from West Virginia. They are putting together a briefing document, reading material for your flight.

"In particular, I have asked them to dig out Isaac and Wohali Lightfoot's connections with the American Continental Board of the Festival of the Earth."

"As far as I've been told, the 'Festival' had been working as a close partner of the Federal Government to deliver on Climate Change policy."

"The last US Government were pushing hard to begin shutting down our oil, gas and coal industries; but since the last election, the new Government apparently doesn't believe Climate Change is happening across the planet. I hear our national policy now, is in chaos."

"Look, George. Just explain, why in God's name, me?"

"Look, John, to be honest we need your creative ability to complete the interviews with Wohali's family. That ain't flattery, John. It just happens to be the truth. To be frank with you, we've assessed all that weird policing experience you've got as an undercover cop in Chicago, together with your seniority. Finally, we put your CV into the mix, and it gave us the confidence that you could flex with a fluid and sensitive mission."

John felt he'd been hit by a train he never saw coming. He was so preoccupied taking in the proposal, he hardly noticed as George slipped in for the kill.

"So, John, I've taken another liberty by asking my Brenda to contact Kay. Over the years Brenda and I have been and done what you're going to do today, many, many times. So, as we speak, our wives are packing a case for you. Then Kay will meet you at the passenger lounge at the Ronald Reagan.

"How's that then, John? You're going back to the field! Time for you to rediscover your investigative instincts again. Much better than organisational restructuring, a dusty office, or a dry conference? Let's be clear, John, the attorney general and Anna McKenna want you to, quote, '*Shut this down fast*' and '*Get the job done!*'."

With that, George was gone, leaving John dazed.

14

So, recovering and adjusting, John spoke to the citywide chief of police, informing him that Phoenix would take over his role; he would stand down in order to travel to Oklahoma.

He just nodded.

"Yeah! I've heard. George has already briefed me. You've sure got a journey ahead of you tonight, John. Thanks for all your help, it's been a pleasure."

Phoenix arrived in the control room.

"Hi, John, I hear you've been asked to lead in Oklahoma. I've taken on your delegated authority and span of control with immediate effect; that's here in the city and overseeing your nationwide workload. I'm reporting to George and Anna while you're away. We'll need to stay in close touch."

"Yeah, Phoenix! I've heard. Actually, I don't want this delegation from Anna. But it seems I have to give way to a unilateral, professional decision. So, I'm just gonna introduce you to the chief before I leave."

Phoenix took John by the arm and led him to one side, speaking quietly.

"John, we don't need any introduction. We know one another. We've worked together back in the day. Look, take care. We'll speak later."

John struggled to find a last word.

"Okay, Phoenix. Just one last direction from me then. The chief and I agree that access to the Undercroft was certainly a vital aspect in planning this assassination. I'm hoping David O'Donnelly's forensic team will give high priority getting prints and DNA results from the national databases to you immediately. In addition, I want Charlotte Linklater to identify the senior manager in charge of Mall maintenance service; find out the name of the manager directly responsible for the Memorial and the Undercroft, then interview them."

Phoenix nodded.

"Okay, got it, John. We'll talk again when you're on the other side. Good luck!"

Returning to the office by Metro, John knew he'd been left with little else to do other than pick up his briefing from Esteban and Drake, then phone his wife, Kay. He was feeling deflated to be leaving the scene at the very heart of the crisis.

Walking along the sidewalk, and within sight of the office, John was immediately struck by a tall guy with a mop of ginger hair striding up and down, on an intense phone call. He couldn't help but overhear the increasing volume of his conversation as he approached the office.

'Okay... So, what do I have to do to pay my father's debts?'

As John was passing, he turned and, holding the office door, he looked over his shoulder before entering; then listening again to the young man, the volume increased another notch.

'And what happens if I say no! Eh? Tell me that, Frank? What happens then?'

15

Arriving back at his service-team room, a young woman, who was a junior investigator, tried to engage John for his opinion about a case she was working on.

John stood for a moment, distracted.

His eye had engaged with the large TV screen delivering the latest news and interviews. John saw a young woman on-screen. John's immediate thoughts were, '*This young woman, she's gotta be a Buddhist nun.*' Her head was shaven. Her robe was simple, worn with bare arms and in deep muted colours of red and maroon.

John looked briefly back at the young woman who still trying to consult him about her work.

"Look, I'm busy! Consult your team leader. It's Charlotte, isn't it? Okay then?!"

The young woman turned on her heels and disappeared across the team room toward Charlotte's room.

John sat on the only available empty workstation in front of the TV screen. All the other workstations were occupied; investigators and administrators heads were either looking down or forward; they were either focussed on typing, reading or talking on their phones. Some, listening on headphones, lay back on their chairs, rocking with their feet up.

On-screen, the young woman with the shaven head was about to be interviewed by Tony Ramires at the FOX News studio.

"So, folks, this is Indira Anand, CEO, International Festival of the Earth. Thank you for giving us your time for this extended interview today. I know people like me have been pressing you and your team for interviews all morning, believe me, we're incredibly grateful for your time.

"So, today has become a day of huge sadness for Wohali Lightfoot's family, and no doubt for you too?

"Can you give us your take on why this assassination has happened at the Lincoln Memorial today?"

"Thanks for having me on FOX News so quickly, Tony. Firstly, I have to give my heartfelt condolences to Isaac, Wohali's father, and Woya, his sister, I know them both well. I know they'll be broken-hearted. I don't know Cary Lightfoot, Wohali's wife, but let me say to her right now, though the screen, *'I am so sorry, Cary! We will meet and talk, face to face, soon.'*

"So, those things said, can you give the people your view on why this tragic assassination should happen here, at this time."

"So, Tony, it's good you've allocated us thirty minutes. It gives us the opportunity to inform you and your public. So, my own take on why this has happened is clear. The USA remains a very troubled and dangerous place. Your nation is showing itself to be both disturbed and divided on the urgent action required to attack climate change and heal our planet. The politicians out there who we will all remember had a three-word Policy a few years back now, threatening to *'Drill! Baby! Drill!'*, are now back in charge. One thing is for sure though, this assassination was an attack on the previous partnership of the International Festival of the Earth and the U.S. Federal Government. I have long predicted this kind of attack would happen, Tony. I fear they are going to accelerate both here in the USA and in other parts of the world too.

"What has happened to Wohali is tragic. You must know

though, as a journalist, what's happened today, happens to many First Nation peoples trying to protect their homelands every day. Illegal miners, loggers and oilmen, they all have their private armies riding shotgun. They kill people."[6]

"What's your instinct, Indira? Wohali Lightfoot and his stallion have been right at the forefront of all your PR and advertising across the continent. Aren't you, as CEO of the International Festival of the Earth, responsible for putting this guy upfront, exposing him through all your publicity? So, my question is, aren't you responsible for creating them as a target for terrorism?"

Indira shifted in her seat.

"So, Tony. We would never take responsibility for this. I ask you, would your President take responsibility for a terrorist assassination of a well-known, close political friend on the streets of DC? No, I don't think so.

"Let's face it, there are now emergent climate terrorist organisations. Some of them are funded by large corporates to operate on the 'colonial' frontiers of the ecosphere we need to protect. They're committed to the destruction of life as we know it. Let me be clear, these loggers and miners, they're crude 'primitives', selfishly shitting in all our nests! If we can't persuade them, human communities and their politicians, we will have to fund policing the biosphere across the planet."

"Well, Indira, surely you and people like you at the COP conferences, you've just gone too far, and too fast? Now you're trying to go further than last COP. You actually want to ban and bury all fossil fuels, worldwide? What about the people who need jobs in logging, drilling and mining?"[7]

"Well, Tony, the problem is, as a species, we're struggling to keep within our one-point-five degrees target! COPs are thirty years old now. We only started talking about limiting carbon way back at COP26! No way was that too fast. It's terrifyingly simple, the human animal *still* lives in denial! Folks out there need to become a kinder creature; kinder to one another; kinder to our fellow species, protecting all our habitats.

"Tony, I don't have to tell you, we need look after this magical planet. It's the only one we've got! Our planet is not some disposable object. It doesn't matter what the childlike, multibillionaires do, playing with their toys to travel to Mars; let's be clear, there isn't a fleet of Starship Enterprise vehicles, parked on another planet poised to rescue us. We are the only ones who will save this magical blue planet."[8]

"So, Indira, what about people's jobs and livelihoods? Aren't you just making our lives a lot worse?"

"There'll be thousands of jobs in the new tech; there'll be new, cleaner markets; people must reskill. The longer we leave this, the worse it gets. Addressing the climate must be at the centre of our being and ambition as an animal; we must get on or go under."

Indira smiled wearily.

"And, Tony, you mustn't keep asking me questions as if everything is normal out there! I am not the one who began this choking and warming through the industrial revolution! What's happening in our atmosphere isn't natural or normal; species who evolved with us throughout Creation must acquire legal rights, indeed an equal right, to live here alongside us. Do you feel their pain, Tony?!"

Still watching the screen, John briefly felt Indira look directly at her audience, through the camera.

"No, Indira. I can't say I do, it's our human pain I'm more concerned with."

"I rest my case, Tony. People watching, they must see your human centricity for what it is.

We have to face it, as a species we are threatened like all the others; carbon is a warming toxin for *all* the species on Earth! You should be telling your audience, the time is *now*, Tony!"

"So, Indira. You've talked about the racial, environmental

and biodiversity narratives for this assassination. Earlier you mentioned the 'colonial' illegal miners, loggers and oilmen. Can you tell us any more about them?"

"Okay. There are two parts to this. Firstly, for years now, there have been many powerful arguments made for the liberation of First Nations people to own and take care of the land they discovered; these lands were so often stolen by Europeans during the last five centuries.

"However, it is the First Nation people who fundamentally understand how to protect and preserve our biodiversity.

"Secondly, the 'Festival' believes we have to undo the 'colonial' idea that the whole of the natural world was created for humans to use as a marketplace. The natural world is being destroyed, under several different human ideologies; all these colonial humans have chosen to dominate, commoditise and destroy the natural world through endless cycles of growth, fuelled by carbon."

"I've heard you speak, Indira, about the Western alliance having followed a fake Jesus Christ, how does that work? I think you call it an 'ideological infection'.

"That's true, Tony. Many of us can see it now; yes, even the Vatican can see, that Columbus and Cabot brought with them a Catholic, man made, imposter. Do you honestly think Jesus of Nazareth would approve of the cruel destruction of this continent's indigenous population and invent the slave trade? Are you a Christian Tony? What do you say? One of the oldest, most destructive clerical ideologies was brought to this continent by Columbus, Cortez, Cabot, and Pizarro. As an 'infection' it is still crackling through the undergrowth of our modern culture.

"It doesn't take a genius to understand the true Jesus, the Son of God, had no interest in an earthly Empire or these European human beings, steeped in murder and mayhem. Come on, Tony, you know the reverse is the truth. They were brutal, evil, colonial subjugators operating from a Roman empire ideology, not the Christian Word of God.[9]

"Listen, FOX News could send you to South America, Tony. Yeah! You could meet and interview the modern-day cavaliers, the 'colonial' pirates on the front line. Pirates who are illegally clearing forest for soya beans, prospecting for gold, coal, oil and rare minerals. You could expose them, kicking First Nation people out of the rainforest. Do some real journalism, get out of your studio!

"So, my turn to ask a question, Tony.

"Will the USA and the British Constitutional monarchies atone? Will they renegotiate their constitutional powers. It's time for them to make reparations with the First Nation peoples. Their constitutions are based on an ancient international law which is a lie.

"Let's be clear there were Founders and U.S. Presidents in the past, who just awarded themselves and the European American people a fake biblical gift called, 'Manifest Destiny'. President Polk was one of them; there has been more than one President, one not long ago who have made speeches about the 'exceptional' American people having the Judae Christian gift of Manifest Destiny."[10]

"Oh no, Indira! No comment! I'll take the 'Fifth' on that one! That question is way above my pay grade. No way!"

"So, Indira, talk us through some of the other challenges after today's assassination."

"I am sorry, Tony; I must finish there. You won't answer *my* questions! Quid pro quo? Let's try it! You answer, I'll answer? Could be fun?"

Tony smiled an uncomfortable smile and began wrapping up the interview.

"One last question then, Indira?"

"No, I think I have given you and your audience a few things to think over. Oh, and by the way, if you and others out there want to, you can either attend or listen in to the Capital One Arena, '*A Conversation Event*' on November 8. I'll be there with the Presidential Envoy. We'll be discussing the problems with the new Government policy in the world as we know it today."

Indira, raising her hand, doubled down on her rules on no more questions.

"No, Tony, my point is made. You play ball with me; I'll play ball with you."

16

Turning away from the screen, John found Esteban Jackson standing behind him.

"Powerful stuff! You must be John Green."

"Yeah. Listen, I'm not sure I know who Drake Collins is or even what he looks like. Where is he anyway?"

"He's a tall white guy with a big head of ginger hair. I met him briefly. I haven't seen him for a while. But you and I, Mr Green, we can just carry on."

John nodded, smiled and shook Esteban's outstretched hand.

"Okay, I've just seen the guy you describe on the street, he's still on that phone call. Let's get on, you lead the way."

So, it was Esteban alone who began to give John a basic understanding about why he was being sent down south. As Esteban spoke, in his own research and thoughts, John begrudgingly began to agree with Anna Mckenna's decision to send him to Oklahoma. At the same time, he was realising he had been drawn in by the unusual, complex dynamics of Indira Anand's interview.

"Right, Esteban, I am here to listen. Tell me what you've found out and what you think I need to know. I am all yours."

"Okay, John. I can tell you that if I ever get to be where you're sitting, as the boss of all this, I'll listen to someone like me. It's great for me to understand you don't know everything."

John squirmed and spurred Esteban on to make tracks.

"C'mon, Esteban, don't make a meal out of this, just shoot!"

"Okay, well, I've found out that Isaac Lightfoot is a pretty unusual character. He's definitely a registered Cherokee Indian. His Cherokee registration record says his ancestral line was in the Cherokee East, 'Deer Clan'. The line goes way back to Dorcas Duncan (formally Lightfoot) about 1760.

"Things get complicated within the registration record. As I've said the record says Isaac was born in the line of the Lightfoot family in 1938, then removed to the Dakota boarding school, aged four; that was 1942. However, I've tried to triangulate his registration information with the boarding school and couldn't make it tally.

"There were five boys, aged four, taken to the Dakota boarding school in 1948, only one began assimilation that year and was given the name 'Isaac'. That boy was a Dakota Nation child, born in 1944.

"Maybe this doesn't matter to us now; but you might feel you want to clarify it. The Cherokee registration date of birth makes him ninety years of age. The Dakota boarding school data makes him eighty-four years of age; quite a difference.

"Worth knowing the boarding schools chose surnames for these children. The surname for this 'Isaac' I've been looking at, is, Reaper. So, teaching reports say this 'Isaac Reaper' was very strong in 'arithmetic and reading'. That tallies with our Isaac, looking at what happened in his future employment much later on.

"For whatever reasons, John, the Dakota boarding school record describes 'Isaac Reaper' becoming a 'runner'; he absconded in 1962. If this was our Isaac, he made that journey of some 850 miles with very few resources. As a fourteen-year-old, he would have had to be personally determined and resourceful to survive. The literature on 'runners' tells us many died trying to escape. Isaac would have had to make tough, but sound judgements, all along the way to survive. After arriving in Oklahoma, we can't see *how* Isaac got a start working in the city bank or how his career progressed. I've found an 'Isaac Lightfoot' just turning up in employment records in the Oklahoma bank as a 'runner.'"

Esteban chuckled as John looked quizzically into Estebans eyes.

"I know, he was qualified in 'running'... bad joke. Sorry!

"How did he progress? He must have had help. Maybe someone spotted his mathematics, then coached him? We just don't know. However, it happened because we know Isaac Lightfoot moved later to the Bank of Cherokee County, employed in financial investment work until he retired.

"The move between banks makes a whole lot of sense to me, given Isaac's history of assimilation. The Bank of Cherokee County was founded in 1907; since it's been rebranded the 'Local Bank;'. Isaac would have been able to use his natural mathematical and money skills in a bank that just served, and ploughed investment back into his own Cherokee Nation community. The original strap-line of the bank hasn't changed: '*Large enough to serve, small enough to care*.'"

Esteban briefly faltered, looked up at John with a question in his eyes.

"I'm still in listening mode, Esteban. I'm with you."

"Coming to Wohali, he has quite an early history of delinquency and drugs. Looks like he became a serious addict, under the control of street dealers in Oklahoma. He regularly came to the attention of local police. Avoided prison sentences though where many others might already have been thrown in the can."

"Anymore, Esteban?"

"Thats pretty much it, John. Oh! Of course, both Isaac and Wohali became *American Continental Board Advisors* for the 'Festival'. I guess you knew that. Isaac turns up in publicly published minutes; Wohali is not mentioned so much, but he is mentioned in dispatches, while he was travelling the American Continent; that's when he was gathering together two hundred First Nation peoples to join him at the Memorial.

"I know, from Phoenix's instructions, you only like short summaries. There's a massive library here in the FBI. So, I've speed-read a batch of academic papers and selected some other attachments which you can read in flight.

"My advice? If you take the time, believe me, they will help orientate you."

"That's great, Esteban. Tell me. You've only arrived here today, where did you find the skills of putting all this together? You've done a great job for me!"

"I studied at the Criminal Justice Institute, Harvard."

John looked briefly into Esteban's eyes and smiled, then slowly turned down the corners of his mouth and nodded in appreciation.

"By the way, Drake? Did he contribute anything to this briefing?"

"Sorry, John, as I say, I don't know where Drake is right now. We've only spoken briefly for twenty minutes. And, no, he didn't contribute a great deal I'm afraid. I'd say he seemed preoccupied and distracted by a phone call he took."

17

John phoned Kay from the office and arranged to meet her at the Ronald Reagan departure lounge.

"Okay, John, let me put you on 'loudspeaker'. You will have to mind your language though; Brenda is here helping out."

"Hi, Kay, and Brenda! I've spoken to George; he tells me, Brenda, you've already spoken to Kay about what's happening. I'm just waiting, reading my briefings before my flight to Oklahoma. I can't say I am feeling that good, but I know I have to go."

In the background, John could hear Kay and Brenda still packing the clothes they thought he'd need. In between, Kay spoke to the kids, letting them know John was on the line. *'Shhh! Daddies on the phone!'*

"Look, John, ever since George phoned Brenda, I have been watching the wall-to-wall news coverage of what's happened at the Memorial. Brenda told me the attorney general has asked for you specifically. Well, you know what I say? I say, *so what?*"

Kay was pressurised in her speech and continued to be pretty much oblivious of anything John said.

"Okay, John. Obviously, it's one thing to be saving the planet but the news channels are saying the activists for the 'Festival' are intensifying a *'climate battle'*. They want to dismantle the

U.S. laws on land ownership, written in the 1800s? I don't know about that stuff; a guy called John Marshall wrote this law based on some 'Doctrine' or other. They're saying this will help resolve climate change. Well, right now, it's impossible for us in the general public to understand that!"

"Yeah, Kay, I know all about their aims. I think you'll…"

"John, it's a powerful, highly charged, strand of their climate change policy; important people don't like it. They call it 'living inside nature'. Their blurb says it's a remedy to our 'centuries of domination of indigenous people and animal species'. Of course, it's all our fault, John; it's all about the pollution from our Industrial Revolution.

"Basically, their strategy is to get us, the public, to immediately stop doing all the shit that damages and destroys other species and their habitats. Who's gonna wanna do all that? Our country is addicted, John; this nation drinks oil, breathes gas and eats coal?!!"

"Look Kay, I think you're…"

John continued trying to respond, even though Kay hadn't finished.

"Well, darlin', thanks for the heads-up. Look, I was *at* the International Festival of the Earth event. I saw it all from about fifty yards, the assassination, and the chaos. I ain't got a choice here! The company bosses' director, Anna McKenna, and the White House, think I am the guy to lead the investigation in Oklahoma."

John could hear Kay and Brenda continuing to pack his clothes from inside his headphones. He could hear Brenda's voice goading Kay in the background, *"Go on, Kay, you tell him your fears, lay down the law. Who the hell does George think he is anyhow?"*

Somehow, John knew there was still more to come.

"John, look, I know you are not stupid, darling, but, by the same token, neither am I! I'm worried about two things.

First, 'politically' you could just be an FBI tethered goat here. You know what a scapegoat is?! If you fail to *'shut it down'* or whatever else it was George said, you could easily become toast! What good is that going to do us? And don't forget that time you were away and had an affair! We had only just got together after that time! Can't they send Phoenix?"

"Kay, look, I *want* to be in Washington, I *want* to be home with you and the kids, right? But there ain't a choice! Shit! It don't matter what fancy psychodynamics you apply, or how you pose, wearing that colourful psychotherapist hat of yours, it makes no difference Kay! I arrived in my job two years ago as an Executive Lead at thirty-five years of age. Hell, Kay, that's never been done before!"

"But, John, you're not listening…"

With a fast-diminishing attention span, John took yet another breath for a final blast.

"Look, Kay, we are talking about rules of the state here. My job involves finding justice for people across our nation; don't matter who they are. We're not talking about the theories of psychotherapy here, if we were, it would take months to make a decision! I'll stay in touch. This task could take two days, it could take more. Let the kids know, Kay. Tell them I love them."

At that point John rang off.

Later, Kay arrived early at the Ronald Reagan Washington National Airport departure lounge in person. She handed over John's suitcase. Instinctively he caught her hand as she moved to leave, still annoyed.

Then, pulling her close, John tried to make the peace, kissing her before saying goodbye.

"Look, Kay, stay close. This is the life we chose, for better or worse."

Finally, waving as Kay left, John was still left feeling he had failed.

Day 1   18

Norman
Cleveland County

Saturday
November 2

Kamama Catawnee had just finished leading a one-day, Saturday community seminar in her department at the University of Oklahoma, Norman Campus. She was making her way along the corridor toward her office thinking she must find a way to take some time out from the burden of teaching.

As the emeritus professor of Native American Indian culture and politics she was in high demand within her busy department. She had closing deadlines for research papers, students to meet or chase and the Cherokee Nation communities always wanted a piece of her time.

In the back of her thoughts that afternoon Kamama just had been realising that the time had come for her to travel again, take time out; be alone in the mountains. Often, she needed to debrief and plug in spiritually to the natural world. She needed to centre herself, spending time sleeping under the stars. Sometimes her yearning to connect with her roots in the soil physically hurt! She knew though, if she didn't make space for this downtime, she'd soon become dull-witted, uncreative, even depressed.

Arriving at her office door, Kamama got her hand on the door-handle but was thwarted, hearing her PA call out:

"Kamama, when you get in there, I am putting a call through to you. It's the FBI in Washington DC."

Kamama agreed to take the call. Picking up, she found herself talking with George Stanhope, Executive Lead for Homeland Security and Terrorism. Kamama listened as George sped through introductions and gave his customary thanks for her time.

The main question in his spiel, however, suddenly lifted her interest.

"Have you seen any of today's national news about the International Festival of the Earth Day in DC?"

Kamama explained there hadn't been time in her day to connect with the news.

George continued, candidly explaining that national security had been seriously breached at the Lincoln Memorial; a Cherokee Indian guy, Wohali Lightfoot had been assassinated.

As Kamama heard the news she was overcome by a wave of emotion; she heard herself gasp. Her immediate thoughts raced to the Lightfoot family; to Woya, his sister; Isaac, his father; Cary Lightfoot, his wife and their young son, Danuwoa. Kamama knew this family well.

Kamama asked George for more detail. He told the story of the events from his limited knowledge. He explained that a significant investigation had immediately been opened.

Kamama tried to steer George to the reason for his call.

"Well, Mr Stanhope, it's good of you to call and let me know about the assassination of Wohali Lightfoot, but I really can't see what any of this has to do with me."

"Well, Kamama… can I call you Kamama? We're sending a high-level investigator to Oklahoma to meet with Wohali's family tomorrow. We understand they live in Smiths Village? Our FBI investigator, John Green, wants someone to advise and work alongside him on Native American Indian matters.

"So, Kamama, to cut to the chase, we urgently need to commission you to be that advisor. Would you meet our investigator, John, at around 11.30 p.m. tonight at the Will Rogers Airport and get him to the Skirvin Hotel? I think we're talking about five days' work in all; we'll pay you the best grade we can for all the work we ask you to do. Oh, I forgot, I'll get HR to send you a contract."

Kamama remained silent while George continued to try and close the deal. As she spent time weighing the pros and cons, she could hear George breathing, waiting for her decision on the line. Then, thinking more quickly, Kamama reflected again on her earlier thoughts about the need for a break in routine. On the face of it, this commission sounded important, certainly something she *should* do for the Lightfoot family. More than that she was, of course, aware that the material resonated deeply with her own history, her work and her political agenda.

Kamama eventually replied to George after all her thinking and consideration. On replying she smiled to herself and found some humour in the darkness of Wohali's death.

"Well, Mr Stanhope… can I call you George? Your daily pay grade sounds good. I don't want to be paid into my own account though. I'd want it paid as a donation to the International Festival of the Earth. I support their political aims for my people, our land and the planet. I do know the Lightfoot family well. I do think I can help. So, if you and I are agreed, I'll pick up Mr Green at 11.30 p.m. Thank you for your consideration of me and hiring me for this role."

Putting the phone down, Kamama briefly smiled through her distress. She was momentarily enjoying the irony of her small FBI earnings going into the coffers of the International Festival of the Earth.

Kamama buzzed through to her PA and asked her to make a large, three-by-one multicoloured notice on thick card which she could hold up in the arrivals lounge.

"The notice should read, 'ARE YOU JOHN GREEN?'"

Returning to her room and her desktop computer, Kamama pulled down the blind on her door and chased up the national and local Washington news online. She found footage of the final moments of the procession when Wohali was on his stallion, reared regally on his hind legs, right in front of the Lincoln Memorial. She physically flinched as the shots rang out, brutally blowing Wohali off the back of the horse; at the very same time, the stallion himself, fell.

Kamama stood up in front of her computer and switched it off. Sitting back down alone, she broke down into floods of tears.

While her heart broke, Kamama felt the political resolve within her spirit stiffen. As she recovered from her first dive into grief, Kamama picked up the phone knowing she must make contact with Isaac and Woya. Standing holding her office landline phone, Isaac's telephone at home rang out. Isaac never carried or used an iPhone, so Kamama looked through her iPhone for Woya's contact number. As the line rang, Kamama prayed that Woya would pick up.

"Hi… Kamama? Thank the Great Spirit Himself, it's you!"

"Listen, Woya, I've just heard what's happened. Where are you, you're not at home are you?"

"You've seen the news? Isaac and I, we've quickly packed bags. Our dog, Ylva, is with us. We're all at the airport. Isaac thinks the *'Predator'* is seeking to eliminate us all. You know how he thinks. Well, for once, I agree. Whoever these bastards are, we feel they might want us all dead."

In between her words Woya started sobbing.

"Well, Kamama? That's… that's right… They want us dead, don't they!? We're on our way to the retreat. We're worried about Cary, but she's decided to stay put."

"Listen, Woya, the government are sending a high-level investigator to find out what's happened to Wohali. He's flying down tonight from Washington DC. They want me to help him.

Can we both fly over to the retreat, see you as soon as possible? Talk to Isaac. What does he think? Send me the zip code for the retreat."

Kamama listened in to Woya explaining the situation to Isaac.

"Hi, Kamama, the answer's yes. He says we shouldn't be at the retreat alone. Before you travel, Kamama, can you call into Smiths Village and check everything is shut down, put out some food for the birds? We just panicked and fled in a hurry!"

"No worries, of course. Look, Woya, don't worry about Cary; I have an idea we'll see her tomorrow. Okay? Safe journey! See you soon."

As Kamama cut the call, deep down she heard the inevitable questions burbling through her soul. *'How much longer is this journey going to take? How much pain can our Indian nations sustain? When will we ever find our way back home to Turtle Island?'*

The returning whisper from a hard kernel of truth inside Kamama spoke softly back, saying,

'The search for justice takes just as long as it takes.'

19

Around 11.00 p.m. Kamama left her city apartment, jumped into her RV and drove south-west, through downtown Oklahoma City, to the Will Rogers Airport.

Kamama felt at home and boundaried within the cocoon of what she referred to as her 'van'. It was *the* single thing she owned that was capable of transforming her city life, taking her away from concrete and tarmac, to the living earth. Taking time to support Woya and Isaac in the Great Smoky Mountains meant she'd be killing two birds with the same stone.

Arriving at the airport arrivals lounge, Kamama could see there were about a dozen people on the same kind of mission, all waiting for the arrival of the midnight plane from Washington DC. For a while she stood with her large, colourful notice by her side.

A random guy wandered over and, standing too close to her, looked sideways to Kamama and said, '*Hi, there's a delay. The D-D-DC flight could be a-a-a-arriving, s-s-s-sometime after midnight!*'

Kamama nodded, briefly observing this guy from the corner of her gaze. His clothing was looking unkempt and dishevelled, his hair was greasy, and he seemed to have a physical tic of nervous energy coursing through his head and neck. This made him appear as if he was either about to move on or was just perpetually trying hard to settle.

Kamama tried her best to ignore him.

"*L-L-Look, can I get you a c- c- coffee or maybe you'd like something s-stronger? We could sit somewhere and relax?*"

For Kamama that was definitely a, 'No!' She gave him a steely look directly in the eye and firmly declined.

"What do you take me for, a hooker?"

Midnight came around.

It was then a further fifteen minutes until the arrivals board showed the Washington DC flight had landed. It wasn't long before a few of the first tired, straggler passengers began making their way through.

Kamama lifted her notice and smiled the best smile she could give for the time of day.

Day 2 — 1

Oklahoma City

Sunday
November 3

When John stepped off the plane, he realised it was already the next day.

He walked, zombified, toward the airport arrival lounge. He knew he was looking out for the Cherokee Indian expert George had commissioned as his advisor. John cursed George under his breath, thinking to himself, '*Hell, George, I don't even know whether this person is a man or a woman!*'

Collecting his case from the airport carousel, John dragged it behind him further into the arrival lounge, its wheels humming on the flooring. Looking around, John noticed a large, colourfully painted board, which was asking:

'*ARE YOU JOHN GREEN?*'

Looking underneath the noticeboard John saw a young woman who was smiling broadly. Pretty soon it became clear that George had linked him up with a young woman in her mid-thirties, about five feet six, 125lbs, thick, long black hair worn well below shoulder length. She wore a black leather jacket, a bright green-and-yellow cotton top and jeans. In the poor light John noticed, through his tired gaze, that she had a warm, reddish-brown complexion. Her dark-brown eyes shone from an oval face, portraying chiselled features and high cheekbones.

As he approached, she gave John a warm glowing smile for a welcome. As she smiled, she held out her hand and shook John's with a confident grip.

"Hi, you must be John Green? Welcome to Oklahoma."

"Thanks. Yeah, that's right. Great noticeboard! But I am afraid I don't know your name. George, my colleague, who arranged for you to meet me… well, it seems it was below his pay grade to have even emailed me your gender, let alone your name and contact details."

"That's okay, John. I understand from looking at the TV news that you, the local police and the FBI in Washington DC are under huge pressure tonight. My name is Kamama Catawnee. I am an Emeritus Professor at Oklahoma University; seems George hired me to advise you. I'm sure it's going to be great working with you. I am looking forward to what seems an unusual and very interesting commission.

"But look, its past midnight, we've both had a long day. I've blocked out my calendar for the next five days. Should you need me starting tomorrow, I'm ready and able."

As they turned to cross to the exit of the airport, John told Kamama that he had been booked into the Skirvin Hilton, in Oklahoma City.

Kamama briefly smiled, stopped on the tarmac and turned to John.

"John, your 'highly intelligent, very well-paid senior government official' has briefed me a bit more than you credit him for. George told me where to take you!"

John cursed George under his breath.

"Good for George then, that's something."

As John walked across the parking area with Kamama he saw she was leading him to a cream-and-blue coloured RV with a bike strapped to the back and an aerial on the top. She opened a luggage compartment underneath and stored John's case. Soon, they were making their way through the city.

"Hey, Kamama, this is some vehicle."

"Yeah, isn't she great! Apart from my work at the university, I need to get away. This wonderful van helps me do that. The city is okay, and I love my work, but often my soul demands that I need refuelling, living in the natural world."

"Just to put a note down in the back of your mind, John. I have an academic and political interest in the work of the International Festival of the Earth. To their credit they're doing something new…"

"Yeah, I heard an interview today, someone called Indira Anand? FOX News were asking her about all that. Then my wife briefed me. Seems like it's big news. Tomorrow, Kamama, I'll need you to introduce me to Isaac, Woya and Cary Lightfoot."

"Oh, John! I forgot to mention to you, Isaac and Woya Lightfoot fled Oklahoma yesterday. They'd become terrified, fearful right after Wohali's assassination; they felt there could be people out there who would also want them dead. They've gone to a retreat they use in the Smoky Mountains. We'll need to talk tomorrow about taking a flight to meet them."

They spent the rest of their journey in a tired but comfortable silence. When Kamama dropped John off they said their goodbyes and arranged to meet the following morning at 10.00 a.m., after breakfast.

Having booked into his room, John just needed to crash. But still, even though he was tired, it was John's habit, no matter how wrecked he was, to unpack and put all his stuff into drawers and hang the rest in the wardrobe.

Finally, he showered, before falling into bed.

Before switching his bedside lights out, John scanned the room itself, perhaps in an effort to remember where he was; so often in the past, John had woken up in rooms like these, not really knowing where he was.

2

So, the morning came too soon, squinting through John's blinds and curtains.

As he opened his eyes, within a few seconds, he remembered he was in Oklahoma City. John rested his head briefly back on his pillow. Staring at the ceiling, he mulled over his mixed feelings about leaving both his family and Washington DC behind. But the way George had set things up with Phoenix, really rankled.

Getting out of bed, he shaved, showered and called room service for an 8.30 a.m. breakfast.

After breakfast, John got himself into clean clothes. He pulled down a different, grey, dry-cleaned suit, white shirt and a different-coloured tie. Picking up the black shoes he'd worn the day before, he considered the other two pairs Kay had packed, then decided black would have to do. Before going down in the elevator John ate his breakfast and packed his small business case. He included the equipment he would need later for the interview with Cary Lightfoot. The digital interview recorder was, perhaps, *the* essential tool which transcribed and transferred interviews onto an FBI-wide, accessible electronic record in seconds.

So, with his breakfast finished, John automatically followed one of his long-standing 'investigator' routines and logged into

Wohali Lightfoot's case record. The record showed John that the evidence CSI forensics had bagged and labelled was the shooters' detritus from the Memorial. He knew this was valuable crap. They had begun to assume this evidence was from two, even even three individuals. John would be wanting confirmation of just how many individuals were hiding out in the Undercroft. Everything would be forensically analysed for DNA and prints later on that day, then the results would be checked against the national databases.

On the audio record John found himself listening to the unmistakable, deep-throated voice of David O'Donnelly, FBI Senior Forensic Scientist. He was objectively describing and summarising immediate results to date:

'The bullet killing Wohali Lightfoot entered his forehead and travelled out through the back of the skull, blowing out a huge exit wound. Death was instantaneous.'

'A fingertip search across the paving of the Mall at the bottom of the Memorial steps has located the bullet killing Wohali Lightfoot. This bullet, though, is in poor condition from striking hard surfaces after passing through Lightfoot's skull. We could be looking at an AK 47, probably the deadliest weapon on the black market.

'The bullet killing the stallion is still embedded in the animal and will be removed by the veterinary surgeon performing the post-mortem tomorrow. This bullet should be in much better condition and carry some precise, unique identifying information about the weapons the assassins were using.'

David's final comments went on to summarise the high-quality work Phoenix and the CSI had done securing the the Memorial Undercroft crime scene.

No suspects had yet been identified.

3

Day 2

Washington DC

Sunday
November 3

Phoenix was at home with her husband, Trent.

They'd both taken their time over breakfast before leaving to attend their Sunday Service at Nineteenth Street Baptist Church. Afterwards they'd planned to drive to their local mall for some weekly groceries. Beyond there they had planned a relaxing day, visiting Phoenix family on the other side of the city. Just before they could get out of the door Phoenix's phone rang. John's name lit up on her screen. Phoenix looked across at Trent and showed him the name on her screen.

She smiled, shrugged and whispered, "Sorry, I gotta take this, honey."

Walking back into her kitchen she took a seat at their dining table.

"Hey, John, we gotta make this short, we're just heading out the door to get to church. What does Oklahoma look like?"

"Phoenix, it was dark when I got here, I've just showered and had breakfast. Pulling back my blinds, all I can see out of the window is a hotel parking lot and an inner-city freeway snaking through some tower blocks. I could be fucking anywhere in most major cities of the world. It's good to hear your voice though, Phoenix."

"Okay, John. Before you ask about how the teams are doing, don't. Yesterday they did a great job. I know you'll have listened to David's audio, so no need to labour those points."

John asked what else was happening.

"Well, we're gathering in all the CCTV we can. We're checking out if there might have been some kind of manipulation or tampering with the CCTV installation. The very early morning footage when the assassins must have left the Undercroft, seems missing. Maybe it's a technical fault but then again, maybe it ain't, we'll see and follow up for any foul play."

"The CSI followed through on the shooter's escape routes. There are witness reports from members of the public seeing two figures running in black tunics and hoods. They must have changed somewhere. Seems these assassins were professionally researched though. They knew about CCTV blindspots. We're still trying to identify where they changed clothing. We figure they might have dumped the black tunics, hoods and equipment along the way, so city police are searching the bins."

"Right now, they seem to have disappeared off the face of the Earth. But I guess they will have had a driver waiting for them."

John momentarily changed the subject.

"Before you go on, Phoenix. What's going on with Drake Collins? Strictly between us, Esteban Jackson told me he has been, quote, 'distracted by a phone call', unquote? I gotta say, Esteban and Drake, well, they seem to me to be like apples and oranges. I'll tell you now I saw Drake yesterday pacing up and down the pavement outside the office. He was arguing with someone about, *'paying his father's debts'*."

"My view on Drake? I've only met him briefly, just once, John. He seemed to be doin' good.

"But thanks, John, I'll bear it in mind. I'll keep an eye on him, don't you worry about that!"

"Oh, and not long after you left for Oklahoma, Anna McKenna phoned me about where she wanted the interns placed, saying, 'With John gone, I'm sure you have a lot on your plate, Phoenix'. So, she's placed the interns with team leaders already. I guess she was just trying to be helpful. So, just to let you know, Esteban is with Charlotte and Drake is with Jason. That choice will no doubt please you. If you think Drake needs knocking into shape, you'll be agreed that Jason is *the* best professional role model, for Drake. As I said, the team leaders are fine."

"I've tried to reach Jim Coogan, he seems to have gone missing for the moment. I guess he just works differently to everyone else, John?

"Charlotte is personally connecting with your own request that we need to make fast inroads into the Mall Maintenance Service. Her plan has been to do a lot of the early information-gathering by phone and then conduct an interview about access to the Undercroft and how things hang operationally, with the maintenance manager.

"So, Charlotte has already done some of that over the phone. She's spoken to a guy called Greg Tranter. He's told her that someone arranged for him to meet an FBI officer called 'John Green' two months ago. I've checked your calendar, John. It never happened, so something is adrift there.

"Charlotte has got a description and this man, he was tall, grey-haired, well turned out, carrying impressive and believable FBI ID. So, your imposter, 'John Green', said he was checking on the Memorial security arrangements prior to the International Festival of the Earth event. Significantly, Tranter showed him round, including the Undercroft!"

"That sounds great, Phoenix. Were there any other additional identification factors mentioned in the phone call with this Tranter guy?"

"Funny you should mention that. You're in luck there too, John! Charlotte has reported that when Tranter and the imposter parted, then they shook hands. As this 'Mr Green' reached out to shake hands, his jacket sleeve rose up his arm a couple inches, revealing a tattoo of a cockerel's head on his forearm.

"Look, John, I gotta dash now. I'll catch up with you later on in the afternoon, from my parents' house. I've checked your calendar sitting here, right now you've got to meet your emeritus professor, in five, at 10.00 a.m."

"Good luck with that!"

Day 2 4

Skirvin Hotel
Oklahoma City

Sunday
November 3

Kamama Catawnee arrived in the Skirvin Hotel lobby to meet John Green, right on the stroke of 10 a.m. As she made her way to the reception desk to announce her arrival, John came across the lobby from inside the hotel.

Kamama was wearing her same black leather jacket and jeans, however, she'd changed wearing a crimson blouse and black, silver-buckled and zipped-up ankle boots. She shook John's hand as he welcomed her, showing her the way through to a quiet spot in the hotel restaurant, where they could grab a couple of coffees and talk.

"First of all, you need to hear this, John. I told George, I have known Isaac Lightfoot for two, maybe two and a half years now. He and I met not long after I was appointed to my professorial chair. Isaac had a previous working relationship with my predecessor in the department. In my time here I have met Wohali and Isaac on several occasions, purely business. Coincidentally we were in the Smokies at the same time once and I met them at the retreat they use.

"Isaac still turns up in my department as a volunteer, supporting student learning. To us, he's a respected survivor from the trauma of assimilation, following his compulsory removal from his parents to a boarding school. Isaac was in a seminar just last week, adding the kind of experience students just can't get a feeling for from books. He's the real deal. He can talk about post traumatic stress, his experiences of boarding school life. You name it, he's just alive with lived history.

"I've let Cary know you want to meet her. So, we have a midday appointment, if you approve.

"Great, I'm ready to rock. We'll soon get to know one another. That's just great, Kamama! Great anticipation, all of this is very urgent. I'm sure we'll be able to strike a balance, work at speed, but hopefully, not so fast we miss stuff!"

"Look, we could just scoot, talk as we drive. I've taken the liberty of renting a car. That RV of yours, love it as I do, well, I thought a car would be easier to get us around the city with."

"Before we go to Cary's place, I told Woya we'd pop into Isaac's house. Just make sure it's secured after they fled."

On the way through the city, Kamama began covering some of the things she needed to advise him about.

"John, there is something you've got to know about Isaac; something he has given me permission for me to disclose to you."

"Okay, hit me with it."

Kamama remained silent until John had negotiated the next set of stop lights.

"Isaac is quite an ill man. He has not long been diagnosed with a form of leukaemia. His prognosis could be okay; from his many years working with both the Oklahoma and Cherokee banks he is financially secure, he can afford treatment. Right now, though, he has a clinical team who are gearing up to treat him."

"This is the reason why he couldn't attend the 'Festival' at the Lincoln Memorial; he was booked to deliver the keynote speech. I guess the Creator must have been looking over him at that time."

"It's possible."

"The consequences of this illness right here and now are that we need to take the coming conversations at his pace. He tires easily. There've already been times when, before I knew he was ill at all, I felt him needing a break and a rest. Initially I just thought it was aging, but it's part of his clinical picture."

"Okay, Kamama, why do I get the feeling there is more to this story? So, what is it?"

"Heh! I am learning fast. You're a pretty full-on guy, aren't you?! You get to the point fast, huh? No, there is nothing more. Woya and Isaac approve of our travelling to the retreat. Interestingly, Woya particularly didn't feel they should be left alone at this time.

"As I say, I've been to the retreat once before. It's impossible not to love it there. But I've gotta tell you, we'll need to find you some thick socks and a pair of walking boots and a couple of items of clothing. We've gotta get you out of that grey suit, the white shirt and the green tie! Those black shiny shoes; we're gonna trade them in for walking boots."

Kamama laughed out loud, then realised she'd begun to feel at ease in John's company.

"I'll take your advice on the Smoky Mountain uniform. From my side though, Kamama, we are trying to work at pace. This ain't a holiday."

"So, John, before we arrive, take me through our task this morning."

"First and foremost, it's a tough time to be interviewing Cary; if you can provide empathy, that would be helpful. Our task though today is getting to know Wohali and his life through Cary's eyes. Understand him looking through the prism of Cary's perspectives.

"We're trying to find his heartbeat, how he thinks and

behaves. What's he been up to working for the 'Festival'? More importantly, who has he been working with? Cary is one of *the* key subjective family observers we have. She'll know more than she thinks, our skill is to unlock it. Then, there are questions about whether she is safe to remain in her own house. So, a risk assessment. Anything else coming to hand in the interview we support her to talk about, is a bonus."

"Oh, John! That reminds me, Woya and Isaac said they *were* concerned about her safety."

"That's good, Kamama… See? We are already working well together."

"John, I think it would be good if we met over a meal tonight, at your hotel. We should speak about my background and knowledge. I need to understand who you are as well. I can't help you if I don't get to know you. I'll need a space to ask you my questions, in my own way. Is that okay?"

John nodded. He looked briefly across at Kamama. She seemed preoccupied.

"Yep! OK, Kamama. Sounds like a good idea."

Day 2　　　　　　　　　　　　　5

Smiths Village
Oklahoma City

Sunday
November 3

Arriving at Cary's house at Smiths Village, it was Kamama who was first out of the car, making her way up to the door.

Kamama rang the bell. Inside she could hear Cary talking, explaining to Danuwoa that she was just going to the door.

"Hi, Kamama."

Cary put her hand out towards John for a firm handshake. She looked wasted. Her hair was untended, and she looked like she needed a good, long sleep. Closing the door behind her, she took orders for drinks and put some cookies on a plate.

Kamama listened as John explained the interview was a 'voluntary' interview. Cary could opt for a formal interview, alternatively, she could see how it goes and stop at any time. John said he'd organise an interview with her attorney alongside, all Cary had to do was stop and ask. Kamama watched as John set his digital recorder down on a low table; he listened carefully to Cary's response.

"It's okay, Mr Green. I want to do everything I can to make

progress toward justice for Wohali. Whoever did this terrible thing has gotta pay, right?"

John began by simply asking how Cary was feeling.

Cary sat, with her head down; her pain was raw, but she quickly came up for air, expressing her feelings.

"How am I feeling Mr Green? What I am feeling is, how am I gonna tell his three-year-old… son…? His father ain't comin' home?"

Kamama moved in closer to Cary and placed a hand on her arm; John briefed Cary on how they could help.

"So, listen up, Cary. We can bring help to you on these kinds of questions. Only if you want us to though. We have access to crime liaison officers, they will listen to you, advise and understand how you feel. Okay? Can we talk about that at the end of our interview? Okay?"

Cary nodded and placed a hand on top of Kamama's.

"So Cary, can you tell us about Wohali in your own words, Cary? How did he appear in the time leading up to leaving for the International Festival of the Earth in Washington DC? Was he stressed? I've heard that in the past Wohali had addiction problems, were there, say, any signs of Wohali relapsing? Were there signs of him having made enemies in his work? Was there anyone you can think of immediately who might then seek to assassinate him?"

Cary looked down to the floor again, allowing a short silence before answering.

"For people like you who never knew Wohali… you'd think he might be stressed, leading all those thousands of people to the Lincoln Memorial. But he wasn't, John. He was up for the gig. As for addiction, we both broke our addictions long ago. Neither of us have ever relapsed over the four years since we got together. Right now, I could use some anaesthetics, for sure. But believe me, I ain't relapsing. We knew about pressure. Understood what it could do. We'd double down on each other. Know what I mean? Protected one another."

Then Cary confirmed Wohali's strengths.

"Wohali became a different person after living with Isaac, before Danuwoa was born. Both of them, working for the 'Festival' was the best thing for him. He became knowledgeable and passionate; he found his authority and the desire to lead. He became a proud, respected member of the Cherokee community; the 'Festival' had lit a fire burning in his belly!

"Long before that, as a child, Wohali told me his relationship with Isaac became abusive. Eventually it got so bad that the family split; they moved into different houses. That was after Isaac assaulted Wohali, aged ten, maybe eleven years old. Isaac punched Wohali unconscious in the kitchen. After that, Adsila, Wohali's mother, decided, she and the kids would live in this property; she left Isaac with no choice but to live on his own."

"So, how did that affect Wohali?"

"Well, the story Wohali told me was he became uncontrollable; he disappeared into the drug world. Drug dealers controlled him, maintained his addiction in exchange for running drugs around the city; sometimes even further afield into other states, West Virginia I think was one."

"Wohali told me, before Isaac had made his peace with him, he'd been out of control as a father. Adsila told me, when the children were born, Isaac didn't know how to be a father. Adsila blamed the boarding school and the abuse he experienced there. If you ask Isaac, he'd agree."

Kamama noticed that Cary was beginning to look anxious. Her long blonde hair was tousled down her face. Suddenly, she looked lost and dishevelled.

John quickly opened up a new line of questioning.

"So, Cary, you've talked about Wohali and Isaac. Tell me about your own family, will you? Were there any difficulties between the families after your marriage? Your marriage was, after all, a mixed-race marriage. Whichever way you cut it; both your families were from two very different cultures. Seems to me that could be a recipe for a stressful collision?"

Kamama noticed Cary's hands had moved back onto her lap. She had slender, worried fingers with cracked nail polish. Some of her nails were bitten to their quicks.

Cary started to paint a picture of her family.

"Last time I saw my mother was just after Danuwoa was born; she was looking older. When I left, I was worried about her. She seemed vague. Detached. I can't put a finger on it. She just seemed different somehow."

"Tell us about your own childhood."

"Yeah. I'd say our childhood always seemed to us to be pretty normal on the homestead. We weren't wild kids; we were given freedom to roam and play in the woods to our hearts' content. I guess you could say we were free compared to the kids I see on the streets in Oklahoma City today."

"And your parents?"

"Well, as I've said, my parents are aging now, John. My father was a good man as a father. He loved us. We always had food. Some neighbours back in those days, didn't. My mother was the warm heart of our home. But truth be told, both did all they could to love and care for us. Have I said they are both still alive? Yeah?"

John nodded.

"I have two younger brothers who are both grown up now. But they ain't married yet. They don't live at home with our parents any longer, they live nearby; sorry, I'm not losing the plot, am I? As far as I know the three men are still very close."

John interrupted.

"No, you're doing fine. Tell me about the 'men'?"

"In the early days, my brothers tried to drive Wohali out of my life. I've always thought my father would have been the one who sent them. John and Charles, they've become his 'enforcers' these days. They do all his dirty work. They would turn up here hammering on the door. Sometimes, they'd be roaring drunk. Screaming and threatening us with all kinds of menaces.

"Wohali was no pushover though. He'd learnt when he was a kid, down in the gutter of the drugs trade, how to defend us and himself. He was a survivor, John."

Cary remained silent for a moment.

Looking up, John saw her eyes shone. Her eyelids rimmed with tears, glistening. Then laughing, she mopped the occasional tear that breached a bottom lid and chased down her face. She shook her head, not welcoming the intrusion of her grief.

"Hell, John. I'm just remembering a day… a day when that door behind you was kicked and hammered so hard… I thought the whole house would fall in."

Cary smiled and whispered,

"My God, John! My lover that day…he was fearless; made of steel."

Her smile unexpectedly burst into a bubble of laughter.

"Ha! First, he'd refuse them entry into the house, bellowing, 'John and Charles, you listen' out there!!? You ain't getting in here. So, you'd both better get used to it, right here and now. Fuck off!'"

By this time, Kamama was sitting on the floor with Danuwoa on her lap. Hearing his mother shout, his head jerked up and he put his hands over his ears.

Cary looked at her son and placed a calming hand on his, then returned to telling her story.

"Then, at other times, Wohali, he'd squeeze himself out of the door and actually go outside with them! See, John, we'd often agree beforehand. I'd lock the door on the inside. Then he'd walk close by them, taking them away from the house. Sometimes, he'd even swagger in between them. He was the taller and broader of the three men.

"On this day, I'm remembering… with no warning, he'd just turned round and faced them both! He shuffled forward.

Went toe to toe with them, his long black hair flying. Then, with those dark-brown eyes of his, he went eyeball to eyeball. To me, I thought his whole body would explode any minute! Mr Green, if I could feel the threat of real violence in him from inside the house, then God only knows what Charles and John felt, staring down the barrel, into Wohali's eyes."

Cary continued her story.

"Then, looking Charles in the eye, he shoved him in the chest, so hard he lost balance and staggered back. Then, looking at John, he shoved him the same. Then, he got into his stride. He repeated the pattern of threats and shoves, and threats and shoves, till eventually, they lost their ground on our property. In the end they actually had backed away so far, they stumbled, right out of that gate."

Cary burst into a peel of laughter.

"Well, Wohali closed that gate out there and laughed in their faces. He came inside and collapsed in that chair; that very chair you're sitting in, saying, '*Fucking white scum!*'.

Cary's mood suddenly slumped, and she sighed gently to herself.

"Well, John, I don't know what I am gonna do without him now. My father, he'll do all he can to force me home. What'll happen to Danuwoa? Well, we are not going back; we're gonna need a future on our own where I can honour my husband's ideas, his memory, raise his little son into a full-grown warrior…"

Watching Cary's genuine determination about her future, John, speaking softly, began fanning the dying embers of her description of her brother's violent behaviour.

"Cary, your brothers, to be clear, they sound like enemies of your marriage, don't they? Trying to break you two up! They were definitely Wohali's enemies, weren't they? What else can you tell me about those men from your family."

"Our family name is Soul. Did either of you know that?"

John shrugged and shook his head.

Cary looked between Kamama and John, as if they should know what that meant. Eventually, she shrugged after neither of them showed any recognition of their surname. Since it didn't register with either of them, Cary went on to explain.

"My father always said our family name goes all the way back to the voyage of the *Mayflower*, sailing from England? Our father was always reading us children the story of the *Mayflower*! The book was actually about Captain Myles Standish. How he was hired as *the* one, English, military advisor to the Plymouth colony. I can hear my dad's voice telling us now, '*And so he fulfilled his promise and protected the original pilgrims from danger...*'[11]

"I told Wohali about this back in our early days. Just like Isaac, he'd research stuff like this; so, he researched the names of the people who sailed. He laughed, saying there was never anyone by the name of 'Soul' who sailed; said there was one man, George Soule, so my father must've grown up mistaken. I don't know. Sorry, Mr Green, I've strayed from your question."

"That's okay, Cary, I'll stop you if I want to ask you something different. Tell me more about the family. We have time. This is a Sunday, mid-morning, it's quiet, there's really no rush."

"Well, my family has a long history of living in Oklahoma District. We were not a wealthy family. My father is still a professional carpenter to this day. He was always honourable in a strange way. The neighbours respected him. He never harmed anyone. I can't remember anyone speaking bad of him.

"We knew he loved and supported us all. As I've said, men who were neighbours, definitely went off the rails. They'd disappear down the local speakeasies and gin joints; anything rather than work, clothe and feed their kids. Some of their women, they'd have to sell their bodies to make ends meet. Our mother was never driven to that.

"Our men worked, no question. My brothers probably still work in the business with my father. They're genuine grafters; they've given all their time in loyalty to their father. "

"Our father told us children, that in modern times the menfolk had served and fought in the First and Second World Wars in Europe. I know that at least one, maybe more of my father's relatives served our country; fought and died in the Vietnam War in the 1970s. Others served in Iraq. We'd talk at the dinner table; he'd be swallowing a mouthful of dinner, then father would say, pointing and jabbin' his knife, *'The menfolk in our family have all been proud patriots. You kids, you'd better listen up! There'd be no America without the likes of them!'* Then he'd go back to eating his roast."

John continued to probe, asking basic questions to fill in the gaps.

"How did you come to meet and marry Wohali?"

"We met in a rehab addictions unit. We were both recovering from double addictions. Both of us had come to love 'Charlie' and then, the beautiful kicking power of 'Horse'.

Cary took a moment, warmly remembering her and Wohali getting their relationship together.

"We got real loved up and close in rehab. Love is what pulled us through. It became our bond of steel, never to be broken. Our marriage wasn't popular on my family's side. My father was 'disappointed'.

"Wohali never said what Isaac and Woya said about me.

Cary smiled nervously. Then looking at Kamama, she chuckled.

"Yeah, I know. Understatement, huh? They couldn't have been happy."

"They've never told me what they think of you, Cary."

"As far as the old man was concerned, I was marrying a full-blood, Cherokee Indian who was also an addict. Double trouble! Back then Wohali and I, we were recovering, telling the world we'd always be addicts. We were just keeping ourselves clean, telling the world we could never go back. Father, though took it literally. '*What? You and that Indian, you'll always be addicts!*'.

My father though, good man or bad, sometimes he loved to just cut me dead when he talked about my marriage.

"Out walking in the woods with the dogs once, he said, '*Time was, Cary, it wasn't even legal in this state for white folks to marry any kinda Indian. Just one drop of blood made a marriage like yours illegal then. Your 'son', Cary. He ain't got just one drop of blood, he's got half a body full!!*'.

"It didn't matter to him that Isaac was a respected banker. It was all a matter of 'blood' to him. Isaac could have been President of the United States for all he cared; it'd still be the same. My mother, she'd never challenge my father out in the open. To this day my mother, father and brothers, they've never even met Danuwoa in person! My father… he just controlled all that."

"So now, you're alone, Cary?"

"You can make what you like like of that, Mr Green. I know my mother wants to see Danuwoa. She's just seen him secretly, from photographs. I've watched her eyes. You know? When she took that picture closer, her eyes melted with a smile of pleasure. As her eyes lit, she wiped a tear. The 'men', Mr Green, they'd never show that kinda love. Doubt they've ever felt a tear rolling down one of their manly cheeks. Not about anything."

Kamama, hearing the volume of Danuwoa's play rising, she turned to John and whispered that she felt Cary might need a break.

However, John had one further question.

"Cary, I am coming toward the end of this first part of the interview, then we want to give you a break. It's simple enough. It's a 'yes' or 'no' question. Does your father have a tattoo of a cockerel or a cockerel's head on his right forearm?"

Kamama watched Cary standing, then bend to lift Danuwoa, balancing him on her hip. John sensed she was on the edge of flight, or fight. He considered that she may ask them to leave her property altogether. He'd seen it all before.

"Look, no worries, Cary, don't you forget this is voluntary. You want to be represented, say so."

John formally advised her again for the record. But he still couldn't see any sign of Cary's anxiety subsiding. Suddenly, she started looking spooked. She looked just like a high-spirited palomino, trapped inside a palisade, struggling kettled up, trying her best to get beyond the fences and into the wide-open land beyond.

"It's okay, Cary. We'll all take that break now."

Having stepped outside, John reflected on what had just happened with Kamama.

"What I can't fathom is what has freaked Cary so badly. I've done what I can to calm her."

"I'm learning, John, for someone who seems a fairly thoughtful man, at times, you also can't see the forest for the trees. This is all about a fear of her father. He's real and alive. It's not only that, he lives *inside* her. She even speaks his sentences!"

John slowly nodded.

"Sounds a likely explanation, Kamama. Good to have your female perspective. You're right, I don't always have twenty-twenty vision. I knew I'd touched a nerve."

Then, John carried on explaining the investigation processes.

"So, to explain, if Cary is unable to answer on this specific question about her father and say, she just stalls; switches into making, '*No comment*'; maybe just says, '*I'd rather not say*', I will have to bring her back for a formal interview later today where she can have her attorney present. This is a murder investigation Kamama. Understood? But it's best she has the chance to talk now."

Kamama acknowledged she was way out of her depth.

"Understood. I'm just worried for Cary. Her husband was assassinated only yesterday."

"This isn't a threat, Kamama. Cary will have to formally sign a statement. The big question this early in the investigation is, was Seth Soul a player in the conspiracy to assassinate Wohali Lightfoot? We need to corroborate her description with the other information we have from a completely different source in Washington DC."

6

Stepping back inside, John noticed Kamama switching her seating. She'd placed more of a distance between herself and Cary. John turned on his digital recorder and looked toward Cary sitting opposite him; she had made more drinks.

"I'm sorry, Cary, you know I have to start this second part of our interview where we left off. I need to ask you, just once again, about the cockerel tattoo. Does your father have a tattoo of a cockerel and branches of leaves on his right forearm?

"If you want to take time to get your attorney involved, we'll stop right here and right now. It's your choice and from my side, this is not a pressure or a threat in any way."

Sitting close by, Kamama could sense Cary bristle. She saw Cary take a sharp, fleeting glance back at John. As Cary continued her consideration and her response, she looked back at John again and blurted out an angry defence.

"I thought you'd come here to help me, Mr Green! You shouldn't be stressing me out! Not the day after my husband has been murdered."

John remained calm while the lounge returned to silence. Even Danuwoa sat on the floor quietly looking up at his mother.

"Cary, as I've said for the record, you can stop this interview anytime."

John looked directly into Cary's eyes.

Time ticked by in a tense standoff.

"*Yes, all right!*

"He has a cockerel on his right forearm. The cockerel actually stands on a weathervane. My brothers have it, maybe on a hat or even engraved on their hunting rifles. For all I know they have it tattooed on their asses! What's more, I don't fucking care! Okay?"

John thanked Cary, then, inevitably asked another question.

"Okay, Cary, thanks. A different question? What's your father look like?"

"My father stands around five feet, eight inches, blue eyes, always had a good head of carefully trimmed hair. Mr Green, what is all this about my father all of a sudden?"

"We have to rule your father out, Cary. What about his hair?"

"It's thick and grey now, of course. And, if I know him well, he still touts a very well-trimmed grey beard and moustache."

Again, John thanked Cary.

"So, Cary, what else can you tell us about your father and brothers?"

"Well, I've already said, they are all members of some kind of 'brotherhood'. My father says he was brought up that way, like all our kind of folk. What do you think? If menfolk are brought up through childhood to do as they're told, generation after generation, did my father have a choice of the brotherhood or not? My brothers, they never had a choice. I get confused, he raised us, worked hard for us, loved us… as I've said, I'd say overall he's a good man who did his best."

"What are you trying to tell us, Cary?"

"We're not supposed to talk about this. It's a 'secret'. I really shouldn't be telling you all this! Womenfolk don't talk to the likes of you about their menfolk…"

Cary began to show signs of more stress.

"Urgggh!! But… my loyalties, they're divided today! It's a

'men only' thing. I don't know what they do or talk about. As a young girl, growing into a young woman, I never liked it; I was outside it. It'll never be a right thing."

"So, what did you and your mother think about this 'men only' brotherhood stuff?"

Cary spat out a reply.

"Any women I've known, including my mother, who married men involved in this so called 'brotherhood', well, they were shut out too. A few have told me, after they got married… they soon learnt they were just supposed to make a home, service their men with their cooking, cleaning, sex and childbearing."

"So, Cary, what kinda things do you think they believe in this 'brotherhood'? When they meet. Do they pray to their God, dance and drink? What happens?"

"I don't know about beliefs. How should I know what he believes? I know what my father said one time, coming back, just after Wohali and I were married. He grabbed my arm, took me to one side, bore down on me; his face so close I could smell his breakfast. Then he made some of his most private comments he'd ever made to me.

"He started talking again about the 'mixing of bloods' being wrong. Wrong in spiritual ways, then wrong because the purity of the Soul bloodline; it was *everything* to him. Further down the line, after Danuwoa was born, he told me this beautiful child you see playing over there was, '*a mongrel! That child has poisoned our blood.*'"

"On that day he went further then, Cary?"

Cary suddenly began to speak with more confidence and a passion; her feelings coming to the surface through her own strength of voice. The sob she'd had in her throat disappeared.

"Yeah, he went *much* further to drive his point home. Believe me, if he got on his high horse – my God, he could lecture us as kids for hours. My brothers and I, we learnt hard lessons on provin' we'd listened!

"After a couple of beatings, believe me, we learnt to remember. He'd say, *'Tell me what I said then. You tell me how much you've been listenin'*. Eventually, we learnt to do it. My brothers and I could repeat it, word for word... just to escape a beating."

Kamama glanced briefly into Cary's eyes. She shook her head at John, as if to say, *'leave this now'*. Then as they looked deeply into one another, Kamama saw Cary's eyes were full of remembering.

Caught in the moment, John suddenly heard himself ask a question he'd never asked anyone before.

"Can you still do it?"

Cary looked back at John, still full of passion and attitude.

"You know... Can you still do it? Show us what your father used to say?"

"Well, I never tried that before except with him... But, yeah, I guess I could try."

John beckoned her with one arm outstretched, as if welcoming Cary to the floor of a stage.

"Well, the floor's all yours then."

So, standing up, Cary gradually took on the mantle of her father's own role. Her body, her head movements and gestures changed. John and Kamama watched her transformation. Cary, as if an 'actress', became inhabited by her father.

As her voice changed, she pointed an index finger; then looking down, she berated her imaginary childhood self:

> *"Cary, look where our family is now? Just look what has happened to our great family! The Lord Jesus Christ Himself sees us; you've brought shame down upon our heads! Us! A family of righteous people an' all. We American people, we are God's 'chosen people'; we have been gifted a Destiny, a righteous purpose; we are the anointed ones! And you, you've mixed our blood with a pagan; this is our Lord's 'Promised Land' the place where we will build a shining citadel on a*

hill that cannot be hid' just like Matthew's Gospel says in the Bible......'

Cary broke down in tears.

Kamama got up. She lifted Danuwoa from the floor and passed him to Cary. Mother and son were held together in Kamama's warm embrace. Quietly, she shepherded them out of the lounge and into the privacy of the kitchen next door.

John sat in the silence they'd left behind until Danuwoa burst out into the lounge and began to play with his toys.

Eventually, the kitchen door opened again. Cary returned and looked up toward John. She wiped her snot nose with the back of her arm, then dabbed the tear-trails off her cheeks with a tissue in her other hand. Danuwoa looked over to his mother and stopped playing; then, standing up, he walked over to his mummy and put his arms around her legs.

"Don't cry, Mummy."

"Is that enough for you, Mr Green? I'm done now!"

"No, not quite, Cary. We need a photograph of your father and your brothers. You can mail me some from your phone, right now if you like? I'd also like a couple of portraits of Wohali please? I need to see him with the light of life in his eyes."

After Cary obliged, John quietly checked the images. She had sent a picture of her father with his sons all in short sleeves. Seth Soul was standing proudly in between his sons, his tattoo was clearly visible. The photographs of Wohali showed a man with a strong, muscular face. One photograph pictured him warmly smiling into the lens. A second, was a side-on portrait. Danuwoa was at play a way off in a forest clearing; both father and son were unaware of the camera. Wohali had a warm smile of a father's pride on his face as Danuwoa was struggling to climb a fallen trunk of a pine tree.

Catching John's eye, Kamama signalled it was his moment to wrap things up.

"Look, Cary, I know today has been tough. I can't thank you enough for the interview and the photographs. You've done Wohali proud. It's important we rule your father and brothers out of our investigation. We've got you on tape, one of our local officers will drop over and ask you to sign off a statement."

"Before we leave, do you know where we might find your father and brothers living?"

"No, I can't help you there."

"Okay. Well, just to let you know, I'll be contacting your local police chief to ask the local force to find out where they are. I'm gonna need to interview them. We'll need a warrant to get into the homestead."

John shook Cary's hand and turned to leave.

"Oh! And finally, finally. I'm mindful that you said your brothers took to hammering on your door. I don't want that happening while you and your son are on your own here. I know Isaac and Woya wanted you and Danuwoa to go with them to the retreat; they respect your judgement not to do that. But we want to provide security for a while. Would you accept an officer in a car outside twenty-four seven. Kamama and I are leaving Oklahoma for the Smoky Mountains, just for a couple of days."

Cary was grateful, agreed to security then showed them to the door.

7

On leaving Cary's place, John asked Kamama to drive.

"I need to make contact with Phoenix as we go."

As the phone rang, Phoenix picked up.

"Hi, Phoenix, are you good to talk?"

"Yep. You go first, John. We're going over to my parents in a minute, so let's keep this short."

"Okay, Phoenix. Kamama and I have heard that description this morning about the cockerel tattoo on Cary's father, on his forearm; the whole image places the cockerel on a weathervane. I've sent you and Charlotte a photographic image of Seth Soul and his two sons, maybe three years ago, but it'll be useful and support Charlotte's work."

"John, I…"

"Be helpful if Charlotte notes the names, Seth Soul is standing in the middle; John Soul as the older brother is standing on the right; Charles Soul, the younger son, is on the left. Charlotte needs to search these guys on all the national databases! I'll be raising the names with the local chief of police."

"John I'll…"

"We need Charlotte and her team to bottom out how this imposter was set up. Does the ID photograph match this family photo and confirm Seth Soul as the imposter? Also, will this guy

Tranter participate in an ID parade of photographs including Seth Soul in this one? Then, the question is how this 'brilliant' ID was set up for the imposter. Which of our departments can support our investigation on that?"

"John, you're right and we have many of those things in hand. Great progress, hitting the jackpot first interview. Leave this one with me, I'll sort this out."

"Look, Phoenix, both George and I agreed there must have been a high degree of planning, funding and internal support. Oh! But, before I forget, you'll need to brief the directo…"

Phoenix cut in to stop John finishing his sentence.

"Okay, John. Being candid, you need to slow down. Right now! I know you mean well; this situation is weird for both of us. But I know my role, John. I don't need you to tell me all this stuff! I'm in daily contact with Anna."

Without listening, John moved on to talk about a hunch.

"Looking round our service, Phoenix, I consider Jim Coogan to be the most serious corporate risk. I think he is *the* one natural candidate right now to be our 'leaker' or 'mole'. Just look at him, he's a loner; loose on procedure; personal life and family are a mess; he may still be an alcoholic for all I know! All of which makes him vulnerable to compromise…"

John began to hear an ominous silence on Phoenix's end of the line. Finally, he realised these were signs of Phoenix brewing up for a battle.

"Okay, John let's try again. You know that George has made a full delegation of authority as well as responsibility to me? It's *my* job to lead and manage the service while you're away? Right?"

"Right!"

"It wasn't my choice, John. I didn't make that happen, right? So, it makes sense, just until you get back, that I follow George's and Anna's instruction. I'll report to them on your hunch. But if I feel Jim needs an intervention, I'll call him in and interview him; maybe suspend and investigate him. But, I decide Right?"

"Okay, Phoenix, I get it, I'm not leading on this. But yeah! Of course, I'll have to respect your decisions."

Phoenix clarified her position.

"My take on this hunch? Neither you nor I have one shred of real evidence and, therefore, no right whatsoever to call out Jim Coogan as a suspect, in being the internal 'mole'. I know these team leaders so well, John!"

Phoenix soon became aware that her strong position on Jim Coogan was annoying John. But that didn't deter her from expressing her position.

"John, I'm sorry to say this, but you're behaving like an old-fashioned male investigator from the sixties or seventies. I can't believe you've become a man with a 'hunch'; you've got a feeling in your 'gut'. Suddenly, your male internal organs are speaking instead of your reason! Research shows this kinda practice nearly always leads to illegal outcomes. It's old news, man! Come on! Wise up! This stuff was happening back in the day when men did the investigating, and women typed their fucking reports. We've got science and equality now. Haven't you heard?"

John, somewhat defeated, asked Phoenix for clarification. "I'll take it that's a 'no' then?"

"Yeah! You're dead right you can! I'm not excluding anyone, John, but I'm not setting anyone up either! Do you know what the FBI corporate mantra is about where the 'spy' or 'mole' will be found?"

For once John was silenced by Phoenix's question.

"Well, no, Phoenix, but I get the feeling you're going to tell me anyway."

"The answer is, '*You always find the* spy *or the mole in the worst possible place.*' That's a line of learning which comes from previous internal reports about leakers and moles. Ask yourself, John, where *is* the 'worst place'? Is it more likely to be an investigator or a team leader? Or could it be someone with, both lateral and vertical influence. Someone who can coldly walk through security clearance at the White House carrying senior ID and authority, for example?"

"Look, Phoenix, I don't care what you say, we gotta find out how these guys accessed the Memorial Undercroft through an incredibly secure door and spent a comfortable couple of days lounging and laughing at our nation. They had a latrine sited directly underneath the statue of President Abraham Lincoln itself. From where I'm standing, it is your job to sort this out."

Phoenix chuckled down the phone. "Oh, and John. Before you go, one more thing. You definitely need to know this; we both know Jim Coogan is unconventional, right? He has just emailed me as we've been talking. It's a good one, John! You listening…? I asked you, John? *Are you listening*?"

"Yeah, I'm listening, Phoenix!"

"He's asked to see me for a personal one-to-one meeting. I've booked him in for Monday. He wouldn't say what it was about. So, right now my friend, he remains inside the fold, okay? He's still reporting to me. He ain't gone rogue yet. Okay?"

Phoenix finally looked across at her husband, Trent, waiting at the door and she smiled; soon they'd be on their way.

"Okay, John, speak soon."

In the silence ensuing after John's call ended. Kamama smiled and glanced at John as she turned off the freeway into the city.

'I'd sure like to meet Phoenix someday. She's some woman."

John looked out of the window as the city flickered past.

"Yeah…"

As the city buildings rushed past his gaze, he realised he was becoming consumed by his conversation with George about the Memorial. Amidst the priorities to interview everyone in the Lightfoot family and 'get the job done', he felt a growing pressure to find and excise the 'mole' from their midst. Trouble was it wasn't his job anymore; but he couldn't stop being concerned; the service he'd just built with Phoenix, had been compromised.

Kamama interrupted his thoughts.

"The time's come, John. I'm driving, right? Time to get you out of that grey suit and those black shoes. I'm taking you to an outdoor clothing outlet. We're buying that Smoky Mountain uniform, remember?"

"You okay with that?" Kamama turned off the freeway towards a shopping mall she knew.

8

In the space after interviewing Cary Lightfoot, phoning Phoenix and shopping, John arrived back in his hotel room trying to catch up with Kay, Ava and Theo. In between attempts he was trying to scroll through the reports and the research Esteban had packaged for him. He reminded himself to book the flight tickets for the Smoky Mountains and a hire car for the other end at Gatlinburg-Pigeon Forge Airport.

Finally, John made contact with home.

"Hi, Kay, good to hear your voice at last. I've been trying to reach you for a while."

"Hi, John. Yeah, we've been out in the afternoon sunshine at the Beauvoir Playground. Emma and David brought their kids. It's always been our best playground in the whole city, hasn't it?"

"Nice one, Kay. I sure wish I'd been there with you rather than working down here."

Kay asked for an update about how things were going. John filled her in with the story and concluded with Kamama having insisted on taking him shopping in preparation for the Smoky Mountain trip.

"Kamama sounds as if she's making a good working partner, John. I've looked her up of course! She's a good lookin', hard workin' young woman, John. Quite a list of academic research and achievements in her professional journey!"

"Yeah, well, less of the good-looking observation, Kay. She has clicked into the work well though. Dealt with the victim's wife and child today, with warmth and care. Impressive. I'd say you'd rate her psychological understanding highly. Tomorrow morning, we're headed to the Smoky Mountains. I'll let you know when I've arrived."

John asked to speak with Ava and Theo. As they came on the line, John melted on hearing their voices and began answering their questions. He talked through the trip to the playground and school the next day. Theo asked John about his trip to the mountains. Talking to them both John asked them to look after their mum until he returned.

In his final few words with Kay, she wished him a safe journey and told him to come back in one piece.

9

In the evening, Kamama arrived in the restaurant dining hall at 8.30 p.m. John was already waiting. He bought drinks for them both as they waited for their food orders. Kamama asked John's opinion about how the day had gone.

He gave an uncommitted smile.

"It's early days for this investigation, Kamama. It's been good working with you today though. Your inside knowledge of the family was invaluable. Your empathy with Cary and Danuwoa was crucial. You created trust and you skilfully built confidence in me. So, that's a good sign for the next couple days with Isaac and Woya. Oh! And my wife has looked you up and admired your research achievements; getting that response from her takes some doing.

"I've booked our tickets for tomorrow and a hire car the other end.

"One thing I wanted to ask you. Can you shed any light on this contradiction between our government records and Isaac's own story about his heritage? Is this something that you can look into for us?"

Kamama listened carefully to John's question. She knew nothing about Isaac's family history all the way back to his childhood assimilation aged four. Kamama decided she couldn't really see where John was headed with this question anyway. She politely skirted and avoided John's enquiry, until curiosity got the better of her.

"I don't understand, John. Why is this question about Isaac important? All I know is Isaac is a registered Cherokee Indian. I know nothing about his life when he was four years old, he has never spoken to me about it."

John looked back with a sense of puzzlement.

"Why is it important? I'd say a cops disciplines are not the same as a professor. In our early routines of investigation, it's just a vital part of building a whole picture of someone's life. If you lift 'stones' in any of our lives, unmoved for years, often it reveals a lot. We're looking to see whether there are contradictions, enemies or conflicts in Isaac's background which could help us see more clearly who might have killed his son. It's a long shot but there could be historical relationships going back a long way.

"In my briefing before coming down, a young, bright intern, Esteban, told me Isaac was stripped of both the first name his parents decided for him, and then his tribal surname. Esteban believes Isaac's American name was 'Isaac Reaper'.

"Esteban said he was just one of five, four-year-old boys in a couple of years of admission, who was given the first name 'Isaac'. So, when Isaac ran from the boarding school, I imagine he would have been responding to his imposed, American name, 'Isaac Reaper'. My imagination about a child's development, in the middle of assimilation tells me, the renamed Isaac, by the age of fourteen, could easily have forgotten his birth names by then.[12]

Kamama nodded and agreed. Knowing the whole of Isaac's past could be important. She began to realise this assignment could challenge her understanding of the Lightfoot family.

"I'd never really considered that, John. Intellectually I know it, of course. Even in my practice I've interviewed assimilated adults. I just haven't questioned Isaac's years of assimilation; I've listened to his history as described by him. I guess your interns rummaging around could have picked up something which tells us a very a different story."

"Didn't you know Isaac was a 'runner'?"

"Well, I don't know the story in detail. I just never doubted Isaac's description of his journey home to the Cherokee Nation; with him coming in to help with students, I guess he's been more of a colleague than someone subject to one of my research programmes."

"Esteban put an academic PDF in my research. I've been reading in the late afternoon about Indian Nation children in boarding schools who became so desperate they couldn't tolerate assimilation and ran. Many runners died and were never found. But then, you'll know that history better than I."

"Of course, I know the research, I've interviewed adults who survived running. Seems Isaac's past is more complicated; it's hard to imagine the fear that drove him to make such a long journey; on the surface he always seems so together, maybe even at peace with himself; when he's talking to my students, he always seems so thoughtful and balanced."

A silence settled while Kamama and John ate. Carrying on the subject, John asked about the meaning of names.

"I don't want to sound ignorant, Kamama, but all these Indian Nation names, do they have meanings? I guess all cultures have this stuff. When Kay and I had our children, we thought about names and their meanings. I remember we checked my daughter's name, Ava, in several cultures. In Latin, it was 'bird'; in Hebrew, 'life' and in Persian it meant 'voice' or 'filled with the spirit'. I particularly liked the Persian version 'filled with the spirit'. So, she became Ava."

"Yeah, well, we Cherokees consider the meaning of names for our children too. "

"So, looking at the Lightfoot family, I happen to know the

Hebrew, biblical name of 'Isaac' means 'he will laugh'. Of course, we'll never know how his parents named him. But, as you'll find out, Isaac remains possibly the most serious, least humorous and most stoical thinker you can imagine. Isaac... well, he ain't a bundle of laughs, John.

"The name Wohali means 'eagle'. The eagle is, for us, the highest spiritual and all-seeing animal in Creation. As we've heard today, Wohali was a fearsome protector of those closest to him. So, I guess there's something in that.

"Woya means 'dove', universally a creature of peace. In real life, I can tell you, Woya is the 'seer' in the family; she's one who looks back through the veil of history to understand the truth in the present. I've heard her do this. Sometimes she can seem a cynical unbeliever.

"Danuwao, we met today, means 'warrior'.

"Adsila, Isaac's wife who died? Means 'blossom'."

John turned his attention to getting to know more about Kamama, her background and how she thought she would be able to advise him.

"So, you were right this morning, Kamama; me knowing about how you can support this investigation is important. So, who the hell are you, Kamama Catawnee, Emeritus Professor of Oklahoma University!

"In your own life, are you married, have children and do you have a wider family? I have found in my own journey that people bring all sorts of strengths and perspectives that aren't necessarily on their 'billboard', if you know what I mean."

"Well, John, you already know I am a First Nation heritage, Cherokee Indian. I have always been fundamentally driven by truth and understanding of our people's journey. What happened to us as First Nation peoples in history is one of my drivers. So, I love exploring our human stories."

"What else can I tell you? I definitely need the natural world. That's just how I roll. I'm a bird who needs the freedom to fly; I like 'roosting' out in the open, under the stars. It's in my blood.

"I'm an academic, so I research, complete fieldwork and publish peer-reviewed papers. I'm published on the broader politics of North American Indian nations. There's a lot more to know.

"For example, part of my mission is to go on understanding the European ancestors who sailed here. As we know, they've never left. As I see it, the descendants today, well, they're still destroying our land; they call it the United States of America; we call it Turtle Island. They're continuing to assume power and ownership of a land that was never, ever *promised* them by their God.

"I'm sorry, John. I didn't mean to go there. I guess you're learning I'm a spiritual and a political animal. You might as well know that now. How about you, John, tell me a bit about yourself."

"That's okay and understood. Sometime, I'd like to know more. There's not much to know about me. I am, as you say, a third-generation European descendant. Just like so many others. I was never much of a sportsman growing up. Probably a bit bookish if the truth be known."

"So, how'd you become a cop?"

"I'm not sure where the root of becoming a cop comes from. Like you, I am very interested in people. What is it that makes us tick? Like you I'm interested in how we became the modern humans we are today, walking the streets of Manhattan. I learnt a lot observing people, undercover on the streets of Chicago. I guess I learnt there's a lot of us who ain't so modern after all."

"That's dangerous work, John."

"Yeah. I have some stories; stories of surviving in places where other cops have died. I guess, as I say, we all have many layers. Truth is Kamama, I haven't stayed still for long, getting married and having children has settled me down a bit."

Kamama took a sip from the glass of dark-red wine in her hand.

"So, what about your own name, Kamama? What's the origin and meaning of that?"

Kamama smiled broadly.

"So, I'm Kamama, which means I'm the 'butterfly. That could tell you I am still a growing caterpillar, munching and feeding on leaves of knowledge; it's all leading to my time of chrysalis dormancy. But I guess I could just be taking a bit longer in the being born again stage; then I'll become that beautiful butterfly.

"When I am reborn, then it'll be a short day or two of flight in the sunshine, then sucking sweet nectar from the flowers of life; eventually I'll amaze with my aerodynamics; then send out a scent to attract the right mate? Did you know that butterflies did that, John?"

John laughed. "Nope!"

"Whatever happens, John, I'm determined to hand on a legacy of whoever this magical being is, living inside me. You know, I'll lay some eggs, hand my knowledge on to some other caterpillars to evolve and learn more."

John smiled. "So, there *will* be children then?"

Kamama smiled back and ignored him. She began to say more about herself.

"So, both my parents are still alive, and I have two sisters and a brother. I am the 'baby' of the family.

"Unlike you, John, I've never married. So far, I've lived as the river flows; sometimes flowing fast and free to the sea, after the spring thaw; at other times my lifestyle loves dawdling and dreaming, through the hot summer sun; my relationships, they've come, and they've gone. My focus now is not marriage or children. I am motivated and determined to make a difference on our planet before leaving it. But, like the butterfly, I'm thinking that I'll know who my mate will be, whenever I meet him."

"So, changing the subject, John, what do you know about the *'Doctrine of Discovery'*?"

John looked into Kamama's eyes after she'd swallowed what was left of her glass of Merlot.

"I've only just heard of it, Kamama. Never read it. But strangely, in the last two days, since I have become involved in this investigation, someone, somewhere has popped up and mentioned this mysterious Doctrine.

"First time I heard it was in my office yesterday on TV. Indira Anand, CEO of the 'Festival', was on FOX News. She linked First Nation liberation to dismantling the 'Doctrine' and then linked it to the USA laws on land ownership. How did she say it? These laws… 'justified the theft of North America.'"

"So, what did you think."

John shrugged.

"How can I possibly have a view on something I don't know anything about? I listened to the TV interview with Wohali in mind. I'd say, talking with you now, I'm feeling this *'Doctrine'* must have been carefully submerged in my education. As a kid, no one in my schooling or university education ever said, *'Now, listen up, John! The laws from the sixteenth-century Vatican, sealed our steal of North America – making our country great again!'*"

Kamama looked at John and thought she saw a dyed-in-the-wool pragmatist. A man who'd spent the whole of his professional life reducing events, rationalising human behaviour into the rules, power and the framework of the U.S criminal justice system.

"Okay, John. You need to know people like Isaac, Wohali, Woya and many modern-day indigenous authors and scholars, have taken huge risks every day analysing, publishing and talking publicly about this stuff. The political, 'colonial arena', of the *'Doctrine'* shows us the very root of European, bloody, domination; Wohali's modern day martyrdom is one such example; my first piece of advice is you need to be prepared, Isaac will be talking about it, for sure.

"I'd say one place you need to start looking, John, is to the white nationalists on the far right. They're insecure; they fear their 'white' entitlement to power and ownership is at risk; the demographics of migrants, people of colour and strangers, becoming the majority in the U.S. population are growing. They are both frightened owners of the land; indeed they are frightening people in their own right, John.

"You'll know more about the storming of the Capitol, January 6, 2021, than I do; you know police officers died. Not only that, but they also erected a noose to hang Vice President, Pence. They reportedly told the FBI in an interview, if they'd found Pence alive', they'd have killed him to stop the election being stolen. You must have heard about that? You're FBI, aren't you?[13]

"You've just got to listen back to that interview today. Look at the somersaults Cary did in that conversation!"

John shrugged and waited.

"Look, Kamama, this street, right-wing politics is just a fashion. Anyway, where's the real evidence of a successful challenge for the 'liberation' of First Nation peoples?"

Kamama adopted a mischievous smile.

"The crows are chattering, they're all coming home to roost, John. The International Festival of the Earth is joining the dots together. They see the planet has needs for the traditional knowledge of the First Nations peoples to hold onto other species and habitats; traditional knowledge is a key part of the human spectrum of knowledge needed to cool the planet; it's what the 'Doctrine' and other such ideologies, have tried, but so far failed, to exterminate."

Kamama stood up, frustrated, needing to take a break, she saw John was deep in thought.

John nodded very slowly. As he looked up from staring into

his glass, Kamama could see the dime gradually drop behind those dark-brown eyes of his.

"Sorry, Kamama. I was somewhere else entirely."

Kamama looked into John's misted eyes as he looked back across the table. She fancied she could see someone else in there. Someone who wasn't just an 'investigator'.

"Are you with me, John? Are you still listening? Otherwise, there ain't no point in my even trying to get you up to speed."

John managed a weak smile and sighed.

"Yeah, Kamama, I'm listening and I'm thinking!"

Kamama looked at John with her head to one side.

"Hey, John, c'mon, another drink? Or maybe something sweet to eat?"

John's eyes lightened up a bit.

"Yeah, Kamama, okay, another drink! Mine's a double, single-malt whiskey with a small jug of water." So, John put down his napkin on their resturant table. Looking around, he made a beeline for a comfortable, private corner of the lounge. Returning, Kamama set down John's glass and jug, then went back to collect her second glass of Merlot."

Making herself comfortable, Kamama smiled back at John. She felt she had made a pretty good stab at providing some advice and context to Wohali's assassination. They talked for a while about their trip for the next day.

Sitting in the quiet privacy of their wingback chairs, they reflected on the separate skills they'd used throughout the day. They both picked out the different aspects of the learning they had taken from their interview; both of them acknowledged how brave Cary had been to give her interview the day after Wohali's assassination.

Looking forward to the next two days, they anticipated how they would need to continue working closely together.

Concluding their evening, John broke a comfortable silence and proposed a toast.

"To tomorrow, Kamama! The Smoky Mountains!"

They reached across the low table together and touched their glasses together.

"*The Smoky Mountains!*"

10

John got back to his hotel room at around 10 p.m. He put a call through to George Stanhope.

"George, the advisor you've organised knows her stuff; she's helped me see why we thought, within the first hour of Wohali Lightfoot's assassination, that home-grown terrorism could have delivered it."

"Kamama added a line about the 'Festival', freeing indigenous people's from the historic domination and subjugation of some Christian Doctrine or other. I need to know more about it. That's right, it's the '*Doctrine of Discovery*', George"

John loosened his tie, undid the top button on his collar and kicked off his shoes.

"This ain't going to unravel quickly, George."

"John, it's good to have that 'conspiracy' theory crystallising so soon. We need to get David O'Donnelly on the case urgently, working with the CSI results. He needs to chase harder for refinement of the DNA evidence we've got."

"George don't worry! Really! Phoenix and I like to keep everything 'in-house' as much as possible."

George then announced he had taken an immediate, unilateral action of his own.

"John, let me tell you, you can't deal with a 'mole' by '*keeping everything in-house*'. I have emailed all our senior managers and investigators announcing that we have a 'mole' on board. That'll smoke them out!"

From John's point of view this at once seemed a dangerous strategy for someone at George's level to take on alone.

"Look, George, you gotta be extremely careful. If this is a deep criminal and political 'conspiracy' there will be key targets. They'll be able to flex and deal with emerging threats. That includes you and me, George. I don't need to tell you, George, you're the national expert."

George listened. He knew enough from John's own level of practice and experience to at least give him that moment of respect and airspace.

"George, you ain't listening. Charlotte's already spoken to Tranter by phone.

"Tranter's identification painted a picture of a guy with grey hair, trimmed beard and a cockerel's head tattoo on his forearm. Today, George, I've also found a candidate for our imposter. Cary Lightfoot has identified her father, Seth Soul. He has a cockerel standing on a weathervane, tattooed on his right forearm! What does that mean, George? You're the expert."[14]

"John, I hear you. It means we're probably dealing with 'Proud Boy' membership in this case. A serious risk! As you say, my kind of territory. I did a huge amount of work on the assault on the Capitol, January 6. All the more important I go to meet Tranter at the Memorial tomorrow morning. There you are, I knew we'd agree in the end."

"Before you go, George, I've let my group of closest line managers know, I'll be travelling to the Smoky Mountains tomorrow. I have copied you and Anna McKenna in and given my contact details and address. Speak tomorrow, George, 10.00 a.m."

"Okay, John. Sleep well."

John signed off on the call and began to think more about the day's work. In short, John realised that his skills and experiences were required at this end of the investigation. George and Anna had been right.

He returned to going over the practical agenda of actions he needed to take from the day. John made a mental note that he must speak to the City Chief of Police, Walter Banks, about finding the men in Cary's family. He needed Walter to circulate Cary's photograph of the men in the Soul family to to put out an all-points bulletin.

Eventually, John looked at the screen of his mobile and saw it was 10 p.m. He decided to turn in early after requesting a 7 a.m. morning call and room service for breakfast.

John knew tomorrow would be a demanding day; as his head hit the pillow, he fell asleep.

Day 2   11

Washington DC

Sunday
November 3

It was 11.35 p.m. and Frank Denman was just settling down in his hotel room for the night. It had been a successful day; he had enjoyed travelling to Washington DC. He'd held a series of meetings with his contacts, celebrating the success of his plan to assassinate Wohali Lightfoot at the Memorial.

Thinking back through the day, he was particularly pleased that he had met Drake Collins for lunch. They had both finally come to a clear understanding about how he may be asked to help his father clear his 'debts'. Frank had quietly reminded Drake that he would also be helping to protect his mother.

He had also caught up with Suzanne Woodman working at the Mall Maintenance team. She had shared her concerns with Frank about how a very senior FBI officer was going to meet with her manager at the Memorial the next morning.

"Look Frank, I know you always say, '*Don't worry, Suzanne, we're well ahead of the game,*' but this guy tomorrow, he ain't meeting Greg Tranter for the fun of it. We're talking about George Stanhope, FBI Executive Lead for Homeland Security and Terrorism. It won't have taken them long to put two and two together. They'll have searched the Undercroft, then at least they'll want to investigate who provided the access. With that in mind I've arranged to be there with Greg Tranter on the basis that I might be able to help the investigation. But you know full well I'll be protecting our backs, Frank."

"Suzanne, what can I say, I just know I can rely on you to do the right thing for me; I don't know where I'd be without you."

In the middle of his conversation with Suzanne, Frank's phone rang.

The number was withheld and the voice he heard on the other end of the line was electronic, distorted, and disguised. To Frank, it sounded like a male voice, but he'd long since learnt that software for modern mobile phones could disguise gender.

"Hi, Frank. You don't know where I'm calling from. I know how you love a burner phone yourself. All you need to know is I am one of your 'friends' giving you reliable information which you'll need to act on fast."

"Okay, so what you got for me?"

"We've just heard that the FBI investigator, John Green and Professor Kamama Catawnee are both travelling together to the Smoky Mountains tomorrow for two days. They'll be living in a very remote cabin retreat with Wohali Lightfoot's father and sister."

"I'll be texting you the zip code of the retreat and information about the property layout."

The phone line went dead.

Frank apologised to Suzanne for the interruption and put a call through to Seth. "Hi Seth, listen, I just had a tip-off from one of our supporters. Looks like an FBI investigator, John Green, together with a Professor Kamama Catawnee, are headed to the Smoky Mountains to stay in a mountain retreat. You're gonna need to talk about this with your boys right now!"

Back in the Thurmond workshop, Seth nodded and smiled.

"Well, at least two of them are agreed targets. If you want the professor and the investigator taken out that's a financial discussion. You and I know we've been collecting intelligence on this family for a long time now. The professor is well engaged in the politics of the International Festival of the Earth, just like the rest of them. She'll be the next generation coming in, after Isaac Lightfoot has gone."

"Okay, Seth? Money is just no problem; we want all four of them in the bag."

"So, John and Charles are back from Washington DC. They arrived here half an hour ago. I'll get them on the road tomorrow. Reckon we're looking at five-hour drive from here. Leave the details with me, Frank; they'll aim to enter the retreat, after lights out. I'm assuming the boys will take the Ford Raptor?"

"Seth, yes of course, the Raptor is ideal for this task. Oh! Wait… Okay, here we go, Seth, my informant has just this moment sent a text with the zip code, there's also the layout of the retreat from the letting agent. I've forwarded it to you."

Day 3   1

Oklahoma City

Monday
November 4

A man has a child within, still locked in time.

> 'Grown men may learn from very little children, for their hearts are pure, and, therefore, the Great Spirit may show to them many things which older people miss.'
> Black Elk – 1863.[15]

On waking, and in the quietness of his triple-glazed hotel room, John found his concerns about George from the previous evening revolving over and over in his mind.

'Hell! Why wouldn't George just see it?! Do what was asked of him? The investigation just doesn't need his trip to the Lincoln Memorial.'

John went to his room window and opened his blinds. He looked out onto an early morning cityscape. The freeway and its traffic were on the move. Looking down to the hotel parking lot below, there were a few early morning empty spaces; only residents' cars had remained parked up overnight.

A group of crows danced on a resturant rooftop; they flew up, then down, settled and flew up again. As John watched, he saw they were fighting their skirmishes for perches on some food-waste bins. The dominant birds who had persisted, punctured the overflowing black plastic bags, stood and necked their booty; then flew away with yet more scraps in their beaks.

Eventually, securing his blinds, John turned back into his room. He showered. Then, sitting on his bed, he dried his hair. Gradually, John was surfacing, finding his energy; he needed coffee and breakfast. While he waited, he tried to contact Kay. Both his home landline and Kay's mobile rang out, both repeating their customary instructions to leave a message. Realising it was Monday November 4, John knew Kay's home routine would have kicked in; she would have prepared breakfast for Theo and Ava, then be out on the school run.

He glanced again at his mobile screen. It was 7.30 a.m. the pressure began growing inside him to contact George for a second time. He waited and waited, but George just wasn't picking up.

The next time John tried to call was around 9 a.m. By then he had breakfasted and arrived at the airport departure lounge and was waiting for Kamama; but still there was no reply.

Finally, taking a step he'd never taken before, he phoned Brenda, George's wife, on their landline.

John began pacing, waiting for Brenda to pick up.

"Oh! Hi, John. That's a first for you to phone this line! What can I do to help?"

"Hi, Brenda, has George left yet? I just needed to speak with him before he leaves the house. Feels like I've missed him though."

Brenda confirmed, George was long gone.

"He was up early, made his own breakfast and was gone well before 8 a.m. I could see he had that sort of tunnel vision of excitement in him. You'll probably know what I mean. I've seen it more times than I care to count. There was a preoccupied, high mood in him, even though the weather was foul. When he was operational, he'd be like this often; particularly if he thought he was on a roll."

"He's not picking up his mobile, Brenda, I'm just calling on the off-chance. Look, no worries. I'll try later. See you both when I get back later this week; maybe Kay and I could get out with you both for an evening meal."

So, John phoned again on George's mobile at the exact time they'd agreed, 10 a.m. By then Kamama had arrived and there were just ten minutes before they would be called to board their flight. John smiled to Kamama, as he waited, raised a hand, nodded and mouthed, '*Hi.*'

Still, there was no George.

So, John put out an urgent call to Phoenix at 10.10 a.m.

Phoenix picked up immediately.

"Hi, Phoenix, hope you're, okay? Sorry to bother you. Look, I spoke to George yesterday evening. I've just been trying to ring him since 7.30 a.m.; last night he and I agreed I would call him around 10 a.m. but there's been no reply.

"Ever since I woke and opened my eyes, I've been ghosted by the feeling that I must do everything I can and stop him going to the Memorial. I spoke to him last night and told him there was no need to go to his meeting with Tranter."

There was a long pause on the line.

"Hi, Phoenix, are you still there?"

Phoenix's voice came back, low and slow. "Hi, John. You gotta brace yourself. There is no easy way for me to say this. I've just got to say it. Right?"

"C'mon, Phoenix, let it go!"

"We've just heard from Anna; George died this morning on his way back from the Memorial. We don't know all the details yet. He did make that journey to the Memorial by Metro well before his 9.30 a.m. meeting was due. You'll know how fastidious he was about being punctual. We've confirmed with someone called Suzanne Woodman, a team leader in Tranter's office, that the meeting did happen.

"Anyway, on the face of it, the story is that George seems to have tripped and fallen off the platform and gone under a Metro train at Foggy Bottom, making his return journey."

"It's been one of those stormy, wet November, DC days. We've immediately accessed CCTV on the platform and, on the face of it, it *does* look like George just tripped accidentally.

"So, given our thoughts on 'conspiracy', I've asked Esteban Jackson to analyse the footage in more depth from the Memorial to the Metro. The platform was incredibly packed and chaotic; I'm banking on him finding an angle for us.

"The Metro, of course, was shut down for a time. George's body has been recovered and is being transferred for a post-mortem by city police forensics. The post-mortem will rule in or out any physical health issues or signs of foul play.

"Anna is doing the corporate touch with Brenda."

John muttered, as if speaking to himself. *'Unbelievable. Not long ago I was speaking to Brenda.'*

"What's that, John…? Look, I know Kay and Brenda used to meet up. So, if you're letting Kay know, she could give Brenda some support time?"

John was distracted for a while, shocked, and preoccupied by the news.

"Sure… I know Kay will want to help. We've both got to be really vigilant about our teams. We ourselves could be on their hit list now, Phoenix. We gotta build that practice of conscious vigilance into our staff. I'm just sharing thoughts now, Phoenix. I'm not telling you what to do, okay?"

John began to talk about returning to Washington DC, but Phoenix had already thought through that John would instinctively seek to rush back.

"John, no need, really don't. I've rescheduled your Monday

management meeting for 11.30 a.m. I agree with you, John, on vigilance. I'm already on it; I've established a heightened awareness across all teams on risk. They've been sent a risk checklist, and I've delegated team leaders to undertake an immediate task to conduct urgent safety reviews.

"Everyone with leadership responsibility, including myself, will make any necessary changes to our practical, operational risk systems. I've told them I'm looking over their shoulders on this; they are instructed to adjust team risk assessments; they'll deliver these adjustments back to me for final approval and my agreement to go ahead and implement changes.

"I have cancelled my one-to-one meeting with Jim Coogan. Thinking through your advice, he is now currently suspended from the workplace without prejudgement. It's for his own good.

"The tech department are instructed to go through his desktop with a fine-tooth comb; one of our senior administrators is looking through his calendar and his methods of management; Jim's staff are being interviewed. The way I see it we should be interviewing Jim no later than Wednesday, maybe sooner. Robin Seacourt is acting for George; he and I will be getting evidential reports back.

"He and I will do the interview with Jim. HR will sit in to record and advise. Obviously, keeping an overview on the 'conspiracy' end of this investigation is now a regular routine for me. We've got an overview as a senior management team under Anna's leadership. I'm reporting our experience here and yours down there on a daily basis.

"Before you recommend it, I've already spoken to David O'Donnelly about keeping us both in the loop about his test results. He's onto it. Being candid, you just gotta forget us, John. Believe me, we won't forget you. Hell, we do miss you though.

"As Anna has said to me more than once, John, you have to focus on what's going on down there. You can trust the rest of us to do the miles up here. Anna McKenna and Robin Seacourt are supporting me; you hear me now?"

John ghosted a reply.

"Yeah... I am listening..."

Still distracted, he quickly thanked Phoenix, and immediately hung up on the call.

Throughout the morning John was consumed by reasoning; he considered the likelihood of foul play; then the likelihood of an accident. Overall, he felt George falling under a Metro train just after he'd sent out a corporate email about a 'mole', there just had to have been a malign influence. A red light of regret continued flashing in John's thoughts, but on balance he felt had done everything he could to stop George travelling.

After a few minutes John felt driven to phone and reassure Phoenix about her new role.

"Look, Phoenix, you don't need to feel I am cramping your style. I completely support you acting up into my role in DC now. I know I've been prickly; that's done with now. Whatever you decide about Jim Coogan, I completely trust it. I know now, I need to be here. I am continuing to communicate with Anna. Believe me, she's been chasing me, giving me a lot of grief. You know the stuff: *'Look, John, this has got to be shut down...'* Fucking ridiculous."

Next call, John got through to the director. She was in a meeting.

"Sorry to interrupt you, Anna, do you have any more news on George?"

"No, John. However, I can't emphasise strongly enough, we gotta get this case of yours wrapped up!"

"Surely, Anna, the death of an executive lead who sent out an email about a 'mole', right across the firm, including you, has gotta change the 'shut it down' message from the attorney general; the situation is much more complicated now. Listen, one of the members of our own corporate family is regularly leaking stuff out there. What's the attorney general saying about that evidence?"

Anna hissed a reply.

"Look, John, I can't discuss this now. The pace and scope of this investigation hasn't changed. I'm as gutted about George as you are! I will be in touch with Brenda later this morning. But that doesn't change what we're doing or how you're supposed to be delivering the work. You've had our instructions, okay? Now, stop bucking the system; get on, and help us conclude!"

"Before you hang up, Anna, my answer is no! Not, okay? The idea of shutting this investigation down just isn't practical. I trust we'll talk again."

After boarding his flight with Kamama, John spoke to the Oklahoma Chief of Police – Walter Banks – asking for his help to seek out any of the Soul family men, in particular, the head of the family, Seth Soul.

"Walter, I am forwarding you a photograph of the men in the Soul family. These guys may well be known to you. They are the menfolk in one of your local homestead communities. This photograph could help you and your officers locate them in day-to-day operations; be grateful if you'd send it out on an all-points bulletin?"

"That's fine. Don't you worry, John, we'll locate the Soul family."

Day 3   2

Smoky Mountains

Monday
November 4

It had been a quiet and thoughtful flight for John.

George had been a key figure of stability; he had anchored John's big transition from his work in Chicago, undercover, to his executive role within the FBI. He had been on the appointing panel; when John had left the 'torture chamber' of his interview, he felt George had been *the* key interviewer assessing if he could make the leap, from Chicago to DC.

A part of John's reflection about George was thinking back to his first week in Washington DC; they had found themselves talking about his appointment over lunch. John asked George to explain the background to his appointment.

'Well, John, the truth is one of our difficulties internally was, we knew we needed new blood. Frankly, we were just recycling water from the same stagnant pond, year in, year out. So, when the opportunity came to recruit to your post, it was seen as a great chance to renew a whole division.'

With his head well back in his headrest, John remembered asking George, *'Why in hell's name appoint me?'*

George's reply was typical of the man:

'At the heart of the decision was the fact you'd just survived a

very dangerous role. You'd worked undercover where others had died. I remember asking you three or four questions about why you thought you'd survived. It was clear, amidst the chaos and the danger on the street, you had three strong disciplines; first, you had strong instincts on risk; second, you were a relentless observer; but more importantly, you were constantly creative in the way you delivered solutions.'

Stepping off their four-hour flight at Gatlinburg-Pigeon Forge Airport, Kamama told John she'd deal with his arrangements to pick up their hire car. She saw John was in shock. So, having collected the car, Kamama set up the satellite navigation with the retreat's zip code and quietly began the drive.

The mood between the two of them was eerily quiet until John broke the surface.

"I'm sorry, Kamama. It's been a really busy few hours for me. It began at around 7.30 a.m. There hasn't been much downtime for the two of us to talk. You'll remember George Stanhope?"

"Yeah, John. I couldn't help but overhear some of your conversation before we boarded. George is dead, right? You want to talk about it?"

"Personally, Kamama, I'm both saddened and frustrated. After our dinner at the Skirvin Hotel, I spoke to George at length; I did everything I could to protect him, but he was stubborn as hell; still, felt he was right. Today, I'm certain the 'conspiracy' that killed Wohali Lightfoot, killed George. My own thinking now is, we all have to raise our game; realise we are all at risk."

"That includes us, John. Yeah?"

"Yep. If you want out of this, Kamama, just tell me and you're out! You can return on the next flight. Okay? You won't find me cutting up rough. I can deal with stuff, done it many times."

Somehow, he soon began to feel more grounded than he'd felt for a long time. There was a quiet sense of concentration in John's mind. Despite a growing sense of anxiety about the higher risk, he felt cool.

On reflection, John knew there had been many times in his career when he had experienced a calming, 'trickster' effect kicking in at times of crisis. Oftentimes, he'd find himself feeling strangely relaxed amidst the crescendo of other people's stress and panic going on all around him. Time and experience had taught him, though this relaxed response signified that his body and mind had made an immediate, hidden adjustment, by speeding up. Strangely, though, the effect on his pulse rate being raised and his awareness heightened, the overall feeling to him, paradoxically, was a state of calm.

Kamama drove out of Gatlinburg-Pigeon Forge Airport at around 2.20 p.m. Eventually, they began to wind their way out through areas of magnificent ancient forest, under canopies of branches and autumnal leaves. John watched as leaves drifted silently on the breeze, like so many cartoon, pastel-coloured paper shapes.

The mountains themselves were showing off their famous blue haze; the landscape itself seemed to be speaking its 'Smoky' name, loud and clear. John soon began to understand how Isaac, Woya and Kamama could be magnetically drawn back to their Cherokee ancestral land. For sure, they would want to immerse themselves here, particularly in the circumstances like recovering from Wohali's assassination; hiding out here to think and grieve was instinctive.

Travelling the road leading to the retreat, John literally felt the reality of his outside world disappear. The cities of Washington DC, Oklahoma, and the Gatlinburg-Pigeon Forge Airport, all gradually receded.

Kamama, feeling the excitement of 'arriving,' began to explain to John what he would see drawing closer to the retreat.

"As we approach the retreat, John, you'll see it across a winding mountain road. The undercroft is built of brick and stone; it has been dug, cut and anchored on a foundational mountain ledge, looking down on a wooded mountain valley."

John looked across the valley's carpet of colour; it reflected the russet browns, pinks, oranges and greens of the season. Catching his first glimpse of the retreat itself, he saw it stood serenely, facing uninterrupted views, toward some other peaks on the horizon.

In the sunshine, clouds drifted across a blue sky; as they moved on the breeze, their shadows glided, as they moulded themselves to the rise and fall of the valley's canopy. The view was crystal clear; simply breathtaking. Leaning forward in his car seat, John looked up through the windscreen to see behind the retreat. John saw that the land rose higher, providing a backdrop of taller trees, including red spruce, mountain ash, maple and yellow birch.

Kamama had been right. John began to see for himself that this was an exceptional setting to meet and interview Isaac and Woya.

Driving closer toward the retreat, Kamama drove up to the undercroft's electronic door and parked. Then, stepping out of her driving seat, Kamama reached back into the cab and gave the horn three loud bursts.

Almost immediately the undercroft's up-and-over double door began to roll up. Gradually, Isaac and Woya were revealed from their feet to their smiling faces. Ylva, their German shepherd, padded out to the hire car to sniff out who the visitors were, then padded back to sit quietly beside Isaac, tongue lolling. Leaving Kamama to deal with Isaac's and Woya's emotional welcome, John drove their hire car into the undercroft alongside Isaac's.

After more introductions they all collected items of luggage; then, climbing the internal metal 'elbow' staircase, they opened a door, entering a long lounge and a kitchen area. Kamama took her luggage straight to one of three bedrooms on the second floor. John and Woya were sleeping in the remaining two. Isaac's master bedroom was in the loft space; from there he could access his own personal veranda and private view over the valley.

It was John's habit on arriving anywhere new to quietly set down his luggage and take a look around. Often, he would find himself gazing out of windows, sitting on seats and taking in views. Woya busied herself behind him in the kitchen area.

"Woya, you mind if I just take a look around?"

"Yeah. That's fine, John. Make yourself at home, it's been a long journey for you. I'm just sorting out our food for this evening."

John quietly opened the lounge double doors, leading onto a veranda. Looking along the veranda, John counted six swinging seats hanging from the rafters of an overhanging roof, two on each of the three elevations of the retreat; he took time out to sit and quietly swing himself on one of the seats.

Looking out over a sloping wild-flower meadow that reached down to the edge of the forested valley, the trained, security driven part of John's brain kicked in. There were no signs of any neighbouring cabins; in that moment, he recognised that they were truly alone.

3

It wasn't long before Isaac came down to sit with John on the veranda.

"My people, John, named these mountains 'Shaconage', *place of the blue smoke*. If you ever want to say that John, it is pronounced, '*Sha-Kon-O-Hey*'. As a people, we owned and inhabited a vast area of this land before the white man came. It was they who named the area the 'Great Smoky Mountains'. We lived here for many thousands of years before Columbus sadly got lost at sea, found what we now call Hispaniola today, then exterminated the Taino Indians. Both the British and the Americans gave us a lot of grief here, John."

Kamama soon joined them. She declined Isaac's invitation to sit for a while. Instead, she insisted they all take a break after their long journey, to stretch and walk. Isaac, however, decided to take a break on his own. Kamama and John went to find Woya. She'd begun to bring an evening meal together.

"Our meal won't be long now, Kamama. We can't go far, okay?"

Eventually, Woya relented to Kamama's powers of persuasion.

"Come on, Woya, Isaac is staying behind. We need to find a way for you to breathe fresh air; talk to us away from that kitchen of yours. Let's get Ylva's lead and get her out onto the meadow. Surely, she'll enjoy some time to just run and play."

So, Woya washed and dried her hands. Taking one last look inside the oven, she put her oven cloth down, smiled and agreed to take just fifteen minutes.

On their way out, John picked up Ylva's lead, ball and thrower. She circled John with her ears pricked and, with a bounce in her step, they all walked down from the retreat and out onto the wild-flower meadow. Though Woya had been reluctant to take a break from the kitchen, she soon linked arms with Kamama on one side and John on the other.

"It's so good to see you both. We've had mixed feelings about being here alone. But at once after Isaac and I saw Wohali… murdered, we just instinctively knew we mustn't be caught out and slaughtered in our own home."

Briefly, all three of them stood together knee-deep in the last blooms and grasses of the fall. Kamama took the ball thrower and sent Ylva off on another search, while John and Woya talked together.

First of all, John wanted to know if Isaac was actually tiring.

"So, Woya, is Isaac showing us he is tiring and unwell by staying behind? Will he be able to engage and have me ask him some questions after our evening meal?"

"To me, John, disregarding his leukaemia, Isaac is very energetic about you both being here with us. We need space to talk with outsiders. As I'm sure you'll understand, we're both very committed to doing every single thing we can do to help you find justice for Wohali."

Kamama, now listening in, chimed into the conversation, asking a different question.

"What is it that *you* need from this investigation, Woya? We need to listen to you as well as Isaac."

"Well, Kamama, no one has ever asked me such a question! Only you, a woman, could ask me that. What I want is to find whoever did this terrible thing to Wohali. They must be brought to justice. All the other 'big picture', dreaming stuff you and

Isaac talk about comes very low on my list of priorities. We need action, not what you call the blue-sky thinking; you two love that stuff, so much."

"You know how determined Isaac is. The Creator knows, as a people, we've clung to every crag of rock, while history has thrown us enough shit and near-fatal blows, as they tried to wipe us out. Yet, we are still here, against all the odds."

"We women, John, have done a huge amount to keep ourselves and our culture alive; that is a miracle in itself. Here we are, still continuing to struggle for our freedom. And us women have done all this, since surviving; we're still having children and creating a destination for the future. We did this having faced so many different methods they deployed to exterminate us; many of us along the way, of course, have lost all hope of justice."

Kamama linked arms with Woya again.

"Look, Woya, what you say is true. But we need hope, above all else. Surely, even with Wohali's assassination, we still need to move forward?"

Kamama saw again an opportunity to ask Woya about the work toward their liberation through the 'Festival's' policy, working with the First Nations as allies.

"Kamama, you know me well. I'm sick and tired of you and Isaac and your naïve talk of 'liberation'. I'll promise you now, if this damned 'Doctrine' you both talk about, enshrined in U.S. law, is ever dismantled, you and I will be the first women to dance down the street like giggling sisters."

"In the meantime, I'll need to see the colour of the white man's dollars for reparations before we talk about a new Constitution; having our own first and second Constitutions, they didn't stop the Trail of Tears, did it? [16]

John found himself looking on. Passions were running high and he knew he just needed to hang back and listen.

"But still, Kamama, I don't think you get it! I'm raw from just losing my brother; the back of his head blown out! So, I don't want to be talking about these fake Christian laws and these ideas of liberation you keep ramming down our throats!"

Woya turned on Kamama, even though she was trying to respond. Her sense of fiery anger and indignation in her bereavement shone through her face and visibly racked her trembling body.

"Us Cherokee women, we would have to be either saints, complete idiots, or both to believe that the justice you imagine for us is a real possibility! It ain't anywhere near the surface of our government's mind. Even I know, the least political amongst us, this white man's government suffocates us with silence.

"And don't talk to me again about what Pope Francis did or didn't say. I've read the Vatican's weasel-worded statement on so-called 'repudiation' of that goddam 'Doctrine'. I tell you, it was written by a lawyer, not a man of God.

"That 'repudiation' was no better than any of the white man's Presidents; whether it's been a black one or a white one, it's made no difference. No one cares about whether this fascist, so called, religious law is based on their Bible-bashing truth or not! Truth? What is truth to all these sickly, fake Christian politicians? They wouldn't know truth, not even if it came up and bit them on the ass."

Woya turned on her heels and started storming back to the retreat. Ylva loyally padded beside her. Woya, still driven by her fury, stopped for another bite of Kamama's ear.

"Just get real, Kamama! They don't care for the truth! All they care about is votes and money! Oh! Oh, yeah, and protecting their stolen land! Hell, a while back we've seen one of our Presidents, sign a fake apology to our Indian Nations. Did he stand on his feet in the White House to speak it? No, he couldn't even get to first base, look us in the eye and say, sorry. How screwed up was that?[17]

John listened, soaking up this spat between the women.

Woya's passions were overwhelming. Kamama attempted several times to get a word in edgewise but failed.

Woya remained on a roll, and she was in no mood for listening or taking any prisoners.

"You and Isaac, you can talk all the bullshit you like about the 'Festival' as our allies. I ask you, when have we *ever* had a loyal ally? An ally who didn't have their hearts full of betrayal from the beginning! Tell me!"

Woya's passion continued to flow while Kamama tried to marshall a reply.

"Okay, let's look at one simple example from our history. Imagine that excuse for a man, British Major, General Proctor? A *fine* upstanding example of a brave ally he was. A snake in the grass more like! What happened? He fled the field of the Battle of the Thames; abandoned our greatest leader and warrior; left Tecumseh with his many braves. Left him to die like a dog in a ditch with so many others of our brave men. Is that not so, Kamama?

"Where were our yellow-bellied British allies on that day then? I'll tell you. Having milked us for their own ends, trying to keep their grip on their ill-gotten Empire, they left Tecumseh to die alone."[18]

Kamama nodded, linking one arm into Woya's arm.

"Hey, Woya, come on! What good's an apology anyway? What we need is international justice for all to see! We don't need no mealy-mouthed apology for the Trail of Tears, Sand Creek or for Wounded Knee, we need to win the recognition and the dignity of ownership, power and governance of our own land; we need Turtle Island back, safe in our loving arms."

With tears in her eyes, Woya put her arms around Kamama's neck. Kamama looked over Woya's shoulder toward John as he stood by.

"That's all very well, Kamama, but how soon will justice be delivered? Where is this 'justice' you talk of be coming from? And, not only that, if you say it does come, when does it come?"

Woya pulled away from Kamama's embrace and stood with her back straight and her fists clenched.

"Okay then, Kamama. Answer me this, who else am I gonna lose? Tell me that? Soon we'll all be gone."

4

Sitting up in the front veranda of the retreat, Isaac watched as Woya, John and Kamama began to make their way back from their walk. He saw Kamama take Woya in her arms and he could see the love and warmth between them.

For himself, he felt the chill from both his ill health and his age, deep down in his bones.

In these last days, since Wohali's assassination, he had begun to think, *'Who can I possibly hand the future on to?'* For now, Isaac was looking toward his stem-cell treatment in the next few days. He desperately needed the five extra years the doctors had talked of. But today, in one of his darkest hours, Isaac realised that he couldn't see further than just three days; he was staring down the barrel of his own life.

Trying to banish fear from his soul, Isaac gave all his concentration to the here and now. More than anything, Isaac loved the sweet clarity of the mountain air. Today, it was as clear as crystal; it never failed to help him see.

Listening, with his eyes closed, Isaac heard the familiar sounds of a persistent breeze blowing through the trees. At first, he heard the sounds of the valley below him as a running, burbling, incoming tide. He imagined the foaming sea, gurgling into rock pools as it rushed further up a beach; then slowing, as it turned on itself, he heard the sound of the tide suck back, to join yet another, rippling incoming wave.

Then, as his ears tuned in more closely, the sounds from the leaves on the trees became more like a sparkling river; its waters singing and laughing on a shallow gravel riverbed, along its journey to the mighty sea. Isaac felt himself naturally draw in a deep breath; he held onto it and, then letting out a long deep sigh, he felt his body empty and relax.

He repeated this several times until he felt fully centred inside himself.

In this one place on Earth, Isaac felt there were occasional glimpses of hope; a hope that, after all he had been through, he could eventually heal. Then, opening his eyes, Isaac gazed skywards where the highest, thin white clouds moved more slowly. These clouds were unhurried; not driven by the stronger currents blowing below. Lower layers of clouds were busier, and a bald eagle circled, gliding on the air currents and thermals. Isaac watched as she swooped and spiralled, scouring the floor of the valley for her next meal. Having laid her clutch in early November, her young would soon be hatching and demanding their late-afternoon meal before sundown.

Isaac smiled with his eyes closed. He and Woya had known this female member of a bald eagle partnership for several years now, they mated here every year.

Then, in his meditation, Isaac felt himself lift and fly with her. Looking down, he manoeuvred at speed, felt his spirit soar; he felt the grace of riding the thermals; then, reluctantly, with legs and feet dangling down, Isaac swooped out of his meditation and 'landed' back on the veranda.

Opening his eyes and looking along the veranda, Isaac saw John and Kamama making their way to join him. Back indoors, Isaac could hear the soulful 'voice' of a Cherokee red cedar, wooden flute playing the 'Death Song', as Woya prepared their evening meal. Behind the melody he could hear Woya humming her own prayerful responses.[19]

Isaac remained in a reflective mood.

5

As John spoke gently, Isaac listened, sitting in between both John and Kamama, as they rocked back and forth.

"It's hard for me to find the words, Isaac... it doesn't get much tougher than being a parent facing the death and burial of your own child."

"These last two days, Woya and I, we've been listening to the 'Death Song'; music we brought with us to help bind and heal our wounds; the sounds of this red cedar flute behind us, flows through us like a meditation; sometimes we feel Wohali's spirit is moving; I pray to the Creator that maybe he'll be gliding as the bald eagle glides; maybe, one day, Wohali and I will reunite and fly together."

In the silence, John turned to quietly focus Isaac on his work to find justice for Wohali's assassination.

"So, Isaac, now we are here in the land of your ancestors. I can see why you've both come here to retreat from danger, to think and recharge. But, as they say, there is no rest for the wicked. I'm here to work and I have many questions to ask."

"The first question in my mind is about what help you feel you can give to me and my teams of investigators in DC? How can you help us find who has done this terrible thing to your son and your family? How can you help us deliver justice for

Wohali? Where do you think, we should start looking to find his killers?"

"John, I'm not so sure how to cover all that ground myself. There's a lot of it! Part of me says you just gotta ask me stuff and see where an answer can take us. What is it you think you need to know?"

"Okay. Let me try and ask it in another way. I've got a colleague and close friend. His name was George Stanhope. Like Wohali, just today, George has died a terrible and sudden death. He went under a Metro train at Foggy Bottom, Washington DC. Against my advice he went to a meeting with a couple of managers from the Mall Maintenance Service at the Memorial. I tried, but I could not stop him."

Kamama nodded in her recognition of George's name.

"Before George died, he and I had talked about Wohali's assassination. As an FBI man, George was *the* most senior, specialist executive lead. He was so experienced; his job was keeping our nation safe from terrorist threats; he was involved in leading our investigation of the January 6 assault on the Capital building.

"George was one of the senior officers painstakingly directing, leading, and making sure forensic evidence was collected, tested, and carefully archived to make it stick in our U.S. courts to obtain a whole bunch of people sentenced for seditious conspiracy.

"George was absolutely certain there was a deep 'conspiracy' behind your son's assassination. I found him to be a man who could be believed. But on the day before he died, he told me he'd written an email message, warning a lot of our own FBI staff that there was an active 'mole' at work leaking information from the firm. His theory was he could flush the 'mole' out, by telling the whole system about its existence.

"Looking at it today, it seems to me, the 'mole' came straight back at him and silenced him."

Isaac nodded slowly and looked sideways at John, listening as to whether there was any more to be said about where John's question was headed.

Then, unexpectedly, Isaac guffawed out loud.

"It's sure good to hear someone else talk like a paranoid person instead of me for once. All that suspicion, that 'mole' stuff? Well, John, it makes me feel almost 'normal'!"

"Let's come at this from another direction then. Before Kamama and I travelled over today, we interviewed Cary on Sunday morning. There is stuff I need to follow up on. So, what can you tell me about the marriage of Cary and Wohali? Then, I need you to tell me what you know about the Soul family?"

Isaac, sobering up from his laughing, began his answer.

"First thing I want to say, answers what you asked first. The people you're looking for are people I identify as 'infected predators'. In this case, I mean people who are still infected by a 'white man ideology' which was an ideology dressed up as a righteous scripture. So, these people you're looking for, they could be people who still believe it's their right to defend the supremacy their God bestowed them; some of these people still consider themselves to be on a Holy crusade on this continent. They believe in their right to dominate and subjugate anyone who ain't either white or a Christian."

"Five centuries ago, the 'white man' ancestors, back then compelled us to hand over our lands to the Kings and Queens of Spain and, Britain; they did this by speaking the Word of their God and enacting through brutal invasions, warfare, genocides, and slavery, they said their God approved of."

"Our story tells us that our First Nation ancestors discovered this land many, many thousands of years ago; the Europeans were just a bunch of psychopaths and gangsters; let us dispense with their propaganda about them being the civilised and us the savages and heathens.

"You ask me why are they getting twitched killing George on

the Metro? Well, the 'Festival' is committed to the evidence that nearly all of the biodiverse lands on Earth are protected by First Nations people; we know how to look after the land, keep the seas, the lakes, the rivers clear and clean; we are one of *the* keys to turning around climate change. The big joke is now, across the planet, we neither own or govern these lands; the 'white man' stole it and they're still trashing it as a commodity.

"You people love your mobile phones, don't you? Type in a question into your other 'God,' Google: '*Who protects all the most biodiverse lands on Earth?*' Answer is: '*Indigenous communities protect eighty per cent of all biodiversity!*' Yet still, there are 'colonial predators' who are trying to kick us out of lands they want to exploit, just so they can rape them and create yet more wastelands and warming.

"Me, John, I am starting to believe that us First Nation people might need to plan for the climate crisis; maybe then our peoples can survive that and start again, living inside nature again, safeguarding those other species and habitats that are left.

"So, John, that's why Wohali has been assassinated; the 'Predator' believes it has to strike now, there's much more to come."

John looked sideways at Isaac's profile. His face was a storybook of furrows; his hair was thick, white and grey; it was unbraided, falling over his shoulders.

"So, Isaac, let's get back to the Soul family. First, tell us about Cary."

"We know Cary well; she loved Wohali. They came to us and told us they were in love and intended to marry. We approved of their marriage. It was clear, John, they helped one another to drive the scourge of heroin and cocaine from each other's lives. The way I see it, Cary brought Wohali back to us as a family. For that alone, I cannot give her enough thanks and praise; she's a great mother to Danuwoa. I love my grandson, and, through Cary, I get to see a lot of him. He plays in our garden; he feeds the birds; runs faster than me now and rightly laughs at me when I can't catch him."

John returned to Isaac's thoughts on the Soul family.

"Anything else to say about the Soul family, the parents or Cary's brothers? Cary has told us about the brothers trying to break them up. Were you aware of all that going on?"

Before Isaac could answer, Woya called time on them to come to the kitchen for their evening meal.

"C'mon you three, evening meal is on the table! There's lots of time to continue afterwards."

"Hold that question, Isaac. We'll return to it."

Day 3   6

Thurmond
West Virginia

Monday
November 4

When Frank Denman arrived back home in Thurmond after his flight from DC, the West Virginian night sky was clear and without cloud. He breathed a sigh of relief and stretched his stiff limbs, glad to be home. Looking through the layers of twilight, the first stars had begun to twinkle through.

Trying to take in the sky all around the horizon, Frank remembered times he had spent with his mother after his father had died. She had been an inspiring woman, full of wonderment. She'd say, '*Frank, West Virginia is one of the best states for stargazin'*. Even after the events of the Springfield Mine disaster, the loss of her husband and her firstborn son, she still filled him with that sense of hope and wonder in the world around them.

Today, Frank thought to himself, '*being alive in these times, on this planet, after all is said and done, it sure is a magical place.*'

Deep down, Frank had come to love these moments of calm ahead of a complex plan coming to fruition. It reminded him of the complex operational plans he had devised during his days as a mining CEO. Since the success of Wohali Lightfoot's assassination he'd begun looking forward to celebrating, by blacking the other eye of the International Festival of the Earth.

After dumping his travelling bag, Frank took a shower. Then, feeling refreshed from his journey, he walked across the yard to the barn to see if Seth was still at work. The lights were on and, making his way to the workshop door, Frank could hear one of the woodworking machines still whirring. Knocking on the door, Frank entered. Seth looked up, smiled and switched off the sanding machinery. He had been smoothing a large post of burr oak. He switched off the current and brushed himself down, then ran his hand along the surface, feeling the warm softness of the sanded wood, as the engine of the sanding machine slowly came to a standstill.

"Your boys have been and gone since early afternoon then? They must soon be arriving at the retreat and settling in for night-time. I have to say, Seth, I am smiling inside with anticipation. What are the chances of these particular enemies all being found dead in the same place? Your boys and the two of us will be long gone in hiding, after we've all covered our tracks? Well, it feels such a great opportunity; feels like it could have been given to us from above, doesn't it?!"

"Yeah! I agree. The good Lord is movin' with us, Frank. This has been a dream of mine for some four years now. I want my daughter, Cary, back in the fold. It's been far too long since we were a whole family; we were broken up by that Cherokee Indian, Wohali Lightfoot.

"The boys are keen. They plan to arrive around dusk, take a look around at the lay of the land. They've researched the layout you sent through; if they're careful and moving with stealth, the FBI investigator, the two remaining Lightfoot family members and the professor, should all be silenced in their beds. That being the case, could be several days before any alarm is raised.

"Good. Well, if you three pull this one off that'll be your

targets met; your payday will be made good soon. I guess we should just wait and hear the boys' news though?"

"This is a great workshop, Frank. Time was when my own machinery at home was the best I could find. But now I can see it was nothing by comparison."

"Thanks for the compliment. I'm sure you were a craftsman in your own right, Seth, doing the best you could to make ends meet. What are you making anyway?"

"Oh, I am just working on another plan in case this evening don't come good. I'll explain all when I need to, Frank. It's nothing you need to be concerned about right now."

"Well, amen to that, Seth! Good to hear you're working on a contingency. Shows me you're a careful, well-prepared, and diligent man. Let's put it this way, Seth, you're a good man. Guess you're right after all, we're two sides of the same coin; both of us passionate about defending the rights of our own people."

"You hear anything Seth, you wake me. All right?"

"Oh! Seth, by the way, I haven't forgotten that we need that discussion about you, John and Charles coming onto my payroll.

"Goodnight, sleep well."

Day 3   7

Smoky Mountains

Monday
November 4

Having finished their evening meal, Isaac stood by the open lounge doors. He could feel a chill wind blowing from the north, across the mountains. While November was often a dry month, Isaac noted the clouds scurrying across the night sky; the moon was only momentarily visible, blinking on and off, shedding its light before disappearing again, behind another cloud.

Isaac turned and watched as Woya and John brought in a supply of logs from the undercroft, then busied themselves getting the fire to light.

"We're high-up here, could even be that snow's on its way tonight. That hearth, John, when it blazes and becomes a red-hot living heat, it can warm any soul. As we have at least another day ahead of us, it might be worth our being open to more of your questions tonight."

"My problem, Isaac, is keeping you on track. Remember, I need to hear more about the Soul men."

Isaac chuckled. He seemed in good spirits.

Soon the fire was lit, and its early sparks flew; the different woods from the valley gave off some of the many scents of pine, birch and oak. Eventually, it did as Isaac predicted, radiating a natural and comforting warmth out into the room. For a while all four sat in silence, just staring into the grate.

Out there, somewhere in the distance, a pack of coyotes could be heard lifting their heads to the skies, their eerie chorus floating on the mountain breeze. Then, just as Isaac was moved to speak, several unearthly howls drifted into the lounge from close by.

Isaac saw an expression of surprise pass across John's face.

"It's our local family of screech owls, John. There's a folk tale from our own mythology about their howling; it's a warning that someone we know is about to die.'"

Isaac smiled.

"Their screeching has come a little late. I suppose we have only just arrived back in our spiritual 'home'; it could signify a reminder of Wohali's death. I hope all your folks, John, and yours, Kamama, are okay!"

John quietly gazed into the fire's early glow, wondering if the owl was screeching for George.

As Isaac began talking, Ylva, who was lying down beside his chair, suddenly stood up. She looked through the lounge double doors and, barking, looked back to Woya, asking to go out.

Sitting on the veranda, her ears were pricked.

Woya followed her out; speaking softly and gently, she put her hand on Ylva's head. Ylva turned to look up at Woya, whining through her nose. It was as if she knew there was a threat out there, yet she was not spooked enough to raise a loud alarm.

Isaac called out to Ylva from his chair:

"Ylva, come on! Lay down!"

Ylva padded back to lay down by the warmth of the fire, her head between her paws, resting beside her master; her eyes soon closed; in time, she began dreaming, soft barking, paws twitching with her eyelids flickering, chasing her prey.

It wasn't long before Isaac began to introduce his childhood story of his admission to the Dakota boarding school. Back at the Skirvin Hotel Kamama had advised John that this was sure to happen. '*Choose your own moments, John. You'll get to cover your own agenda.*'

"I'm eighty-four years old now. I am told I was born in July 1944. In Europe, the Second World War was in its last year. But here in America, the U.S. Federal Government were still stealing us Indian Nation children from our parents; still with the aim of destroying our culture through a mass assimilation policy. The USA was fighting fascism abroad but continuing a fascist policy of cultural genocide at home."

Isaac paused and looked between them.

John asked a question.

"Just to remind you, Isaac, I'd like to start where we finished before dinner? In my mind your story about the Dakota boarding school comes much later in my priorities."

Isaac, a little impatiently, tried to continue to hold the floor with a single sentence.

"John, I thought we had covered the Soul family. Listen, I also need you to understand the impact of climate change policy and the connection with U.S. laws of land ownership, based on the 'Doctrine' of Discovery!"

Isaac, thinking he had re-established relevance with John returned to his main theme.

"The infection of the 'Doctrine of Discovery' empowered the early European colonial descendants. Captain Henry Pratt coined the boarding school system's motto, '*Kill the Indian, Save the Man*'.[20]

John, thinking he was joining a conversation, began talking about his own research.

"On the plane coming down, Isaac, I read some briefings on my laptop about the bigger picture of the U.S. Federal Government boarding schools. You'll know the kind of reports. Also, Kamama here has advised me about the 'Doctrine' at dinner before we came down. Look, Isaac, I am just letting you know, I don't need you to relive your painful past. I want to return to my earlier questions about the Soul family; the area we started before dinner."

John continued while Isaac sat back watching him, biding his time.

"Kamama advised me that virtually the same Policy being enacted in the U.S. was being pursued in Canada and Australia. In Australia these children became known as the 'Stolen Generation'. The U.S. Federal Government have also been reviewing and reporting on our own century of Policy…" [21/22/23/24]

John looked around and became aware of an uncertain silence in the room.

Isaac, at first, seemed to smile broadly. Then, speaking with a large dollop of straight faced, angry sarcasm, he leant forward, facing John directly.

"Well, John, sounds like you know it all already then! You won't be needing to hear from me at all, coming all the way across here was a waste of all our time!"

The fire crackled and spat in the grate.

Isaac nodded to himself. He looked from Woya to Kamama, then stood up, towering over John's chair.

"John, you don't seem to understand, I am doing everything to feed you, lay down for you, several layers of real, deep truth. I'm speaking from the dimensions and streams of my thinking about what I consider the cause of Wohali's assassination.

"I would say, John, you need to 'listen', then, 'learn' and 'understand'. Then, and only then, finally find your 'adjustment and action'."

Isaac's anger flared and grew as he spoke; his face came even closer to John's ear.

"Be still, man, until you *know*!"

Suddenly, it was as if Isaac had finally heard his own voice as truth, then snapped.

"Actually, John, I can't continue with this. You tell me your dead friend George believed there's was a 'conspiracy'. I thought you believed that too."

"Listen, Isaac, my business here is about the assassination of your son, Woh…"

"In the end, John, you're turning out to be just another 'suit' from Washington DC, with your black shiny shoes. I don't know why you bothered to come here! Get the hell back to Washington DC where you belong! Go and *invent* the truth, why don't you! We've seen it all before."

John looked across at Kamama for shelter or just a small, helpful intervention as his advisor. She in turn, looked away. Then John looked up at Isaac as he stood looking down on him.

"My apologies, Isaac, I wouldn't want to, and never intended to offend you in any way…"

Right now, didn't matter what John said. Whatever he said sounded pathetic. He felt like a small child pleading with a wounded and angry parent.

Isaac, moved to leave the room, calling Ylva to join him.

John turned to Woya in desperation.

"I think we could all do with a break! What do you think?"

John tried to rescue the situation by calling after Isaac to return.

"One day, Isaac, while we're here, I must speak to you about my own heritage. I think you and I could both benefit from that…"

But Isaac steadfastly continued on his path, taking himself out of earshot.

Woya stood up, rolled her eyes, and nodded.

"Yep! Okay, let's do that then."

8

Meanwhile John and Kamama found their jackets. They switched on the veranda lights, then took time out; trying to make sense of what was happening.

As they made their way through the double doors of the lounge, they could hear Woya arguing with her father.

"*Look, father, take a break yourself! Lighten up a bit! As usual, it's all too intense.! Have a hot drink why don't you! Believe me, you've got to leave these people feeling better than they do right now.*"

Not long after John and Kamama stepped out onto the veranda, the early winds died down and the air was stock still. Then the storm Isaac had predicted opened up in the darkness; there were rumbles of thunder and flashes of lightening streaking across the sky.

As John leant on the balustrade, large drops of rain began slanting under the veranda's roof cover, falling onto his head and arms; drops of rainwater trickled down John's face and hands, where he stood.

John took to muttering to himself out loud. "*Seems to me I'm getting crap from all directions.*"

Kamama remained unresponsive and silent. Behind him,

John could hear Kamama breathing as the swinging seat slowly rocked.

"So, John, what's the story on your own ancestors? I felt the tension suddenly building in there; but John, you just stumbled on; continuing to blindly press self-destruct buttons as you went. You were just being clumsy, even offensive.

"I thought, back at the hotel, I did brief you about who this guy was. As I said there ain't a great deal of humour in the world of Isaac Lightfoot. Tonight, there's even less."

John choked on that and spat his words out into the dark.

"Well, Kamama, I did look to you as I was going down the pan. And you, my very own 'advisor', what were you doin'? You were looking out of the lounge doors with nothing to say! Hell, I was stranded in there!"

As the seat rocked slowly behind him, John sorely spoke his words out across the valley, fully intending them to reach Kamama's ears.

"Look, you're here to help me with this stuff. Ain't that right? Seems I'm probably in this right up to my neck and drowning. I'm feeling less and less of an investigator unearthing evidence; increasingly more and more I'm like a sponge soaking up sack-loads of historical misery! All stuff I can't do anything about!"

John muttered to himself again, reflecting on his last phone call to Anna McKenna. *"This investigation is just taking too long! I need to shut this down and report back. Move on! Get on with my work; get back to my family back in DC. Maybe there's nothing more I can do here."*

So, eventually having vented, John looked over his shoulder and sat down next to Kamama. He was drenched by the rain that had been driving underneath the overhanging roof.

"So, what's the story, John? Why is all this shit getting in the way? How have you got to this point? It's one thing to interview Cary Lightfoot, quite another to interview either Isaac or Woya; even I came unstuck with Woya this afternoon.

"Oh, and by the way, I knew you were trying to work fast but what's with these new words you've just been mumbling? Now you're trying to 'shut down' this investigation, 'move on'?"

John took his time, considering whether to tell Kamama about his own story, which he knew was troubling him.

"Okay! Look, I never want to explain this stuff, but it seems I have little choice. Part of my own story, that almost no one knows, is I have a Jewish ancestry. My wife, Kay is perhaps the only one, for sure, in Washington DC. I had a close, trusted friend, Simon, in Chicago who knew. Kay, she understands my dynamics on this."

"The truth is, Kamama, I can't afford all these doubts. Hell, I was requested by George to take this investigation on. The attorney general in the White House is still taking reports from my director on what we're doing. Here I am, though, crumbling tonight, stewing in my own juice.

"I told Isaac before and after dinner, I wanted to return to my questions on the Soul family and all I did was try to hold him to my schedule. I am part of a team working at the same stages...

"You've gotta understand, I haven't been in the field for a while now. And, right at the beginning, before coming here, when I described the work, Kay said she knew this particular case could press my personal buttons. Annoying though it is sometimes, she knows my weaknesses back to front."

Kamama listened in the silence.

"Look, John. None of this helps me understand what's really triggering all this tension. How can I advise if I don't understand? I thought back at the hotel we shared a bit about who we were so we could work well together."

"Okay! Look, I've never had to explain this to an outsider. Never had to discuss this story outside my relationship with Kay and one close friend."

"Why don't you try me, John. I can listen. It might help."

"Okay, well my great-grandparents were living in Paris in the summer of 1942. When the Nazis occupied France, my great-grandparents, along with other Jewish parents, decided to arrange for my grandfather, a small boy then, to be smuggled across the Pyrenees to either Spain or Portugal. He became one of what is known historically now as the 'One Thousand Children'; having crossed the mountains they found their way to the USA, safe from the dangers of the European mainland.[25]

"My great-grandparents, like so many, did not survive. They were transported to Auschwitz concentration camp.

"I don't know the true story of attempts made by U.S. citizens and politicians to rescue many more Jewish children. Within the inner sanctum of my family, I remember there were often conversations over dinner. My mother and father would sometimes passionately debate this, saying, *'Look at the size of this country!'* *'Why did they not take ten thousand of our children? A number like this could easily have been saved and grown up here!'*

"So, my grandfather, having been saved as a child, eventually married a young girl he had travelled with, across the Atlantic. She had become his soulmate and, he hers. Eventually, this fine young woman, my grandmother, through her marriage to my grandfather, gave birth to my father.

"So, I guess am living proof of how a political policy of compassion and acceptance of diverse cultures can safeguard people in a spirit of tolerance. Look at my own family; three generations have flourished. I have two children, Ava and Theo. Our bloodline will go on. One day, Kay and I will have to share our family history with my children; our story of survival will live on in them, and so on.

John stopped talking for a moment; Kamama then reassured John she was still listening.

"I'm sure an educated academic like you will know all about the Holocaust history. I think it's likely that Isaac, in all his research, will have thought through his '*Predator*' theory and aligned it somehow to Nazi Germany. You'll know that millions of my people living in communities across Europe, in several other countries, were invaded; all became European funnels for the compulsory 'cattle truck' train transportation that carried my people and others, considered subhumans, to Nazi death camps.

"My people were dispossessed of land, wealth, professions, families and, ultimately, their lives. Others fell into the hands of the 'Angel of Death', Dr Josef Mengele, and became subjects of his cruel Nazi 'research'. Eventually, as history tells us through the Allies advancing through Germany, they found the system of 'Final Solution' death camps. The whole world then heard about Hitler's huge, industrial scale, genocidal machine."

John stopped talking for a moment. He could feel Kamama's warm hand was on his arm. As he turned, he saw Kamama's eyes were looking deep into his.

"John, it seems to me, tonight, you've just made the connection between your own history and Isaac's story as a child and the wider story of First Nation peoples, dispossession, domination and genocide. Can we get to that please?"

John, hearing what Kamama said, continued his story.

"As I've said, my great-grandparents eventually died in Auschwitz concentration camp. But they died knowing they had done all they could to replant their seed and save their culture.

"Coming to the point you just made, my own story has been brought to life again here, through a kinda... well, what can I call it? A 'reverse resonance' with Isaac's story? My ancestors' story is about great-grandparents being forced to protect their son and all that they knew, in order that my Jewish nation and our culture could find new roots and survive; also, very brave people risked their lives to enable children, like my grandfather, to survive.

"I'll be straight with you, Kamama, what is deeply troubling me is that hundreds of thousands of children have been systematically removed from their parents not just in the USA, but in other countries like Australia and Canada. I have read the investigations, reports submitted to our Federal Government and the others; the stories recur over more than a century; the story of 'colonial' powers attempting to destroy the very existence of First Nation people's. Then meeting Isaac and beginning to hear his story has brought it all to life.

"Also, my father and mother told me that the British played a heroic role in the *Kinder transport*, some British people took huge risks to rescue ten thousand Jewish children making them safe from the Nazis. Yet now I'm hearing that elsewhere in the old British Empire and the Commonwealth, British colonial descendants were, behind the scenes, systematically 'stealing' First Nation children from their parents in their Australian and Canadian territories; these were parts of the world where the British Monarch has been continuously in role, to this day, as a Head of State.

"I just don't get it. Did the British Monarchy know? Were they informed of these, so called, Policies, about the thousands of 'Stolen Generations' in their own 'colonial' lands?"

"The investigator in me cannot separate the basic evidence; these powerful countries, have been fundamentally connected in over a century; trying to eliminate First Nation peoples through the systemic theft of children from their parents, their tribes and nations; this behaviour has all been connected to the destruction of cultures and the 'colonial' theft of land, all over the world.

"Am I right so far?"

Kamama nodded.

"I am here to advise you, so listen."

"You're right thinking these are all interconnected; they've all been adopting very similar strategies. John, you think you've got a serious conspiracy on Wohali's case; John, well the level of colonial conspiracy between these five highly respected countries, is so huge, so monstrous, it's almost impossible to see it for what it is!

"These are five countries the U.K., USA, Canada, Australia, and New Zealand, they are all members of the oldest, modern day strategic, security alliance in the world today; they call themselves the 'Five Eyes'. Recently the USA, the UK and Australia have a new alliance to equip Australia with nuclear submarines.

"The tip of the whole iceburg can be seen on September 7, 2007 at the United Nations. The member nations of the world were voting on the Declaration on the rights of Indigenous People; 143 voted to adopt the Declaration; those few opposed included the USA, Canada, New Zealand and Australia; they voted *against* the Declaration.

"All these four nations, as we know now, had brutal histories in their treatment of indigenous people and their children; little wonder they initially voted against, they had no record in affording indigenous peoples rights because they had stolen all their land; all four of them, including the USA, had been part of the British Empire.

"It's a good example of the 'Five Eyes', almost entirely, voting as a political, 'colonial' block, only the UK from the 'Five Eyes' voted for; We know now even New Zealand has its own dark history of compulsory removal of children from their families.

"So, you are right to conclude, John, all the 'Five Eyes' members have dark and menacing histories; they have all adopted a similar behaviour pattern to try and consolidate their 'colonial' land thefts, through the destruction of indigenous culture; truth is they had all run out of effective extermination Policies and, instead, looks like they decided as a block to dominate and subjugate by trying to eradicate indigenous culture, through the abuse and assimilation of children.[26]

"Eventually, they did all come to endorse the Declaration

on the Rights of Indigenous Peoples; it's important to say it only carries moral force, it has no binding legal powers; got to tell you, all five countries, plus the British Crown, have, in their histories used the 'American Doctrine of Discovery' through the precedent of U.S. Supreme Court law, 'Johnson v Mcintosh.[27]

"John, you are trying to assemble a jumbled jigsaw. Kay was, in a way, right to be cautious about you coming here. Coming to investigate this case, completing some interviews, and listening to our history, you're hearing it resonate with your own story. My advice, John, for what it's worth? You must go on listening to your own story, it's your own 'truth' and your own roots."

"The truth is, Kamama, I'm back in my parents' lounge; their telling me I'll never be safe, and I must always be vigilant. Like Isaac, my name had to be changed for good reasons. They told me why my 'chameleon' name, John Green, had to be changed; told me how our real family surname would attract antisemites."

Kamama's hand still rested on John's arm. The dark night seemed to have soaked up John's emotions and questions, but it spoke no answers in return.

Kamama, however, spoke gently.

"Look, John, I understand, you're stirred up. You're trying to deal with a lot of painful stuff on your own. I had no idea! Like a lot of guys, you give very little away. I get it, though! It'll take time."

John quietly considered Kamama's psychological advice.

"Okay. Well, that's a very different way to look at it, Kamama. These days, back in DC, I tend to try to bolt it down; all my life I've been trying to digest it. Nowadays, Kay wants me to let it rest in peace; leave it all behind. Seems, deep down, I'm learning I can't do that."

"Lots of people, just like you, me and Isaac, we're all living with an ancestry packed with events of invasion, war, pestilence, dispossession, slavery, and genocide. You ain't on your own, John."

"I gotta be professional, Kamama. I can't allow a whole heap of this stuff to cloud my judgement."

No sooner than John had spoken, Woya called them back.

9

Isaac watched as John and Kamama came back into the lounge.

He was already seated with Woya. New logs had been put on the fire and yellow flames had begun to blaze again.

Woya had put together a tray of refreshments.

Isaac looked more relaxed and the emotions in the room had calmed. Aware of John opposite him, Isaac noticed he was about to make a move, break the silence, and explain himself.

"Look, Isaac…"

Isaac, however, leant forward in his seat and raised his hand, quietening John.

"No, John. You gotta let me speak first. All of this that we're dealing with here, my friend, is hard. It's all part of the deadly poison we in the Indian nations have had in our system for centuries now; Wohali's death has been the last straw."

"Fact is, not only have we lost Wohali, but we have also lost his urgent energy, passion, and confidence as an activist. I suggested he research so many of the stories of shaman, warriors, women and poems from the past; I'm proud to say of him, that on my recommendation, he did it."

"My son read about Tecumseh travelling to all the Indian nations to unite them against the Americans. Wohali was inspired by that; it was he who proposed that the 'Festival' send him to contact and involve other First Nation peoples across the continent; Wohali's idea was to try to unite as many of our nations as possible to help heal the Earth. As we know now, many responded to him."

"Wohali sometimes grew tired of my obsessions about what that boarding school took out of my brain; I still listen for that four-year-old child inside me; you see, yet, as I listen, I can never hear or see clearly through the dense fog drifting into my memories. Wohali, he told me, '*Put these things to one side for a while, father. I put my old self to one side and got drugs out of my system. Now I'm going to lead and fight…*'

"There are times though, John, when I'm living on the edge these days."

Isaac looked across at Woya.

"What I wanted to do was to tell you some of my childhood story. John. How I suffered; being held down on the floor aged four; them cutting off my four-year-old braids; forcing my mother's handmade clothes from my back, stripping me naked, laughing; their cruel faces, grinning. Then, one day, how I was rescued by a Black Panther when three 'white man' staff leathered me with their straps in a corridor."

Woya quietly chided Isaac.

"Isaac! You can't always do what *you* want. John's here to investigate. Let him get on with it! Let's face it, father, the time for your own justice is long gone; the time for Wohali is *now*! We need justice for him."

"What I wanted to say now, though, hasn't got any bearing on your work with us here, John. You don't even need to stay and listen. Kamama told me you'd asked her about my records not matching up…"

"You're forgetting, Isaac, it's for me to decide what's relevant to this investigation. I have to consider if there are factors from your distant past acting out in your world today. Maybe the past is still active in your life today, maybe not. But I have no idea until I hear it. I just need you to work in tandem with the priorities of my team in DC, that is all. The Soul family comes first."

Isaac nodded and backed down.

"Okay then. Come thunder and come lightning, we're gonna cover the Soul family now."

John set down his digital recorder.

"Thanks, Isaac, for giving ground. I'm including you in this, Woya; Kamama said on our walk, we need to hear from you in this investigation, that's true. Cary gave up a couple of difficult, painful hours to tell us about her family; gave us evidence we need to check out with you. I want to respect the effort she made.

"Turns out my team in DC have similar evidence about this mystery man at the Memorial who was impersonating me a few months back; Cary bravely confirmed some of that. We're gonna see if we can corroborate any of what she was talking about, through you as well. Kamama will tell you in a private moment about Cary. I don't need to tell you, she was grieving; however, she dug deep into her own painful history and did Wohali proud."

Kamama nodded in agreement.

"John is right, Isaac. Having sat with Cary on Sunday, I'd say you need to give him time to cover this ground tonight."

"First up then, did your family ever meet with Cary's family?"

Both Isaac and Woya said they hadn't.

"So, you never saw Cary's father? Did you ever see a tattoo on any part of his skin at any time?"

Isaac and Woya looked at one another and confirmed they'd never seen him or any tattoos.

John looked across at Kamama.

"Looks to me like this ain't gonna take long, Isaac. When you saw Wohali or Cary did they talk about their marriage?"

"Wohali never spoke to me about Cary's family. If I asked him how his life was going, he rarely said anything much; told me once that Cary's family didn't much like him being her husband."

Woya chimed in.

"Look, John, the truth is Wohali and I have always been close. Ever since our own family split over Isaac's abusive behaviour toward Wohali, he and I would talk to one another about anything and everything. Cary told me once the brothers would do anything to separate them. Her mother, well, she never had anything to say for herself."

"So, Isaac, you say Cary brought Danuwoa round to your house. You played with him in the garden. But life for them was hell at home? Did you know that?"

Isaac shook his head, then looked at Woya. "Sounds like I wasn't in the loop."

"Woya, this is all about a huge racial clash, isn't it? They wanted Cary out of there didn't they? Maybe not so much Danuwoa. Cary says her father thought of him as a 'mongrel'. Did you know that?"

"Yep."

"So, all the male thoughts and feelings in the Soul family were for ending Cary's marriage and breaking up their family. I'm right there, aren't I? How on earth Cary coped with all this alone when Wohali was away on his field trips, God only knows."

Woya and Isaac remained silent.

John looked to Kamama briefly; he read the look in her eye as a visual shrug; so he ploughed on.

"This sounds to me like racial hatred, Woya. Don't you think? These people weren't Wohali's friends or family they were his enemies; they were also your enemies. We heard that Seth Soul, and probably his sons, despised the mixing of bloods.

"We know we've got a 'conspiracy' going on here; right now, we can't see how all the pieces might begin to fit together but the truth is, it's possible they could have conspired to assassinate Wohali, couldn't they?"

Woya and Isaac agreed that could be possible.

"Okay then. Isaac, I'd like to know how you and Wohali talked and planned the work you were doing for the 'Festival'. Did you talk at your house, Isaac, or at Cary's place?"

"Always at my house, John. We never wanted to disrupt Cary and Danuwoa at home."

"Did you ever feel anyone could be listening in to your discussions."

"Never thought about that."

"Any building or electrical work going on at your house over the last two, three years?"

Isaac looked at Woya.

"Yeah, the house was rewired, couple of years back. Can I ask, where are all these questions leading to, John?"

"I can't say yet, Isaac. Wohali's assassination was a carefully planned event. Using our imagination, can we consider that when the electrics were done, listening devices were installed? Seth Soul could easily have become aware that Wohali was working for the 'Festival.' Maybe Cary proudly told her parents; maybe she defended Wohali in an argument about her husband and told them about his work with the 'Festival;' who knows?

"We already know now, the man who impersonated me at the Memorial months before Wohali's assassination could look like Seth Soul. It could be him who successfully convinced an experienced Federal Official he was completing a security check, while he was casing the joint.

"So how do we know that this man could have been Seth Soul? He had a tattoo of a cockerel's head on his forearm, as a minimum, he had blue eyes and a neatly trimmed head of grey hair and a well-trimmed beard. We know already that while you and Wohali were planning for a successful day together with the American Continental Festival Board, others were planning to destroy it.

"So, let's put it this way. If someone was listening in, what plans would they have heard you making?"

"Well, they'd certainly have heard us build a new position on the 'Doctrine of Discovery' and the U.S. law, *Johnson v Mcintosh*. We began to imagine constitutional reform because the law on land ownership was built on a clerical ideology, not a true religious theology. This came after the Catholic Church told the world the 'Doctrine' was a man-made ideology and not the word of God. The Vatican stated the 'Doctrine' had been used as a justification for colonialism. We needed a new position.

"They'd have heard our support to lock up all future carbons in the ground and under the sea. They would have heard all our plans for Wohali and his two hundred First Nation people to lead the event, with him on horseback."

"Okay, that's me done tonight, Isaac. Maybe you can think in what ways your '*Predator*' would feel threatened by hearing all that. If you were them, what would you do? All I can say to you both is, if you think of anything else, keep talking to me."

Everyone decided to retire for the night; Woya bedded Ylva down, made the fire safe and switched off all the lights.

Day 4   1

Smoky Mountains

Tuesday
November 5

Since the events of November 2, John had begun counting the days since Wohali's assassination. It felt to John like he had been away several weeks, but as the clock passed midnight, he had only just arrived at the beginning of the second day of his investigation.

After showering, John stood by his open window. Apart from the sound of wind in the trees in the valley, to him there was just darkness and silence; it didn't feel like a friend.

As John looked out into real, unpolluted darkness, he began explaining to himself; he was craving the streets; the bustle and noise of traffic; the human crush and rhythms of the Metro; the hubbub of the office and, finally, the banter of being at home.

Feeling cut adrift and alone; John tried to phone Kay. The landline phone rang and rang… He tried her mobile which he knew she kept beside their bed, but it quickly went to answerphone.

He left her a message: '*Hi, Kay. Just touching base. Where are you? Out here in the mountains, it's so goddamned quiet. Just wanted to hear your voice! Tell me how the kids are doin'. Feel I've been here for weeks and it's only the second day. Ring me? Please?*'

Determined to speak with someone beyond the mountains, John phoned Phoenix. She picked up.

"Hi, Phoenix, sorry to phone so late. There is a reason to speak, but first I gotta tell you the silence out here is driving me nuts!"

"Okay, John, you want me to sing, maybe quote poetry? What can I do for you?"

"No! Tell me about, Jim Coogan?"

"Well, our investigation is interesting. We're not finished, but its already clear, things are adrift; you know, with some of Jim's practices and disciplines. No smoking gun yet though. Jim has been in touch to say he has evidence of his own to bring in on his interview tomorrow. Then there's Charlotte, she's making progress with Mall Maintenance."

"Okay, Phoenix. So, here at the retreat there's no further corroboration on the forearm tattoo and Seth Soul. However, there is a lot more corroboration of the Soul family on racial hatred. Comes into the narrative through Cary's family and their attempts to separate her from Wohali. Woya, Wohali's sister, gave us that narrative tonight. Wohali spoke to her alone about what was happening. So, for me, Cary's father and brothers are still very much in the frame. Look, thanks for picking up. I'm missing my day-to-day… look, I gotta turn in.

"One other thing, Phoenix, there is toxic stuff in this investigation on racial matters which is very powerful. This 'Doctrine of Discovery' stuff is a revolting can of worms. It has unsettled me. Part of the racial story even speaks to the history of the transatlantic slave trade; it has stirred something from my own background today, which I'll share with you sometime."

"We've got to be there for one another, John. Just call if you need me; you're on the front line of this investigation right now."

Soon all the lights, downstairs and up were off and everyone including Ylva, were at rest.

2

In the early hours John was woken by the sound of loud barking; as he got up, he slipped on his trousers and went downstairs.

By the time he made it down, Ylva had begun low, deep-throated growling; then barking loudly at John. She began charging around the lounge; then pawing and whining at the bottom of the door to the undercroft.

Woya soon joined them.

She tried hard to try to calm and even instruct Ylva. Then, as Woya knelt, she rearranged Ylva's bedding, talked softly, patting, and encouraging, but still, Ylva just would not get back into her basket and settle.

"Look, John, this is unusual. Something beyond that door just ain't right."

"Yeah! Thinking back, she was unsettled in the lounge earlier this evening, wasn't she?"

John quickly ran back upstairs, dressed and pulled on his bullet-proof waistcoat. Finally, he strapped his shoulder holster on, then quickly checked and lodged his 9mm service weapon. John considered that Ylva's agitation could be just a skunk or a cougar; but he needed to check it out. At the top of the stairs, a fleeting thought crossed his mind: *'There's no access to backup.'*

Before they opened the door to the garage, John asked

Woya to fetch the house flashlight. They decided to allow Ylva to go down first; by then, she was bursting to get through that door. No one could have held her back; going through the door behind Ylva, John looked along the beam of the flashlight; she had absolutely flown down the elbow of the metal flight of steps and was searching inbetween the two cars and the undercroft floor.

Arriving at the bottom, he saw Ylva intensely following her nose across the floor; soon she was barking at a smashed side window of the undercroft. John held her back by her collar to protect her paws. Clearly there had been an intruder, but it looked like they had got no further and left again by the same way they'd come in.

John looked over his shoulder and shouted up to Woya.

"Switch on all lights in the garage, and the external lights; then release the electronic entry for the garage door."

As the door ratcheted open, John could see that Ylva was again pressing to get through the wide door as it slowly ratcheted itself higher.

At her first chance Ylva crawled, first on her belly, then flew out onto the retreats approach road. John did his best to follow her at pace. He found himself catching up as she occasionally stopped, her nose seemingly fixed to the ground; then, she would suddenly stop, turn in circles, nose fixed to the ground going round and round, then finding new scent trails and charging off again.

Along the way John tried to use the flashlight to search the ground; occasionally, he'd check to locate where Ylva had got to. Pointing the flashlight to the wetter ground John quickly picked up two sets of bootprints. As well as these footprints, there were freshly snapped grasses, broken by the intruders on their walk to the retreat and now, running away.

Still jogging behind, John eventually caught sight of the backs of two figures running in and out of the beam.

He drew his handgun; knelt and shouted:

"Police! Stop or I'll fire!"

Still the shadowy figures ran on. There was just the sound of a male voice shouting, "*C'mon! Keep up! Run!*" As John chased onward, he considered he could easily be dealing with the Soul brothers.

John knelt with his gun aimed along a line of fire established by the flashlight beam; he fired three shots along the illuminated corridor. He heard a vehicle door open; there was one yelp of pain coming after his last gunshot; this was followed by the sound of Ylva barking; soon after, there was the sound of a diesel engine desperately trying to ignite but failing.

As John reached the driver's door, he tried to force it open; the slit eyes of a balaclava hood looked back through the window at him; the engine continued to turn over, repeatedly. But still, it wasn't firing. Trying to pull the driver's door open again, John yanked it furiously, his left foot levering into the Raptor's side panelling. Suddenly, the guy in the driver's seat released the door lock and it flew open, catching John off balance; the force of his own weight threw him backwards to the ground; struggling to stand and get back to the four-by-four, he could hear Ylva barking close by; as he reached out to grasp the door handle again, John felt a huge blow to his head from behind.

Then, semi-conscious, he sensed himself being dragged up into a kneeling position by his collar; somewhere in the distance he could still hear the echos of Ylva barking and growling again; in the chaos he felt himself falling backwards, then heavy blows kicking into his face, ribs and stomach; gasping for breath John heard a male voice screaming out, "*Get in!*"

As the four-by-fours engine finally ignited, John passed out.

The next thing John heard was Woya's voice and he felt her shaking his shoulder.

"John! John! Wake up, John!"

John slowly opened his eyes; struggling to sit up, he reached to examine his throbbing head; he gasped with the sharp pain from touching a bleeding wound. Then, looking at his bloodied fingers, he fell back into the soft grass again; then, trying to sit up, pain shot from his bruised stomach and ribcage; he fell back a second time; turning his head to one side, John looked along the beam of the flashlight he had dropped. He could see a clear set of tyre tracks in the soft ground.

"Now that, Woya, is a piece of gold dust. I gotta get back to the retreat… get me up, will you? Gotta call in the CSI to come in first thing in the morning and secure all this evidence. This is a crime scene. Come on, Woya, help me to get up, can you!"

Getting to his feet, John leant on Woya; he insisted she stay beside him while he searched the undergrowth with the flashlight. John looked around where Ylva had caught up with the intruders by their four-by-four vehicle.

While John steadied himself Woya couldn't stop talking and talking, explaining what she'd seen.

"Look, slow down, Woya. You're not making sense."

"When I got here the lights of the four-by-four lit the area. I hid in the grass over there. One of the attackers, held you by your collar with one hand, he balanced you onto your knees; he had a gun in the other hand, pointed at your head; then Ylva arrived from nowhere. She leapt, barking, then growling, grabbed the attacker's arm in her teeth. She shook her head from side to side. The guy screamed in pain, as he pulled his arm away; I saw some of his sleeve tear off from his jacket, leaving it in Ylva's mouth."

Woya explained to John that his attacker had got into the passenger seat, supporting his wounded right arm. With the four-by-four's engine revving, its rear wheels left the grass verge, then gripped the tarmac, burning and screeching; once both the front wheels began to grip it left the grass, and they had sped away.

Supported by Woya, John and Ylva searched the grass where he had been assaulted. John pointed the flashlight at the grass in front and around the roadside.

"Look, Woya. There you are. Another nugget for the CSI! There's the piece of torn sleeve you mentioned; looks like it's got blood on it. Pick it up by the very edge of the material, Woya, we must bag it somehow."

Woya gently bent down and carefully picked up the fabric, handing it to John.

"That's DNA, Woya. The tyres and bootprints have got to be cast tomorrow and the rest of this grid of ground must be systematically walked by our forensic team. Thankfully, the rain has stopped, and the cloud has cleared."

Making their way back to the retreat, John was excited that the new evidence might show how this event was directly connected to Wohali's assassination.

"I promise you, Woya, if they're a match, we'll track 'em down and lock 'em up. I'm going to stay up now, Woya, phone Phoenix, and get her to contact the CSI team for me for tomorrow."

"C'mon, Woya, we need a stiff drink, and I need you to have a look at my head; probably just needs you to bathe it; it's probably just a gun-butt wound."

Getting back inside, Kamama was sitting with Isaac making sure he was okay. He looked shaken but stoic in attitude. Isaac clearly attributed the first ever break-in to the retreat as part of the continuing attack on both his family and the International Festival of the Earth.

John, supported by Woya, smiled through his pain as he took a seat in the lounge. As Woya inspected John's head wound, Kamama came over to check with John whether there were any other serious injuries.

Feeling uplifted by events and evidence, John joked with Isaac.

"Okay, Isaac, let me guess now, could this attack have anything at all to do with your '*Predators*' with a capital P?"

3

Rested, John struggled upstairs to make a secure phone call to Phoenix; her phone rang and rang. John, however, showed no mercy and kept the phone ringing until she eventually woke.

"John! What in God's name are you doing waking me up at this time of day?"

John heard Phoenix scrabbling for a bedside clock.

"For God's sake, you've woken up Trent now. I can tell you, he's an ugly cuss when he hasn't had his beauty sleep! This better be good or you'll be apologising to Trent next time you see him!"

"Good morning, Phoenix! The hell I'll apologise to Trent for waking him up! Tell him 'hi' anyway. However, tonight the Lightfoots, Kamama and I are lucky to be alive. You said it 'better be good'! Is that good enough for you?"

"Shit, John, you know well enough when the chips are down, we are there for one another. I'd be destroyed if anything and, I mean anything, happened to you. Are you okay?"

"Yeah, well, with a couple of heavy blows to my head plus a good kicking in the ribs, I've felt a lot better than I do right now. If it wasn't for the Lightfoots' German shepherd, we'd probably all be dead in our beds."

John told her the story.

"Look, Phoenix, rather than you just getting back into bed,

I desperately need you to stay awake. You've got the national CSI network to hand there? Yeah? They need scheduling right now to attend here in early daylight hours. They'll need to walk the grid here and fully secure the retreats undercroft and outside.

"At the very least we have got tyre tracks and bootprints, plus I've found a piece of torn sleeve with an intruder's blood on it. There's almost certainly more at the side of the retreat where they broke a window and climbed in! Could be prints inside."

John took a moment to change his sitting position, supporting his ribs to ease his pain. Woya fussed around him, bringing painkillers and water.

"Oh! I also need you to ask CSI to complete a sweep of Isaac's Oklahoma property for listening devices. I'm pretty damn sure that their properties have been bugged during their preparation for the 'Festival' event.

"Then, the next thing, please brief David O'Donnelly for me; ask him to contact me; he'll need to coordinate with CSI forensics while they are here; also, he needs to press them to pass across their results as soon as they've processed them. As always, Phoenix, we need David to urgently do the comparative work done between results here and the Memorial detritus, plus the national databases.

"The other thing is, if you haven't realised already, neither of us can trust anyone inside the 'firm' going forward.

"This conspiracy stuff is kicking off, Phoenix. The 'mole' has to be one of those trusted people named on the email I sent out, telling you I was here. Could be anyone sitting at our own table; let's face it, that includes Anna McKenna, Robin Seacourt, any of our team leaders, even Dina, my PA. You gotta take care, Phoenix. We'll talk more in the morning."

Phoenix quickly interjected to stop John from closing the call right down.

"By the way, John, I think we've covered Jim…"

"I've already said, I trust you, Phoenix – no one else though! That's my position tonight, Phoenix. Right now, we're in a situation where the FBI could have lost two executive lead officers in two days, all because one of our own has gone rogue."

After his call to Phoenix had concluded, John phoned home to Kay. As the line rang John slowly sipped from his hip flask of malt whiskey.

Eventually, Kay answered.

"Hi, John. It's very late. You, okay?"

John heard Kay switch on her bedside lamp.

"Hi, Kay. I tried to contact you earlier. Just need to keep in touch. First thing to say is, I am okay. I know if I don't tell you the truth, you'll worry more. I've been assaulted tonight by a couple of guys attacking the retreat here in the mountains. I've got a sore head, cuts and bruises elsewhere, but, everything seems in working order. A dog came to the rescue while some guy held a gun to my head; had that not happened we may not have survived the hit."

"Oh, John! Are you sure you're okay? Get yourself checked over."

"Yeah, physically bruised, but I'm fine in spirit. Gotta tell you, you were right about the psychological profile of the mission. It's been getting to me. Ideally, I really do wish you were round the corner; you know those times when we get to bed, it's the end of the evening, and we always share the day we've both had. But you're not here. I'll be fine though."

Kay sighed down the phone.

"All I can say to you, John, is shut out any personal horror right now. You know what I'm gonna say. When we first got together, we went through all this stuff in that early antisemitic case in Chicago. As you well know, this all came to a head just after we'd got married; but that stuff is all in the past now.

"We're all carrying stuff we can't handle, darling, day to day we've just gotta get by. So, don't let it consume you. You and I have talked this through for hours. Just shut it out, John. Do your job and get home to us, eh?"

"Um … well, right now I feel it's too late for shutting this stuff out, Kay, doing just that hasn't worked for me. I've got no idea when I'll get home now, Kay. The retreat mission is all over the day after tomorrow, when the forensic investigation completes. It ain't safe to stay here now. But I know already there'll be more to do back in Oklahoma, tracking down the prime suspects; so, love you, Kay, love to the kids

"Don't worry about me, John, we're okay; just finish what you set out to do and get back."

4

Isaac woke later than anyone else.

Coming downstairs he could hear a buzz of conversations; John's telephone was constantly ringing; the CSI had already arrived.

Isaac realised he needed to catch up on what was happening.

As he got halfway down the stairs, he was just in time to hear John shut off his mobile, claiming that he needed some peace and quiet to take his breakfast. Woya and John were engrossed in a conversation, they didn't know that Isaac was nearby.

"Woya, is Isaac, okay? Is he up for more work today? He looked incredibly wiped out by the events of the early hours. Look, if he needs Kamama to advise him about how much he can take on, ask her privately to get alongside him."

"John, you just don't know my father. There is no way Isaac would allow Kamama to advise him. Isaac and Kamama, they're in all this political, cultural, protest stuff, right up to their necks! Didn't you know that? She's just not capable of being a calming 'keeper'. Isn't that right, Kamama?"

Kamama, eating her breakfast, just laughed; from where she was sitting, she could see Isaac was listening in.

Woya continued.

"Knowing Isaac, he probably feels like this is the battle of his life. I just know he's gonna say, '*Woya, this is just the beginning! We're moving out of the* foothills *to take up our battle lines!*'"

Isaac, smiling to himself, coughed and made sure everyone knew he was down.

"Well, Woya, you're right! I am afraid it's definitely a 'no' to anyone wrapping me up inside some kinda academic absorbent cotton! Oh! By the way, John, I'm coping under the strain thank you; yes, I *am* excited. We might, sometime soon, see the '*Predator*' out in the light of day."

Coffee was a lifesaver for them all. Isaac joined Kamama and Woya for breakfast. John left them to it, gingerly nursing his aches and pains upstairs, to then shower and change.

Downstairs, the landline phone for the retreat was ringing.

Woya took the call. It was from the CEO of the International Festival of the Earth, Indira Anand. She was considering travelling by helicopter to visit the retreat, together with the USA Festival CEO, Grogan Small. They both wanted to give their personal condolences and discuss the future.

Woya responded for Isaac.

"Look, Indira, I think you've forgotten Isaac will be in hospital in a few days. Also, I can't possibly say whether Isaac can travel to London in the spring. This treatment's a big deal."

Isaac smiled and listened.

Woya put Indira on hold and spoke to him.

"What do you think, Isaac? Would these people be safe here?"

Isaac shrugged and pointed to John.

"Look, Woya, I think it's best to consult John on this."

John advised Woya to close down the call, he would call back. "Well, look, Woya, we've just had a dangerous attack on the retreat. I think it's quite fair for me to say to you, '*We're lucky to be alive!*' So, I'd respectfully say no."

"But, John, they say they are bringing their own security with them…"

"I'll call her, Woya! Okay? The answer has gotta be, 'No.'"

After showering and a change of clothes John returned downstairs to make the call.

"…Look, if you insist on coming, Ms Anand, I want you to understand that I won't be responsible for you or your staff. My own personal assessment today is you're almost certainly going to be a target on the list of this 'conspiracy' in your own right. We've got hunches about who we're dealing with; we have some evidence but, as yet it's not matched to suspects.

"I can tell you, Ms Anand, I listened to your interview on FOX News after the assassination. I agree with you, we are probably seeing the growth of an international network of climate terrorists. So, I can't agree to you putting yourself at risk."

Isaac looked up from his coffee feeling relieved that John was taking charge of these decisions. While he and John had disagreed yesterday, right now Isaac felt safe. He could see John knew what he was doing.

"John, you certainly don't mix your words, and these people can be in no doubt, they are responsible for themselves now. Maybe they'll decide to meet up another day back in the city."

Woya, however, thought their final decision seemed to be that they were coming.

Day 4 — 5

Washington DC

Tuesday
November 5

Phoenix was busying herself around the breakout room she had chosen for her first full-service meeting as the acting executive lead. She'd been awake during the night arranging CSI support for John; right now, she looked deep in thought and a little anxious that everything was well done and set up before her staff arrived.

John's PA, Dina, had helped sort out the basics, getting chairs and tables in place, putting glasses and water onto the tables and finally placing Phoenix's agenda for the meeting in front of each person attending.

Phoenix placed herself and her team leaders, Charlotte, and Jason, at the head table. Dina had arranged herself to sit with them to support them by taking verbatim notes on her laptop.

Gradually the room began to fill up with Charlotte's, Jason's and Jim's investigators, as well as their interns. When the time reached 11.30 a.m. and the majority of the service was assembled, Phoenix kicked off on the agenda on the dot.

The priority area of discussion was clearly the Wohali Lightfoot investigation.

Phoenix briefed the team that there had been an aborted assault on the Smoky Mountain retreat where John and the

Lightfoots were based; John had been injured but he was okay. CSI forensics were there combining and securing all the evidence, together with some items John had secured the night before; David O'Donelly was working closely with the local CSI.

"There will be a need for Jason's team to pick up the search for all the candidate four-by-four vehicles once we know the make and model from the tyre-track castings. Jason, I'm relying on you to keep on top of that. Also, there should be an excellent DNA sample from the piece of torn jacket sleeve material, John rescued after the assault on him. The results will need comparing with the DNA collected at the Memorial Undercroft.

"I am going to be candid with you all. We're concerned that there have now definitely been three breaches of information from this office now. Firstly, a breach setting up the 'John Green' imposter to meet the Mall maintenance manager at the Memorial at least six months ago. Secondly, there was the leak which resulted in the death of George Stanhope at the Foggy Bottom platform. Thirdly, a leak from John's email informing and timing attackers that he and Professor Catawnee would be travelling to the retreat in the Smoky Mountains. They'd arranged to interview Isaac and Woya Lightfoot who had fled Oklahoma City after Wohali was assassinated.

"Things don't get much more serious than this for the FBI. I'm hoping the culprit is not in this room right now. But believe me, if the 'mole' is in this room, John and I will root you out. Whoever the traitor is, they'll be charged, prosecuted and locked up for a long time."

The room was silent.

Phoenix looked around and sensed the need to allow what she'd said to settle; keeping her own counsel, she felt the tension in the group grow. Jason was the first to break the silence; his response was to raise other concerns about workload.

"Look, Phoenix, the Lightfoot investigation is growing now. We're gonna hear from Charlotte and Esteban about their work later. Surely, we're gonna need extra resources. And where's Jim? Our most experienced team leader? Charlotte and I are picking up supporting his team as well as our own. What are you gonna do to manage these pressures, Phoenix? If John was here, he'd have a solution for us right now."

Jason looked around the room as he spoke. Phoenix saw others start to nod in support of his comments.

As she looked around the room, she saw others rallying around Jason.

Phoenix knew Jason had a way of making trouble while seeming to lead; he had a way of sounding responsible while undermining others. John could never see it.

"Look, Jason, you're a team leader; John's forever telling me how good you are. So, you're someone John and I need solutions from right now. What I won't accept from you is a list of operational problems for me to fix for you."

Phoenix looked around her staff, eyeballing them.

"Before anyone here starts following the line Jason is treading, there are no added resources; you've got what we've got. You guys as team leaders, you have to be resourceful and manage well. Jason, my response to you is you need to dig deeper. This service is under scrutiny now, Anna and Robin are very aware of what's happening; they're watching.

Jason looked around at colleagues, still seeking vocal support; Phoenix felt a sudden charge of professional anger.

"Listening to you, Jason, I am getting concerned for you. While I'm talking about a security breach in this service, you, Jason Colbeck, you're busy picking fucking holes in my leadership. John might well think very highly of you, but I'm not so sure. Got that? I'm proud John and I built this service together with you all; staying tight when times are hard was a core value, Jason. I remember you were in the room when we laid the foundations together! So, I don't want to hear any more from you, Jason, unless it's a solution.

"You know the score, Jason, right? If I ain't made myself clear to you and your team, *find that fucking four-by-four!* Shit, John Green could be dead this morning!"

As she spoke, Drake made his way into the room, head down as if trying to make himself invisible. Phoenix stood up and put her hands on her hips, pointing at Drake, she hammered home her message to Jason again.

"Yep! And that's another thing, Jason! Get your intern to tow the line. He should be arriving here keen as mustard; he should be on time to show *me* some respect! So, you get him on message, he could also start completing the tasks we give him! He certainly failed on George Stanhope's delegation to produce a briefing for John. So, get on his case, Jason, and get off mine! Next item!

"Robin and I have brought forward our meeting with Jim Coogan to 2 p.m. today; you'll all know that I am not at liberty to disclose the details. What I do want you to know is that Jim is suspended, at this stage, for his own protection. I'd do the same for any of you."

Finally, Phoenix moved on and asked Charlotte and Jason to take responsibility for getting the team's electronic whiteboard up to date.

"We need to be mapping the investigation, posting evidence, keeping it up to date, okay?"

"You can both delegate this to our interns; Esteban and Drake, here, involve them, they're both bright students with new ideas, get them involved. They'll probably have some new ways of presenting data; we need to learn their new methods; they need to learn from our experience. Next time we meet as a service we'll use the electronic board as a focus to analyse and visualise where we've been as a service and where we're headed. Make sure this happens! I want to use it to take Anna Mckenna through out progress regularly."

"Before we finish, Esteban, I know you have got a few words to say about your CCTV examination regarding George and the

Metro. What happened to George affects us all deep down. I've watched Esteban here, sitting in front of his screen trying to do right by George and his wife, Brenda."

"Over to you then, Esteban."

"Shall I do that now?"

Phoenix nodded.

"Well, the reason I wanted to raise this piece of work here is I think we need some extra forensic expertise on this. I've watched the clip we've got, gone over and over it. My thinking is we need footage from another angle.

"So, I want to ask you, Phoenix, can you bring in the resource I need? I've talked to David O'Donnelly, so I know he has a CCTV specialist; we need her involvement. I'd like her to work with me to review the film we received first. But then, I'd like us to go down to Foggy Bottom with our specialist, meet the Metro CCTV officials, make sure we haven't missed some footage."

Phoenix agreed to link with David O'Donnelly and fix additional support for Esteban.

Finally, Phoenix then asked Charlotte to get the teams up to speed with her work on the Mall Maintenance Service.

Charlotte referred to her notes as she spoke.

"Okay. Well, I have been working with Greg Tranter who leads the whole service. As Phoenix has said we are certain now there has been a breach in internal security between our own service and theirs.

"So, what do we know? We know a fake, very believable, FBI ID was made for the 'John Green' imposter to meet Greg Tranter; the imposter was shown into the Memorial and the Undercroft on the pretence of him making a corporate FBI risk assessment for the International Festival of the Earth event. Tranter says during a parting handshake he saw what looked like a tattoo of a cockerel's head on his forearm. We also know Tranter didn't meet George alone, he had one of his team leaders with him, a woman by the name of Suzanne Woodman.

"John has now corroborated this tattoo from an interview within the Soul family. He has sent through a full photographic image, provided by Cary Lightfoot, Wohali's wife."

Charlotte flashed the photograph image on the screen behind her.

"You can see the photograph shows us Cary's father, Seth Soul, standing with his sons, he's wearing a short-sleeved shirt. There's a cockerel standing on a weathervane tattooed on his forearm. The whole image is an important part of the jigsaw. I'm meeting Greg Tranter later on today to show him this photograph for ID.

"We've made some other good progress from the Oklahoma end. Cary's family, surname is Soul. In this image, the father, Seth Soul, is standing in the centre, the next guy on the right is John Soul and lastly, Charles Soul standing to his father's left. John has asked Oklahoma, Chief of Police, Walter Banks to issue an APB to urgently find Seth Soul and his sons and bring them in for questioning.

"We're still investigating the details about who in our own service was involved in making the ID. Phoenix, you're leading on this and who made the appointments for the 'imposter' to meet Greg Tranter; he says that George was very impressed with Woodman, she had talked through the detail on how the meeting was set up through our own offices here at Pennsylvania Avenue."

Phoenix nodded and then, looking at Esteban and Drake she pointed to the image on the screen.

"Yeah, that's right! This is a real breakthrough. Never forget that a high percentage of murders are committed by people known to the victim. Cary Lightfoot has let us know her mixed race marriage to Wohali Lightfoot wasn't sitting easy with the Soul family; she's identified occasions when her brothers were trying to pressurise, separate and destroy her relationship with Wohali."

Charlotte continued to finish the briefing on her item.

"As I've said, I've interviewed Team Manager, Suzanne Woodman once about all the systems, breaches we think must have occurred to get the assassins into the Undercroft in advance of the Festival of the Earth procession. We've followed up on all the potential breaches she has given us. She has confirmed she spoke to a male officer in this office about arranging the 'imposter' meeting with Tranter and there is an email trail we are following up on with Woodman to establish what happened back there.

"I've learnt through Woodman; she has recently recruited a team called the 'Ranger Tour Guides'; this team now provide tours into the Undercroft itself. Woodman was appointed to establish this team and get them up and running. I have to say the creation of this team was an ideal opportunity for an insurgency into the Mall Maintenance Services; George himself said to John on the day of the assassination there must have been a lot of preparation and internal breaches of security."

At the end of Charlotte's report, Phoenix closed the meeting down. She congratulated her team around the core items of progress. Then she motivated them on the urgent 'must do' items to add to the growing picture of evidence accumulating from the three locations of Washington DC, Oklahoma and the Smoky Mountains.

Day 4 6

Smoky Mountains

Tuesday
November 5

The hubbub of the CSI investigation continued through the morning.

John was busy orientating the CSI forensic team outside. All of them were masked and dressed in their white forensic gear and walking the 'grid' outside the retreat.

Isaac waited for a quiet moment so that he could propose a walk for them all to take time out. However, as he waited, he heard another phone call wing its way in from David O'Donnelly for John; Isaac couldn't help but overhear the content.

"David, I am asking the CSI forensics to establish a sweep of Isaac's property at Smiths Village for listening devices. Yeah, I am fully convinced now, 'they', whoever the members of this 'conspiracy' are, they've been listening to Isaac and Wohali for well over eighteen months."

After all the phone calls and breakfast finished, Isaac pressed Kamama and John to go for a walk; he felt they needed to catch up between themselves about the events of the night before. Woya remained at the retreat while Isaac called Ylva from her basket to join the walk.

Isaac led John and Kamama to the rear of the retreat, taking a well-worn route to the higher ground, thinking they might find some of the streams and waterfalls making their way down into the valley. Isaac walked close by Kamama and asked her if the International Festival of the Earth people arrived, would she agree to sit in with him.

John was walking behind them.

"I've heard enough this morning to know that you two are definitely close, secret partners in the same 'crime scenes.'"

Kamama chuckled, bumping shoulders with Isaac, then laughing.

"Oh yeah, John! Is that what you've heard? And who'd you hear that from, eh?"

"I don't need an informer, I've got eyes. I just got to listen to the three of you in different combinations, you're all always plotting and scheming something.

"As far as I can tell, you – Kamama Catawnee – you often seem to be in the Lightfoot house for some reason or another! But, being serious for a moment, Kamama, we're working in a very high-risk situation here; we could have all been dead this morning."

Isaac and Kamama chuckled again like small, naughty children railing against a bossy parent. Kamama replied loudly for them both with a dollop of mirth in her voice:

"Yeah, but we're not John, are we? You, Woya and Ylva, you *all* kept me and Isaac safe in our beds. We didn't even wake up straight away. Ain't that right?'

With the light-hearted atmosphere, Isaac suddenly threw a curved ball for John.

"Well, John, you're doing stuff, but you're doing it in secret without consulting me! This morning you were talking to someone called David about searching my house for 'listening devices!"

"Okay, Isaac, well, we broadly talked about this yesterday. We do need to go ahead on this."

Isaac chuckled and gave his approval.

As they arrived back at the retreat the CSI team leader and another officer were bent over examining animal tracks on the ground at the side of the retreat where the attackers had entered by a window. John introduced Isaac and, turning, the team leader reached back, shaking his hand.

Pointing to paw prints they'd been examining, the team leader stood up and said to Isaac.

"In all your days, Isaac, you ever seen anything like these prints?"

"Yep! They look like cat tracks to me."

"And, if you had to guess which of the bigger cats you think these paw prints belong to?"

"Well, officer, I'd say they are likely to be the prints of a black panther. Like humans, they have five 'fingers' however, only four of them get to register in their tracks. They don't live here in the Smoky Mountains though; haven't done for a long time now."

"As a child, I did have a passing acquaintance with a black panther. But that was seventy-six years ago."

"Well, Isaac, you're right. The black panther is on the edge of extinction now, living in Florida. So, there are huge questions about how this animal and its prints got here.

"By the way, John, we're going to have to alert the local chief of police. He may want to send a notice out to the community and send out some trusted local people out for a search. If I am right, it'll be difficult, but they'll need to find a way of returning it to Florida, if they can retrieve it alive."

7

Once inside the retreat, Woya came over and told Isaac and Kamama she'd spoken to Indira Anand by phone again. They had decided to organise a Zoom call, having listened to John's security concerns.

Woya took Isaac through to the lounge where she had organised their laptop; they were both waiting on the split screen. Isaac thanked them both for reaching out.

"Well, Isaac, it's been a while since we met in person. It's probably been a whole six months or more, but in that time you and Wohali had been meeting with Grogan preparing the way forward for the Memorial event.

"First thing both of us want to say to you, Isaac, Woya and you, Kamama, is how we feel so deeply for your loss. We, of course, are feeling our own sadness through our relationship with Wohali.

"Oh! By the way, I'd like to speak with John Green before we go."

Isaac nodded in agreement.

"As far as Wohali is concerned and the campaign here on the American continent, we need to hold onto his legacy, Isaac. The advances he made building alliances all over the continent must must be preserved.

"I announced to the press immediately on November 2, that we have booked a stadium event for November 8, at the Capital One Arena. The U.S. special presidential envoy on the climate and I will lead that event to make sure that people can still find hope and continuity for the climate change agenda going forward; tickets are available online. We'd love to see you there, Isaac."

"Well, your condolences are welcome. We don't know yet when Wohali's body will be released, so no news on our celebration of his life and funeral arrangements."

Grogan Small added his own thoughts and prayers about Wohali but then, like Indira, also sounded a practical note.

"Hi, Isaac, Woya and Kamama. Listen, when you have the time we'll need to get practical with you about Wohali's contact list of all the people up and down the continent who he recruited. We will want as many of these people to stay involved in the future.

"You, more than anyone right now, Isaac – you know that the work we all have to do for the planet is like a generational relay race. No one single person or group of people can see the planet through to a state of health.

"So, no offence, Isaac, we know you are unwell. We need to be mindful and take your advice about continuity of the future campaigns while you're with us. In short, though, we're trying, perhaps badly, to explain we want to secure Wohali's legacy. We need to replenish our culture carriers all the time; get new blood to take us along the next leg, toward another point in time.

"That contact list of Wohali's will be a vital first place to start looking for First Nations people who can carry the torch you've both lit. I think you and Wohali used to refer to these new recruits as your 'bundle of twigs', a quote I believe from the great Tecumseh himself, referring to strength in numbers."

"Okay, Grogan, that's understood. I'll ask Woya and Kamama to look into this. I'm starting hospital treatment next week. Don't worry, we'll look into this for you. They'll need to speak with Cary about Wohali's records and how he kept them. Would you like to speak with John now?"

Isaac asked Woya to call John on his mobile and ask him over. Isaac thanked John for joining and made the introductions. In John's own mind his intentions were to keep this part of their meeting very short.

"Good afternoon. Good to meet you both. Firstly, I have to say that there are severe limitations on what I can say, no fine detail but a couple of broad thoughts. What I do say, however, is still highly confidential."

John saw both Grogan and Indira nodding on-screen.

"That's fine, John. We understand. We wouldn't dream of doing anything to lose your trust and jeopardise the November 8, Capital One event."

John then pitched into his briefing.

"What I can tell you following on from this morning is that we are pretty damn certain that there is a well-organised conspiracy involved which will, I'm sure, be well-funded. I listened on TV to your interview with Tony Ramires, FOX News the other day, Indira. I heard all your own comments about climate terrorism; so, just to let you know, we broadly agree.

"This 'conspiracy' could have a very deep root. I'm certain now it has flourished in our public service corridors on the ground. Looking at the American continent, we should expect it has entered many corridors of influence and power in other countries. For all we know they could be capable of multiple assassinations. I'm sure they'll have target lists.

"You *must* seriously plan for the eventuality that you are both on such a list. I can only advise you to heighten your awareness, make yourselves and all those around you as safe as possible. I must tell you we have just survived an assassination attempt. We have CSI forensics here now securing evidence in a crime scene."

Indira and Grogan listened gravely to this news.

"Later on, Indira, Phoenix Shultz, who is acting into my national executive lead role, will need a conversation about your plans for the Capital One Arena. She'll want to risk assess and determine whether the event should take place at all."

Indira responded. "On one level, John, it's shocking to hear you talking about this 'conspiracy' as a reality. All I can say right now is we'll listen to your advice but, almost certainly, we'll still have a job to do on November 8; people expect to join us, person to person, in the work we do together."

"Well, you'll know your own practices of corporate risk assessment and risk management. We all have jobs to do. But there are practices we have to imbed to make ourselves and the public as safe as possible.

"As my deputy, Phoenix Schultz, said to our staff as preparation for your Memorial procession, '*There are people out there who just love to hate.*' The message for us and yourselves is, '*Be vigilant.*'"

At that point, John, looking at his watch, saw the time was nearly 2 p.m. He thanked them, saying he looked forward to further contact, and left the lounge.

After a few further best wishes and hopes for the future, Isaac closed the call down.

8

Isaac watched John leave the meeting. It was about 2.45 p.m. He had gone out onto one of the swinging seats, taking in a few quiet moments to think alone.

Eventually Isaac, Woya and Kamama all came to join him.

Isaac and Kamama sat either side of John and Woya leant against the veranda balustrade with her back to her father. Isaac was on good form, he said it felt good to feel them all back together, smiling and laughing, and taking in a few thoughts about the day so far.

While Isaac and the three others rested together for a while, they heard footsteps coming through the lounge. It was CSI lead officer who came out onto the veranda to find John and say goodbye.

"Okay, folks. We're all packed up and making our way back. Gotta thank you, Isaac and Woya for your hospitality, keeping us going with snacks and drinks. John, I've booked the team and all the packed evidence materials onto a flight back tonight; someone from the office will meet us at the other end to take our 'booty' back to our laboratory.

"There's a lot of stuff there. I've got a good feeling about it though; we've checked the digital records of the Memorial CSI team's work. I think there's a good chance there'll be linkage.

John, you don't need to worry, David O'Donnelly is already in touch with us. When we've made our report, we'll connect with him.

"Also, we're completing the sweep for listening devices at the Smiths Village property as we speak. Should be able to feed back by phone end of play today or first thing tomorrow morning."

John stood up and went with the officer to thank the team before they left. Isaac took an opportunity to speak to Kamama and Woya about the evening ahead of them.

"John hasn't asked or spoken to me about this evening. I guess he's been a bit preoccupied."

As John returned from seeing his forensic colleagues off; he sat down with Isaac and Kamama. Isaac looked across at John, trying to pick his moment to ask a question.

"John, we were just talking about whether we should meet up again this evening. It has been a busy day. What's your thinking?"

"First thing that comes to mind is we've covered a lot of ground today. I think we should take some time out in our own ways, have a meal and get to bed soon afterwards.

"Just to let you three know, Wohali's records back at Cary's place will be of interest to us in the investigation as well as Grogan Small. I'd be grateful if one of you could speak to Cary asking her to look for what's there and ask her to prepare them for tomorrow for me to take a copy away."

Isaac asked Woya to call Cary and organise this.

"There'll be time in the morning as well to catch up on any last things you want to feed into my ear after breakfast. I'll be happy to leave here at midday before we go our separate ways. There is one thing I want all three of you to turn over in your thoughts; I have formed my own assessment of your risks.

"My view is that Phoenix Shultz needs to establish twenty-four-seven security for Isaac while he is in hospital, then also establish a safe house in Washington DC for Isaac to eventually join Cary, her son, Danuwoa and Woya. Can you consult Cary about this please? Tell me what she says? Kamama, we also need to talk, okay? The events here speak to me about your own personal high levels of risk."

John then moved into the lounge to make his call to Phoenix. He updated her on the CSI findings. Phoenix knew that they were still waiting for the results on embedded listening devices at Isaac's property in Smiths Village. John mentioned the fact that there was a stadium event booked into the calendar.

"Look, John, I'm aware that Jim Coogan and his representative have arrived. Let's catch up again later on."

Day 4　　　　　　　　　　9

Washington DC

Monday
November 5

Phoenix and Robin Seacourt had discussed and planned their formal interview; Jim Coogan and his attorney arrived at 2 p.m. for a 2.45 p.m. start.

They had agreed a clear agenda. HR were scheduled to sit in, record and provide professional advice should it be necessary.

When Jim and his attorney were brought into a small interview room by the HR partner, Phoenix looked up and at once noticed that Jim had aged. She knew that over his long career Jim had gone through a very difficult time trying to hold together the stress of the work, often failing to anchor a marriage and a family with three kids.

The truth was Phoenix also knew, like so many investigators, when fully exposed to the darkest side and dangers in human behaviour, they often found it hard to hold the boundary between the toxic elements of the work seeping into them, which then created the pressures in their own lives.

Jim had been a good example. Phoenix knew all too well Jim had ended up staring into the bottom of a glass, alone in a bar with a bottle; just before getting the hearing up and running,

Phoenix found herself reflecting on whether, as senior staff, they'd done enough to protect Jim.

Jim arrived suited, booted and shaved. His thick head of salt-and-pepper hair was neatly trimmed. Looking into his clear-blue eyes she saw a man who was in the moment; he was motivated, riding along seated on the 'wagon' of an alcohol-free existence. At the back of her mind, Phoenix knew Jim was doing all he could to salvage his career.

Introducing the meeting, Robin Seacourt explained to Jim that the Wohali Lightfoot investigation was throwing up definite evidence of a 'mole' or a 'leaker' inside the camp of the service. He described the three incidents, in which 'leaking' information by an internal 'mole' had led to three serious incidents in which assassination, violence and murder had all occurred during the short three days including the events at the Memorial.

"So, hearing that, Jim, you'll know I'm talking to you from my role as acting executive lead for George Stanhope; it's not long since he died falling under a Metro train. Right now, as I speak, I can tell you that you're in a very precarious position this afternoon. So, Phoenix and John are still investigating George's death as a murder investigation, in conjunction with the Lightfoot assassination.

"John Green is taking a lot of interest in these proceedings. So, we need to take you through some scenarios and evidence together; we'll be recording your responses.

"We know from your contact with John's PA, Dina, you're holding onto information about a strong lead which could help us. I know Phoenix has explained to you, this information must be passed across to us this afternoon without delay.

"Important to be absolutely clear, Jim, this information you're in possession of, it ain't a 'bargaining chip', we are not dealing in favours."

Jim nodded and looked to his attorney to determine if there

was anything further to say from their side. The attorney shook her head.

"Okay, well let's see it, Robin. Show us what you got!"

Phoenix flashed an email process from Jim's desktop, arranging a meeting for John Green through Suzanne Woodman, the Mall Maintenance team leader. Robin explained, Suzanne Woodman had provided this evidence. In addition, Robin switched the screen display to the high-quality, fake FBI ID which had convinced Suzanne Woodman that the 'John Green' imposter was legitimate in requesting a meeting with Greg Tranter; eventually, as we now know, they had gained access into the Undercroft of the Lincoln Memorial itself this way.

"Look, Jim, I'll say it again. Suzanne Woodman provided this fake ID as evidence."

Robin asked for Jim's response.

"Well, Robin, I've never seen these items before. I can be categoric that I never sent these emails across to this Suzanne Woodman person you've interviewed. I don't even know who she is."

Robin's response was to continue explaining that an FBI internal IT expert had investigated Jim's desk top computer.

"For the record, Jim, you say you've no knowledge of these items, but they were located and saved from your email inbox. The fake ID was found in your photographic records. You'll see on the screen display here your second email includes the attachment of a photograph of the 'John Green' imposter, to be included within the the fake ID documentation.

"Suzanne Woodman says she spoke with you on the phone, Jim. Have you spoken with her to confirm arrangements for a risk assessment of the Memorial and the Undercroft?"

"No. I haven't. I just told you! I don't know this Suzanne Woodman woman. Never met her, and never spoken with her."

Both Phoenix and Robin took Jim through a series of detailed, searching questions about Jims's security procedures for operating his desktop. For example, corporate logging on and off procedures and routine use of username and password security. Jim's responses clearly demonstrated that he wasn't following company policy to maintain his daily security.

Phoenix dispassionately gave a full picture of what they'd found.

"The truth is, Jim, we've interviewed your team members, they say it isn't unusual for you to leave the office, your screen on, having not logged off. To us it seems this is the norm, not the exception in your pattern of behaviour. Everyone in your team confirmed it; it's probably across all our teams, many of them describe how they could actually access your security information. It can be found in your workstation drawer. What have you got to say about this, Jim?"

Jim remained silent.

What was becoming clear in the hearing was there were easy opportunities for anyone in the office to use his desktop; his email account services, like data storage, were wide open; telephone calls in Jim's name from the office were easy to make and fake.

Robin passed across a slip of paper to Jim.

"Are these your security details?"

Jim nodded.

"Can you speak for the record, Jim."

"Yeah, that's my bit of paper and my handwriting."

"We know they are, Jim! We've used them and we've been able to access your account and send emails from your desktop. It's easily done. We've also accessed your confidential reports, photographic documents, your staff supervision records, and case data without any difficulty. We were even able to go into important documentation and evidence you've been assembling; we've proved for ourselves how it can be falsified. Your desktop, Jim, well, it's been like a swinging gate for years. The facts are that you put yourself and the service at risk.

"As I've said, the photograph of the imposter 'John Green,' it is still stored in your photographic records. IT staff are still investigating your desktop, but we think it is certain your desktop has been used to contact organised crime, ordering and providing the fake ID to be processed for the 'imposter's' use. Do you recognise this photographic evidence and our conclusions that you've used your desktop to order fake FBI ID?"

Jim looked chastened.

"I see the evidence you've collected, but I didn't do this illegal work myself. So, what's next, Phoenix?"

"We need you to provide us with evidence giving a detailed log of your movements over the last eight months. Your online calendar is not informative at all, we cannot see how you know what you're doing from one day to the next; there is no method; neither your team PA, nor your staff can access your functioning calendar; they say they can't track you when they need to. This is another breach of company policy; again, it puts you, your team, and the firm at risk.

"Your PA has told us she has informally maintained a personal log of your movements because it's been the only adaptation to policy, she could manage ad hoc to provide some kind of safety for the team.

"So, when we have your handwritten log, we'll get the tech guys to correlate these against your PA's evidence of where you were, at times when your desktop may have been accessed by another operative. You simply better hope the evidence they find is in your favour. If it does not there will be profound consequences."

Robin pronounced a brutal five sentence summary.

"I have to say for the electronic record, as the chairperson of this panel, the evidence here is damning. We're looking at a gross disregard for company policy and professional methods. You've put our service at risk. Our decision will need to reflect the serious, woeful level of professional neglect and disrepair your conduct has fallen into. Little wonder your executive lead's suspicions fell upon you; John Green was fully justified in his basic assumptions that you were the 'mole' inside his service.'"

Jim requested time out.

He and his attorney took time in an empty interview room next door to discuss the details.

They returned after a ten-minute break.

Jim agreed to providing a log of his movements across the time span identified. He and his attorney looked across the table to Phoenix, then to Robin and HR.

"Are we done on the formal issue regarding my own conduct?"

Phoenix nodded.

"So, before we finish and go our separate ways, Phoenix, I need to cover that one other matter. Okay to do that now?"

"Go ahead, Jim."

"On the Sunday after International Festival of the Earth Day, around midday, I went to a restaurant with a friend. By a complete coincidence I saw your new red-headed intern, Drake Collins, in a meeting with a very well-heeled guy I've never seen before. I don't know Drake, I've got no axe to grind with him, I only met him on Saturday.

"I'm no snitch myself. But my gut told me that something about this lunch date was wrong. They were deep in conversation. Drake didn't see me. I took these six photographs and, for the record, I'm sending them to you now, Phoenix."

Jim pressed his send button.

"So, don't get me wrong, this could have been completely innocent, social and above board. Maybe this guy is a rich uncle! But the other side of the coin is, I asked myself, *'What in Hell's name is a lowly intern from West Virginia doing meeting this 'well-heeled' guy and having lunch?'*

"If I were you two, and John Green, in light of all these 'conspiracy' theories and serious incidents, I'd want to know who this smart-looking guy is with Drake? I can tell you, Phoenix, this cool mystery guy had an aura of power and privilege about him. Could have been a politician; just as easy, he could be a mobster."

At the back of Phoenix's thoughts, a red light flashed on and off. She began thinking back to her 11.30 a.m. meeting; in her mind's eye she heard herself chiding Jason Colbeck about Drake and needing to rein him in.

"Well, thanks for the information, Jim. I'll get Charlotte's team onto searching and providing identification for this guy in the photos. I'm also going to send the photos over to John. He can ask the chief of police down in Oklahoma to get a request out to his local network. Drake's home state is West Virginia; maybe this guy is well-known down there. It's worth a try. So, you leave this with me now."

As the interview concluded Phoenix and her HR partner made it clear to Jim, and his attorney, that they would give a verbal response in thirty minutes and the next day he'd be given written confirmation of their decision together with any further action.

Phoenix asked them to wait outside.

In their after-meeting discussion Phoenix made clear that she wanted Jim's suspension lifted. He needed to be brought back into operation alongside a comprehensive retraining programme aimed at Jim getting refreshed on modern security systems, practice, policy and procedure. She looked to her HR partner for comment.

"If you do that, Phoenix, you'll need to walk the walk yourself. Jim's practice will have to be reviewed at every stage within your weekly supervision; we'll need summaries from your supervision notes to record in HR. You'll need to demonstrate change, his attendance at retraining; then you'll need to monitor change and implementation in his conduct; this process will be mandatory on both of you.

"If Jim fails, or lapses, the conversation will turn back to you, Phoenix, and we'll reconvene to decide on dismissal. From an HR perspective we'd be looking for summary dismissal for him with a loss of pension rights. All this needs to be in our final letter of warning; this sets the context for you to dismiss Jim. When you feed back, Phoenix, you need to make it clear this outcome is conditional on him meeting the requirements of his calendar movements matching the team PA's personal record."

Robin and Phoenix agreed to this process and the HR partner left the room.

"One of us, Phoenix, will need to meet and formally interview Drake."

"Yeah, I'll organise that. He's on my service, Robin. Leave that with me. Thanks for your support!"

Robin looked across at Phoenix before leaving the room.

"Look, Phoenix, we are sitting here as equals, we're both acting executive leads. But I have to say I think Jim's supervision has been weak. My advice is you need to seriously reflect and examine your methods of supervision at the very least. This goes no further right? What I said about John Green's instincts, they were right. Jim turned out not only to be a serious risk to our service, but he could also have been a risk to your own career."

Phoenix made her way to John's room; she'd begun to feel a sense of safety and refuge there.

She took a moment to gather her thoughts. Phoenix felt bruised by Robin's comments, but on reflection could see that the weakness of Jim's practices had led to his workstation being exploited; she saw this had happened on her watch.

Then, phoning through to John, she gave him an important update from the Washington DC side of their operations.

"Hi, John. I got some updates for you, some of which you'll need to process for yourself and also with Isaac, Woya and Cary. You free to do that? I'll just reel 'em off."

"Yeah, go ahead."

"Firstly, we met Jim, you may not like it but subject to him corroborating his movements his suspension is lifted. There were significant failings, but not failings that lead to dismissal at this time. Jim will attend a corporate refresher; I've agreed to take full responsibility for Jim entering a training programme. If he fails, he will be dismissed.

"I owe you an apology John. I gave you a hard time on your instincts about Jim. You were right, he was a risk.

"The other thing is he's given us an important new lead involving Drake which Charlotte is following up. Jim photographed Drake in a city restaurant on Sunday. Could have been innocent but looked suspicious. Jim talks like you, he's another guy who has got a hunch in his gut!

"I'm organising an audio recorded interview with Drake for us to consider. I'm also posting six photographs of Drake, Jim provided for you to share. It shows Drake on a lunch date with a well-heeled guy. In this atmosphere, we're looking at everyone and everything, right?

"Secondly, CSI report the sweep for listening devices. Well, it's just more evidence of conspiracy, John. Isaac's property has been bugged for at least a couple of years. To be thorough and, with Cary's consent, they swept her property. Nothing found there.

"So, as we've been thinking, all the Lightfoots will need to be moved into the safe house up here in DC while the investigation gets closer to confirming the men in the Soul family are guilty of murder and are part of a wider conspiracy. We just don't have that yet and we don't know where they are."

John agreed.

"That all checks out. Isaac says the house was rewired a couple of years back. So, they've listened into pretty much all of Isaac and Wohali's preparation for November 2.

"Got Jim's pictures by the way. Thanks for your apology by the way. My advice is that you need to acknowledge that staff do go off the rails, if Jim fails you've got to get shot. I will be talking with Chief Banks about them, getting the pictures out across his network. Someone has to know who this guy is."

Phoenix continued with her catch-up.

"I'm speaking with Jason later on the safe house and security for Isaac at the hospital."

David and the CSI are confirming already that evidence collected at the retreat matches evidence collected at the Memorial. So, the connection is clear. We know now that Seth Soul and his sons are currently our prime suspects; this will become more concrete after Charlotte completes an ID meeting with Tranter on Cary Lightfoot's photograph. Again, John, we need Chief Banks and his team to help find them and bring them in for questioning et cetera.

"I have Jason and Drake completing the search for the four-by-four used at the retreat. It has been confirmed as a Ford Raptor F-150 from the CSI castes of the tyre prints taken at the retreat."

"Thanks, Phoenix. Look, we are leaving here tomorrow midday; you and I had talked about switching over so I can get back to Kay and the kids; increasingly though, I'm feeling like I have to see things through here. I have a sense that we've both become immersed in complex work that needs continuity at both ends, switching compromises that continuity. Of course, I want to get back home, but I'm not professionally happy with it. Are you okay with that?"

"Yeah, I am fine with that; I agree. Thinking about it right now, that gives me the chance to get experience on completing some things I have begun to deliver on. I'll let staff know."

"Okay, that's sorted then. I'll let Kay and the kids know."

Now that John knew for sure he was staying the distance in Oklahoma, the first thing he did was call Chief of Police, Walter Banks to find out if there were any results from his search on Seth Soul and his boys. John described all the events at the retreat and confirmed that Seth Soul and his sons were definitely prime suspects.

"Sorry to hear about your trouble John. The short answer to your question is 'no'. I'm sorry John, we drew a blank. There was no one at the Soul homestead property at all. One of the officers who has had occasion to visit there a long time back said it had since become a ramshackle place, vacant looking; maybe they all moved on?

"So, we'll keep looking for you, John. Anything else I can do for you?"

"Guess not. By the way, we're finishing up here tomorrow and I'll be staying on at the Oklahoma end of our investigation. Our Acting Executive Lead, Phoenix Schultz, will continue to lead in DC. Maybe, if the Soul family are still not visible, we can both work together on a search the next day, 'many hands make light work'? Be good if we could have a warrant to enter and search the homestead while we're at it."

"Yeah, let me know when you're back."

Day 4   **10**

Smoky Mountains

Tuesday
November 5

After, Phoenix's news on the installation of listening devices, John headed back to the kitchen to find Isaac, Woya and Kamama; as John got nearer to the kitchen, he could hear their laughter; he knew his news was about to change all that.

Standing with his back to them, John made himself some coffee and waited for them to finish, then invited them over.

John fed back to them most of the update Phoenix had given him which would concern them.

"On top of all this, we're also doing a wider and more detailed search of the Metro CCTV footage, trying to catch a glimpse of George Stanhope's killer."

John looked across at Kamama; just looking at her, he knew she was learning how to read him; she could see there was more to come.

"The CSI team conducting the search for listening devices have found a system which has been installed for at least a couple of years, at your place, Isaac. About the time period, Isaac, when you and Wohali had been working together as advisors for the 'Festival'; you said you had rewiring at the house; probably would have been installed then."

John could see both Isaac and Woya were visibly shaken and gave them space to respond.

As he watched their reactions unfold, John could feel for the first time they hadn't completely emotionally engaged in their loss of Wohali; this news on bugging Isaac's property at Smith Village harked back to the time when they were happily living together again as a family unit; a time when Isaac's abuse of Wohali had been healed.

Woya was the first to respond.

"Wow! That makes this all so much more real; they've been listening in to our house all this time. John, I can't tell you how hard this is to take."

Woya stood up and walked out onto the veranda and stared out across the valley. John watched Kamama as she stood up and moved her chair back; he could see Kamama was pretty much tuned in to working as a 'partner' and left the room, following Woya onto the veranda.

In the background he could hear Woya opening up to Kamama about feeling defiled.

Isaac, however, seemed to remain calm. John was always amazed how remarkably focussed Isaac was in his analysis of the '*Predator*'; he always seemed to be struggling to stand up from one heavy punch, only to stand up in the ring to face another.

"I think you know where I am, John; Wohali's death, the intruders last night and now this. I think I've known almost all my life, the '*Predator's*' breath has been hard on my trail; don't know if I ever told you, I became a runner from the Dakota boarding school after watching the gardener dig a grave for a friend; then the gardener stopped and lit a cigarette and hummed a tune; after he finished he just tipped the wheelbarrow and my friends body rolled like a lump of meat, landing with a thump. I've never forgotten the gardener just picked up his shovel, refilled the hole he'd dug and levelled the ground. Finally, he just scattered grass seed to grow over where my friend lay.

"You'll understand, John, I could never go back there; I had escaped knowing where the *'Predator'* actually lived. Sometimes I'm thinking to myself, *'Isaac, you've been fighting all your life.'* But just maybe, the truth is, I never actually stopped running? Adsila and I, we tried to fix it when the new Cherokee registration system came in 1975/76. But still, the 'Predator' never leaves me alone for long."

"I understand that, Isaac. Given what you've been through, well, your feelings are gonna be complicated. Good to have the context for my intern, Esteban, who sussed out your dates of birth were suspect."

"But John, what you're telling me is the *'Predator'* actually wants me dead, right? Not just me though, my family as well. Am I right, John?"

John nodded thoughtfully.

"Yeah Isaac, talking man to man, without the women in the room, I think what you're saying is a real possibility. But we also know it could also be so much more than just your family, Isaac. The hit list could be extensive. We're warning all the higher-ups; I'm ready for anything.

"You heard the conversation with Indira Anand; the 'Festival' leadership and the Special Envoy on Climate, they also could so easily be high-level targets. I've said this more than once, Isaac, their motivation will be political, but there'll also be financial gains from destroying the government policy to address climate change; could be gold, could be gas or oil; could be soya exports or just stealing another section of land indigenous people are living on, but don't own."

This was an ideal moment for John to raise safety and risk matters with Isaac.

"Isaac, you are the head of this family, right? This is as good a time as any to tell you. Phoenix and I, we've agreed there is a need for us to arrange twenty-four-seven security for you in hospital; then also for Woya, Cary and Danuwoa in Washington

DC. I'm just confirming something we've talked about; now it's going to happen."

Isaac nodded.

"But in the end, it don't matter what I think. You, Isaac, are the person who will discuss and lead the decisions for your family. You'll be the guy who persuades Woya, Cary and Danuwoa to move into a safe house in Washington DC."

"Will you be heading back to DC, John?"

"Nope, I'm staying on in Oklahoma City. I need you to consult your doctors; then, I want you to consult your family to help me bring this security plan together, Isaac."

Isaac soulfully looked down into his lap.

"I know we've crossed swords, John. Still, you must know I'm truly very grateful for all that you're doing. This news has hit Woya and I very hard…"

John placed a hand onto Isaac's shoulder.

"Never mind us arguing, Isaac, that's all a part of the work; there ain't nothin' personal in it."

At that point Woya and Kamama came back in.

"Now you two are back, Isaac will speak to you about security arrangements. On a personal note, I've just let Isaac know I am staying on for a while in Oklahoma to bring all this to a conclusion."

Woya went straight to her father, and they held one another close. Quickly, she began to share her thoughts. Woya said she felt personally contaminated by the listening devices. She was clear, she never wanted to return to the house at Smiths Village to live.

John was clear with everyone that tomorrow morning they needed to be travelling back by midday.

"We've seen off one assault on this place, collected a lot of helpful evidence, but this is no longer a safe space for any of us."

Isaac asked if there could be time straight after breakfast tomorrow for a final conversation.

"Definitely, Isaac, it won't take us a moment to pack, lock up, then scoot. Our flight tickets are booked. Woya, Isaac's going to talk to you about security. I hear what you're saying about Smiths Village and what Isaac's gonna talk to you about will, I am sure be helpful."

As they broke up, John took some time out to contact Anna McKenna and then Kay.

John briefed Anna about the attack on the retreat and the assault on himself. Then he began linking clear evidence from Wohali's assassination scene, the assault on the retreat, the listening devices in Isaac's house.

"None of this, Anna will go away until the 'conspiracy' has been completely unmasked, charged and decapitated. We'll need Robin Seacourt and his specialist teams on Homeland terrorist threats to join us in this work as soon as possible. I can tell you now Anna, George would agree with me on bringing his specialist terrorist service into play."

John explained that Jason Colbeck was organising security for the Lightfoot family who were going to be moved to a Washington DC 'safe house.'

Anna quickly interrupted John's update.

"While this is not what we've asked from you, John, I am going to support Phoenix at this end. I'll talk directly with Jason Colbeck. I know he's experienced, but I will operationally support his task. I want to take pressure off Phoenix; I'll help pull any strings, remove bureaucracy, find the budget and provide immediate safety for all the members of the Lightfoot family."

"Anna, you're at liberty to talk to any of your staff. Phoenix and I don't need your help though. As you know well, we like to keep everything in-house under our own control."

"All I'm saying, John, is I can see you're both stretched. I'll speak to Phoenix and iron something out. She's in charge up here at the moment; it's not your call to control this, you're a long way from home. For once, I'm trying to be helpful!"

On that note, John let Anna know he was staying on in Oklahoma.

"Arrangements between Phoenix and I need to remain the same. She'll need to carry on in her acting executive role."

"At the same time, John, I take it from what you're saying that there are increasingly fewer opportunities to wrap this up and move on. It's the reverse of what the attorney general and I have asked for, isn't it?

"Gradually, this investigation is widening. You're not shutting it down! I'm right, aren't I? I am going to have to alert the attorney general; he won't be happy, John! If he starts talking about a suspension for you and new leadership, I may not be able to do anything other than act on his instructions."

John had grown used to Anna McKenna's threats and lukewarm responses.

"All I'd say to you, Anna, is, *'listen to yourself'*. You said it's widening, you're right! It's widening not because Phoenix and I are incompetent or purposely widening it. The criminal intent is wider and deeper than we first assessed.

"You want to suspend me; you can try it; see where it gets you, Anna! My conscience is clear, I'm doing a good job; I'll face you and the AG down in any goddam kangaroo court you put up!"

The phone went down at Anna's end. This left John free to speak briefly with Kay to say his return to home and DC would be delayed.

Day 4   11

Thurmond
West Virginia

Tuesday
November 5

Both Seth and Frank were growing more and more concerned that they hadn't heard anything from Charles and John.

As the silence persisted Frank persuaded Seth to phone. Eventually, Charles picked up.

"Hello, boy. Frank and I are getting a bit twitched. We need to know how your trip to the Smokies went. What's going on? I've got Frank with me and you're on 'loudspeaker.'"

There was a brief silence on the phone while Seth looked to Frank and shrugged.

"Truth is, Dad, we got rumbled and we're on our way back. We broke a window on the side as planned; we got into the garage; then the dog woke upstairs. There was a hell of a commotion, the door opened up at the top of the metal staircase releasing the dog down.

"To cut a long story short, we had to get out of there fast. With us racing away, well, the garage door opened; the FBI guy gave chase together with the dog; brother John has taken a flesh wound to his right calf.

"I gave the FBI guy a good kicking and was just gonna put a bullet in his head when the dog attacked me; locked onto my arm. I got a nasty wound from dragging myself free, then we had to get out. So, in summary, Dad, we live to fight another…"

At that point the Soul boy's phone went dead.

Frank looked to Seth.

"Okay, Seth, what's your plan now?"

"Well, Frank, you'll remember I asked you to buy in some strong bur oak posts and equipment. On and off, since arriving here, I've been working on my original idea. I've always had a hankering, as a carpenter, to build this thing. Basically, it's all ready now to transport by the Raptor and a trailer. We'll bolt it together in situ."

"Okay, so what is this thing you've been making?"

"It's what I call a 'Columbus gantry'; it's a device described in our ancestor's history after arriving in the Americas. One particular Catholic priest, guy called Las Casas, he sailed with Columbus in 1498; he took on the job of recording what he saw.

"His record shows us that one of the many early celebrations Columbus and his cavaliers designed for the Taino Indians was this gantry. They were designed to both hang and burn thirteen savages alive at any one time; as a carpenter and a Christian believer, I have always had an ambition to build one of these devices. So, now I have the chance to build it and use it."

"Why thirteen, Seth?"

"It's said the number thirteen was in honour of the Lord Jesus Christ, Himself. So, thirteen represents the twelve apostles plus Jesus Christ, Himself, makes thirteen.[28]

"I'm building a similar model of this gantry, but just for one person on this occasion. Columbus's cavaliers dug trenches and lit fires underneath these savages. If you want to, I can show you. I can dig out the detailed engravings online so you can see them."

Frank moved uneasily in his seat while Seth put the screen image in front of him.

"All we need now, Frank, is for the right moment to present itself and, believe me it will. We know that from listening in to his house, Isaac needs to get into hospital asap before he dies; he's hell-bent on extending his life by five years.

"I have a hunch that this moment will come soon…""

Day 4   12

Smoky Mountains

Tuesday
November 5

Right at the end of the day John found Kamama sitting in the deepening twilight on the veranda; he sat down beside her and looked over the veranda as dusk descended on the valley.

There was a comfortable silence between them.

Looking out, he had to acknowledge to himself it had been a difficult day. But right there, in that moment, he'd begun to feel there was something different about ending a difficult day in the Smoky Mountains.

Here, the backdrop was one of perspectives; the planet was so plainly spinning and hurtling through space-time; John had seen for himself that, right after sunset, it was possible on a clear night, to see the Milky Way. Now, this city boy understood that the Earth he lived on sped and spun on its way through space, while everything else seemed to remain the same. For the first time ever, he felt there was some relaxation in knowing he was but a mere speck of space dust.

Sitting next to Kamama now, the only sore feelings he had were the physical ones, from the beating he'd taken the night before.

"Where're Isaac and Woya?"

"Oh! They're back in the lounge. I think they are trying to get their heads around what's happening to them from tomorrow after we leave here. Sounds like Isaac will be admitted to hospital as soon as we arrive back. Then Woya, Cary and Danuwoa will be travelling back to meet one of your FBI investigators. Everything is changing, John. Changing for them, and for you and me.

"We are all separating at a time when us human beings, need to hang together. They're frightened, John. I am frightened for them."

John looked directly at Kamama.

"I keep saying, Kamama, we need to assess your risks, but we ain't making much progress."

"Have you had any feedback about the black panther from the CSI or the local chief of police?"

"No. It's been one hell of a day though, what I need is a couple of beers and to chill. Why are you askin' anyway?"

Kamama looked away, swinging her legs.

"Twice today I have felt haunted, John; I've had to literally pinch myself, but I *did* see her. I saw the black panther, this evening. She was over there on the open land at the side of the retreat, just sitting on her haunches, completely relaxed. As I looked back, she calmly watched me with those piercing amber-green eyes of hers.

"I closed and opened my eyes more than once. But each time I opened my eyes again, she *actually* was there. When she eventually moved away, she flowed like a fluid; melting through the grasses and the shadows as only big cats do. Then, she morphed into the tree line over there and was gone.

"John, I've never seen any creature so beautiful. She literally took my breath away; she was living inside me, and I in her."

John felt Kamama touch his arm just as she had the night before.

"I know I am supposed to be an academic and a scientist,

John. I should be driven by data, history, physics, and biological reality; but I'm a Cherokee Indian woman as well. I know I've just communed with a powerful force from the spirit world.

"Isaac said to us a black panther protected him from a childhood beating; she licked his wounds. Long ago, I read Tecumseh was born into the Panther Clan."[29]

"Yeah, I've heard Isaac say that."

"So, Kamama, this is all a bit out of my league. I'm neither religious nor spiritual. None of our Hebrew prophets were playful, that's for sure."

"The black panther in modern times has been a great symbol of power, liberation, love and of the protection for people of colour."

John held up his hand, like raising a red flag.

"Woah! Kamama, your thoughts on this are way out of my understanding. Shit, we've been through one hell of a day, this sounds like you're in the foothills of another steamroller preach!"

"John don't make this all about you! I know you're carrying a heavy load, organisational pressures and all." Kamama laughed aloud. "It doesn't matter what you say, the black panther is on our side, John. You hear me? She's on our side!"

As John went to move away, Kamama reached out and grabbed his forearm. Then pulling him closer and reaching up, she kissed him; her other hand tracing the back of his neck. Feeling himself melt in that moment, they shared that kiss together and briefly held on with tenderness, and with care.

Coming out of their embrace and looking at one another, eye to eye, John pulled back.

"Kamama, this is crazy. I'm just an investigator; an FBI man ordered down from Washington DC by the attorney general to deliver results for Woya, Cary and Isaac. I have a wife and kids at home. No offence to you, but this makes no sense at all."

Getting up and without looking back, John went through

the lounge and climbed the stairs to his room, leaving Kamama on her own. Reaching his room, he closed his door behind him and rested against it.

As John eased into a reclining chair by his window he could hear music. To his untrained ear it sounded like a primitive war chant. Then, listening more carefully, John recognised it as the 'Honor Song'; the song which had been sung on the procession just before Wohali's assassination.

Having listened to the music from Kamama's room, he rested in the silence, while the darkness descended; eventually he went to shower. When he'd finished, he heard his room door open and close.

Returning to his bedroom, Kamama was standing by the window with her back to the room.

Then turning round, Kamama spoke.

"John, you gotta work out what you're doing here. I'm concerned for you. You're in danger like the rest of us. Look at your bruised face, the pain you're in with your ribs. Last night you were just lucky to survive; only Ylva saved you."

"Are you sure you're not just an imposter investigator? Giving us a sham investigation on behalf of the establishment; maybe you are here just to 'shut us down'. For all I know, you're even a part of this 'conspiracy' you talk about all the time."

"Believe me, John. My people have seen it all. The U.S. government, the FBI, the CIA, we've done all this shit before. Hell, the CIA have even imposed the political leaders the U.S. Government approve of on whole countries. Do you really fully appreciate what happened to Wohali? Was George really murdered? Why *have* you survived the attack last night on the retreat?"

"That's all for you to decide Kamama. I know who I am and what I'm doing. There's no way I am going to waste my time convincing you I'm genuine."

Though Kamama had spoken with a powerful challenge,

at the same time she did not speak in anger; she had spoken through a heartfelt conviction.

"Deep down I've felt your own wounds, John; I've listened to you speak of your ancestors and felt their pain; as your wife said, this mission is full of risks and high pressure for you."

Within the shadows of the room, Kamama looked up into his eyes.

"But I can help you, John, you know I can. Help you to listen to your own pain. Make your pain a friend; make it live at peace within you; no one need ever know."

As Kamama stepped forward they held one another again; John looked down through the windowpane and saw the deep purple black of the impenetrable night enveloping the valley. The sky was dusted with stars; it was a sky that was only just faintly lit by a sliver of a crescent moon, resting on its back.

Holding that hug, John felt himself sinking and drowning into Kamama's warmth, the scent of her hair and the warmth of her skin; he felt the power of their emotions and the demands of that moment. Suddenly, he felt Kamama gently pull away from their embrace.

"John, you get into your bed. I'll be back in a minute."

John leant back on his pillows, as he waited for Kamama to return. Then, silently, the shadow and shape of Kamama made its way across the shadows of the room and slipped into bed beside him.

Kamama smiled and, with the gentle palm of her hand, she lightly traced John's bruised eye, down to the healing surface wounds on the side of his face and round his bruised ribcage. Holding one another more closely, their kisses became more urgent within the physical warmth of their embrace.

Day 5   1

Smoky Mountains

Wednesday
November 6

It takes one to know one.

> 'European observers of the 1930s all recognised that black-white conflict was only one aspect of the history of American racism. Indeed, Nazis almost never mentioned the American treatment of blacks without also mentioning the American treatment of other groups, in particular Asians and Native Americans.'
> 'Hitler's American Model: The United States and the Making of Nazi Race Law' by James Q Whitman. With new preface by the author. Princeton University Press, Princeton and Oxford 2018[30]

Not for the first time since leaving Washington DC, John woke with a feeling of apprehension; to date, neither Phoenix or Chief Walter Banks had not located where Seth Soul, or his sons, were. As John continued to surface to a clearer state of consciousness, it soon became evident to him that Kamama had returned to her own bed overnight; for a moment John found it hard to believe they had slept together.

However, in the double-take of waking, John began to live with the fact that he and Kamama had allowed the boundaries of their feelings to become blurred. At the same time, John now felt anxious; Kay had already reminded him twice about an early affair in their marriage; truth was, what should have been laid to rest years ago, had come to pass again. He had failed his marriage again for a second time!

Getting up and dressed, he went into his en suite and looked into the mirror; he checked out the progress of his bruised and bloodshot right eye and face, then he checked out his bruised ribs and stomach areas. Opening the bathroom cabinet, he fumbled for the packet of painkillers Kamama had given him. Then, pressing them out of their packaging, he swallowed a couple.

Returning to his room, he looked out of his window. The sunrise was lighting up the canopy of the trees across the valley.

On the skyline and on the land, it was now possible to see through the beginnings of the dawn; two, maybe three of the simplest lines of landscape were just visible, naively drawn amid the growing mystery that was infusing the darkness. These childlike lines depicted three mountain ridges in the distance. John felt pangs of sadness knowing, in such a short time, he'd come to love this place. He realised he had no idea when he would ever see the Smoky Mountains again.

As John watched, he looked up again from the valley to those simple, ridge lines. The living image before him continued to morph, spreading its ancient, most primal colours. The sun's peeping rays of yellow, orange and red were now running together, like watercolours soaking into a page of soft, grainy, porous paper.

As the sky changed again, sunlight began to flood the upland mountain slopes. The sunrise, momentarily holding itself between the opening curtains of its terrain, simply continued to perform its magic light show.

John slipped quietly down the wooden staircase. He was halfway down when Ylva's head popped up from her basket of warm, chequered tartan blankets. As he went over to pick up her collar and lead hanging from a hook in the kitchen, Ylva immediately scrambled out to greet him; standing still, she waited for her collar to be attached. Then, while everyone else slept, Ylva and John walked out together down the wild-flower meadow. After John let Ylva off her lead, she led the way, down into the forested valley below.

As a self-confessed veteran city dweller, John hardly knew how to respond to, let alone know, the names of trees or flowers. However, on their walks together, Woya and Kamama had been naming and introducing him to some. The one tree John loved best was named the 'heart-leaved paper birch'. Actually, he loved its name as much as the tree itself.

Entering the edge of the forested valley, John looked up into the canopy of autumn leaves; while many had fallen, those that remained were still displaying the many shades of autumnal colours; they were like nature's leaded stained-glass windows in a place or worship. As the light began to pool and shimmer on the 'cathedral' forest floor, John realised while walking in and out of the light and shade that a part of him had begun to move and breathe differently; he realised he could see and feel nature in a way he hadn't experienced before.

As they walked, Ylva still led the way, and John realised she knew exactly where she was taking him. Soon, they arrived at a waterfall with a pool which then streamed through the forest, out along the valley floor.

The water in its pool below, rippled, driven by the splashing surge of the stream's current; the images of the trees above the falls, the rocks and the clouds in the sky above, were all reflected on its surface; underneath the surface, long strands of water-plants' leaves swayed horizontally with the current.

Ylva stood beside the pool and looked back at John, tensed

and alert; with a growing expectation she stepped into the shallow water of the pool and barked while John found her a chunky branch of birch. Sitting down on a comfortable low-lying rock, he tossed the branch almost to the other side. Ylva plunged in, swimming to the other side again and again. Each time she arrived back on land, John delayed just a few seconds, Ylva would soon speak up, barking loudly.

Eventually, John decided the next throw must be a final throw before they returned for breakfast, "Last one, Ylva!" This time Ylva just carried on swimming to the other side, clambering out onto a crop of low-lying rocks. Suddenly, she just dropped the stick like it could have been a hot flaming branch. John watched her as he saw she was looking up the waterfall to the rocks above. Ylva became more animated, barking, stooping, and bouncing, up and down the bank and in between the rocks.

Following Ylva's line of sight, John looked up to the top of the fall; there sitting on the topmost rocks, was the black panther Kamama had described. She calmly blinked back at John. Kamama had been clear, this was the black panther Isaac had described more than once from his childhood. Now, John saw her for himself; she carried her body with a calm, regal power, nosing the air with an unperturbed air of arrogance, looking down toward Ylva, barking up toward her from the ground. The panther remained cool, almost dismissive. In those short seconds, she unblinkingly gazed into John's own eyes, her glowing black coat shimmering against the autumn colours of the falls.

Briefly distracted, John heard Ylva barking on the other side of the waterfall pool. Feeling a concern that he needed to have sight of Ylva, he looked away. Having located Ylva, John looked back up to the top of the falls but saw only an empty rock space of doubt where the black panther had once been.

Overwhelmed in his emotions, John became tearful.

With his head held down, tears quietly rolled uncontrollably down his cheeks. In the immediacy of the moment, he felt an inexplicable sadness, maybe a feeling of personal loss sparked by the black panther's sudden disappearance; truth was, for whatever reason, he felt exposed, not knowing at all what was suddenly happening deep down in his soul.

John thought to himself that maybe the black panther's piercing gaze had stripped him back again to those unresolved emotions from his past. He reviewed the recent untoward events of the last few days. He considered he might still be feeling raw about being hustled out of DC following the assassination of Wohali Lightfoot; ruling that out, he considered there had been the death of his friend and close colleague, George Stanhope; then, John also acknowledged that he had been assaulted and rescued from a gunshot to the head, a near miss; in the mix he also thought through having been emotionally stirred up through Isaac's life story and its resonance with his own ancestry.

Finally, John reflected on his emotional encounter with Kamama. During the rain and thunderstorm, she had helped him vocalise his pain and turmoil. Then, as a woman she had come to him, given love and care to him during the night. John hadn't forgotten Kamama's prescription for his own cultural pain; he should 'know it', 'listen to it' and make a 'friend of it' not try to bury it through denial.

After his tears, John became centred within his own feelings and was momentarily at peace. Remembering the night of his childhood tears being shed when his parents prepared him, as a child born into the Jewish diaspora in the USA; they recounted the story of the Jewish people, the centuries of discrimination, destruction and genocide.

John remembered his father's voice, *'You must be prepared, John, for these dark days to return. Even though we have Israel, and we live here in the USA, it can all happen again at any time, anywhere. Like your great-grandparents, you may be called to decide something far-reaching in your own life one day; you will not know it until you see it.'*

John reflected that Israel had been at war again. Hamas terrorists had breached Israel's security, tortured, raped and slaughtered Jewish people and their children; in the brutality of the days that followed much darkness and grief had entered the lives of thousands of innocent Israeli and Palestinian men, women and children, alike.

Sitting by the waterfall, John continued assembling the personal jigsaw Kamama had spoken of. There was no doubt in John's mind that Isaac's story had reopened his parents' stories; the talk of an invading 'Predator' resonating with his great-grandparents' loss of land and property; then of mass slavery, war and death through industrial genocide.

Finally, there were the stories of two innocent children separated from their families; one separated to save the Jewish culture from the Nazis, to rebuild a nation; the other child forced to separate from his parents by a US government policy, aimed to destroy Native Indian culture and their nations, only for them to steal yet more land.

Listening to the sounds of the waterfall, John felt the spirit of his father again. He knew now his father had passed him an ancient cultural 'baton'; the certain knowledge of a well-known human '*Predator*' whose behaviour was driven by the human evil of racial supremacy. This baton of his own 'truth' and experience had been handed down from time immemorial; great-great grandparents, to great-grandparents, to grandparents, to his parents and then to himself.

Suddenly, an unexpected question popped into his mind. How could he do what Kay asked of him and just bury the true warnings of his ancestors' experience? Wasn't the handing on of this 'baton' essential? Wouldn't any good, loving parent want to convey their 'truth' about such a '*Predator*' ? Wasn't this act of love, the necessary, fundamental response he needed in order to live well or even just to survive?

Surfacing from his thoughts, John gazed clear-eyed into the

waterfall, grounded in a moment of consolidation. He heard Kamama's voice again, advising him not to shut down his own history and feelings, but to befriend them, make them a part of himself.

Suddenly, a dripping Ylva dropped her sodden stick at John's feet. He reached forward and stroked Ylva's wet head.

"You and I, Ylva, we're troopers. C'mon, let's go and get breakfast!"

Returning to the retreat, John's spirits seemed unusually lighter and at peace. It was as if he had left a weight behind him at the edge of the woodland. For once he felt immersed in a sense of pleasure and harmony, in the moment.

2

After John and Ylva finished their morning breakfast together, Isaac approached him in the kitchen.

"Hi, John, we agreed we'd get together one last time this morning. Woya and I are packed and ready to leave."

"This morning, Isaac, this is your time to tell us what's on your mind. Fair's fair? I'll need about ten minutes to ask a couple of questions."

As John sat together with Isaac agreeing his ground rules, Kamama joined them.

"This time, this morning, Isaac, is yours. All I want is a couple of minutes. I just want to focus on what the 'conspiracy' will have known about now we know they were 'listening'.

"Nothing I haven't already told you, John. Isaac and Wohali needed academic references, they needed articles and the work of new indigenous authors across the American continent."

Kamama gave John more insight into the advice and information she gave.

"I advised on educational video, documentary film, basically a bucket of things to watch. Isaac will confirm Wohali was growing, reading more and more; he was fast becoming a knowledgable leader and an activist.

"As we've said, Wohali was talking about searching out and

collecting together the two hundred First Nation continental representatives for the November 2 'Festival' event. He talked about things he saw and heard; First Nation people in the rainforest showed him how the colonial enemies were only interested in nature as a commodity; their whole activity was about finding and sucking out more and more products, scarring the forest, releasing carbon from the planet to burn.

"Wohali talked first hand about illegal logging, forest burning and mining and the search for minerals and gold. He had learnt much about processes, the poisoning of rivers and the food chain; how some First Nation people's prenatal babies were affected. Wohali saw it, heard it and was changed by it.[31,32]

"Wohali was being transformed from a hopeless addict into part of a new generation of First Nation activists; he was opening up, seeing the world around him for what it was. At the same time, he'd begun talking about wanting to live on the 'front line', living in the rainforest to help fulfil a practical mission for its protection; he talked of living inside nature himself; he'd told us he'd begun talking to Cary and Danuwoa, wanting them to go with him."

John thanked Kamama for embellishing Wohali's story.

"So, those 'listening' in were hearing all this?"

"Yeah. I guess they were, John. But we didn't know they were listening. What were we supposed to do? Sit quietly and take no action? I still don't think you get it. We saw everything so clearly in those days; we even watched video and film about how the deepest seabeds are being destroyed by machinery, drilling and vacuuming up minerals.

"Isaac will tell you. We understood that these human *'Predators'* would never make the evolutionary leap without a massive investment in aggressive international laws, policing and protecting of other ancestral lands. They're still dominating, still destroying, John; still making a Hell on Earth for all peoples; taking powers over all the other species and their habitats."

"Look, Kamama, I'll say it again, I'm investigating an assassination here. I make no comment, no judgement about what you're doing or saying. I'm simply drawing the conclusion that those listening in could easily have been motivated to become Wohali's assassins, possibly linked up with climate terrorists."

"Like so many people from the establishment John, it seems you just don't get it! This isn't a game in which 'indigenous' people on the front line can be expendable. The modern day, colonial '*Predators*', they are a purposeful and destructive vanguard, funded by those who possess real power, consuming everything they can in their wake."[33]

"Look, Kamama, I've been doing all I can, all the time, to be clear with you; I know the emotional boundaries between us have gotten confused. But I remain a simple FBI investigator, collecting evidence from yourself and the Lightfoot family. I have listened to the whole story of the human animal thing, the dominating colonial '*Predator*', destroying the planet.

John looked across the lounge toward Kamama.

"Isaac said he understood this yesterday; now it seems I need you to get that same message too! My role is to investigate and deliver justice to Isaac, Woya, Cary and Danuwoa."

3

John handed the final thirty minutes over to Isaac; he went out of his way to look at his watch.

Isaac chuckled.

"I know, John, don't worry, I'll be quick.

"So, what I want to say, John, is Kamama has told me about the impact my own story has had on you; it has brought back the painful story of your own ancestors from the Holocaust. I hear you wept on the veranda during the storm on the night we argued.

"I know all you want to be is the 'investigator', John. Of course, you'll want to be 'Mr Objective'. But that's a 'professional' straitjacket; a uniform; it's not what makes up all of who you are.

"Last night, I got to thinking; I just want a few minutes to try and make the connection between our personal stories. I thought I'd like to leave here today thinking both of us could become soulmates along our different journeys into the future.

"So, what I want to say is person to person, it ain't evidence of any kind; it's just you and me, being human.

"My own 'research' over the years has all been about me trying to find a way to repair myself; make myself whole again. But I know, John, it ain't gonna happen.

"So, as a much younger person I knew I was desperate to

understand human supremacy; you know, the mind of the human '*Predator*'; where did the 'infection' begin?

"Turns out, John, a small tribe of us Homo Sapiens crossed the Red Sea, leaving East Africa seventy thousand years ago. My own ancestors walked from Siberia to Alaska across the Bering Straits.[34]

"Then, in blink of an eye, just five thousand years, we became the only species of the whole human family left on the whole planet; we had lived with other human species along the way; we hunted with them; ate with them, made relationships with them, had children with them. Then we outcompeted them and drove them off the face of the Earth. In short, we had become the most formidable apex '*Predator*' on the planet; we had even learnt to train and tame wolves to hunt with us.[35]

"The shadow of that history can be found in our DNA; both the Neanderthals and Denisovans are still snuggled inside us. Only a few of us humans who are African descendants of ancestors who never left Africa, don't possess the genetic inheritance of other human species."[36]

Isaac paused and looked over at John and smiled.

"Okay, let us fast forward in time.

"The first European version of this apex, human '*Predator*' accidentally washed up on our shores in 1492; they didn't even know our people or our continent, existed; of course, this was Columbus and his cavaliers. Over the next five centuries wave upon wave of these same '*Predators*' successfully invaded, passed over their viruses, enslaved my ancestors, imported slaves from Africa, tortured, maimed, made warfare and enacted genocides on all our nations across *our* continent.

"Science today tells us, during the first century of the European invasion our continental population of one hundred million First Nation souls was reduced to just six million; whole nations were forced off the face of the Earth.[37]

"Sound familiar?

"Everywhere the European *Predator* went it carried with it the stench of death; indeed, death and the deadly infectious diseases travelled in their vanguard ahead of their journey. But they carried in their heads another kind of infection, established by a different of virus. Its code had been buried within their dark souls. This 'code' had been written down by Catholic Popes of the fifteenth and sixteenth centuries. I know you know, John, that the 'code' was the *'Doctrine of Discovery.'*"

John sitting quietly, suddenly leant forward.

"But Isaac, how did this code, this 'virus' and this 'infection' establish itself?"

"Well, we know now, the Popes of the Holy Roman Empire from 1450 were like blowflies. They laid their eggs of corruption into the very body of the Holy Bible itself; these eggs hatching into first-stage pupae crawled and feasted on the Old Testament. As second stage, their maggots of corruption forced their way into the New Testament; they tucked into the teachings of Jesus Christ, hollowing Him out from the inside; crucially, they were careful not to disturb the façade of Him; they preserved the believable features of the Son of God Himself.

"This shell-like image of Christ, however, now taught from a Papal script on, domination, slavery, death and theft; cavaliers and conquistadors, came to believe in this *'Predator'* as the Way and the Truth for Christian humans with white skins; however, this script was the Way to perpetual Slavery and Death 'for' the subhumans the Popes had named as 'savages' or 'heathens' or 'enemies of Christ'; it had been decreed in a 'Doctrine', therefore *'Promised';* European Christians were the *only* humans allowed to discover and own the 'Promised Land'; the enemies of the Son of their God possessed no rights of ownership; only the right to 'occupy'.

"Today this fake theology in law, remains in force; it defines our relationship to our land as one that allows us to 'occupy';

the power of ownership remains within the European Christian executive, in the 'American Doctrine of Discovery'.

"Back in the day, if the 'enemy of Christ' did not comply and give up their land, all kinds of threats of warfare, enslavement and brutality would be served upon them. In my mind this has always been the evil face of a Mafia mobster, *'making an offer'* First Nation people could not refuse.[38,39]

"So, John, I named this *'Predator'* the *'Corleone Christ'*; that Hell the Europeans brought down upon our heads, was never taught at any Sermon on the Mount by Jesus of Nazareth; their behaviour and their message came from nothing other than some grubby, psychopathic Popes and Priests who were criminal opportunists; it was the biggest land grab in human history.

"Today, the 'Corleone Christ' slumbers in the U.S. Library of Congress, inside the 'American Doctrine of Discovery'; published under the bland title, *Johnson v Mcintosh*. The 'Predator' is still in control; this mobster Christ continues to act as an enforcer, stripping my people, and others across the world, of our human right to own the land our ancestors discovered.[40]

"Our fight goes on; we must be liberated from subjugation and domination of this oppressive ideology; now it seems Pope Francis has repudiated the 'Doctrine'; the Vatican says it 'renounces the Doctrines mindset of racial superiority'. Now the ball is in the court of the USA and other colonial countries who have used the precedent of the political 'American Doctrine of Discovery. It is time to renegotiate and reconstitute their gross abuses of power"[41, 42, 43]

"So, Isaac, tell me, what's the connection here between you and I?"

"So, all I want to do is to make this connection with you, John.

"Hitler fully appreciated and approved of events in the formation of the U.S. State; events like President Andrew Jackson's compulsory removal of my people from our ancestral lands through the Trail of Tears; he admired how the United States had awarded itself supreme powers of the Christian god's 'Manifest Destiny', to invade, steal and occupy the whole of North America. Adolf must have thought of it as a kind of precedent, *'If the USA can steal the West, then surely I can steal the lands of Eastern Europe'.*[44]

Isaac looked directly into John's eyes, his face was expressionless and without emotion.

"It's important, John, that you connect together the sacred warnings your own father gave about human supremacy through antisemitism and the genocide of your own ancestors, with the ancient predator I have named the *'Corleone Christ.'* The continent your grandfather was sent to in 1942, had been born in wars and waves of bloody genocides.[45]

"So, it is important that you know, John, that several years before your great-grandparents were transported to Auschwitz, Hitler had already sent his lawyers here to the USA. Their purpose was to learn from the U.S. racial blood laws; through them, they learnt how to write the evil Nazi German blood laws they needed. These laws, when finally approved the Nuremberg rallies were given the legal ascent and authority for the genocide committed on your great-grandparents and millions of your ancestors.

"Let's be clear, Hitler is even recorded referring to Eastern Europeans as his *'Redskins'.* He viewed Eastern Europeans as subhumans, living on land he had every intention of invading, stealing and ethnically cleansing.[46]

"John, in July 1935, Hitler rewarded all his lawyers who'd done the work, which led to the Reich's racial laws being authorised, by sending them back to the USA, to the city of New York, on the SS *Bremen*. You can read the history for yourself.[47]

"John, you gotta be careful! John, I hope we can become brothers who understand one another."

Day 5   4

Washington DC

Wednesday
November 6

Phoenix had a spring in her step making her way to the office. In reality she had begun to feel comfortable in the role of an acting executive lead. She reflected on the work she had completed with Robin Seacourt which had led to an immediate decision for Jim Coogan to return to work.

    She felt good about that. By the end of Monday afternoon Jim had quickly provided his calendar movements. Particularly during the six-week period when his desktop computer had been used to send email; arranging the imposter's meeting at the Lincoln Memorial and the imposter's FBI ID and lanyard.

    Phoenix had found out that on each occasion an email had been sent out, Jim's PA had independently recorded Jim's movements out of the office on interviews or journeys to other locations. Gradually, Phoenix had triangulated this evidence with Jim's investigator staff, staff who he was working with at the time. It all checked out along with other dates when John's fake ID had been made!

    In her own mind Phoenix could now clearly see that there was a strong likelihood that the 'mole' was based close by to Jim's desk and would have seen when he was either leaving the building or returning.

As Phoenix entered the doors of the FBI offices, she knew there was a busy day ahead of 'back-to-backs'. There was little time to even breathe; she was pleased that John was staying on in Oklahoma City to tie up more loose ends.

Making her way along a corridor of glass-fronted, soundproofed, breakout rooms, she looked into the room she had booked for the first meeting of the day. Jason, Charlotte and Jim were standing in a huddle, making up for lost time.

Esteban Jackson and one of David O'Donnelly's forensic technicians, Jeanie, were making sure their equipment was working so they could demonstrate some new CCTV evidence regarding the death of George Stanhope.

Phoenix breezed into the room with a warm, "Good Morning."

"Hi, everyone. It's *so* good to have everyone back together. Jim, welcome back! I think this process this morning will pretty much bring you up to date. I'm not sure if you had time to meet Esteban, here?"

Jim acknowledged they had met briefly.

"Okay, Esteban, you've got fifteen minutes. My hope is that you are presenting this evidence to the team leaders may ring bells for all three of them. Okay, Jeanie, let's get this show on the road!"

Esteban stood for a moment of respectful silence in front of the screen with a picture of George Stanhope, freeze-framed. Then, introducing his presentation, Esteban explained that the work he and Jeanie had done was to trace George's journey back from the Memorial meeting.

"In the first section we're going to show you short CCTV footage, demonstrating who was at the meeting, you'll see three people standing at the top of the two flights of steps, between two pillars. You'll see the weather is foul and they're sheltering from heavy rain.

"Secondly, you'll see footage of George being tracked back to the Metro by one of the people he had met.

"The third section is from George entering the Foggy Bottom Metro station, through to the platform; we walked this route ourselves before we edited the video clip. It is important to say that Jeanie and I met with the Metro CCTV staff at WMATA, that's the Metro transit authority; they passed new footage over to us, providing new viewing angles through which to analyse the process."

Esteban turned and nodded to Jeanie, kicking off the presentation to the meeting. The next scene showed members of the public hurrying down a Metro passage.

Watching carefully, Charlotte quickly identified George and Greg Tranter. There was also a female present who had her back to the CCTV camera.

"Do we ever get to see who the face of the woman is in the meeting?"

"Jeanie and I tried a number of ways to get an early view of this woman. It's a wet, blustery, fall day; she's wearing a coat with her hood up. At the end of the meeting, we see George leave. Then, Greg Tranter and the woman remain together briefly until they both go their separate ways; the female goes off in the direction of the Foggy Bottom station at pace. She remains under an umbrella but seems to be following George's general direction.

"Now you'll see Jeanie's edit has switched into a short clip starting from the entrance to the Foggy Bottom Metro passageway leading onto the platform.

"You'll see Jeanie has used spotlighting techniques to show not only George but also the female following him through barriers and along a pedestrian escalator. Sometimes you'll notice the female not only following but arriving near to the platform; she overtakes George, weaving with the passengers until they reach the platform.

"Arriving at the platform you'll see the woman, still with her hood up; she pushes through the growing number of passengers, positioning herself directly behind George; she maintains her own position directly behind him, pushing forward to the very front line on the platform. Our mark still has her hood up.

"Now there's a switch in the footage; we're showing you the original unedited, normal-speed footage which we viewed immediately after we were informed George had died. It's important to direct you to the viewpoint of this clip which is looking along the track as the train is arriving. So, now you'll see the chaos of passengers walking through a busy Metro passageway and onto the platform, you'll see it was very difficult for us to identify our mark, but, lastly, we can see George falling into the path of the oncoming train."

Then the team watched in silence as Jeanie's edit switched again to new, slowed down footage. The viewpoint of the clip was from behind where George and the woman are seen standing one behind the other; in this section Esteban and Jeanie had again inserted spotlighting on the figures of George and the woman who had been tracking him. The last thirty seconds of the video footage was purposely slowed right down, clicking through four static, final photographs, frame by frame.

First frame: Showed the woman behind George holding the umbrella horizontally with the handle pointing forward toward George's right-hand side.

Second frame: Showed several passengers, including George Stanhope, looking toward the arrival of the Metro train they were all intending to board; the woman's hooded head, however, could be seen looking downwards with the umbrella handle extending forward, toward the ground that George was standing in.

Third frame: Showed George beginning to trip. The umbrella handle wasn't visible around George's ankle, but the woman's coat sleeve and hand could be seen firmly holding onto the pointed end of the umbrella.

Fourth frame: Showed the ensuing panic and chaos of

people seeing George tumble forward onto the rails and under the oncoming train. The woman behind George was then shown trying to turn against the tide of the crush to escape the platform. In the growing chaos, the woman's hood momentarily falls back; it's trapped between her head and another person's shoulder behind her. The woman's face was finally revealed, spotlighted on-screen, with one hand trying to desperately reset her disguise. However, Jeanie had freeze-framed her face, leaving it on-screen.

Straight- away there was the sound of Charlotte pushing her chair back and walking toward the screen.

Phoenix watched as she walked up and, standing to one side, so as not to cast her shadow on the fourth and final image, she looked back at Phoenix and pointed at the face.

"I know who that is! That's Suzanne Woodman. She's the team manager at the Mall Maintenance Service. As we know, one of the services in her sphere of management is the 'Ranger Tour Guide' team, showing tourists round the Undercroft."

Phoenix watched as Jim's well-worn face cracked into a broad smile.

"There it is then, Esteban. You've identified a member of the 'conspiracy'. Congratulations! Looks like that little team has been infiltrated, way ahead of Wohali Lightfoot's assassination, and this Suzanne Woodman woman, murdered George, seeing him off the Metro platform. This, Phoenix, is I believe, the same woman who has been providing evidence to you for my disciplinary hearing! Am I right?"

"Yeah, you're right, Jim."

Phoenix, however, did not want to be distracted by Jims' comment. She asked Jeanie an important question.

"Finally, then, Jeanie, can you assure me that you've kept a clear log of all the enhancements you've done on this CCTV footage? I'm hoping I don't have to brief you about the FBI code of practice in this area. It is impossibly detailed. The last thing I want is us to end up in a court of law anytime soon, with you on the stand, unable to demonstrate to a judge and jury, a clear record of what was done to achieve these pictures. We don't want to be undermined by a defence attorney saying that we've manipulated this evidence and see George's assassin going free."

"Yes, Phoenix. I consulted David O'Donnelly all the way through. He briefed me and pointed out all the governance I had to comply with. We do have a detailed log to support this evidence; David has also viewed the footage and scrutinised the log; he has given his technical approval."

"So, that's good. Charlotte, I need you to hang back after the meeting to discuss your team's work in the Mall Maintenance Service.

"Can I thank both Esteban and Jeanie for your brilliant, groundbreaking investigative work, staying with an arduous task! Seems to me, this could have great significance; along with the other evidence on the cockerel tattoo."

Phoenix moved on to the next part of her investigation catch-up agenda.

"Okay. You're next, Jason, I've asked you up to tell us about your work with Drake to identify Ford Ranger Raptor candidates in the Oklahoma District please?"

Jason quickly covered the search that he and Drake had undertaken.

"Well, Phoenix, there really is only one candidate. It's a burnt-out Raptor and fits in with our own timescales of the assault on the retreat. It can't help confirming the evidence of tyre tracks collected at the retreat because it's so badly destroyed by fire. Police are saying that it has now been removed from an isolated piece of waste ground and taken to their police compound."

Jason passed round photographs.

Jim looked across at Jason and asked if it was available for forensic examination.

"Yeah, it's available. We can organise an examination anytime."

"Okay, Jason, that's great news. I'm speaking with John later. Maybe, because this is another important lead of potential evidence, we'll want to establish a joint FBI and city police forensic examination ASAP, even though the vehicle is badly destroyed. We have to follow up every lead. John will make the judgement on when.

"Finally, then, within your team, how's the work on making the Lightfoot family secure? That's the safe house, plus twenty-four-seven security cover for Woya, Cary and her son. I've asked you to organise Isaac's security in Oklahoma Hospital. Twenty-four-seven security cover outside Isaac's hospital room from tonight."

"Yeah, the safe house is commissioned, Anna McKenna has been helpful on budgets. On Isaac, I've commissioned his security through our local guy, Ray Chan."

"Right, that's my agenda for the team today. Well done, folks, on all the progress. Keep it comin'!"

"I just need you, Charlotte, to hang back. I'll catch up with you later, Jim. We need to sit down and talk about what we must do to get you back into the action."

5

When everyone had gone, Phoenix asked Charlotte if she was prepared to enter a highly confidential trio of practice with John and herself. She was pretty sure that Charlotte would leap at the chance, and she wasn't disappointed.

"Of course, Phoenix, you've got my full attention."

Phoenix explained she needed her to establish a detailed report she just may need to present to a judge; the purpose was to agree the use of a wire tap.

"You should be aware, the governance for this is extremely sensitive. This can only be legally achieved through Title 18, U.S. Code Section 2516. I need you to leave our meeting and brief yourself; get one of our corporate lawyers who knows and has got experience and practice to put this report together and take you through the legal court hoops. In some place or other, I'll need to get approval from a judge. You still in, Charlotte?"

"Come on, Phoenix, I am in!"

John's internal desk phone rang. Phoenix answered on loudspeaker. It was Dina, John's PA.

"Phoenix, Drake Collins is here for his appointment."

"Ask him to wait, Dina. Make him some coffee."

Phoenix turned back to Charlotte and picked up their conversation with a high level of intensity.

"This approval is in respect of a lead from Jim Coogan in his disciplinary meeting."

"He's been busy! Is he recovering?"

"Yeah. It's tough, though, him being at the centre of a swirling atmosphere of 'conspiracy'. People are beginning to wonder what or who they can believe."

Phoenix brought up a series of six photographs on-screen.

"Jim provided us with these photographs taken by pure chance in a restaurant. Don't need to tell you this is Drake Collins sitting with a very well-heeled businessman, maybe a politician? Others have wondered if he is a mobster, some kind of power broker. I need your team to identify this guy.

"I want to know everything you can dig up about this man, from birth to now. Who's in his family? What do they do? What does he do? What are his politics?? You name it, I want it. I'm also going to try my own methods with Drake after you've left. The question is, can I get him to help us out and tell us who this man is, himself?

"John has shared these photographs with Chief of Police, Walter Banks to look at what's known locally by police in the State of Oklahoma.

"Depending on what Drake says, whether I think he's cooperating and what your team find out, I may offer him the difficult role to go undercover with a wire tap at some time. I'm considering whether he should join David O'Donnelly on a trip to Oklahoma tomorrow. For all I know there may be an opportunity to ask him to work with John in Oklahoma and to use a 'wire' down there."

Phoenix's HR business partner knocked on her window, she leaned forward, nodded and mouthed a 'goodbye' to Charlotte and buzzed Dina.

"Bring Drake over please, Dina."

6

As Drake came into the room, he noticed Phoenix had brought the HR officer he'd met when he formally signed a contract and joined as an intern. As he sat down some of his red hair fell forward across one eye.

Drake momentarily looked up, giving Phoenix a nervous glance. He was casually dressed in light-brown tight-fitting cord trousers, brown shoes and a dark-green shirt, open at the neck. Phoenix was struck by his stunning blue eyes.

"Well, thanks for coming to see me, Drake. I am not going to lie to you, this is a formal meeting, I am going to record it using this."

Phoenix placed her digital recorder on the palm of her hand and then onto the desk corner nearby Drake.

"This is confidential but as you can see, I have to have HR alongside to witness our interview and make sure what I'm doing is fair and legal. I think you know one another?"

Drake smiled and nodded.

"This digital record will go into your confidential employee notes with our HR department. I will not lie, what you say to me over the next fifteen to twenty minutes will be very important; it could have a big impact on your life going forward. If you can't convince me you're telling the truth, this certainly will be the end of the line for your career right here and now. However, tell the truth and believe me, you could go a long way, Drake."

Drake nodded, sat back and relaxed into his chair.

"You're probably wondering why I have asked you to come to see me. This *is* unusual, normally I'd ask the team leader to manage their intern. Hopefully, this may never need to happen again.

"There will only be three people in this organisation who get to discuss what happens in this conversation today. That's Charlotte Linklater, John Green and myself. After this meeting I don't want you discussing it. Not Jason, not Esteban or anyone else on the outside. Believe me, if I get a sniff of you breaching our ground rules on this, Drake, that will be that! Fired! Understood?"

Phoenix put her right hand in the shape of a handgun, put the 'barrel' to her temple and pulled the trigger.

Drake nodded.

"So, a colleague of mine met with me recently and provided me with a set of photographs. I want to start this conversation by showing you each one."

Phoenix turned her screen toward Drake so he could see the series of six photographs Jim had provided.

While Drake silently looked through the photographs, Phoenix carried on briefing.

"You'll know, Drake, that the Wohali Lightfoot investigation is our highest priority piece at present. Even though some of us are doing other stuff, still, every one of us is connected to the Lightfoot case in some way, right across our service.

"You know from my team briefings, we have at least one 'leaker' or 'mole' in this service. So, we are questioning all those people when we need to, understood?"

Drake nodded "Understood."

"You've become one of those staff today. Our aim is to make ourselves secure again; bolt down all our hatches."

"John Green and I won't rest until we've dragged that 'mole' out of that underground tunnel, blinking into the sunlight and locked him or her up as a traitor.

"You've had a few minutes to look through these photographs. I'm going to ask you directly, who is this well-dressed man you're with, looks like a corporate businessman, maybe a politician?"

Drake looked up at Phoenix with a question in his blue eyes.

"If I tell you, are you going to investigate him?"

"Drake, Charlotte's team are doing everything they can right now, trying to find out who he is. The question is, what does he mean to you? What's the connection? We've got to rule him in or out of this investigation. Tell us who this man is so we don't have to waste any more time."

There was a long silence while Drake looked between Phoenix and the HR officer.

"He's, my dad. Just doing his best for me. He was visiting me from West Virginia. He came up to see how I'm getting on."

"So, what's your dad's name?"

"His name is James T Collins. He used to be a local cop, but he retired early."

"So, what does your dad do for a living now?"

"I'm following in his footsteps. Not the way *he* did things, he made big mistakes. Left the force early and, absolutely everything went wrong for him; life for us as a family became very hard.

"When I arrived here, I was excited, something good was happening. I was amazed to have this chance. Arriving on Saturday, talking to Esteban, I literally thought to myself, '*How the hell did I get here? Esteban got here from Harvard!*'

"I just couldn't work it out. But I have now."

"Go on, Drake, give us the lowdown on that."

"As I say, I met Esteban in the first twenty minutes, we got on, I like him. My phone rang while we were drinking coffee. It was an anonymous call. I took it outside on the street to be private.

"A guy's robotic voice spoke to me as if he knew all about me. He told me stuff about my life only my family know. Said he knew I was very talented with a rifle. Knew I could use a handgun at an early age; knew me well enough to know I was a member of the Duttam Gun Club and Rifle Range.

"He said I was either gonna work for the FBI or for *his* people. He told me it was him who'd got me to where I was now as an intern. Said my father owed his 'organisation' a big debt; told me that my father had agreed that I would pay the bill!

"He said if I decided to work for him, '*you'll be protecting your parents. But you gotta know, I'll ask the questions, but you'll always provide the answer to them. Clear? No questions!*'."

"So, what's the connection between you, your father and the anonymous 'voice' in this 'organisation'?"

Drake looked up and asked for further reassurance that this was a confidential discussion. Phoenix gave him the reassurance he needed.

"All I know is my father has worked with people on the 'dark side'. You know what I mean? I've never been told the details. Sometimes I think, maybe, he's been using his contacts and dealing drugs, that kinda thing?

"When I was a child, people, they'd come to our house; me and my sister, we'd be sent out to play. Now, it seems from what my dad said on Sunday, they've got something else on him. He said they had protected him till now. But I know from what he told me the other day, his life was on the line again."

Drake told Phoenix the level of threat his father and mother were under.

"The voice told me that if I didn't do what they asked, they'd take my dad to a piece of waste ground and put a bullet in his head. He told me my mum was a 'good-looking woman' and they'd 'look after her' and she'd have to 'look after them.'"

"Drake, I'm really sorry to hear all that. The sins of the father are visited on the son. I appreciate your honesty. And I know what it means for you to have to come clean. Facts are Drake, you're compromised!

"Tell me, what were you told? How were you gonna know who, within the FBI, would be connecting with you to do this dirty, illegal work?"

"Well, the voice said I'd be 'placed' with a team leader and whichever one that was, that team leader would tell me what to do, and when to do it."

"And, Drake, think carefully before you answer this. Has your team leader, Jason Colbeck, asked you to do anything for the 'conspiracy' yet?"

"Not yet, we're just getting acquainted. He seems to know a lot of details about me that weren't in my application for the internship. He knew, that as a child, I was a handgun champion at my local club."

"That's all I can tell you now, Ms Shultz."

"Call me Phoenix... Look, time is short, Drake. We've gotta move on this Lightfoot case with all speed. Truth is, even though you're compromised, I may need your help. In so many ways I am so sorry to have to ask you. Your life is already tough.

"Let me just check, you're twenty-five? You've got a Bachelor of Arts degree? You've had work experience with your local police force? We'll need to check your fitness, and you've got a driving licence? Am I right on all that, Drake?"

Drake nodded to all those questions.

"Look, there are a couple of options. I could just fire you! You're compromised and you've lied. You could resign, being an intern and walk. But I could ask you to 'work' for us undercover. I suggest you join David O'Donnelly on the trip to Oklahoma tomorrow. Then, you'd work together with John Green down there. We might even ask you wear a 'wire,' if there's a member of the 'conspiracy' you can help us listen in to; John has worked undercover before; he'd support you to do that. You'd be a double agent, Drake, working on our side.

"Maybe you can even help us bust the man who's threatening you and your father. It would mean flying tomorrow with David, then meeting John at the airport in Oklahoma. What do you think?"

"Can I take a minute?"

Drake stood up and paced around the room.

"So, are you asking me to keep talking with the people, like Jason, who could be a 'mole'? Then talking to you, John or Charlotte about what they're saying and planning to do?"

"Yeah! And when you leave this room, you'll have to stay calm with the likes of Jason. You'll need to listen to them and smile at them. Stay cool and relaxed."

"My father, he's back in West Virginia right now. Will he know about this?"

"No."

"Okay… So, look, help get us through this big case, Drake. I promise you here on the digital record, the FBI is a very big organisation. We'll train you to the highest level we can. If you want it, we'll open that big door to a great career. Who knows, you could become the real deal, a top undercover FBI investigator and a highly respected one. How's that sound?"

Drake didn't seem to need to think about it anymore.

"Okay, Phoenix, I'll travel with David tomorrow!"

"Glad to hear that, Drake. You're gonna have to stay close by David and John. You have got to understand though, you'll be 'smiling' and getting along with Jason. But, from now on, you'll really be working for me, Drake. After we've finished up here all I gotta do is speak to John."

Drake put out his hand; his blue eyes looked deep into Phoenix's eyes. Phoenix nodded and her eyes glistened as she looked back at him.

"Glad we can still work together, Drake; that's all for now. I'll tell Jason about tomorrow's trip right after my call to John. You go right away to Dina, my PA out there, about your booking onto tomorrow's flight and your hotel stay. John will meet you and David at the airport.

"When you've done all that, go on home, Drake. Rest up, full respect to you, young man, for choosing to work with us."

Drake left and closed the door behind him.

Phoenix passed the recording of the interview to her HR partner.

"Look, whatever you do, make this recording safe. Get it onto Drake's record. Mark it with a *restricted access/high security* tag. I don't want anyone accessing it without John Green or I knowing or at least being consulted to give our authority for granting access. Okay?"

In the quiet of her office Phoenix felt a mixture of fear and admiration for Drake. But then for Phoenix, thinking through the interview, the big punch in the gut came through her realisation that maybe, just maybe, Drake had revealed that Anna McKenna, the director of the FBI, had been compromised by the 'conspiracy' herself.

Phoenix thought it through in her own mind. *Yeah, that was right. Anna had insisted on taking over the placement of interns to 'help' me out. She'd even told John about it. Did Anna actually know Jason was a 'mole'? Maybe it was a coincidence.*

Phoenix realised this would be a private conversation with John.

For Phoenix, the consequences and shifting sands of the emerging 'conspiracy' in the service and the wider federal services began to open up her feelings of intense insecurity. With further reflection, Phoenix realised there and then that Jason's security decisions and arrangements would definitely need to be independently verified.

Phoenix picked up the phone and contacted Jim Coogan.

"Hi, Jim. Can you take a moment and call in to see me in my office? I need you to urgently review some security arrangements for me."

Putting the phone down, Phoenix felt relieved that she now had Jim to rely on. Knowing that he had come through close scrutiny began to mean a lot. Having done that, Phoenix picked up her phone and asked Dina to get Charlotte into an urgent meeting.

Day 5　　　　　　　　　　　　　　7

Knoxville Airport

Wednesday
November 6

The drive to Knoxville Airport from the Smoky Mountains was uneventful. Kamama drove John; Woya and Isaac drove their own hire car with comfortable space in the rear for Ylva.

All of John's concerns were now fully focussed on the work firstly with Chief of Police, Walter Banks in Oklahoma; secondly, he needed to hear what progress Phoenix was making in DC.

Reviewing operational factors in his mind, John felt confident that Jason Colbeck, his favoured team leader, would have given all his support to Phoenix. He thought highly of Phoenix's judgement in selecting Jason for such a sensitive task, establishing safe and secure arrangements for the Lightfoot family.

It was just thirty minutes to boarding the flight back to Oklahoma when John's phone rang.

"Hi, Phoenix. Yeah, I'm fine. In three hours' time now, I should be back in Oklahoma at the Skirvin Hotel. I feel like I've been away from civilisation for years! How are you doin'?"

"John, we need to talk urgently! There's been some big developments in the last few hours. There's been no time to talk in between events. Have you got time to talk now?"

"Well, we're boarding in about thirty minutes. But, once aboard I could muscle my way into first class as an FBI executive officer to take a secure call. Give me half an hour and I'll ring you. Okay? Phoenix, just before you go. Did Jason come up trumps with sound security arrangements for tomorrow?"

"Well, all I can say right now is that's part of the discussion we need."

Briefing Kamama, John told her that he'd go to a more secure seat to make a call to Phoenix. On boarding, John showed his ID to one of the flight stewards. He explained what he needed, and she escorted him immediately to a private, executive seated area.

Phoenix picked up John's call.

"Hi, John. Look, we've had a major breakthrough on the 'conspiracy' and the identity of the internal 'mole'. The last two hours have been utter madness."

Phoenix ran through the details about Drake's background, about his internship being compromised right from the beginning. She felt the fallout from Drake's interview was profound, and it was crowding out her thinking.

First, there was Drake's understanding that Jason Colbeck, his team leader, could be the 'mole'. Drake had said someone knew an awful lot of private information about him.

"Well, John, firstly this all implicates Jason Colbeck. Second, Anna McKenna made the 'placement' for Drake with Jason. Does that mean she did that knowing Jason is the 'mole'? Sounds crazy, but do you see what I mean, John? Is Anna, herself, compromised?"

Secondly, while listening to herself, Phoenix suddenly had the dawning realisation that Jason knew from Esteban's team briefing about the CCTV progress, and that Jason knew Suzanne Woodman had been identified as *the* prime suspect for George Stanhope's murder.

John asked Phoenix to slow down.

"So, Phoenix, suddenly the 'conspiracy' is unfolding. Feels like shit, doesn't it? We've got to deal with this a stage at a time."

Phoenix continued talking faster, briefing John further about Suzanne Woodman.

"What am I going to do to secure Suzanne Woodman?"

"Look, Phoenix, slow down! I don't need to tell you, you have to arrest Suzanne Woodman immediately, right now! It can't wait until tomorrow. Not only does she need arresting, but she needs interviewing under caution, charging and detaining on the basis of today's CCTV evidence.

"Don't forget, Phoenix, she herself is at risk. Jason and the wider 'conspiracy' could be issuing instructions, deciding her fate, as we speak. You know, Phoenix, these people are ruthless, they could easily just take her straight out after she leaves her office this evening. Could be in her own home; could be a hit and run; could be a long-range rifle shot.

"If I were you, I'd be getting hold of Jim and picking up two priorities. First, you arrest and charge Woodman. Second, get Jim to review security arrangements…"

Phoenix interrupted John.

"Okay, look John. I'm ahead of you! I agree with all you've said. I've already got Jim on board to review security, he's ringing Ray Chan in Oklahoma as we speak. I'm catching up with Jim now on security and then we'll get on with arresting Woodman."

"Okay, that's great! So, beyond there, well, the question is how we manage Jason Colbeck. I think you'll have to discreetly take the most senior HR and legal advice first thing tomorrow morning. But there's no doubt in my mind he will need to be arrested, interviewed and taken into custody, latest tomorrow."

Phoenix began to feel more grounded with John's input; Phoenix explained Jason was out of the office and wasn't picking up his mobile; she had phoned home to his wife but she wasn't picking up.

"I'm catching up with Jim now on security and then we'll get on with arresting Woodman.

"Oh, John? Before you go, there's another issue with Drake.

To cut to the chase, in my interview with him, I gave him a choice, work with us, pick up a career, or leave. He's decided to help us identify the membership of the 'conspiracy' in Oklahoma; don't forget he knows West Virginia, it's his home state, should the net widen.

"He's agreed to travel early tomorrow morning with David O'Donnelly. He's got a room at the Skirvin Hotel next to you. I know you'll look after him. Charlotte is still following up on the photographs Jim gave us. That's it for now, John, I've gotta go"

While Phoenix closed down her call with John, Jim Coogan knocked on her door.

They both split up their tasks.

Phoenix phoned through to Greg Tranter to find out if Suzanne Woodman was still in the office and would be there till the end of that day. Tranter said her calendar was clear, she was there until the end of the working day. Phoenix asked him to do everything he could to make sure Woodman didn't leave before they arrived.

In the meantime, Jim completed his call to Ray Chan and joined Phoenix in her room.

"Look, Phoenix, Jason hasn't worked through Ray Chan at all; also, he's made no contact with the hospital authorities. As far as Ray knows there isn't anyone scheduled to guard Isaac tomorrow. So, Ray is sorting that out right now. He has guaranteed me that there is an established, permanent, two-handed rotation until Isaac is discharged. Then he'll organise safe armed escort back here to the Washington DC safe house."

Knowing that they had secured Isaac's admission to hospital, Phoenix and Jim raced across the city to make their arrest of Suzanne Woodman.

Taking Woodman into custody, Phoenix charged her with the murder of George Stanhope. She booked a space to interview Woodman together with Charlotte first thing in the morning.

The custody team then processed her, took prints and mug

shots, then assessed her mental state before securing her in a cell. She was advised of her rights to make three phone calls which would be recorded; the custody officer strongly recommended that one phone call would be to her attorney, to support her through the early morning interview.

Day 5   8

Oklahoma City

Wednesday
November 6

Stepping down from the plane onto the Oklahoma tarmac, John was feeling disorientated. The trip into the Great Smoky Mountains had held the quality of an odyssey. The vivid stories Isaac had told from history were still resonating in his thoughts.

The investigative element of the trip had already revealed some important information. Particularly the corroboration between Greg Tranter and Cary Lightfoot's independent verification of the cockerel tattoo, in respect of Seth Soul. It was at the top of John's agenda now to contact Chief Walter Banks to arrange their work for tomorrow.

John had booked a couple of taxis to get people to where they needed to go. As he walked to the Lightfoots' car, he warmly shook Isaac's hand. He thanked him for all his hospitality as head of the family and also for dealing with all the stress of the interviews.

Isaac, standing between John and Kamama, put one arm around John's shoulder and the other around Kamama's waist.

"Here's hoping I get to meet you both again in Washington DC, in your office this time, John."

"Yeah, I'm hoping and praying for you, Isaac; good luck with your hospital treatment; two security guards will be sat outside your door day and night. I'm staying on at the Skirvin Hotel and I'll be in Oklahoma for several days longer yet; I've gotta square that with my wife, Kay, though!"

Woya hugged John tight. He knew she would be struggling with leaving Isaac behind the next day, plus there was all the confusion of packing and needing to leave Smiths Village John knew both she and Cary were taking a fearful leap in the dark.

John stood back, then held Woya in a warm handshake.

"Look, Woya, I know you're a strong woman. Give my best wishes to Cary. Tell her I'm looking forward to seeing her in DC. All this will come right in the end somehow."

John and Kamama turned away and got into their taxi and settled in for the ride to the Skirvin Hotel. John looked across at Kamama, placing his hand on hers.

"Look, Kamama, it's been impossible for us to find time to talk. I have had to take calls from Phoenix, and I still need to speak to her again as soon as I get back to the Skirvin Hotel. Can we get together this evening? Somewhere of your choice, or maybe just revisit the Skirvin Hotel Restaurant, say, for old times' sake?"

"Yeah, John, I've no doubt you're in high demand already. Must be tough for your wife and kids, all this uncertainty. Not sure I like the idea of meeting for what you call 'old times' sake'. Sounds too final for my liking. But, yeah, I'm sure we should touch base with where we've been. I'm a great believer in smooth landings."

The rest of the journey for both John and Kamama was silent, both looking out of their separate passenger-door windows.

John could feel that what had happened the night before at the retreat was sitting uneasily between them like a third, muted passenger.

As the taxi pulled into the hotel drop-off point at 2.45 p.m.

John reached across and again, placed his hand on Kamama's. He kissed Kamama gently on the cheek, then pulled back and smiled.

"Don't get out. I'll see you this evening, around 8 p.m. okay?"

9

Across the city, Woya, Cary and Danuwoa had accompanied Isaac to repack for his admission to hospital; like them he needed to pack the belongings he'd need to use in hospital, then also in his move to the safe house in DC.

Finally, they all travelled to say their goodbyes at Oklahoma City Hospital. During his admission process, just booking in at the large reception counter, Isaac had seemed to Woya to be somehow much smaller, and more vulnerable.

They were directed to the third floor where, as a family, they were greeted by the two-man security detail John had assured them about. Isaac began to settle and unpack his clothes and belongings. Woya tried to help him, placing the things she thought he'd need on his bedside cabinet.

"Look, you two, ain't no good you are fussing around here with long faces. You're making me feel bad! I am safe here. I need those extra five years they've been telling me about and I believe I am going to get them. Right? You two, and this young warrior of the future here, you need to order a taxi and get the hell out of here, then get onto that plane to find your own security. I know, John Green and the FBI will do everything they can to look after the three of you.

"But it ain't no good, you are hanging around here, you're making me feel jumpy."

After his family left, a junior doctor and nurse came in to confirm all his admission details and told him about the phases of his treatment, what would be happening, where and when.

10

Having booked back in at the Skirvin Hotel reception, John took the lift to the third floor and trundled his case along to his room, inserted his plastic key, and closed the door on a welcome silence. He found himself breathing a sigh of relief; he lay back on his bed and drifted off into a shallow sleep.

As his mobile rang, John blindly felt across the surface of his bedside cabinet. He pressed the green accept button, knowing Phoenix was on the line.

"Hi, Phoenix. Give me a moment to surface will you."

"No time for that, John. We've got to quickly talk through where Jim and I have got to on security and Suzanne Woodman."

John responded, struggling to sit himself in an upright position.

"Hi, John, are you still there?"

"Yeah! I'm here! Right. I can tell you, Isaac's security was there at the hospital; they met Isaac and his family as they arrived. "

"So, what about Suzanne Woodman?"

"She's in custody, John. Jim and I cautioned, arrested and charged her on the basis of the CCTV evidence regarding George's murder. She kept her cool with 'no comment' responses in a first short interview. She'll be organising her phone calls later on this evening.

"Of course, we'll get the chance to review all those calls. Could be interesting to see who she calls? Charlotte and I will interview Woodman tomorrow morning; at least she's safe now."

John left a thoughtful silence on the other end of the conversation then responded, "I've been in touch with Chief Banks. His team still haven't located Seth Soul and his sons. I'm gonna be working with him to personally retrace the squad car's steps back to the Soul homestead, tomorrow. Walter will get a warrant for the search of the property. I'll take Drake with me.

"Tomorrow morning I'll be seeing the Lightfoot family onto their flight to DC, then I'll also be around to meet David and Drake as they arrive. Let them know, Phoenix, we'll be heading straight to city police HQ. I'll be leaving David to do the joint forensic examination of the Raptor with Robert White, his opposite number down here."

"I'm glad you've agreed to work with Drake, John. He made a tough decision to stay with us and take on a career. I'm guessing we'll be taking no further action on Anna McKenna. I'll keep you informed about Charlotte's team's findings on those photographs from the restaurant."

"Well, there's little love lost between Anna and me. While I've privately found some of her professional advice and comments offensive to say the least, I can't say you have a shred of the kind of evidence we'd need to inform the attorney general that she's compromised and working for the 'conspiracy'.

"Phoenix, you've got a long day tomorrow. Keep in touch about your interview with Woodman please. I want to know how that one goes."

"Yeah. I'm going home to Trent now. I need the sanity of home; Trent is my rock. He'll be in his studio trying to complete his latest portrait of the next DC dignitary seeking immortality in oil. Our partners, John, they have to put up with a lot."

"Yeah, that may be right. But I can't talk about that one right now."

11

After his phone call with Phoenix, John set his alarm for 7 p.m., then slept for another couple of uninterrupted hours.

When the alarm woke him, he felt well rested.

After showering and changing, John made his way down to the hotel restaurant where he had booked a table. As he waited, John felt a sense of edginess and a wellspring of anticipation bubbling up inside about dinner with Kamama. Then, suddenly he saw her making her way across the floor of the restaurant. She looked stunning; Kamama was wearing a long, flowing dark-blue dress with flat, leather, ankle-strapped sandals.

As Kamama drew closer, John noticed she was wearing a silver chain necklace, on which swung a pentagon-shaped pendant. At the heart of the pentagon there was a dangling turquoise stone bead, looking out like a single eye; three beautifully crafted, silver eagle feathers hung from the pentagon's bottom edge.

As Kamama arrived John commented about how beautiful she looked and they briefly touched cheeks. As John pulled away, Kamama held onto his left elbow, smiled and gently brushed his lips with the back of the forefinger of her right hand.

Sitting down, John found himself mesmerised by Kamama's necklace.

"Does it have any symbolic meaning, Kamama?"

Kamama look back at John with a quizzical look in her eye. "The pendant!"

A light sparkled in Kamama's eyes and, as she settled in her chair, she chuckled.

"Yes, John. It's called a dreamcatcher."

They ordered food and wine.

Returning to workaday conversation, Kamama asked John how the investigation was going.

"Yeah, there have been some significant developments. Phoenix, has done some amazing work with our teams. We seem to be getting closer to the 'conspiracy'.

"We know there are staff who are embedded in both the FBI and one in another federal service which almost certainly provided the 'conspiracy' with public access to the Undercroft at the Memorial. The men from the Soul family are prime suspects. Also, we know one of the city police teams found a burnt-out Ford Raptor F-150. We don't know if it is the one used on the assault of the retreat. So, tomorrow, one of our forensic experts is travelling down with an intern. The intern and I will be working with Chief Walter Banks at the Soul homestead. So, a very busy day."

At the end of their meal, they followed the pattern of their first evening when they met in the hotel restaurant. John ordered drinks; a double malt whiskey and a jug of water, plus a glass of Merlot for Kamama. They sat, as before, unseen in the same quiet corner, with the same wingback chairs, and the same low table between them.

John opened up the conversation about their changing relationship.

"I just want to say, what happened between us back there, Kamama, it was a beautiful thing. I have no regrets. Believe me, Kamama, look at you tonight; you're a very beautiful woman. Listen, I don't want you to feel disrespected in any way. My feelings for you over the last twenty-four hours are strong, but I am confused."

John and Kamama took a moment just honestly looking back at one another, feeling the change that the night before had brought into both their lives.

"Look, Kamama, I ain't just talking about the night we spent together either. Professionally, you've supported me; you've advised me on Cary, Isaac and Woya; on a personal note, you've opened me up on my own conflicts and feelings. You're also responsible for turning this city boy more toward an awareness of the natural world; I can even name a couple of trees now."

John took a moment to think.

"Oh yeah. Then of course, you gave me a basic tour de force of what the *Doctrine of Discovery* might mean. So, my reckoning is, that names three doors you opened: crucial doors. I'd say that's almost access to a whole 'house'; all in two and a half days!"

John watched as he wistfully swirled the remains of his malt whiskey at the bottom of his glass.

Kamama remained silent; quietly relaxed.

"I don't think I told you, when Ylva and I visited the waterfall and its pool yesterday, I too saw the black panther. She was shimmering on a rock at the top of the falls. She just nosed the air and arrogantly looked away. I could have sworn her gaze looked deep into my eyes, but I may be exaggerating that.

"What was strange, after she'd gone, I just broke down and wept; haven't done that since I was a boy!"

As John spoke, he put his head down, feeling the emotions return.

He didn't see Kamama broadly smiling back at him. "I knew it! John, ever since we met I have always looked into your eyes and seen someone else listening. Well, you should know, that glorious black cat doesn't appear to just anyone! Whatever happens, John, you and me, we'll always be soulmates; that's for certain; you and I *knew* one another from the moment we first met after midnight, from your late DC flight."

They both chuckled over the sign Kamama had made and held aloft: '*ARE YOU JOHN GREEN?*'

"Listen, Kamama, in my life I have been a person who has gone through many changes; it often arrives, knocking on my door, unannounced. I can't explain it, maybe lots of people have the same thing. Sitting here though, right now in this moment, I feel more connected; I'm more joined up in myself than maybe I have ever felt. But…"

Kamama raised a finger to her lips, shook her head and frowned. She saw the next line coming from a mile down the road.

"Yeah, I know you've got a wife, John, and two children. Then you've got Phoenix on the investigation, and Washington DC."

"What I am trying to say, Kamama, is I have that feeling in my gut, the winds of change are moving. Believe me, I know the signs; change has never let me stand still in my life yet."

Kamama leaned forward, reached across the low table and grabbed John's hand.

"John, you don't need to say any more. I'm a free spirit, remember? What will be, will be."

Finishing their drinks, they talked, small talk; about the mundanity of being back to work and the familiarity of family and old friendships which were in both their thoughts. Eventually, without a word or a signal, they stood up together as one; their connection just seemed to inform them, the time to conclude had come; what was said, had been said.

John linked his arm with Kamama's, and they walked out to the hotel forecourt. Then, walking round to the RV, in the half-light of the parking lot they held one another close; kissed, then stood together with their foreheads joined. They smiled into one another's eyes and parted.

Kamama's RV fired up first time as usual. John, standing by the headlights, raised a hand to his eyes, as Kamama reversed away. Once the RV was out of sight, he suddenly felt awkward and stranded on the tarmac. Walking back past hotel reception into the elevator, he felt the first pangs of being alone stirring in his emotions.

Closing his hotel room door, John loosened his tie, kicked off his shoes, and slept.

Day 5   **12**

West Virginia

Wednesday
November 6

Frank, Seth, John and Charles had spent their evening having a meal, talking and planning in the barn. It was the first time they'd all been together, in the same room. They had already discussed the debacle of their mission and retreat from the Smoky Mountains. Just before they were about to break up and go their separate ways to get some sleep, Frank's phone rang.

"Excuse me, guys, I need to take this call alone, outside."

Frank could see the caller was using a burner phone number he'd seen before.

"Hi, Frank, we've never met. My name is Jason Colbeck, I got your number from Anna when Drake was placed as my FBI intern. Without you knowing it, I've been your anchor man inside the FBI, inside the Wohali Lightfoot investigation."

"Hi, Jason, just to say, you're wrong there. We have met, but you were way too young to remember. I knew your father back in the day at Springfield Mine. He was a good man. Before he sadly passed, it was him who convinced me you could help me save the mining industry; he could be very persuasive."

"Look, Frank, I don't have long. A lot has been going on up here in Washington DC over the last twelve to twenty-four hours. First thing you need to know is I'm aware a colleague of mine took photographs of you with Drake Collins in a restaurant in DC. Phoenix Shultz, my line manager, has now formally interviewed Drake about who you are. I'm a hundred per cent sure he'll have been shown the photographs. Got no idea what he said in reply to Phoenix's questions. He's avoided me since.

My boss may even have instructed him to avoid me.

"A colleague, Charlotte Linklater, who runs a team here; she specialises in tracking these kinds of images both here and through your local police departments of Oklahoma and West Virginia. Point is, Frank, someone's gonna be on your tail.

"Meanwhile, I've found out through Phoenix's PA she's been booking flight tickets and made a hotel booking for Drake. He'll be working with John Green, our executive director in Oklahoma.

"Next thing, Suzanne Woodman is now in custody. I've seen the photographic CCTV evidence from Foggy Bottom, in a team brief. It's compelling and incriminating her for the murder of George Stanhope. She's due to be interviewed by my boss, Phoenix Shultz, and a colleague tomorrow morning. There is no doubt in my mind, if Suzanne faces prosecution she will be facing a long prison term. There'll be a huge pressure on her to do business, make a deal with the Department of Justice for what she knows, in exchange for a reduced sentence."

"Well, Jason, I need some time to think about that one. Suzanne, well, she's become special to me over the years. She's been that key piece of our jigsaw; for example, getting us close enough to Wohali Lightfoot and blowing his brains out."

"Look, Frank, we *ain't* got the time to think like this! My cover is blown, I've got some slack in my calendar then I'll be out of here first thing tomorrow; gonna need to be clear of DC, otherwise it'll be my head on the chopping block. Okay, here's one way forward. Do you want me to 'visit' Suzanne before I leave? Believe me, she *is* an immediate risk not just to you, but the rest of us too."

Frank knew the answer. Even though he and Suzanne went back a long way, unfortunately this was 'business' now.

"Well, if you can do that 'visit', Jason, I'd be most grateful. If you do, take her some black roses, from me, okay? You know what I mean now, Jason, don't you?"

"Frank, I can't take anything like that into a custody suite, it's not a fucking hospital! Custody officers will be monitoring close-circuit TV from the cell! Their policy is to search me; in reality they ain't done that for a long time, we're friends."

"The black rose is a symbol we've both used, Jason. Even a tiny envelope, delivering strong medicine, she'll understand the time has arrived; I don't want any pain for her, Jason, just sleep. You hear me now? Give her my love and thanks."

"One last reason I'm phoning, Frank. Isaac Lightfoot has been admitted to Oklahoma Hospital. The two Lightfoot family members, John Green and the professor are returning. I left the 'security door' wide open for you and your Oklahoma colleagues to just breeze into Isaac Lightfoot's hospital room. But if they know I am the 'mole', and they will, you'll need to start planning a method of dispatching him. Maybe an abduction? Up to you; I'm telling you, it's now or never because the Lightfoot family will be in a secure safe house in DC. It's up to you."

Frank listened carefully.

"Look, Jason, I'm still in direct contact with Drake, believe me he'll do what I tell him, wherever he is. I'm truly sorry to hear you're compromised. If you want to immediately leave DC after you've dealt with Suzanne, why not come here. I'll text you the zip code. Thurmond is a bit of a weird place, but they'll never find you here. You'll have to be quick though."

Having ended the call, Frank returned to Seth, John and Charles.

"Looks like that second opportunity has come through on Isaac Lightfoot. He's in Oklahoma Hospital. There'll be security in place. Our source on the inside, he recommends an abduction.

"I'm gonna say to you, Seth, you need to consider not just Isaac Lightfoot but also Professor Catawnee. You say she has been working with the International Festival of the Earth as well?"

Seth and his boys were happy.

"Okay, Frank, looks like we have a plan then. I'll need to complete my task in the workshop, and you'll need to source us an ambulance and some believable hospital outfits and a wheelchair. Also, Frank, any ideas of an outdoor venue, way out of Oklahoma City, we could take Lightfoot to? We need to be private. We'll have invited guests and, we won't want to be overlooked."

Frank thought for a while.

"If you want privacy, I'd suggest some disused coal-mine land, Natural Coal Company land at Lehigh could be just the place. No mining going on there now, I closed it down. As I remember there's a section of land there with dilapidated mining equipment, plus a couple of old tin cabins all encircled by a clearing of woodland. Just like here, nature is taking over. I can get hold of a map of the terrain for you."

Seth set his sons to work.

"Okay, boys. You're gonna need to plan and deal with two abductions. One of them is Professor Catawnee. She'll need to be tomorrow evening, then Isaac early the next morning. We know the professor's pattern of working from listening in to Isaac's place; she routinely works alone, late into the evening. Lightfoot, well, he'll be a more straightforward abduction.

"I'll sort out our 'equipment' to transport on a trailer under a tarp. I'll also send out the word and ask our friends for a container consignment of dry bonfire wood. They'll deliver that.

"We're gonna light up that 'dead' Lehigh place for you, just one last time, Frank?"

"Okay, boys, you gotta leave, take my saloon car. It's a long journey. Keep your phone lines open. I'll be in touch with you about the ambulance and uniforms."

Day 6   1

Skirvin Hotel, Oklahoma
The day after the night before.

Thursday
November 7

Somewhere, way back in his unconsciousness, John began to pick up his 'marimba' iPhone alarm signal repeating. It felt to him as if it was grabbing his collar and dragging him to the surface of the morning. Looking at his mobile screen, it was 7.30 a.m. He must have already fumbled the 'snooze' button several times, preventing himself from waking.

John found himself just staring at a blank ceiling, then, looking at the screen, he could see it was Kay; he picked up and instinctively just gave a short, monosyllabic answer.

"Hi."

In John's state of surfacing, he was in no way prepared for a conversation.

He knew Kay would have been up and breakfasted since 6 a.m. She was a person who, once awake, never returned to sleep.

"Hi, darling. I thought I'd just call. I know you're staying on in Oklahoma, but I just thought I'd make sure you're up and about. The kids were looking forward to seeing you tonight, but they know the score, you're working. How you doin' anyway? Somehow, we've just missed one another on phone calls.

"I guessed you've been trading every waking hour to get by and get that job done. I know how all-consuming these investigations can become for you in such a short time. Remember, you used to call these times away, how did you put it? *'It's like a deep dive'.*"

John found himself struggling to respond to what felt like an overwhelming wave of expectation; caught off guard, he started burbling.

"Oh! I'm only just about awake, Kay. Truth is, I just crashed on my bed early evening and disappeared. You know how it is when you wake, knowing you've not moved all night? I've had a long sleep though. When your call came in I was just staring at the ceiling thinking, I must get up."

Clawing his way into the spirit of the conversation, John sat up against his pillows.

"Hey! Yeah, Kay, I do so need to be home. I'm disappointed it's not today. But you know the reality, while I need to be back with you and the kids again, it just ain't possible. It's all a long story, darlin'. It's a story that hasn't finished yet. I can't take you through it right now, we both know the phone has its limitations. But, sometime soon, Kay, we will need time to talk together, one to one. But right now, I wouldn't really know where to start."

John asked a couple of questions, catch-up stories about the kids; but then Kay, precise in her listening as ever, brought him back to an earlier phrase.

"John, I seem to have heard those words you just used, just once before. How do they go now?"

"I don't know what you're talking about, darling."

"You know, John. The words were, '*We do need to talk sometime, one to one, Kay. But right now, I wouldn't know where to start?*' You and me, John. We are *all right,* aren't we?"

John immediately began to panic.

He quickly sat bolt upright. He realised that from his very first attempts at stringing a few words together, Kay had already sensed what was happening from the previous evening he'd spent with Kamama. John thought, *Shit! She has* read *me from a single phrase!*

John began to talk more quickly. "Look, Kay, I've just woken up. I've still gotten yesterday's clothes on. I can't talk right now. I need to shower… We're just going to have to leave this till I get back…"

There was silence on the phone.

Kay, however, was clearly listening to a much deeper, unspoken storyline; a story that had lived in a single phrase from a time long past. John felt a huge cloud of suffocating transparency descend on him; the result was more telephone silence, strung out with tension.

"Okay, John. Right now, I'll take that as a 'no' then, shall I? I'm understanding your silence is the answer to my question. John? It's a 'no', isn't it?"

John, gasping, remained paralysed in his ensuing silence.

"John? We're *not* all right, are we?!"

Then the phone went down at the other end.

Slowly, getting out of the clothes he'd worn from dining with Kamama, John showered, shaved and quickly ordered breakfast to his room.

Eventually, there was a knock on his door.

"*Room Service!*"

John went to the door feeling he'd been hit by a sledgehammer. Opening his door, he looked up and down a deserted corridor. Then, picking up the breakfast tray left on his doormat, he knew he had to bury what was happening in his own life; take breakfast and continue the race for a result on the Wohali Lightfoot case.

Day 6   2

Washington DC

Thursday
November 7

Phoenix and Charlotte arrived in their office within five minutes of one another.

Phoenix sat perched on the edge of Charlotte's desk. She was feeling a twinge of impatience as she waited for her team leader to arrive. The plan was to make progress on the Suzanne Woodman interview and take the next steps in remanding her, then building the case for her prosecution.

Charlotte eventually blew in through the office door; flustered, she looked around the office, then complained to Phoenix about traffic.

"Look, Phoenix. Okay. Sorry I'm late. Where's everyone else? Where's 'Mr Perfection' Colbeck, no sign of him yet then?"

On their arrival at the custody suite, Phoenix asked the officer for Suzanne Woodman to be brought to an interview room. They were shown to an empty room; as they waited, they checked out that the recording system was working; then tested the screen equipment, making sure the room services were functioning. Phoenix had asked Charlotte to show the Foggy Bottom CCTV images Esteban and Jeanie had demonstrated in the team briefing.

Time passed and they waited.

After a while Phoenix got up, walked out of the interview room, then, sensing something was adrift, she made her way into the corridor where detainees were held. She'd walked this corridor with its rows of cells on either side so many times over the years.

As Phoenix approached, she heard the custody officer shouting.

'Look, Doc, it's time we called this. We've gone well beyond time, there's no sign of life.'

'No, don't call it yet! Keep going with CPR! We've got to try a bit longer, get her back!'

Phoenix arrived at the cell door. She watched as the custody officer and the medical officer were desperately trying everything, they could *get her back*, sprawled on the floor. As Phoenix watched, she stood with both arms outstretched, her hands leaning into either side of the entrance of Suzanne Woodman's cell door.

"It's your call, Doc. But watching and listening, I'd say you are telling the custody officer here, who is not a doctor, it's not yet time to call it. If it *is* time and you've lost the battle though, call it!"

Phoenix slowly walked away, deflated. She knew that, for whatever reason, a big opportunity to bust open this investigation, had been snatched away from her.

She called back down the corridor.

"When you've finished, Sergeant, if you and the doctor there, would join me and Charlotte Linklater in the interview room, we'll both have a couple of questions."

Then talking directly to the medical officer, Phoenix asked for an immediate post-mortem and the clinical decision on cause of death to be published as a matter of urgency.

"Sure, we'll get right back to you, Ms Shultz. Right now, though, this looks like a drugs overdose; I'm pretty sure blood tests will confirm that and, of course, which drugs were used."

Five minutes later the custody officer and the medical officer came to join Phoenix and Charlotte.

"Thanks for joining us. We both know it's really hard for your team to lose a detainee. There'll be the inevitable investigation that will soon proceed and, your team will be on tenterhooks, feeling the pressures of corporate blame or maybe even disciplinary action. We know the score guys, but it ain't our discipline, as you both know."

"Yeah, thanks, Phoenix. First thing I want to show you is this envelope we found in Suzanne's cell; it has a black rose image on the front."

The custody officer passed Phoenix and Charlotte a tiny envelope about an inch, maybe an inch-and-a-half square. The officer gently passed a right-handed forensic glove to Phoenix: he then placed the envelope on Phoenix's palm.

"We'll get this tested for drugs and prints, but don't hold your breath for positive results."

"You're right in what you say, ma'am. Your understanding, it's appreciated. But we'll hope to learn lessons rather than be punished."

"Look, all we want to know right now is, has anyone else visited Suzanne this morning, then we'll leave. Do we have any CCTV record or footage?"

"We'll have CCTV footage of her visitor arriving in the corridor. We can all review the footage in Suzanne Woodman's cell in a moment. There are no blind spots in our cell coverage.

"First, I should say we completed our standard risk assessment. There were no signs of Suzanne being a suicide risk at all. There are full recordings of her making telephone contact with her attorney about attending her interview with yourselves today. She spoke to her family members, looking for their support and involvement. When your team come to review these calls, I know the record will show the detainee was upbeat, her mood was positive. She wasn't clinically depressed."

"Who visited then?"

The custody officer logged onto the interview-room screen.

"It was that team leader of yours, Phoenix… Jason Colbeck? He said you'd sent him."

Phoenix looked at Charlotte.

"Truth is, Sergeant, I didn't send him."

The custody officer leant back in his chair and threw out his arms and shrugged.

"But over the years, Phoenix, we've trusted Jason like he's one of our own team. He was always in and out of here."

Phoenix looked at Charlotte and nodded.

"I'd say it's pretty damn certain, Sergeant, he was the drugs 'delivery man'. After years as a 'sleeper' and a 'mole' in our organisation, Jason acted as a well-respected, consummate professional; it was him who got this drugs overdose done and dusted. I'd say he was sent to see her off before she was exposed to an interview with us. Can we look at the cell footage now? We should be able to spot the moment the drugs were passed over."

Before getting the footage on-screen, the custody officer went back to defending his team's practice. "She was throughly searched before coming into custody and she carried nothing in."

"Okay! Look, Sergeant, I'm not here in judgement of you. I'm sure the investigation will decide whether you searched Jason Colbeck by procedure before he went to see Suzanne. My guess is he wasn't, and your staff trusted good old Jason. I can't disguise it Sergeant, Suzanne Woodman was an incredibly important arrest as well as a potential part of our bringing others to justice."

"Let's review your cell footage."

Starting the footage off, the conversation in the cell was unremarkable. On the face of it, all Jason did was check that Woodman had been advised well and accessed her statutory rights. Had she used her three phone calls? He asked her if she had all she needed.

But then there was moment on parting when Jason and Woodman shook hands and momentarily remained with their hands held for a moment as they finished talking. Phoenix asked to slow the footage down through the handshake.

"We can't see it but that slightly longer handshake moment seems obviously to be the moment of the delivery of the small envelope, with the big, black rose message."

As the handshake ended Jason moved to the door, turned, then eyeballed and nodded to Woodman with a cold expression. Suzanne put her hands into her tunic pockets and listened to Jason's message.

'Okay, Suzanne, the 'boss' asked me to say he's hoping you 'sleep well' in here and sends his regards.'

Charlotte turned to Phoenix and the custody officer.

"Obviously, a crudely coded message. The 'boss' won't be Greg Tranter. Let us know the post-mortem result ASAP."

Phoenix went back to her office room with Charlotte.

She immediately tried to call Jason's phone. It went straight to answerphone. Then she dialled Jason's home number to speak with his wife, Patricia.

"Hi, Patricia, it's Phoenix Shultz here. I'm trying to locate Jason; his mobile is just going to answerphone. I need to speak with him urgently. Have you seen him?"

"Oh, hi, Phoenix. Yeah, he was just here, ten minutes ago. Came in, all of a hurry. Packed what he calls his 'away bag', for work trips; he left in a hurry. Said you'd asked him to travel urgently to support an investigation in Eugene, Oregon."

"Thanks, Patricia, I'll be back in touch sometime soon. I just can't reach him. If he calls you, can you call me and let me know please?"

"Sure thing, Phoenix."

Phoenix replaced her office receiver, stood up and kicked her chair over.

"Shit, Charlotte!! Jason's gone AWOL."

Day 6   3

The Soul Homestead
Oklahoma District

Thursday
November 7

The day before, John had put in a call to Chief of Police, Walter Banks. Setting up the work, they talked through what they needed to do, and the resources they required to follow up on Seth Soul and his sons.

In their phone call, John had asked Walter to take a member of their forensic team on board to collect the family's fingerprints and DNA at the homestead. This evidence would almost certainly become another vital reference point in eventually charging and convicting whichever of the Soul menfolk had been involved in the assassination of Wohali Lightfoot. Right now, even after extensive online national database searches, none of the prints and DNA from the Lincoln Memorial Undercroft or the retreat, provided a positive result.

In his mind, John still retained a basic working hypothesis from his very first interview with Cary Lightfoot; she was clear, her brothers did their father's dirty work. John's assumptions had been reinforced by the assault on the retreat; for him the likelihood was this was the work of the Soul brothers.

David O'Donnelly had made contact with his opposite number in Oklahoma, local senior examiner, Robert White in advance of travelling. They would both be examining the burnt-out Ford Raptor F-150. Together they would determine if this was the vehicle used at the retreat.

Having retained his hire car in the Skirvin Hotel car park, John drove to the airport and picked up David and Drake. Woya, Cary, Danuwoa and Ylva had already boarded and left for the safe house in DC; they were meeting Jim Coogan, who would settle them in and take a role of being their contact, formally reviewing how their stay was working for them.

By the time the three FBI colleagues cleared the airport arrivals lounge, it was past midday. John drove them immediately to the Oklahoma City Police HQ and the compound where the burnt-out Raptor was stored.

Chief Banks led the introductions from his staff side.

"Okay, David and Robert, we're gonna leave you here to do whatever witchcraft you have to do with that burnt-out wreck over there. Roxanne here, is Robert's right-hand woman on our forensic team. She's coming with us to the homestead, John, so we'd better get going."

"Oh! Walter, I didn't introduce Drake, he's our intern who's along for the ride."

All four of them crossed the yard and picked up their squad car. It was soon clear that they were going to be accompanied by four other officers following behind. Walter explained this was a contingency.

"If we should find Seth Soul and his sons and there's trouble, we're covered. Right?"

Making their way to the Soul family homestead, it was clear the early morning weather warnings of high winds were bearing fruit. As John peered out of his passenger door window, thick grey clouds scudded across the sky.

"Looks like rain, Walter."

"Yep, it's forecast, for sure. Probably, at the end of this afternoon; could be a November downpour. Let's hope we don't get stuck in mud up to our axles."

Nearing the end of their journey, the two squad cars made their way winding along a wooded, dry dirt road; Walter zigzagged the squad car as it pitched, rolled and avoided the worst tyre-track dips and troughs in the very uneven road. Eventually they arrived to within walking distance of a dilapidated wooden house and outbuildings.

John got out of the passenger side, he stretched and flexed his back. "You sure we're in the right place, Walter?"

"Yep, this is the right place. It's been a long twenty years or more since I've been here in person. Looks like everything has aged somewhat, including me, of course!"

The homestead seemed to be brooding; it wasn't in any way at peace; it was eerie. To John it felt the property was more like a shipwreck with a broken keel; the tides and active waves of time had long since gone out, leaving it exposed, high and dry on a beach, going nowhere, except to wrack and ruin.

Some of the wooden fascia boardings on the front of the house had been missing for some time, letting in rain and rot. There were four panes of glass on the veranda, they were either cracked or had fallen out. Looking through the missing panes, John saw there was a wooden door-frame, which was constructed around three filthy glass panes."

Walter asked his officers in the other squad car to stand by.

John looked across at Walter as he skirted round the perimeter of the house.

"Shall we separate and search? Drake and I, we'll take the outbuildings over there. I guess Roxanne could make a start collecting prints and DNA."

Surveying the outhouse buildings, John saw they were in equally poor repair; they had large gaps in the boarding, and, like the main house, some had missing wooden roof shingles.

He pulled one of the outhouse doors open and looking through the gloom of cobwebs, he saw shafts of light poking through the holes in the roof. They lit up slivers of carpenter's benches and old redundant bits of machinery.

John asked Drake to take the second outhouse.

After a while John stopped by to see how Drake was getting on. He saw that this outhouse had different machinery, this time it was for ploughing and sowing crops. John noted that the more expensive items like a tractor were nowhere to be seen. They'd probably been sold to make ends meet.

Drake was out of sight. He was searching for some smaller rooms at the back. He called out to John to come over and see what he'd found.

When John joined Drake, he'd found a small table, and a crude wooden chair sat beside a window. It was the only area not festooned by cobwebs. On the table, Drake pointed to a bunch of unplugged electrical equipment and headphones.

"Well, we already thought Seth Soul and his sons were the likely candidates for listening into the Lightfoots' property. Looks like there is electric power in this shed. I guess this provides us with the final piece of evidence on that."

Drake motioned to pick up the equipment.

"Oh, Drake, before you touch any of it, get Roxanne over to photograph all this and take prints please? After she's done that, she'll formally bag up the equipment and reference it. Be great if you'd secure it in the boot of our squad car and we'll eventually get David O'Donnelly to take it back to our storage for further investigation."

John made his way across the yard back to the main house. A couple of scrawny chickens scuttled and scratched around the yard underfoot; they were expecting a feed of grain, but there was no chance. On the veranda a wasted hound was lying down low, growling and watching with eyes that moved inside his stationary head.

As John approached the house, he saw Walter and Roxanne hadn't entered and were still looking through household rubbish that had been thrown out of a side door. John diverted Roxanne to go over and find Drake and help with the listening equipment.

Standing beside John on the veranda, Chief Banks hammered on the door and boomed:

"Hello, anyone at home?"

The broken silence echoed, but the rooms inside soon settled back to their spooky quiet; the skeletal hound shuffled away to find another, quieter vantage point from which to observe.

"Well, I don't know what the last two officers did to rouse anyone. But we're gonna give this place a real good rattle and a shake. This time we've got the warrant, so let's get on with this. We've gotta find out if anyone is in here, dead or alive."

Roxanne and Drake rejoined the search party and waited at the foot of the homestead steps until the door was opened.

Then, Walter looked to John and nodded to try the door. He turned the handle and, as he pushed, it creaked open. There was no need for the drama of splintering or smashing a forced entry.

"Hello! Seth Soul! Sal? Anyone at home?"

There was no answer. The four of them entered. John was beginning to feel creeped out.

Slowly, they made their way methodically through the ground-floor area.

Roxanne immediately busied herself with finding prints on surfaces and potential sources of DNA from unwashed kitchen utensils. Later, she planned to scour the upstairs bathroom and bedrooms for toothbrushes, hairbrushes and anything else she could find.

The lounge was furnished with rough, outdated wooden furniture. A large wooden, home-carpentered table still stood sturdy, with trestles to match. It wasn't hard for John to imagine that this furniture was made from the time when the family was setting sail into the future.

Running his fingers across the dusty table surface, John could imagine the sounds of a family long since flown. He visualised, maybe the young girl, Cary, or one of her brothers shouting into the kitchen demanding another helping of dinner.

Dusting off his hands, John felt the images recede until the cold hard reality of this beached and broken era came back into view.

The kitchen stank.

Fumes of several different kinds of archaeological layers of rotten food and dirty water rose from the sink. Some plates and cooking pots were just so encrusted they had ceased smelling at all; flies still buzzed lazily around the paltry remains of a last unfinished meal on the table.

John looked at Drake and shook his head. He called out. His voice, like Walter's, died away throughout the house. He called again.

"Hello! Seth Soul! Sal! Anyone at home?"

Walter nodded and pointed toward a sizeable gun cabinet; its door was unlocked. It had been left, swinging open; Walter sucked in air and gently whistled through his teeth.

"Looks like someone coulda left in a hurry, all that armoury that was in there, is out there right now, in service. So, assessing risk, we gotta take that empty cabinet into account over the next couple of days."

The cabinet showed there was space for four, maybe even five significant weapons. Walter looked at Drake and pointed to the open ammunition drawer hanging out of the base of the cabinet.

Drake looked back at Walter, examining the cabinet himself.

"Yep, looks like those weapons are out there somewhere! When I was a kid, in my family, our gun cabinet was the securest place in the whole house. This one? Well, it's a disgrace."

John suggested Drake went back outside to scout around the surrounding land of the homestead, see what else he could find out.

So, with some trepidation, John began to make his way upstairs followed by the chief.

Instinctively, he had drawn his handgun. There were four bedrooms and a bathroom. He and Walter both silently signalled to one another and took two bedrooms each, either side of the landing at the top staircase. Roxanne followed the men and located the upstairs bathroom to see what she could find to take DNA swabs from.

Opening his first bedroom, the chief jumped out of his skin as a crow, who had taken up residence, screeched and flapped toward him. Then, after Walter had furiously waved his arms in defence and shouted, the crow quickly left through a broken windowpane.

Scanning the room, Walter was clear, no one had lived or slept in this room for years. In the corner there was a makeshift tiny toy crib covered in dust and cobwebs. The face of an old-fashioned ceramic baby doll, with just one remaining eye, peered through the wooden bars.

Walter whispered to himself, "*I guess this had to have been Cary's room, then.*"

John eventually came to his last door.

Opening the door, he poked his head around the corner. He saw a large wooden bed covered with a beautiful, multicoloured, hand-sewn patchwork quilt. It was illuminated by a stripe of mid-afternoon sunlight. It struck John that perhaps this one item was undoubtedly made from Sal Soul's skilful female hand. Out of the whole dilapidated state of the homestead, this was the one remaining living jewel.

As John approached the head of the bed, he was suddenly shocked to find an elderly woman, still warm. As John bent forward, he heard her breathing very shallowly. Her head rested on a grubby pillow, turned grey for the want of a wash. A half-filled jug of water stood on a bedside cabinet next to a dirty glass. A plate of half eaten food on the floor suggested that someone might be visiting.

John realised this was Sal Soul, seemingly abandoned. He looked around the bedroom. There were no signs that any other person was coming in, other than the plate on the floor. Sal looked seriously malnourished; her skin was stretched like thin parchment over the features of her face, which had become wizened and birdlike, with sucked-in cheeks and a protruding nose. John gently reached out and swept away her wispy silver-grey hair from her face. He felt the woman's body warmth, then slowly, very gently, rocked her shoulder and found himself whispering:

"Mrs Soul, can you hear me?"

There was no response except the continuous sound of shallow breathing.

John stepped away from the bed, then bellowed out loudly to Walter searching his second bedroom down the landing.

"Walter, I think I've found Sal Soul!"

As Walter arrived in the bedroom, John was feeling for a pulse in her neck.

"Her pulse is very faint, but it's there! Walter, we'll need an emergency ambulance and paramedics. Could the officers in the squad car outside call them in right now and get Sal checked out? Surely, she's going to need to get medical help and away from this toxic place."

Walter was shocked.

"Good God Almighty, John. That must be Sal Soul, right there. Did I tell you I knew her way back? She ain't waking, is she? There's no sign of the boys or old man Soul anywhere. I can't believe that Sal's family have just left her like this!"

"Yeah, Sal could have died. She still could."

Walter radioed down and asked his other officers to call in an ambulance and paramedics urgently.

"You okay, John? You're looking a little spooked right there."

"Yeah, Walter, I'm okay. I'm just thinking what kind of scum these Soul men are to leave Sal here in these conditions. I know from interviewing Cary; this woman made a home here for her husband and her children for years. She's loyally stuck by them to the end.

"Believe me, Walter, the way of life for Sal was controlled by Seth Soul and his 'boys'. She was little more than a slave with little or nothing to talk about; she was never even allowed to smile and see and hold her grandson, Danuwoa."

After a while the yard and the house suddenly came alive as the twenty-first century burst onto the scene. First, there was the siren of an arriving ambulance; then a paramedic and a doctor were soon thudding up the staircase taking a stretcher with them. They quickly took charge of assessing and establishing Sal Soul's medical needs.

The chief and John went out in the yard and waited; Drake ambled back across the yard to stand with them.

"Nothing else to report, John. Just more of the same. This homestead went to seed a long time ago. The only functioning equipment seems to have been the listening gear. Maybe that's all they've done lately, prepare for the assassination of Wohali Lightfoot?"

Slowly but surely, Sal Soul was brought downstairs, secured safely on a stretcher. John walked toward the ambulance so he could see Sal's face one last time before they left to admit her to hospital.

John asked the paramedics to write down Cary Lightfoot's name as the next of kin.

"Can you ask the hospital to use this number and speak with Phoenix Shultz, my deputy please? She will be able to put your medical staff in contact with Cary, this woman's daughter. She's living in a safe house in DC from today. I will also contact Cary by phone myself later on this evening. She'll want to know what's happening to her mother."

As the ambulance started up, the siren sounded briefly before being switched off. They drove down the dirt road with clouds of dust billowing behind them.

Chief Banks quickly instructed the second squad car to leave and pick up any new general incoming calls and responses required, on their way back to the city. Then, phoning back to the office, Walter asked his backup services to attend the scene.

"Listen, I need them to secure this property, check for vermin. We've got the forensic evidence we need. Get a group of cleaners into the filthy kitchen and remove the animals for veterinary attention to decide about their welfare."

The rain had held off in favour of cloud and sunshine. However, they'd drawn a blank on the Soul men again. Walter, John, Drake and Roxanne made their way back to the city police headquarters. Arriving, John immediately went round to the compound and found Robert White and David, still working.

"Well, what have you two been up to? More importantly, what have you found?"

David climbed out of the service pit underneath the Raptor and, nodding at John, took a spirit-soaked rag to clean his hands.

"Well, John. The serial number of this vehicle tells us it was one of the first F-150's to come off the assembly line in 2010. It's had a long life. We're agreed here that this vehicle was deliberately burnt out with a suitable accelerant, basically gasoline. Probably had to be stoked more than once to achieve this level of total destruction. There's huge paint damage as you can see, and all the soft interior has been burnt to cinders. Windows and windscreen have cracked due to the very high temperatures, and tyres, of course, have blown, burnt and melted away. So, the destruction is pretty global.

"Truth is, John; Robert and I haven't found any evidence of prints or DNA to link this to the events at the retreat."

However, David smiled at John. Reaching to a shelf behind him, he showed John a small plastic tray with two small, blackened metal cylinders three inches long and an inch in diameter.

"These two little metal cylinders have miraculously survived the fire in the glove compartment. The key piece of science here is that paper and other materials in the compartment burnt in such a way that they created a sooty layer on the surface of these cylinders. In forensic science, we've known for a while now that prints on the surface of metal surviving fire like this can be protected by soot and lifted.

"Robert and I are going to deliver procedural tests on these cylinders this afternoon in his lab. If we can, we'll get prints and also see if anything is surviving inside them."

"Okay, sounds exciting, David. Was it worth the trip then? Is it still possible this is the vehicle they used?"

Both forensic examiners nodded.

"Well, guys. Worth knowing Roxanne here just took a whole body of evidence from the homestead today. First of all, she has a collection of prints from the whole family. You name it, she's swabbed and collected it; she's collected the comparators for your cylinders; I got to tell you guys; we really need a big breakthrough on this case."

John spoke directly to Robert.

"David here, he'll tell you what it's like having our director breathing down your neck."

"Well, John, Walter here can get testy if he needs results and we're short of resources."

Looking at his watch, John saw was 4.21 p.m. John left the compound to find a quiet space to put in a call to Phoenix. He needed to hear whether Woya, Cary, Danuwoa and Ylva had met Jim Coogan.

Day 6   4

Washington DC

Thursday
November 7

It was 5.21 p.m. and Phoenix was sitting in John's room at Pennsylvania Avenue. She'd just finished leading a whole afternoon session with all her investigators round the electronic evidence board. They'd reviewed where they had come to date. Then, they had tried to think creatively about new risks and ways to press for more leads. As they worked methodically, they'd been listing all the different ways they could move forward.

As they had worked, Phoenix had looked up briefly to the back of the breakout room. She was surprised to see Anna McKenna putting in an appearance. She sat stock still, quietly listening.

Early in the meeting process, Jim Coogan had raised his own individual concerns and contribution. He talked about the well-trailed, International Festival of the Earth event, at the Capital One Arena, the evening of November 8. Jim's theory was that this event could easily be the focus for another assassination. The room quietened. Phoenix found herself listening closely.

"Fact of the matter is, there's no reason at all why we shouldn't be practically assessing the risks across the whole Oklahoma/Washington DC geographical axis. For example, on the evening of November 8, Indira Anand and the special presidential envoy for the climate are still insisting on hosting a live event; it's advertised online, aiming to compensate all their supporters after the interruption of Wohali Lightfoot's assassination.

"If I was on the 'conspiracy' team I'd be thinking, '*What can I do to really set the 'Festival' back a long way?*' The answer for me would be to place and hide a powerful, silenced, long-range rifle for a 'clean shooter' to locate after entering the Capital One Arena turnstile. Then, if he or she could take down one, if not both these most senior leaders on climate change, wouldn't that be one hell of a victory?"

Phoenix had praised Jim's creative thinking.

"Jim, I gotta thank you for that. That's just the kind of lateral thinking we need in these sessions. Can't think why we haven't tied this one down. My view is one of us needs to speak directly with CEO, Indira Anand at the special envoys office and the Capital One Arena, and to assess the risk. If it's a high enough risk, we could apply to shut it down."

Phoenix looked at her watch, then looked again to the back of the breakout room, just in time to see the back of the director quickly disappearing.

"So, it's 2.30 p.m. now, Jim. I need you to leave the meeting, then get right onto scoping that scenario. Then, bring back your outcomes by the end of the afternoon."

Back in her office, Phoenix's quiet reflection on the afternoon were interrupted by Charlotte knocking to come in. She leant back in her chair and gestured for Charlotte to come in and sit down.

"Hi, Charlotte. What you got for me?"

"It's about Drake, Phoenix. I'm updating you on my team's results. We've followed up, trying to identify the man with Drake in Jim's photographs. So far, we've drawn a blank."

"Okay. So, what else you got? There must be more than that; time is coming when we need some good news, Charlotte."

"Well, it's clear Drake has not told you the truth about who he was meeting that Sunday in the DC restaurant. He told you this guy was his father, James T Collins. Drake said his father is a retired cop from West Virginia. Well, he isn't! We've looked him up in the local force records. James T Collins was dismissed from the force after an investigation found him to have proven corrupt links with local organised crime; a disciplinary panel dismissed him. Looks like it was a big drugs story. Lastly, here's James T Collins's photograph Charlotte placed a printed picture of James T Collins in front of Phoenix.

"So, like father, like son with the ginger hair, eh?"

Charlotte pointed to Jim's photograph from the restaurant.

"But this man. We still don't know who he is!"

Phoenix, looking thoughtful, asked a couple of questions.

"Hmm. Drake said in his interview that the anonymous caller told him he would have to pay the 'debt' of his father's sins. That's right, isn't it? And, in my meeting with him, he voted to come over to our side? Seems to me though, we know Drake is still living in fear and being manipulated by this guy in the resturant. He's telling us they've got him over a barrel, and he can't trust us to hear the truth."

Charlotte looked at Phoenix and frowned.

"That's very generous, Phoenix. You're perfectly within your rights to say he's lied; he's fucked us over and you're going to have to move with HR to instant dismissal."

"It's for John to really bottom this out, one to one, direct with Drake. If Drake is going to work with us, he has to come clean! He must give us the name of the guy in the restaurant and all the details. It's ultimately my decision, Charlotte. John will sort out the practicalities in Oklahoma; don't worry John will bottom this out!

"Okay, Charlotte, leave this with me. I'm expecting a call from John to catch up."

5

No sooner had Charlotte left Phoenix's office than Jim Coogan arrived.

"Okay, come one, come all! Jim, make it quick, I'm trying to get home to see Trent; I still haven't spoken to John yet. Who knows, I might get home by 8 p.m."

Jim explained to Phoenix he had phoned through to the office of the special presidential envoy on the climate and spoken to the envoy's closest advisor. Jim had made it clear on behalf of the FBI he was very concerned about security at the Capital One Arena event. The advisor went on to ask Jim some basic questions.

Jim immediately knew from the way she rattled through his questions; it was as if she had been through it all a million times.

"Okay, Jim, I know the envoy will ask some basic questions himself and he'll want answers.

"Are you okay with that?"

"Yeah, that's fine."

"So, what is the detailed intelligence that informs the high risks you have assessed and are who is advising us about?"

"Well, there is no new intelligence as such. The main problem is the Capital One Arena event is a rerun of the Memorial 'Festival' event where, let's not forget, there was a brutal assassination on November 2."

"The envoy himself will never forget it. He saw the assassination from the Memorial platform. He was set to make his speech, just before the shots were fired. What security measures have been taken to mitigate this risk at the Capital One Arena?"

Jim explained that, given the circumstances, the special envoy could mitigate the risk by cancelling. The advisor to the envoy had been very straightforward in his questioning.

"Sounds to me, from my experience, though, Mr Coogan, you don't have *actual* intelligence, neither do you have a tip-off. Am I right?"

Phoenix then asked Jim how he'd replied.

"Well, I explained we had no active intelligence of an imminent threat. However, we were doing all we could to ensure that if the event took place, it would be safe."

Phoenix nodded and smiled.

"Jim, they're going ahead, aren't they?"

Not to be beaten, Jim went on to explain to Phoenix he'd contacted Indira Anand. Jim had described the very same potential risks and the clear logic to shut down the event. Anand had simply explained the event would go ahead.

"Indira Anand was very straight with me. Jim read from his notes, '*Look, Mr Coogan, I haven't heard anything from the special envoy's office yet. But I can tell you, if we cancelled all our events on the basis of some crackpot people who want to assassinate or threaten us, we'd never get our job done.*'

Phoenix thanked Jim for the work he had done, then cut to the chase. "Look, Jim, you've made sure that they have heard our concerns. Seems to me they are going forward. My decision, Jim, is that we've taken responsibility for our concerns and they're going ahead. Just make sure you work with the Arena management to search the Capital One Arena in advance and get that security beefed up on the night.

"Let's leave it there, I have to call John now."

6

Phoenix put a call in to John knowing he would almost certainly still be at the Oklahoma City Police HQ.

"Hi, John, it's been a long day, let's try to keep this short and to the point."

"Hi, Phoenix, you go first."

"Okay. Well, it's hard to know where to start. I am going to leave Drake till last."

Phoenix worked through her list from the death of Suzanne Woodman, Jason Colbeck's involvement, and finally him having gone AWOL; then she came to the news on Drake and the need for John to establish if he was working with them as intern inside the FBI or not.

"Bottom line on Drake is you've got to get the name of the guy in the restaurant out of him. One thing we definitely do know is he is not Drake's father. The good news though, John, is that Isaac and the Lightfoot family will now be safe and secure."

John audibly flinched.

"First things first then. My preference is I interview Drake together with Walter. We all worked well today, and I think Walter has something in his personality to bring pressure to bear on Drake. Walter is straight down the line."

John heavily edited his own day. He and Walter hadn't

located Seth Soul and his sons. The homestead was a rubbish tip; Sal Soul was in hospital and Cary Lightfoot had been informed so she could connect with the hospital's clinical services.

On forensic evidence, there was only an outside chance the Ford Raptor F-150 was the one used in the assault on the retreat. David O'Donnelly had been brilliant on the science. A full set of prints and DNA had been collected at the homestead and the listening equipment connecting to Isaac's property had been found and bagged. David would certainly test the listening equipment in connection with Isaac's place.

"Oh! And the other headline is my marriage could be on the skids, but I don't want to talk about it."

Day 6   7

University of Oklahoma
Norman, Cleveland County

Thursday
November 7

Since the days of the investigation in the Smoky Mountains, Kamama had returned to working at her university department. She had to admit to herself she was missing both the investigation and also missing John Green.

Kamama's long-time working habit was to remain in the office, often when everyone else had left. She liked the feeling of the calm at the end of the day, the absence of pressure. No telephones and, just sometimes, looking out of her office window, watching the twilight set in until the curtain of darkness suddenly descended.

Kamama hadn't heard from John since the investigation in the Smoky Mountains had ended. So, she decided to take it upon herself to call him, feeling at the back of her mind that he may never take the initiative and call her.

She took out her mobile and rang his number. John picked up, not realising it was Kamama's number calling. They spoke for ten minutes, catching up on the day-to-day.

"So, Kamama, where are you calling from? You must have left the office and be back home by now."

"No. I'm in the quiet of my own department, catching up on emails. Don't worry, I'll be leaving when I'm done talking to you."

At first, John chose not to say where he was, but eventually he thought better of maintaining a meaningless secrecy.

"Well, I did say to you, things could change in my life. I think I told you, stuff happens, sometime Kay knows something's not right; she's so perceptive, picked it up from something I said that reminded her of our early days when I had an affair years ago. If you look through your email list, she's probably contacted you."

"I'm sorry to hear that, John. I have read Kays's email. I liked her style. She's a woman who knows her own mind and speaks it."

John quickly interjected.

"No! Don't be sorry. I'm sure we'll meet up again soon."

"Look, it's time I went home, John. We'll catch up another time. Maybe I'll come to the Skirvin Hotel, or maybe we could do something else other than the hotel restaurant? How about that?"

"Yeah! That would be great! You'll know the best places. Let's make a date to do that."

"Okay, John, we will."

Kamama closed the call down and packed her briefcase. She loaded it with all her commitments, research papers and her laptop so she could go on working at home. Making her way into the university car park, she was felt worn down and needed to rest. Kamama looked fondly across at her solitary RV just standing under a well-lit area of the car park, just waiting to take her home.

As she went to unlock the driver's door, she felt someone grab her from behind. Then a sharp needle injection into her thigh. Kamama felt her grip on her briefcase slip; suddenly, her sense of smell was consumed by the overwhelming smell of a leather glove held over her nose and keeping her mouth closed.

A couple of moments later and Kamama was still pinned and struggling against the door of her RV. Her assailant's arms were held tightly around her waist. The gloved hand was still clasped over her mouth, allowing her to breathe through her nose.

In the darkness she heard the unmistakable sound of a man clearing his throat, then spitting the loosened phlegm, which smacked onto the tarmac at their feet.

"Keep still, bitch! You're all on your own; we've got plans for you."

She could hear her nose exhaling air fast and felt herself physically weakening. Then, hearing the sound of a deep-throated engine pull up behind, she panicked, hearing the sound of a car boot opening. Kamama struggled as hard as she could, trying to stamp and kick back at the man holding her captive; she felt a warm weakness surging through her body as it slipped down onto the tarmac.

Just before losing consciousness, Kamama felt her mouth being taped; her hands were secured behind her back and her feet were taped together. Finally, with no control, she felt herself being lifted and rolled into the car boot.

Then the lights went out...

Day 7 — 1

Oklahoma Hospital

Friday
November 8

> 'They erected certain Gibbets, large, but low made, so that their feet almost reacht the ground, every one of which was so order'd as to bear Thirteen Persons in Honour and Reverence (as they said blasphemously) of the Redeemer and his Twelve Apostles, under which they made Fire to burn them to Ashes, whilst hanging on them:'

(Author's Note: Just one of Christopher Columbus and his Spanish Cavaliers' treatments of the original peoples of Hispaniola from 1493)[48]

A Brief Account of the Destruction of the Indies by Bartolome De Las Casas. First published, 1552 printed by, Sebastian Trugillo at the port of Seville, Spain. The Project Gutenberg Ebook (giving access at no cost under the Project Gutenberg Licence). The original archaic spelling and punctuation has been retained.

Isaac was a light sleeper in his own home, let alone in a hospital room. He was woken in the early hours by what sounded like a scuffle outside his room. Listening out, and more or less awake, all he then heard was silence and he put his head back down, telling himself to go back to sleep. He told himself, '*Isaac, this is strange place. Maybe it's a cleaner, a wheelchair or a patient going by on a trolley.*'

He was fortunate to get back to sleep.

Sometime later, being woken again, Isaac saw that two male nurses had entered his room, dressed in hospital fatigues. One stood at the foot of his bed and the other was standing beside him. As he surfaced fully from his sleep Isaac noticed they had lanyards swinging from their necks with their photographs smiling out of them.

"Good day, Mr Lightfoot. Your schedule for further tests has been changed this morning and brought forward. We need to take you down to the stem-cell clinic for a test that needs to be done before you eat and partake of breakfast. We apologise for the inconvenience. Unfortunately, this wasn't explained to you yesterday."

The nurse at the bottom of the bed pushed round a wheelchair while together they went to help Isaac to make the transition from the bed. Sweeping his arm in front of his helpers, Isaac insisted on making his own way to the wheelchair.

"Okay, guys, stand aside, I ain't some invalid. I don't need your help to get out of bed!"

"This should be quick and easy, Mr Lightfoot. Very soon you'll be back here having breakfast."

As they left the room Isaac saw that the two security men were seated, slumped in position either side of the door. They seemed to be dozing, and Isaac thought no more of it.

Arriving at the elevator, one of the men pushed the button to go down to the ground. Arriving at zero, the elevator doors opened, revealing the early morning hubbub of a busy hospital reception. Isaac's wheelchair was quickly pushed past reception and the people waiting, then across to the entrance. They quickly took him outside and into a waiting ambulance, via its hydraulic lift.

"Hey, you guys! What's going on here? Why am I travelling by ambulance?"

"The department you need is a bit further than we can manage by simply pushing you all the way."

Isaac's wheels were locked into place, securing the chair. The back door was locked just before the ambulance pulled away.

Day 7 — 2

Oklahoma

Friday
November 8

John, Drake and David O'Donnelly were having breakfast at the Skirvin Hotel. They were discussing the results in the search for Seth Soul and his boys and the forensic results from the burnt-out Raptor. David announced their hopes that the metal cylinders would reveal prints identifying members of the Soul family, had not been born out by examining the comparators from the homestead; neither had there been any results through the national databases.

John began to feel the only small gain so far was that they'd found Sal Soul alive. At least she was getting the medical care she needed.

David reminded John how important processes of elimination were.

"I don't need to tell you this, John. But at least we know the real Raptor we took tyre prints from is still out there, in use."

The three men discussed their plan for the day.

First item they agreed was that David would return to DC. As always, his breadth of knowledge and skill had been invaluable.

So, the plan was for John and Drake to return to Oklahoma

Police HQ and continue the joint working with Walter Banks in their search for Seth and his sons!

John informed Drake he needed to have a short three-way meeting with Walter. John lied about the purpose of the meeting, telling Drake it was to decide what action was needed to protect his father back in West Virginia.

Drake nodded.

3

Arriving at Oklahoma Police HQ, John and Drake made a beeline for Chief Banks's office.

"Hi, John, good to see you."

"Hi, Walter. Before we do anything else, can we take five, to meet with you? Just the three of us. Won't take long."

Walter nodded. "Okay. But it's gotta be quick, there's been two major events overnight. I've already briefed Phoenix Shultz, your acting executive lead. Right now, you're not sighted okay?"

Walter then shut his door, sat down and looked between John and Drake to find out who was going to make a start.

"Okay. What's this about then?"

"So, the issue you and I have here, Walter, is that we're still trying to find the identity of that guy Drake met in a DC restaurant last Sunday. You'll remember we sent you some photographs?"

Drake turned in his chair to face John as he spoke. John continued speaking directly to Walter while maintaining his gaze directly at Drake, eyeball to eyeball.

"Thing is, Walter, Drake here told Phoenix back in DC that the guy in those photographs I sent you was his father, James T Collins, a retired cop from West Virginia. Our team in DC has established Drake is lying. James T Collins was dismissed from the force for proven links to organised crime. Now, one of my team leaders has sent a mug shot by email this morning of Drake's father, James T Collins."

John shared the photographic image with Walter, then with Drake.

"Look, you compare them; this photograph of James T Collins isn't the same man with Drake in the restaurant, amongst other features, the hair colour is a giveaway."

Walter leant back in his chair, comparing the photographs. He swung his chair slowly from side to side, looking between Drake and John.

"So, Drake, you've been lyin' then?"

John nodded slowly.

He arranged the two photographs on his phone screen side by side; he handed his phone to Drake. John continued looking at Drake with an intense gaze, then led out with a crushingly simple question:

"So, Drake. We have got urgent business to get on with here. Phoenix said to you back in DC, you're either with us, or your gonna be gone! If you don't tell us right now who you've been meeting with, I'll put you on a charge for wasting my time and put you in custody. Then, Walter and I will get to work while you remain in a cell here. For the last time, who is this guy you're meeting in DC?"

Walter looked at Drake, then at his wristwatch.

"Look here, young man, we've got to get on! There are people out there at risk today! Who *is* this guy? Where does he live? What's he got on you?"

Drake looked back at Walter.

"He's Frank Denman. He's a retired mining man living in Thurmond, West Virginia. Somehow, and I don't know how, he's been given the control that organised crime had over my father; now Denman is controlling me!"

As Drake spoke, Walter was looking up the name online; first on the police record, then on the internet.

"Well, this Denman guy, he ain't got a police record. On the internet he's only known mainly as a mining man with a great reputation. His last job was CEO at 'Natural Coal', West Virginia. He reluctantly led the closure there; says here, he was seen in the community as a very fair man. One thing you're right about is, he's retired now.

"His history says he's been in the mining business all his life. I'd say if miners say he was fair as a CEO, he definitely earnt that respect the hard way. There's a news article online here about the Springfield Mine disaster. There's a photograph of a young sixteen-year-old Frank Denman, leading the men back to work. Something pretty big must have happened to make a radical change to this man, Frank Denman."

Drake looked urgently back to John.

"Look, John, nothing's changed. I am still with you and the FBI! I'm not working for Frank Denman; he's got me down as a childhood champion marksman who they can control for an event in the future. I've lied to Denman just trying to protect my parents. Honest, I'll wear a wire, John. I'll do whatever you want."

After a short heavy silence John stood up and went to Walter's window, standing with his back to Drake.

"Okay, Drake, I'm gonna ask Walter what he thinks."

Walter, swung in his chair and looked back at John.

"Listen, John, we don't need no snake in the grass involved in this operation. Not today of all days. If you think he's genuine about staying with us, it's your call; this is your parade, right? Drake is your responsibility, not mine; it's on your own head."

John continued looking out of the window. Then he suddenly turned and grabbed Drake's jacket and pulled him face to face.

"Okay, Drake, listen to me! I remember now. Right after Wohali Lightfoot was assassinated, I returned to the office. You were outside on the pavement, pleading with someone. *What happens then?* you said. Was that Denman on the phone?

Denman, he's imported you into my fucking service. Well? Hasn't he?"

"Yeah! But I didn't know until that moment when he phoned me. I thought the FBI had just genuinely accepted my application. Honestly, I didn't know until then. I'm sorry! I know it looks like I haven't been straight. I didn't know what to do! I've been trying to work it out for myself, John. What I told Phoenix was true. I'm with you, one hundred per cent! I'm my mother's son, I'm here working for justice with you guys. I want a career!"

John looked at Walter, then out of the window while he thought.

"Okay. You're in! But just one step out of place, Drake, I'll have you on a charge. You'll be working close beside me, where I can see you, right?"

John turned to Walter.

"I've just gotta make a call…

"Hi, Phoenix. This has to be quick; I can't stop. Just had that conversation with Drake we talked about. The name of the guy in the resturant is Frank Denman, you got that? Lives in Thurmond, West Virginia. He has daughters living in California. I want you or Charlotte to organise a joint squad of Charlotte, operating for us with the Beckley City Police and forensic support. They're a city force just a few miles from Thurmond where Denman lives.

"This guy, Denman, must be found, right now! They've gotta get a warrant to search his property. Charlotte and the Beckley force, they've got to get Denman into custody and question him. Let's get this straight, Phoenix, Denman's property must be pulled apart room by room. No stone left unturned. You understand? If he ain't there, of course, you'll break down the door and search."

"Got that, John. This will be tomorrow now. Either me or Charlotte have got to book a flight, organise accommodation, you know the score. What do we know about Thurmond?"

"Walter says Thurmond is a coal industry ghost town.

Just three people living there… that's a fact. Local police must know this guy Denman, he was CEO in Natural Coal before it went down. Listen. I want you to sort this now, Phoenix. Not tomorrow! Right now! You are still my Deputy as I speak to you today, Phoenix, okay?

"I want Charlotte on the ground in Beckley ASAP; I don't want your attention on this to slip today! Charlotte's gotta leave as soon as Dina has booked the flight; hell, Charlotte can find herself a hotel room somewhere on arrival."

John briefly stopped talking, thinking more carefully.

"Okay. I'm gonna say given the doubts you raised about Anna McKenna's role in placing Drake with Jason, I want you and Charlotte to maintain silence; for now. I don't want Anna McKenna knowing anything about this, Phoenix; just a precaution, I'm not accusing her of anything; but we don't want to get there and find that Denman has been tipped off and 'flown.'"

4

Walter eased himself out of his chair. "Okay, can we move on?"

John pocketed his phone and sat down.

"First, John, we've had a report from the University of Oklahoma campus at Norman. Professor Kamama Catawnee is missing. Her RV never left the car park overnight. Her briefcase was found standing beside her drivers' door.

"So, question here is, what's happening? My thoughts are, we're looking at an abduction. The RV, the briefcase and the surrounding parking lot are secured as a crime scene; as far as we can see, there are no additional prints around the door to the RV other than the one set we assume belong to Professor Catawnee.

"Given what else has been reported, I'm even more confident about that hypothesis that this is abduction.

"So, second event reported is, Isaac Lightfoot has likely been abducted from his hospital bed this morning. Witnesses report they saw him wheeled into an ambulance by two men in hospital fatigues and wearing lanyards. The other news on this, John, is your security guards were found dead in their chairs on either side of Isaac's door. Looks like they were both simultaneously restrained and stabbed with stiletto blades to the heart. Ray Chan, your security lead in the city, reported on this.

"I've appointed one of our best team sergeants as the incident commander. Our police officers, Robert White and his forensic team will cover the ground, interview any other witnesses et cetera.

"So, let's agree these two events are coordinated."

Walter went on to explain that a police helicopter team had begun the wider search for the ambulance carrying Isaac.

"I think we must assume another vehicle is carrying Professor Catawnee. It's possible we'll find two vehicles are travelling in convoy to the same destination. I'll also concede, John, it's possible by the time we find them they'll be dead."

Walter looked at John.

"Sorry to ask you this, John. Are you okay? You are looking a little pallid in complexion."

"I'm fine, Walter, I've spent a lot of time with both these individuals lately."

"Okay! Just as long as we understand one another, wherever they're headed, none of it sounds good."

"So, what do we do, Walter? I am out of my area but, you and me, we're gonna jointly lead this operation together, right?"

"You ain't going to like this, John! I'd say, we initially need to show patience. We need to wait and hope we get a call from the 'copter team, after they break cover. We were notified around 8 a.m. by Ray Chan at the hospital; the 'copter team went up fifteen minutes after.

"Waiting is hard, John."

"My deputy, Phoenix, had a theory about the 'conspiracy' kicking off in DC and here, at the same time. Now it looks like it's actually happening. Our thoughts are they are looking to deliver a huge blow to the International Festival of the Earth, decapitating the leadership team, all on the same day."

"Could be, John. One thing is for certain, they almost certainly mean their victims actual harm and suffering; as far as we know, they've kept them both alive."

"Okay, I'll catch up with Phoenix again; find out what's happening about the Capital Arena in DC. Tomorrow night, the special envoy for the climate and the CEO of the 'Festival' are leading the arena event."

5

As time passed, Walter walked through the office to where John and Drake were sitting.

"How's things going down at the Capital Arena?"

"Looks like Phoenix has the situation under control. The arena has been searched; no hidden or placed weapons have been found. The 'Festival' CEO and the special envoy insist it's going ahead; we've arranged enhanced security on entrances and inside the Capital One Arena our own officers will work alongside the Capital Arena staff."

Walter's PA interrupted them; the message they'd been waiting for had come in from the helicopter crew.

"They're saying it's taken them time to emerge on the road; looks like they're headed, in an ambulance and a saloon car, toward Lehigh on State Highway Three. If they're headed all the way to Lehigh itself, it'll take them about an hour. I gotta get my squad of officers together and you and I, John, we'll need to brief officers and get on the road."

Walter put out a call for everyone to meet in their large briefing room.

"Be glad, John, if you'd kick off the briefing, tell our officers what you think we're dealing with."

Soon, John was summarising the story from the Lincoln Memorial to the two abductions.

He finished with a warning:

"You men and women, you need to be fully prepared and tooled up for combat. This mission today will almost certainly involve imposing physical controls, making arrests and bringing people in. We definitely want Seth Soul, and his sons brought into custody alive; there are aspects of this FBI investigation which indicate that we could be coming up against members of a far-right, armed militia today.

"That being the case, us working together today as a tight team will mean everything. We must, at all costs, aim to get Isaac Lightfoot and Professor Catawnee out alive as well as detaining Seth Soul and his sons."

"Thanks, John.

"Okay! Along the way we'll be guided on the ground by the helicopter officers. Keep your radio channels open!"

6

The squad car John, Walter and Drake travelled in, led the rest. A whole team of officers were travelling in squad cars, some in four-by-fours with capacity to secure arrests. A black Mariah vehicle followed up at the rear as they headed out onto the State Highway.

After an hour, or so, on the road, the helicopter crew announced that an ambulance and saloon car had come to a halt.

The helicopter crew spluttered and crackled onto Walter's radio.

> "They've come to rest in a circular clearing surrounded by woodland. They're within the old disused, Natural Coal Company land. We can see couple of disused corrugated iron coal mine buildings in the clearing; light is failing but we can see other vehicular lights, approaching the site. There are others on foot arriving, some carrying flaming torches; bonfires have been built in an arc in front of the two derelict cabins.
>
> "There be could twenty, maybe as many as thirty people on-site. Over."

Walter responded:

"That's fine. Let's be clear, we don't want you to land in the clearing. What I want from you, is to land somewhere safe and discreet on the Lehigh land where we can call you in a moment's notice. I have a feeling in my gut that we're gonna need you for urgent transportation."

"Okay, Walter, we'll be there and respond whenever you call us in."

"By the way, when you arrive, this clearing has an entrance about two cars' width. When you arrive, you'll need to block it off. Most of the people have parked inside the clearing. You block 'em in then you'll corral them and get as many as possible into custody."

Day 7   7

Disused Natural Coal Company Land – Lehigh
State of Oklahoma

Friday
November 8

Isaac sat in his wheelchair waiting inside a dilapidated corrugated hut. His mouth was taped, and his arms and legs were strapped to his wheelchair.

Watching people coming and going. He could smell bitumen in the air and the burning of unseasoned wood. He could hear drunken laughter; the loud sound of beating drums filled the air. Isaac's concern, however, was not for himself.

Looking over to the corner of the hut, Isaac saw Kamama had been summarily dumped; she was slumped, drugged and unconscious. Like him, Kamama's mouth was taped. Her long black hair was wet and matted with sweat; her head fell forward onto her chest.

The sight of Kamama broke his heart. When he had first arrived in the cabin, Isaac had seen Kamama when she was awake; he saw the terror in her eyes. Eventually a guy came in. He ripped the tape from Kamama's mouth and, holding her head back by her hair, forced a drink down her throat. Kamama gasped, gagging and spluttering water down her blouse. When she had finished, she tried to speak. Isaac watched as the '*Predator*' taped her mouth up again and kicked her with great force in the thigh.

"Shut up, bitch! You're lucky you're getting anything to drink at all."

Then, not long after Kamama had been given water, he injected her again; soon she slumped back into unconsciousness. On the way out, Kamama's minder turned to Isaac and ripped the tape from his mouth.

Soon, two other guys came in and they began pushing Isaac's wheelchair out and across rough ground to the cabin next door.

As they pushed him, Isaac looked around the clearing. When they had arrived, the sun had all but set; parts of the clearing were so dark now there was little to be seen. Isaac looked around the parts of the clearing that were lit by an arc of bonfires. He spotted a line of a half-dozen men and women using oil drums, drumming out new, more urgent rhythms. Isaac saw drunken people dancing, their twisted faces emerging between dark shadows and the flickering light from the fires.

Moving into the second cabin, Isaac looked around. There was a three-legged stool standing in the middle of the room; a pressurised kerosene lamp, lit the cabin; the lamp hissed loudly as it burnt its fuel. For a few moments Isaac watched, mesmerised, by the lamp, its light throwing shadows off his captors, moving around the walls.

Eyeballing the three men standing around him, it was Isaac who eventually spoke.

"I've seen guys like you in the newspapers; they were Russians though. I watched a video clip, from the war in Ukraine; their captives were all blindfolded and tied together and were being dragged across a road for their execution."

Isaac spat out another line.

"I know who you are; your 'infected' human beings, just

like those Russians. All '*Predators*'. I knew people just like you in my childhood. They killed and buried my best friend in a schoolyard, barrowed him into a hole in the ground, covered him with dirt and put down grass seed."

As Isaac spoke, he saw them waken. The three of them stepped forward and surrounded him. Suddenly, they dragged him out of his wheelchair and sat him on the stool in the middle of the room.

"There you are you fucking savage. Yeah! We know *you* so well! We Americans, we spent all that money on your 'education', cut your braids off, clothed you and now look at you! You've grown them back again."

They all laughed and jeered; their faces distorted in the yellow light of the lamp.

"You just can't get the 'savage' out of these folks."

One of the guys, taking out a knife from a sheath on his belt, stepped forward and cut Isaac's braids off, discarding them on the dirt floor; they laughed and forced him off his stool, kicking him in the face. Isaac spat out the grime and dust he had inhaled; blood poured from his nose. He dragged himself up, knelt and tried to get back onto the stool; he resumed his eye contact with each assailant.

Soon, they surrounded him, punching him to the floor; he spat broken teeth from his mouth at the feet of one of the '*Predators*'. Isaac forced himself to stand up so he could look at the men eye to eye. He swayed like a knocked-down boxer, looking each of them in the eye.

They laughed and pushed him to see if he would fall, but Isaac held his ground.

They grabbed Isaac's arms and dragged him back to the stool, his legs trailing behind him.

"Come on. You ain't standing now."

The door suddenly opened and Isaac, sat bent double on the stool; raising his head and saw a hooded '*Predator*' enter the cabin; he was wearing a leather mask with a breathing hole and slits cut so he could stare out into the room without being recognised.

"Okay, guys, that's enough! We don't want him dead yet. Get him back in his wheelchair and we'll take him out to see our other friends. Before you go, I've just got one ritual to perform."

Before they left the cabin, Isaac watched as the hooded man approached him with a thick black felt pen and wrote 'PAGAN' in big capital letters across his forehead. Then, walking over to the corner of the cabin he brought back a fake Indian headdress and secured it on his head while others tied his hands behind his back and bound his feet.

"There you are, *'Chief of the Pagans'.*"

On the door being opened Isaac felt a few spots of heavy rain; he saw the area was surrounded by plumes of smoke and bonfires. There was an avenue of men and women with distorted faces, men and women with lank hair, some with missing teeth. Beyond them he saw a gantry had been erected with a noose dangling from a heavy beam.

The crowd had come prepared with bags of rotting food and excrement, bottles of urine and fetid animal entrails. Isaac was dowsed, pelted and smeared.

Isaac ducked and weaved as best he could; he understood what had happened to these people; this was not their fault. In his mind, he understood their minds had been 'infected' by the twisted and evil Catholic 'Doctrine' of the past; they'd grown into adults from children who had suckled their mother's breasts, while their heads had been filled by the teachings of the *'Corleone Christ'*.

The executioner turned back to examine the gantry as two other men supported Isaac to stand on a thick metal sheet spanning the trench with the glowing embers of the fire below.

"So, this isn't just a simple hanging contraption that we 'honour' you and the 'professor' with today. As you can see, we've lit a fire of wood and coals in the trench underneath, just to warm the proceedings; this isn't a gantry with a quick 'drop' to break your neck and it's all over. It's a gentle drop for you to take on the battle against death, from the burning fire below or strangulation from the noose above.

"Of course, Spanish cavaliers invented these executions in groups of thirteen. They were sacrifices made in honour Jesus Christ and His Apostles.

The hooded man stepped forward. His blue eyes shone through the slits in his leather hood.

"After you, Isaac, comes the 'professor'.

"Of course! What am I telling you this for, you know all about it, Isaac?"

Isaac looked through the leather holes of the mask, deep into his eyes.

"We know from when we listened in on you, Isaac. You and Wohali, plotting with the 'Festival', you had both read all about Columbus and his cavaliers. You encouraged Wohali to read the recorded events from the invasion of Hispaniola; we know you and Wohali both read what the priest travelling with Columbus, wrote down.

"We know all about your scheming ways; you're planning with the 'International Festival of the Earth', for your people's liberation; you want to force us into law reform and constitutional change. You want your land transferred back into your ownership. The 'Festival's' idea is that First Nation peoples', all over the world, will stop the Earth warming. See, Isaac, I know all about it.

"All I'd say, Isaac, is this is *our* 'Promised Land' and *our* Lord, Jesus Christ anointed us with the power of 'Manifest Destiny' to rule it for eternity; the long line of Presidents who have led our great Nation, not one of 'em spoke otherwise! Truth is, Isaac, if us white people weren't here, there would be no America!"

As he spoke, the people lurking in the darkness surrounding

them, cheered as they listened. Then, getting bored, they shouted, '*Come on! Less of the talking! String him up! String him up! String hi...*'

As the fire spluttered into life beneath Isaac, he felt more heavy spots of rain begin to fall again. He could smell that wood soaked in bitumen from the old mine's railway ties, the billowing smoke and the fire crackling below him.

The hooded executioner's eyes glistened and shone, lit by the red glow of radiant heat.

"One last piece of advice. I've read those executioners dealing with their charges' executions by fire in Medieval times; they often gave some kindly advise."

Isaac smelt the alcohol-soaked breath of the hooded man as he came level with his ear, whispering his advice in a hiss:

"*Breathe in the smoke, Isaac. Breathe in this filthy black smoke, deep in those old lungs of yours. Pray it will see you off before the flames catch your feet!*"

"Any final words, Isaac, before you leave?"

Isaac looked again past the crude leather holes, into the blue eyes of his executioner.

"If you truly saw yourself, you'd go hang yourself from a sturdy branch in that woodland over there. If you were a Christian, you'd know Judas did the very same; once he was 'shown' by his God, who he had truly become; famously he hung himself. You, my friend, are a betrayer of your God's Son, Jesus Christ; evil men in the Vatican poisoned you and your ancestors, they made a fascist ideology just for the likes of you; they were criminal men who loved the Roman Empire, *not* the Holy Roman Empire."

Suddenly, the drumming stopped.

The men behind Isaac pulled his head back by his hair, far enough for him to look skyward; peering upwards he saw in the dark shadows two shining golden eagles gliding above him. In that moment he knew the Great Spirit and the Great Mother would hold him close. Then, as the men behind him slipped the noose over his head, they lifted Isaac's bruised body off the warming metal sheet he stood on, letting him swing above the fire.

Suddenly, the drumming recommenced and strides of heavy rain streaked onto the fire below.

Men and women danced and laughed, as Isaac began to breathe the acrid smoke deep down into his lungs.

8

The force that Walter and John led to the derelict coal land had found their position at the head of the clearing. Officers were instructed to encircle the edge of the woodland maintaining a silence.

Walter gave his instructions. "When you're in position, standby. Await my orders."

John could see through the trees and the failing light, to the flaming bonfires and the revellers, their bodies jerking and dancing to a primitive rhythm. John could see four, maybe five men and women all hammering out their beats on empty oil drums.

There were, as the helicopter pilot had described, two corrugated cabins which hadn't yet been consumed by the surrounding woodland. Behind the cabins there was a silhouetted, rusting pit head and its winding wheel; an unsecured steel cable swung lazily from the rusted mine shaft winding gear. As it swayed and clanked while heavy rain began to fall in the evening breeze.

Suddenly the drumming stopped.

In the shock of silence the police officers, standing on the edge of their wooded boundary, began to understand for themselves what was being created in the clearing; it was a vision from Hell itself.

Walter, hearing the drums go silent, ordered his force to move forward in an arc; all wore helmets and visors, some carried their riot shields and batons, while others sported automatic weapons.

Eventually, the crowd of revellers, seeing that an organised police presence was armed and advancing, tried to take the battle to them. As the opposing sides clashed, and in the cut and thrust of the action, police officers took blows on their shields, but at the same time began making arrests, immobilising assailants with their batons; a few, in the chaos of battle, made it into the surrounding woodland and melted away.

Meanwhile, John and Drake had quickly advanced through the battle-lines, toward the two cabins. Their mission was to find and release Isaac and Kamama. As they stood at the arc of the bonfires, John immediately saw the erected gantry that had been built and a man's body hanging from it, hands tied behind his back.

Drake had never met Isaac; he saw a body that had been left to struggle and swing on a short length of rope and noose; his bare feet reaching down toward the heat of the fire below.

Drake found himself transfixed; he was rooted to the ground.

John shouted his orders to him.

"Drake, move yourself! Take two officers alongside, lift Isaac's weight and cut him down."

Drake, taking John's orders, sprang into action, rushing toward Isaac and, standing astride the gantry's trench of fire, held up Isaac's weight. His height enabled him to lift and cradle Isaac's body weight, lifting his feet from the fire; the two officers worked together cutting the rope, to free him.

John radioed through.

"Walter, we've found Isaac. Drake and a couple of officers are making him safe now. You need to call in that 'copter right now."

Drake, having taken the strain of Isaac's body weight, safely lowered him to the ground, away from the smoke and fumes.

As Drake checked Isaac's airway was open, he found a faint pulse in his neck, then immediately began CPR. The welcome sounds of the helicopter landing were soon accompanied by the arrival of two paramedics; they brought oxygen with them and immediately took over clinical responsibility.

John, however, found himself distracted now that Isaac was safe; he was doing all he could to locate Kamama. He shone a powerful flashlight all over the ground. In his mind he'd begun to think the unthinkable: *Has Kamama already been executed?*

Turning back to the cabins, John suddenly thought he saw a dark animal shape moving through the smoke. Its head seemed to him to briefly turn towards him, showing a glimpse of two amber-green eyes. He dismissed it as a trick of the firelight and smoke, then continued to search for Kamama, either dead or alive.

John entered one of the cabins, illuminating all corners with his flashlight. Looking through the beam, there was no sign of Kamama amidst the grime and rubbish of the cabin. Making his way out, John ducked a hurricane lamp and tripped over a blood-spattered three-legged stool.

He made his way into the second cabin.

Again, looking around in the gloom, John was again spooked as his flashlight beam picked up the reflected movement of two amber-green eyes moving away from the back of the cabin. Shining his torch in that direction, he saw a man standing over what looked like Kamama's body; he was smacking her face and shouting, "*Wake up you bitch! Wake up!*" John ran forward. Grabbing the man by the collar, he pulled him away, then taking hold of his baton, clubbed him unconscious to the ground.

Kneeling, John quickly reached out to find a pulse in Kamama's neck. He found one! John screamed into his radio, "Walter! She's here! Kamama's in the second cabin."

Then, lifting her up in his arms, John carried Kamama out through the corrugated iron door. As he carried her, Kamama's head and legs dangled over both of John's arms; those nearby watching could see tears and rain streaking down through the grime on his face, as he walked carefully through the swirling smoke and pouring rain. As he walked carefully forward, and in what little light that was left from the bonfires, the gantry still cast a fearful shadow.

The line of drums was silent; the drummers themselves had fled.

John carried Kamama to where the helicopter had landed; he gently lowered her down into the care of the paramedics. Looking down, John bent over to tenderly move strands of hair that had stuck to her face, mixed with the muck and dirt from the cabin floor, knowing he had to leave, he stroked her face.

"Please look after her."

Quickly, John made his way back to the cabin, and there he cuffed the man he'd left unconscious, lying on the floor. As he cuffed him, he glanced down to the man's right forearm, as he snapped the cuffs tight. John saw the man's right arm carried an infected bite wound; he immediately knew this was one of the Soul brothers. It was the brother who'd assaulted and clubbed John at the retreat. John looked around the cabin and found a bucket of water. Standing astride the man's head, John doused him until he stirred, then, dragging him to his feet, he took his detainee to the black Mariah parked in the middle of the clearing.

"Lock this guy up good and tight, on his own. He's one of the Soul brothers. We've been looking for him for days."

On his way back to the cabin John found Walter. He'd begun to realise he'd lost contact with Drake.

"Have you seen Drake? I've lost sight of him. I found Kamama, she's alive; but now I've lost Drake."

Walter said he hadn't seen Drake since he had carried Isaac to the safety of medical attention. "John, you need to know, Isaac is still alive; probably touch and go. Drake and a couple of my officers did a great job getting him off that gantry.

"By the way, we've arrested seventeen, eighteen of them. I've called in the CSI. I've nominated a commanding officer to lead and another shift of officers to secure the scene once we've finished here. I'm hoping Seth Soul, and his sons are amongst them."

John extended an arm around Walter's shoulders.

"Well, I've just taken the nineteenth. He's definitely one of the Soul brothers; gotta say now, your officers have been the best, Walter. But I've got more to do."

John made his way back toward the helicopter thinking Drake might still be there. As he approached the cabins again, he heard a diesel engine start up. A vehicle had been hidden there on the blind side to the cabins, furthest away from where all the action had been taking place.

Instinctively, John drew his weapon and approached the vehicle; its engine was running in the dark. As its headlights switched on, John positioned himself in front of what looked like a dark-green four-by-four. In a flash, John knew this was *the* Ford Raptor F-150. He knelt down with his right arm and handgun extended alongside his left-handed flashlight beam, shining directly onto the windscreen.

Suddenly, the vehicle's blinding, full main-beam headlights were switched on.

With tyres spinning, the four-by-four careered toward John; he leapt and rolled aside. As he landed and broke his fall, John saw into the front and rear passenger windows passing by him. As he shone his flashlight, the beam briefly illuminated Seth Soul's grinning face; as they passed, he waved. In the back seat, John caught a glimpse a younger man, forcing Drake's face by his ginger hair against the window with the barrel of a handgun pressed to his head.

The Raptor sped toward the two squad cars, blocking the entrance to the clearing. Briefly, it stopped while the driver revved the engine. From a standing start the Raptor took off from the wet ground, bursting into the two squad cars; the driver reversed, revved the engine again and tried again to force their way from the clearing, this time making almost enough space to escape.

John contacted Walter through his radio.

"Walter, I'm pretty sure I've just seen Seth Soul and one of his sons trying to screech out of here in the dark-green Raptor. They've got Drake hostage. I can hear them trying to smash through the squad cars at the entrance for a second time. Won't be long, they'll be through and on their way. We need to understand, Drake's a traitor in their eyes, Walter; he's in serious trouble. I gotta do all I can to make him safe. I need a squad car and a couple of officers to get into pursuit. Okay?"

Walter's response spluttered, almost indecipherable to John's ear.

"*Yeah! Take what you need, John!*"

John quickly sourced a squad car and recruited the two officers he needed. They raced after the Ford Raptor which had now broken through the squad car cordon; then they raced down toward the entrance of the Natural Coal Mine land. As they made their way on down John saw the Raptor in the distance take a left turn onto the highway. One of the officers alongside looked across at John and gave him a clue as to where the Soul men were headed.

"Turning that way, they're headed north, back towards Oklahoma City, John. Reckon they could be defaulting back to their homestead? Surely, they have no other option."

John agreed.

"Yeah! Makes no sense for them to try and reach Thurmond. Our information is they've possibly been hanging out with a guy called Frank Denman. That brand-new Ford Raptor F-150 ain't Seth Soul's vehicle, that's for sure. Okay, guys, c'mon. We've gotta rescue Drake and bring in Seth Soul and whoever is with him."

John asked his police colleagues to contact Walter immediately.

"Tell him we need him to order another police squad vehicle, a four-by-four and four more officers as an emergency. We need a vehicle with the capacity to safely detain Seth Soul and three others. They need to make their way to the Soul family homestead right away. We need the four-by-four and officers to park at the homestead, out of sight, lights off behind the outbuildings.

"Inform Walter that we can't intervene on the road, they still have Drake Collins with them. Tell him we're quietly following them. The plan is we'll be coming up from behind and block off the homestead dirt road as an escape route.

"It is coming up to midnight. It has been a long night, guys and we ain't finished yet. It could be about to get a whole lot longer."

Eventually, the message came back from Walter.

"No worries, John. Good luck with the detention of Seth Soul. Just to reassure you, the helicopter has left here with Isaac and Kamama on board. They're in good hands, John. No worries about the four-by-four and additional officers from H.Q. They're on their way and will wait for you to arrive at the homestead."

Day 8

1

The Soul Homestead
Oklahoma

Saturday
November 9

I AM the Great Spirit
'I AM the Great Spirit,
I AM Khoi San,
A Cherokee, an Inca
And an Iroquois.
I AM an Inuit,
A Kuru,
A Warlpiri and a Chu.
I AM a Hebrew,
A Canaanite,
A Saxon and a Celt.
I AM Taoist,
A Buddhist,
A Hindu and
A Sikh.
I AM a Jew,
A Sephardi and
An Ashkenazi.

I AM Muslim,
A Sunni, a Sufi and
A Shea.
I AM Christian,
A Protestant and
A Catholic.
I AM the One
Eternal story
Spoken through
Creation's voice.'

Crossing the Red Sea – A Creation Anthology.
Isaac Lightfoot 1997.

It was past midnight.

John remembered the road the Ford Raptor would have turned onto to get to the homestead. He turned to Eddie, the officer in the passenger seat.

"Not far now. I'll leave a delay when we turn onto the dirt road; we'll wait while the Raptor makes its way and parks up. Our job then is to block the road and quietly hurry on foot. We'll then locate and join our support force who are hopefully, quietly hiding on-site."

John looked in his rear-view mirror and noticed that the officer seated in the back had drifted off to sleep.

"Hey, Chuck! Wake up. We're nearly at the Soul homestead."

Chuck jumped, instinctively reaching defensively for his weapon, then realised where he was and who he was with. He straightened out his helmet and uniform.

Halfway up the narrow dirt road, John turned and parked the squad car, blocking the single-track road for any oncoming vehicles, coming in or going out. All three of them got out of the car and shut the doors quietly. The night was quiet. There was a heavy cloud cover and no moonlight.

Gradually, they made their way through the surrounding woodland. When within a stone's throw of the homestead, they could see the Raptor's headlights; they had been left on, lighting the yard. There were three men; Seth Soul, almost certainly one of his sons, and Drake were making their way into the property. They left Drake to shuffle towards the door, his legs tied loosely together.

Seth looked behind him.

"C'mon boy, don't take all night getting inside. We got a plan for you to mull over. You made your choices, turned out to be a snitch, boy! Ain't that right?"

With the three men now inside, John, Chuck and the other officer, Eddie, ran bent double across the yard, attempting to locate the other officers. John and his team began skirting around the yard to find the additional officers and the four-by-four they had requested; the three of them moved slowly. Hugging the outline of the outbuildings, they tried not to be lit up by the Raptor's headlights. Then, cutting round the side of the last outbuilding, they found their four fellow officers sitting calmly in the dark.

John, Eddie and Chuck gathered around the four-by-four with the windows open, while John quietly briefed them and agreed a plan.

"Look, I know this building and have searched it recently. There is a back exit; two of you guard that exit, yeah? Good. The rest of us will enter the homestead with maximum force. That should be that. However, one of them could try and leave by the back. So, you guys will have that covered. If no one comes out the back, you'll join us to add more force to the raid. Okay?

"If we can't see Drake, Eddie, I want you to take personal responsibility for locating him. There's always the chance they'll use him as a hostage. They could have secured him upstairs in a bedroom. The layout is, at the top of the staircase there are two bedrooms either side on a landing."

On moving to take up their positions, someone had been out to turn off the Raptor's headlights. The driver and the two Soul men were lit up and visible with the house lights on; they were sitting at the wooden kitchen table. Drake was nowhere to be seen.

John, having left enough time for the back exit to be covered, counted the raid into action, on a count of three. With John leading from the front, the six officers exploded into action, first through splintering the frail front wooden doorframe and smashing the glass. Eventually the two officers at the rear entered, blocking off any escape route.

"Police raid! Get face down on the floor! All three of you, now! Hit the deck; I said face down, on the floor; hands behind your head where we can see them. Now!"

While the officers cuffed and secured Seth, his son and the driver, Eddie searched upstairs to locate and free Drake. John, meanwhile, loudly cautioned Seth and the driver. John clarified their names, leaving the father to explain his son's name was Charles.

At the same time, John read them their rights on arrest; he informed them they would first be charged with criminal conspiracy and the assassination of Wohali Lightfoot.

"Then we will be charging all three of you with the attempted murder of Isaac Lightfoot and Professor Kamama Catawnee. However, when we left Lehigh, both were in a state of unconsciousness; if either or both of them should lose the battle for their lives, there'll be two more murder charges on the sheet.

"This'll be presented to court where they'll decide your prison remand without bail; there ain't a court in the land that would ever agree bail arrangements."

While Seth, Charles and their driver were led to the secure transport in the police four-by-four, John asked Eddie to radio

Chief Banks, give him the news and also to request that this crime scene was secured for forensic examination.

"I suggest he could decide that a couple of the supporting officers stay behind to make sure the Raptor and the homestead are safe, waiting for the forensic team to arrive."

John crossed the yard and went over to see Drake. John smiled and shook him by the hand. He examined Drake's burnt trousers from his rescue of Isaac, then the burn injuries on both his legs.

"We'll need to get those examined and treated straight away. Good to see you though, Drake. Can't tell you how well you've done; not just today, but yesterday. I can tell you Isaac and Kamama went to hospital. Thanks to the work we all did, they're alive. The work you did to rescue Isaac was exemplary; you showed us what you're really made of.

"You should also be aware that later on today, because you told the truth, there'll be a raid on Frank Denman's house in Thurmond. Hopefully, we'll arrest him and eventually collect the evidence which will tie him into the pattern of prosecutions on the 'conspiracy' as we move forward.

"When we've got these guys back to police HQ, we'll need to get you to the city hospital to dress those burns. After that we're both gonna need a long sleep."

Before everyone got into their vehicles to leave, John remembered there was one quick call he needed to make.

"Hi, Phoenix, I know it's late. I'm just phoning in to report that Seth Soul and both sons are headed into custody for charging and remanding. By my reckoning this is the eighth day both of us have led this investigation, a great achievement. Of course, later on today the raid kicks off in Thurmond. I'd be grateful if you'd continue to maintain silence with Anna McKenna. Keep me informed."

"That's wonderful news, John; we'll debrief formally later. Sure thing, I ain't even gonna answer my phone any more tonight.

Charlotte kicks off from Beckley City with her assembled force at 9 a.m. Be so good to wrap all these arrests up; getting Frank Denman under lock and key for interrogation could mean we've decapitated this as a terrorist threat."

"Before we finish up, Phoenix, can you get a message through to Cary and Woya saying Isaac and Kamama are in hospital being treated for their different injuries. They're both alive but I don't know details. Isaac's clinical condition was described as 'touch and go'.

"Also, I have it in mind for you to ask Dina to arrange flights and hotel stays for you, Cary and Woya to travel tomorrow to visit Oklahoma Hospital. Oh, plus boarding arrangements for Ylva. I suggest we all meet up at the Skirvin Hotel tomorrow sometime late afternoon or evening."

"Will do, John. And, I have to tell you, you've done a great job!"

Day 8   2

Thurmond
West Virginia

Saturday
November 9

It was 8.30 a.m. and the weather was set fair; the sky was one unending stretch of blue; Frank Denman felt blessed by the morning sunshine.

Frank stood on the doorstep of his house; he was looking out for a visitor. He'd been busy over the last twenty-four hours. He could feel the winds of change blowing across the ghost town that was Thurmond.

As Frank stood on the doorstep, he was anxious to get news of what had happened to the second plan he and Seth had agreed to dispatch their enemies at the Natural Coal Mine land in Oklahoma. Silence, as always, was troubling him.

As he turned to go inside, make coffee and cook some breakfast, Frank heard a vehicle approaching. It was a yellow cab, delivering Frank's visitor. He walked toward the taxi passenger door and opened it for Jason Colbeck to get out; they shook hands; Frank warmly put an arm around Jason's shoulder.

"Welcome, Jason. I was just wondering what had happened to you. I know, you're a great stickler for time, but today, you're late."

Jason smiled broadly, then just went to the open passenger window, collected his bag and paid his taxi fare. Together they walked into Frank's kitchen where Jason sat on a high stool, catching up, while Frank made coffee.

"Well, Frank, good to meet you at last. Of course, I do feel I know you well; you've told me about working with my father back in the day. Of course, I know you knew my family well down here when I was a young boy. It's strange I have no memory of you in those days. But it's good to be with a friend right now and good to feel safe at last.

"As I said to you on the phone, the local police and the FBI will be hot on our tails. If you're still leaving here and travelling to South America, I'm sure looking forward to becoming your travelling companion and right-hand man, if you need me."

"Look, Jason, your father would be proud of you today. We will have some coffee and breakfast, then I'll take you over to the barn, show you your accommodation. We'll talk about the plans for us both after you've settled in."

"Sure, Frank, breakfast would be great, I'm really hungry."

"I won't show you round the house, right now it's all under wraps in preparation for us leaving; cleaners and decorators are coming over later today to spruce the place up. I want it to look its best to attract someone who will pay for a rental and live here for a while."

3

After breakfast Frank stood up and both he and Jason cleared up and filled the dishwasher with the dirty crockery and cooking utensils.

"Okay then, Jason, let me get you over to the barn. After I've settled you in, I need to drive over to Beckley City, get some supplies and talk to my real estate agent to get this property on the market and hand over some keys."

Frank went to the back of the kitchen where his coats were hung. He lifted a black leather jacket down and gestured to the door so Jason could go ahead.

"Looked like rain very early this morning, but now it's just glorious."

As they walked over to the barn Jason asked how the work was progressing at the Natural Coal Mine land.

"Well, Jason, I'm a bit concerned that I've heard nothin' this morning. Don't suppose you know anything from an FBI intelligence point of view, do you?"

"Well, no, Frank. I'm on the run now. They'll have known for twenty-four hours now that I was responsible for the death of Suzanne. I know exactly what they'll have done; Phoenix Shultz, she'll have reviewed the internal footage from Suzanne's cell and the custody suite; there'll be an internal inquiry and a post-mortem; Phoenix will have spoken to my wife, she thinks I'm in Eugene, Oregon. But soon my wife and children will know I have defected."

"So, do you think they have my identity, Jason?"

"I have no idea, Frank. It depends what Drake told Phoenix in his interview."

Frank opened the door to the barn and ushered Jason in.

"Never mind now, Jason, that's the past. Now we're both going forward to a different future. Let me show you our woodworking machine room. Seth Soul, you know him of course, he made a gantry in here for last night's event at Lehigh. But whether his gantry executed Isaac Lightfoot and Professor Catawnee I have no idea as yet."

Jason was impressed and admired all the new equipment. As they turned to go upstairs to see the living space, Frank stopped in his tracks.

"Oh! I almost forgot. I showed this little facility to Seth which he thought was neat; I must say I am really proud of this feature."

Frank bent down, lifted the square of wooden covering with a small brass ring; he pulled on the ring and revealed the stairs and storeroom underneath.

"Have a look, Jason; it's a neat addition for any storeroom and took a bit of digging out and building."

Jason made his way down the steps, marvelling at the engineering.

"Wow, that *is* a clever addition. A room like this will be hard for anyone to find. No one would ever know it was here."

As Jason turned to climb the stairs out, he saw Frank standing at the top of the flight. Frank's face was unsmiling; he held a High Standard HDM pistol with an integral silencer in his right hand. He held Jason's travelling bag in his left.

"I'm sorry about this, Jason, you just got too close to me. You're carrying the whole story of the 'conspiracy', Suzanne

Woodman, let alone Wohali Lightfoot. You know everything we've ever talked about. Maybe you'd say I coerced or threatened you to kill and silence Suzanne. Maybe you'd make a deal? You even know that I'm headed for South America; so, you'll know I can't risk leaving you alive.

"You're my first, Jason."

"Frank don't, you do… "

Frank threw Jason's bag down the steps, throwing Jason off balance back to the bottom. Then he pumped three bullets into Jason's head, closed down the entrance to the storeroom and secured the brass ring in place. Finally, he inserted the disguise for the wooden flooring, hiding the brass ring below.

Ever cautious, Frank had organised a contingency; a private jet charter at Beckley City Airport was waiting for him; he had just a couple more tasks to complete. He locked the doors to the barn and the house. Then he crossed the yard, and then drove his car to the nearest auto salvage yard to be destroyed; Frank had organised a taxi to take him and his hand luggage to the airport.

4

It was 9.30am and Charlotte Linklater had arrived at Beckley City Police HQ.

She was welcomed by Chief of Police, Joe Brandon. He showed her through to their briefing room, where a force of some ten officers and their head of forensic services were waiting.

Joe introduced Charlotte to everyone; then he spoke to his officers about Frank Denman. He told them about his history as the son of a mining family.

"Some of you are old enough and your families will have spoken about Frank Denman. As a young lad of sixteen after his father and brother died in the Springfield Mining disaster, Frank became a local 'poster boy' leading the men back into work. Then some of you may know that he had a long career in local mining. Frank's last working role was as a CEO managing Natural Coal, finally through to closure."

Joe Brandon turned directly to Charlotte.

"Let me be clear, Charlotte, many of us find it hard to consider that this local man may have become the leader of a home-grown terrorist conspiracy, with the aim of destabilising the nation's efforts to abandon coal, in favour of the climate. Many of us here in this room, well, we have family roots in coal. Frank Denman is a significant figure amongst the roots of our community."

Joe Brandon turned back to his officers.

"Today, though, we've got to work with our friend and colleague, Charlotte Linklater from the FBI. We'll be raiding Frank Denman's property in Thurmond by force. Anything you want to add, Charlotte?"

Charlotte stepped forward.

"Thanks, Joe. Well, I can hear this is a difficult mission for you all here in West Virginia today. I'm hearing it's hard for you to consider that Frank Denman should warrant this attention. To you, he's a man of high integrity. He ain't on your radar, but he is on ours. Some of you in this room might remember Suzanne Woodman, another local person. It was Suzanne who provided Frank with huge support at Natural Coal as a PA.

"After the closure of Natural Coal, Suzanne continued to support and work for Frank. But this time she'd bought into his plans to rescue the coal industry, and their work became a criminal enterprise.

"We have clear evidence that Suzanne was our prime suspect for the murder of George Stanhope, one of our most senior and distinguished executive leads; she never got to interview, let alone trial. Suzanne sadly died in custody in Washington DC from barbiturate poisoning. We believe that Frank Denman ordered her to be silenced by an FBI internal 'mole', Jason Colbeck. In the last few hours, we've learnt that Frank Denman knew the Colbeck family from way back as far as the Springfield Mine disaster. Jason himself, previously a well-respected FBI officer, is on the run.

"For all we know, Colbeck could be hiding out with Frank Denman. My orders today are that we use the warrant you've obtained to pull his property apart. We're looking for IT devices, papers, bank accounts, weapons, anything which will help us to convict the people we know have worked within Denman's conspiracy. On the forensic side we want all the usual technical evidence; prints taken, DNA and any other materials removed and bagged for testing and examination. Our most senior forensic scientist, David O'Donnelly, will join forces with you from our DC Offices to help complete the work."

Chief Joe Brandon thanked Charlotte. The assembled force then moved into action.

The force arrived at Frank Denman's property at 11.53 a.m.

On arrival Chief Brandon hammered on the door. There was no answer. He then stood aside while force was applied. Before entering, Chief Brandon ordered that the barn across the yard be opened by force and searched.

In the main house all the rooms were covered with dust sheets. The generated electricity was shut down. It was immediately clear that Frank Denman had left. In the kitchen the officer looking through drawers, cupboards and the pantry noticed the dishwasher was still cooling. Charlotte and Chief Joe Brandon increasingly began to see this as evidence that Frank Denman had just recently left at speed.

Charlotte turned to Joe as they practically assessed the abandonment of the house.

"Chief, I think we've got to call the airports, send the photographic likeness we have of Denman; we need him arrested and detained for questioning."

Gradually the officers searching the main house began to bring out boxes of materials, devices and papers from the property's small office. The forensic officer searching for prints declared the kitchen and surfaces had recently been professionally cleaned and prepared for closure.

As they began to conclude their search of the house, the forensic officer examining the barn came over to speak to Charlotte and Joe.

"Look, we need you both to come over to the barn."

They were shown into the woodworking machine room.

The forensic officer on-site explained that a diligent rookie who felt he could hear a difference in the sound from walking on different parts of the floorboards, persisted in finding a disguised entrance in the floor. Joe and Charlotte were shown the rectangular wooden insert that had disguised the entrance to an underfloor storeroom.

As they lifted the secret entrance to the storeroom, Joe stood at the top of the short flight of steps; he looked down and he saw a man's body who had clearly been shot in the head.

He turned to Charlotte.

"You know this guy?"

Looking down into the storage space she saw Jason Colbeck lying at the bottom of the steps.

"Yep, that's my ex-colleague, Jason Colbeck. He went AWOL from work yesterday. Told his wife he was headed to Eugene, Oregon on FBI business. I can tell you with some confidence, Joe, this man is our FBI 'mole.'"

Charlotte stepped aside and phoned Phoenix so that Jason's wife could be informed.

After speaking to Phoenix, she phoned John.

Day 8 — 5

Oklahoma City

Saturday
November 9

It was 7 a.m. John Green woke in his hotel room. He remembered he needed to ready himself for a joint press conference with Chief of Police, Walter Banks at the Oklahoma City Police Headquarters at midday.

After breakfast was delivered to his room, John showered and dressed formally in his corporate armour for the occasion. His grey suit, white shirt and green tie was laid out on the bed. His black shiny shoes still sat on the floor of his hotel wardrobe.

At the back of his mind, he was aware Drake Collins was sleeping next door. John knew he didn't intend to expose him to the media circus; he left him a note under his door.

Before he left he knew he must phone through to Kay. Tomorrow he would be travelling back to Washington DC. John and Kay hadn't spoken for three days and last time they spoke, they hadn't parted on good terms.

As John made the phone call, Kay picked up.

"Hi, Kay. I'm just phoning to say I'm wrapping up the investigation with a press conference for the national news today and I am back in DC tomorrow. Of course, the work isn't finished by any means. But if you watch it, you'll hear what's been achieved and what's still left to achieve.

"For ourselves and our marriage, I know we've got a lot to cover."

"Okay, John. Thanks for letting me know. I will watch. I might sit with Brenda Stanhope and support her through it. George's death seems a million miles away now, but what you're telling me is it's coming back into focus.

"When you come back, you need to know I'm not ready for us to just resume our lives. I'm taking legal advice. I'd appreciate it if you book into the Lyle Hotel, and we'll work from there. The kids just think you're at work, which is true. Good luck with the press."

John knew this wasn't the time to say anything more. From his side of his personal life he knew his own feelings weren't at all cut and dried. Deep down, his feelings were confused.

6

As John and Chief of Police, Walter Banks entered the conference room there were rows of flashlight photography and microphones as they took their seats on the platform.

Walter, knowing the local press made a plea for calm, told everyone to be seated.

"Listen you all know the score. Ain't no good you all shouting questions. First of all, John Green, FBI National Executive Lead for the FBI, beside me, will make a statement, then I'll open the floor to three, maybe four questions, no more."

John made his statement.

"This all started with the assassination of Wohali Lightfoot at the Abraham Lincoln Memorial. Wohali was a respected, local Cherokee Nation leader who was working with the International Festival of the Earth, across the whole continent. It was he who gathered together two hundred First Nation representatives to lead the largest ever human gathering the world has seen, in support of healing our planet.

"His assassination was the starting point of a significant investigation over the last eight days. I feel it is important for me to say at this time, that assassination as a human communication is deeply imbedded in our culture. A while ago now President Trump was shot and wounded at a rally; a little later another assassination attempt was shut down by security services, on one of his golf courses! President Reagan survived an attempt. In the 1960s there were three unprecedented assassinations: President John F Kennedy in 1963, Dr Martin Luther King and presidential candidate, Robert F Kennedy, both assassinated in 1968. Further back in time of course, there have been others, most notably Abraham Lincoln himself, in 1865.

"On behalf of the American people, the FBI, together with the Oklahoma State Police, Chief Walter Banks and the Chief of Beckley City Police, Joe Branden, have uncovered a national and potentially an international, climate terrorist conspiracy.

"I have formally passed my own risk assessment to the attorney general, through my Director of the FBI, Anna McKenna. Today there are still others at risk; perhaps most notably, our own President who, like all Presidents, decides climate change policy, the presidential envoy for the climate and the CEO plus boardmembers of the International Festival of the Earth. That's just a preliminary risk assessment, there could be others.

"This conspiracy has tried to disrupt and destroy the vital work of our democratically elected, national and federal government. This includes the worldwide work of the International Festival of the Earth across our Continent.

"Over the last few days, I have personally witnessed at first hand, an attempt to eliminate a whole Cherokee family; the Lightfoot family. As I speak, Wohali Lightfoot's father, Isaac, remains at a secret location, in a critical condition after an attempt to execute him in a public lynching; a close friend and colleague, Professor Kamama Catawnee, was abducted from her university campus, drugged with ketamine and assaulted; she was next in line.

"Both these individuals are in an intensive care unit still fighting to recover from their ordeals: they are under tight security. Like Wohali Lightfoot, both his father and Professor

Catawnee, they were both actively supporting work on the American Continental Board of the Festival of the Earth.

"The rest of the Lightfoot family are currently residing in a safe house.

"Three individuals are in custody here at police headquarters charged with conspiracy to murder Isaac Lightfoot and Professor Kamama Catawnee: then also the murder of Wohali Lightfoot. The men detained are Seth Soul and his sons John and Charles Soul, all resident in the State of Oklahoma.

"While I'm mentioning the two individuals in hospital, I want to commend the action of Drake Collins, an FBI intern, who risked his own life and rescued Isaac Lightfoot from a gruesome execution. Behind the scenes all the members of my national service and local state police have undertaken their roles with bravery and distinction. I must also make mention of, and commend, the two-security guards we commissioned to protect Isaac at the Oklahoma Hospital; both lost their lives, murdered by John and Charles Soul, during Isaac Lightfoot's abduction. Our thoughts today are with their families.

"A joint Beckley City Police and FBI force raided the house of a suspect, Frank Denman, in Thurmond, West Virginia yesterday! During that raid an FBI officer, Jason Colbeck, who we now know was an FBI 'mole', was found brutally murdered in a disguised underground storeroom, probably only known to Denman himself.

"Unfortunately, the joint operations in Thurmond missed detaining Frank Denman for formal questioning. We have reason to believe Denman has fled the USA. Police inquiries tell us that he put his car in a local breakers yard where it was destroyed. Beckley Airport report that an older guy, meeting Denman's description, left on a pre-commissioned private jet.

"The FBI officer, Jason Colbeck, dishonoured his family, the FBI and the American people. In his activities as a 'mole' he was responsible for the breaching and misdirecting of restricted information; conspiring with others and coordinating the fatal attack on Wohali Lightfoot. Colbeck and his fellow conspirators then changed focus, to destroy Wohali's family and Professor Catawnee, who were assisting us, in the Great Smoky Mountains; then he also conspired with others and coordinated the murder of George Stanhope, FBI Executive Lead, a highly valued national servant, an expert in keeping our nation safe through the fight against terrorism. Our thoughts are with George's wife, Brenda and his family today.

"Colbeck worked behind the scenes with Denman and his closest colleague, Suzanne Woodman. She had infiltrated the Mall Maintenance Service, managing tourist services at the Lincoln Memorial. It was her who gave access for Wohali Lightfoot's assassins to hide out in the Memorial Undercroft. It was she who later murdered George Stanhope, tripping him onto the tracks of the DC Metro station, at Foggy Bottom. In the end Colbeck was responsible for Woodman's death in custody, delivering a fatal dose of barbiturates just prior to her interview with FBI agents.

"So, finally, there is much more to do on this case. For myself I will work tirelessly with state police to continue the work. I won't rest until this 'conspiracy' is fully dismantled. My opinion is that FBI and local state police have achieved a huge amount to get to this point in just eight days."

After John's statement, the press had a hunger and a desperation to find answers to their difficult questions. Eventually Walter allowed ten questions before calling time and thanking everyone for attending.

7

Following the press conference, John drove over to the Oklahoma Hospital. Arriving at reception, John was informed that a member of the medical team, Dr Kramer, wanted to see him before he visited either Isaac or Kamama.

Meeting Dr Kramer, John informed her that there was a party of three others coming down from Washington DC to visit later on in the day; Phoenix Schultz, Woya and Cary Lightfoot. Dr Kramer made it clear that both he and other visitors could spend just five minutes with Isaac and Kamama each. She made it clear that Isaac's health was very delicately balanced; while he was highly motivated to recover, there was much smoke damage to his lungs and significant burns to his feet and shins.

"These things will take time to heal. On top of these problems Isaac still needs access to his stem-cell treatment. Kamama, on the other hand, has suffered less physical injury. She is, however, showing signs of a deep psychological trauma; she needs rest and therapy further on to secure recovery. We can see that she was physically assaulted, there are no signs of any sexual assault occurring in the twenty-four hours or so that she was drugged and held hostage."

Before travelling on the escalator, up to Isaac's and Kamama's corridor, John phoned Phoenix.

"Hi, Phoenix, just wanted to touch base with you on visiting arrangements. I've spoken to Isaac's and Kamama's doctor. I don't know if you're going to visit yourself, but Woya and Cary can only visit giving Isaac and Kamama individually, five minutes to each.

"The same rules apply to me; I'm going to visit now; I'll see you on returning to the Skirvin Hotel."

"Good to hear your voice, John. No, I don't plan on visiting myself, I'll stay and work at the Skirvin Hotel. I'll use the time to catch up with Charlotte, she's done a great job down in Thurmond. That was a great press conference, John. Good job. I think Anna McKenna might be in touch with you, not sure she agrees with me though on your conclusions. We can talk more this evening and debrief over dinner."

"Talking of dinner, Phoenix, I've booked a room and a table so we can all gather together. I'm going to invite Walter Banks; he's become a good colleague and a friend. I want him to meet you, and also, I need to thank him personally for everything, even though the jobs not completed. The contribution of his local police officers on their confrontation, control and arrests at Lehigh was an exceptional operation."

"While you're on, John, I've got to ask you about Drake? Wow! That was an amazing thing you did, publicly highlighting his brave conduct."

"Yeah, well, I didn't see him before breakfast; I left him to sleep and rest. I'm hoping that like Esteban, he'll remain on our intern programme and work toward a long-term career. He has a lot to thank you for, Phoenix! Look, I have to go. See you tonight at dinner."

8

Coming out of the elevator onto Isaac's and Kamama's corridor, John found himself feeling anxious. On the way up he was thinking back to the traumatic images at Lehigh. The bonfires and the smoke; the drumming and the wild dancing of the revellers Seth Soul had assembled to witness the executions; then the scenes of both Isaac and Kamama both wounded, tortured and humiliated. John recognised his fears were about coming face to face with how these tragic events were affecting them now.

As John made his way along the corridor, he stopped for a moment to thank the two security guards looking after Isaac and Kamama; before entering, he checked with them which room Isaac was in, then knocked.

There was no answer, but John entered.

Taking a chair with him to Isaac's bedside he was shocked by his appearance. Gone were his long, elegant braids; his head had been shaved since being admitted to hospital. One of his eye sockets and his face were badly bruised; the doctor had explained Isaac had taken a kicking to his skull; his brain function was being carefully monitored. Isaac's neck, feet and shins, though, were loosely bandaged to support the recovery of his burns from both fire and the effects of the rope around his neck.

As John sat down beside Isaac, he quietly listened to him breathing oxygen through a mask. In the silence he looked into Isaac's face. John imagined Isaac the four-year-old child, bruised and battered from the corridor of the Dakota boarding school.

The banks of clinical monitoring systems beeped and flashed. Living graphs of light that sound-tracked Isaac's heartbeat, blood pressures and other vital signs; Isaac's situation was precarious, the machines just placed John on the edge of that cliff. During two of his five minutes John found himself reflecting on just how much he wanted to be in Isaac's living company again.

Eventually, John took Isaac's hand into his, feeling its warmth. Then, he found himself talking for a minute, updating Isaac on progress.

When his five minutes were pretty much used up, he still spoke a while longer.

"Hi Isaac, it's John. I'm here with you hoping and praying the Great Spirit, and that beautiful Tecumseh soul inside that black panther are here, looking over you. You are, after all, their witness for justice. So, if it's down to me to tell you, I'm gonna say, '*your job ain't finished yet, my friend*'."

Finally, John gently began to move his hand, preparing to leave. As he did so, Isaac's hand closed on John's, his eyes opened; moving his head sideways, Isaac looked John in the eye. As he tried to speak it was clear the oxygen mask prevented him from doing so. Responding to Isaac's eye movements, John pulled down the mask.

John listened as Isaac's haunting voice tried to speak in a rasping whisper. Isaac tried to clear his throat and tried again…

"The '*Predator*', John! I saw into the '*Predator's*' eyes…"

John nodded, holding Isaac's gaze.

"Understood, Isaac. We have some of the '*Predator's*' attack dogs, locked up now. We have arrested Seth Soul and his sons. I know you'll remember the name of Cary's family; it was his ice-blue eyes behind the jagged holes of that leather executioner's mask. I'm afraid the top dog *'Predator'* himself escaped us. That's my problem, Isaac. You can rest on me.

"I need you to get well, then you need those five stems-cell years. I'll see you again on the front line when you're ready."

John squeezed Isaac's hand.

"Take care, I'll be back."

John took time out in the corridor, leaning against a wall. He needed to clear his thoughts.

Then, knocking on Kamama's door, her weakened voice responded.

"Come in."

As John entered the room, he saw Kamama's tired smile shining out from her pillow. There were fewer monitors and no oxygen mask to obscure Kamama's face. Her long black hair had survived and framed her face as she sat up, resting on a large white pillow.

As John approached Kamama, he felt a tear trickling uncontrollably down his face; reaching forward, he gently kissed her bruised cheek.

"C'mon, John, you're supposed to be cheering me up, not shedding tears."

Kamama shuffled across her bed, making space for John to sit beside her. As he sat down, he reached forward and put the palm of his hand warmly onto her cheek. Kamama turned her head and kissed it.

"I know medical staff have given me just five minutes to see you. So, I know it's not *you* that is in a hurry. Not this time. It ain't Kay, Phoenix, Jason or Drake. It ain't Anna, Walter or Charlotte demanding your time; now it's those damn doctors restricting our time together."

John went to speak, but Kamama put a finger onto his lips.

"Shush! I'm guessing you're back to DC tomorrow."

Kamama nodded with a quizzical look in her eye.

"Am I right, John?"

John nodded.

"Well, in the two minutes we have left now, I gotta say a few words. I've been told you saved my life, John. When you found me, you clubbed some goon unconscious who was slapping my face and injecting me. Then, you carried me to safety. As if you hadn't done enough, I've heard you went back into that cabin, arrested my minder and locked him up."

"Yeah, you're right. That 'goon' was John Soul! All Cary's menfolk are locked up. Sal Soul, Cary's mother, remains in hospital herself."

Kamama smiled, a guffaw of laughter bubbled through the tears welling in her eyes.

"Good! What took you so damn long? You and me, John, we know we're soulmates now; we've got time ahead of us. But, right now, I must thank you sincerely, from the bottom of my heart."

They took each other, into one another's arms and held the warmth they shared for one another.

John stood up, still holding onto Kamama's hand.

"I'm going to be on your phone, Kamama; you know I've got some things to fix at home with my family. I won't be living at home; I'll be at the Lyle Hotel in DC; Kay has told me that. I think we'll be spending time discussing separation details. I'll be back, Kamama. I'm feeling we've both earnt some time together by then, but only if you'll see me.

"But, there *is* more to do, Kamama. We didn't get everyone we needed to get; I'm still going to need an advisor though, when you're good and ready."

Kamama smiled.

"I hope my pay grade has improved."

John leant forward and kissed Kamama on the lips, and Kamama reached her hand around the back of John's head, then, holding his forehead against hers, she whispered:

"C'mon, John. You've got to leave now. See you soon. Make it soon, *very* soon!"

9

In the evening at the Skirvin Hotel, John had booked enough table space for everyone who could get together. By John's estimation there were six people, including Walter Banks, to join him, raise a glass and give thanks to those involved; he had organised drinks, fruit and canapés, all laid out on a separate table. There was space for them to move around, talk and spend as much time as they needed.

After everyone had arrived, John, having given enough time for people to pour a drink and settle, tapped an empty glass with a small spoon, pulling everyone together.

"Well, tonight's a night for just saying, 'thanks. The last eight days have been some of the most difficult days of my career.

"In the present company of Woya, Cary and Danuwoa I first want to raise a toast of respect in the memory of Wohali Lightfoot: *'To the memory of Wohali, he was a husband and a son, a father and a leader of people.'*

"Then there are those who can't be here; Isaac, Kamama and Cary's mother, Sal; they remain in hospital.

"So, just a few words of thanks. Walter. Thanks so much for everything you and your officers have done, working this case with us. The same applies of course to Chief of Police, Joe Brandon at Beckley City force, who can't be with us.

"I want to say thanks to my own team. Phoenix, David, Charlotte, Jim and all our investigators.

"We know we've got so much more to do. Firstly, we have to organise and tie up all our evidence as we take forward our charges to secure sentences to fit crimes. Then finally, we have to find, arrest and charge Frank Denman, the mastermind of all the misery and pain we've seen created. We'll need to locate him, possibly in South America.

"So, I suggest now, we take time to enjoy our company tonight…"

John's phone rang.

"Excuse me, I've gotta take this…"

Moving into a private space John took the call.

"Hi, Anna. I was wondering if you would put in an appearance."

"I've got to remind you, John, it's taken eight whole days for you to close this case down. I would congratulate you, but you took too long!"

"Well, Anna, I hear you've still got that foul mouth of yours. If you listened to the press conference, you'll know the FBI and the local forces have done a good job.

"I am gonna say this only once, Anna. We ain't finished yet. There's the small matter of our needing to find Denman and decapitate the 'conspiracy.'"

"I have read your interviews on Wohali Lightfoot's record, John. All the 'political' stuff about the 'Doctrine of Discovery' the constitutional and legal questions about who owns North America, are not in our national interest to pursue. Also, I need to correct you here and now, there's no more work for you to do on this case. Denman is not your problem. He's left our country and we have no jurisdiction in South America.

"Indira Anand has spoken to me already. She's been asking for your further involvement. I've told her to work with her other partners in Brazil or any other country he may have flown to; she may approach you, but the answer is, n*o!*"

"Okay. While we're mopping up, you'll know Jason Colbeck's been found dead in one of Frank Denman's properties in Thurmond. Jason did a lot of damage, poor George and Suzanne Woodman and then a whole lot more!

"Then there's another small matter of your name being connected to the placement of Drake Collins with Jason Colbeck. Both of them were 'conspiracy' imports. Phoenix and I kept quiet about all that. We couldn't make up our minds whether your own integrity was compromised or not. We still don't know. At the time we gave you the benefit of the doubt. But neither of us trusted you then. Listening to you, I certainly don't now.

"Phoenix briefed me about your attendance at the service briefing on the 'Festival' event at the Capital Arena. All our intelligence was that further assassinations were likely at the Capital Arena. When nothing materialised, we decided not to inform you on the bust of Frank Denman's property in Thurmond. For us that was a precaution, just in case you might tip him off. Even then, Denman still got away."

Anna was silent. John let it ride.

"John, you don't have a shred of evidence."

"Not right now, Anna. But just wait until Denman is found and extradited to face U.S. justice. When we've got him back in DC and we come to charge him, we'll maybe listen and adjust his sentence in exchange for information. Let's not forget, Anna, FBI directors are political, presidential appointments. Under our constitutional arrangements, presidents can sack and investigate people like you, establishing the FBI directors *they* want. When I've finished escalating my concerns to the attorney general, our current President in office, might just decide you're far too high a risk for him."

As the call ended, John returned to speak with Phoenix.

"Hi, Phoenix, I have to get some rest soon. I know you'll look after these people for me. I need to take some time out, so

I'm putting in for leave from tomorrow. I'm sure Anna will want to keep me at arm's length and keep you acting in my executive role.

"I owe Kay and the kids some time now. Kay and I have a lot to sort out between us, our marriage is in trouble, it could be the end of a chapter.

"I have complete confidence in you, Phoenix, acting up into my role. You'll continue tying up these cases, formally charging them, racking up all the evidence, with David O'Donnelly preparing the prosecutions on Seth Soul and his sons. Between you and me, Anna has instructed me there'll be no further work on Denman, not our 'jurisdiction.'"

Phoenix thanked John for everything.

On leaving Phoenix, John went to spend time with Woya and Cary. He personally thanked them for their patience and said he wouldn't rest until everyone who should be brought to justice was found and punished.

Woya put an arm around John's waist and pulled him close to her.

"It feels like an age since Isaac, and I raised the electronic undercroft door at the retreat to find you and Kamama standing there. I'm glad you both came. Isaac and I are very thankful. Obviously, I haven't seen them yet; we're both praying Isaac and Kamama come through their ordeals."

John turned to Cary.

"Good to see you again, Cary. Isaac and Kamama weren't the only casualties. How's your mother, Sal?"

"I'm seeing her for the first time tomorrow. Yeah, thanks to you, she's recovering; she's rehydrated and though she is frail, she is strong in heart and soul. It's hard, John. My family as it was, is destroyed. Those men I truly hope will never see the light of day again. My plan is that my mother will live with Danuwoa and I; she'll become a real grandma now. A part of our lives."

"Sounds good, Cary."

John smiled a weary smile.

Cary put out a hand to shake with John, holding onto him before he could escape.

"So, finally, I've gotta thank you, John, for bringing the men to justice! Crazy men who planned and assassinated my husband. It's a hard lesson for us all that this evil lived inside these men who considered themselves to be Christians. Of course, they're nothing to me now."

John smiled and told Cary he was pleased some things had worked out for her. Then, taking his hand back from Cary's grip, John gave his apologies, saying he needed to make a call home and get some sleep.

"We will all talk more when we travel back to DC tomorrow, together. If you'll excuse me, though, I have to get some sleep."

Taking the escalator to his room John's phone rang. It was Indira Anand.

"John, sorry to bother you tonight; I've heard you've been closing down the first stage of your investigation."

"That's okay, Indira, I just need some sleep, then I'll be back on form. What can I do for you?"

"Well, I've been speaking to Anna McKenna about extending your investigation to bring Frank Denman to justice. She and the attorney general are adamant, they've finished.

"So, I can kinda see the points Anna described to me; the U.S Federal Government has no interest in pursuing Denman now. They have no constitutional interests.

"I understand that nations, built on the fake foundations of Christian theology and brutal colonial values of the 'Doctrine of Discovery' are going to find it hard to work with the 'Festival' on this? They just ain't gonna renegotiate their constitutions; agree genuine power-sharing institutions and values to heal the planet just like that. The Australian government has been through a referendum to reconstitute and share power with their Aboriginal communities; the Australian European descendent electorate failed to agree a single legal step away from their colonial roots.[49]

"But still, I've been talking to our chairperson of the 'Festival' Board. We want you to join *us*, John; please consider a secondment into a very highly paid role as our undercover investigator. We want you to seek out where Denman is hiding in South America, then bring him back to the U.S., to face justice and life in prison. If you're successful, we'd want to employ you on our international board as our security advisor, long term."

"Sounds like you're looking for a 'bounty hunter'. You'll need a lot more money than just funding my salary, Indira."

"Anna is prepared to consider a secondment for you, John; plus, she has agreed cooperation and information from the FBI in tracking Denman down. A few board members will want to meet secretly, away from the gaze of public minutes and reporting, with you and me. This will be about the task, the risks, the resources you would need and, ultimately, what it will cost.

"Okay, Indira, I'll do what you ask. I'll consider it and let you know."

Ending the call, John made his way wearily along the corridor to his room; he took out the plastic entry card from his wallet, closed the door, went to bed and slept.

References

1. Tecumseh. Shawnee Chief and Warrior. 1768 – 1813
2. Dum Diversus, Papal Bull, 1452. Pope Nicolas V
3. Trove of damning Xinjiang police files leaked as U.N. Rights chief visits China. Published: Washington Post May 24 2022 at 8.55 a.m. EDT. By Lily Kua and Cate Cadell.
4. 'The Honor Song.' Jeremy Dutcher and Yo Yo Ma: Album, Notes for the Future, Copyrighted to Sony Music Entertainment / Sony Corporation.
5. 'The Burning' The Tulsa Race Massacre of 1921. Tim Madigan. Published 2001. St Martins Publishing Group.
6. 'Amazonia': Life and Death in the Brazilian Rainforest.' Tommaso Protti. Reliefs Foundation Carmignac and authors. Language. French, English · Publisher: RELIEFS. Publication date. November 7, 2019.
7. 'Four Steps for the Earth.' Published CelPress, 'One Earth' 4 January 22, 2021. Lead Author, Professor E.J. Milner-Gulland / Oxford University
8. 'The Pale Blue Dot', A Vision of the Human Future in Space. Author, Carl Sagan. First Published 1995 by Headline Book Publishing. A division of Hodder Headline PLC, 338 Euston Road, London, NW1 3BH
9. 'The Vatican repudiates 'Doctrine of Discovery,' which was used to justify colonialism' MARCH 30, 2023 1:38 PM ET by Bill Chappell, NPR
10. 'Trump Uses Speech to Deliver Divisive Culture War Message.' Published with video: New York Times. July 2020
11. Myles Standish (c. 1584 – 1656), Captain of the Pilgrims. Author, John Stevens Cabot Abbott (September 19, 1805 – June 17, 1877). Digital Edition published by Stingray, June 2014. First published 1872, Cornell University Library's print collection, scanned on

APT BookScan and converted to JPG 2000 format by Kirtas Technologies.
12. Education for Extinction. David Wallace Adams. American Indians and the Boarding School Experience 1875-1928. Published 1995 by University Press of Kansas
13. Informant Told Feds Proud Boys 'Would Have Killed' Pence on January 6. The Daily Beast. AJ McDougall / Breaking New Reporter. Published Jun. 16, 2022
14. Proud Boys and the White Ethnostate. How the alt right is warping the American Imagination. Alexandra Minna Stern. Published Beacon Press. April 7, 2020
15. Black Elk, 1863.
16. Constitution of the Cherokee Nation. (first Constitution 1827) Second, Passed at TAHQUAH, CHEROKEE NATION, 1839. Printed by Gales and Seaton Superseded in 1976. 2021 Cherokee Nation Reservation treaty rights approved Oklahoma Court of Criminal Appeals.
17. A sorry saga. Obama signs Native American apology resolution; fails to draw attention to it. Indian Country Today. By Rob Capricossio. Published January 13, 2010.
18. Tecumseh. A life. Dr John Sugden. Published: 2 July 2013. Henry Holt and Company.
19. C Nakai: Death Song: Changes: Native American Flute Music (Canyon Records Definitive Remaster) North America 1983: Lossless
20. 'Kill the Indian Save the Man' Gaylord College of Journalism and Mass Communication, University of Oklahoma. By Addison Kliever, Miranda Mahmud and Brooklyn Waylord. Gaylord News.
21. 'Truth and Reconcilliation Commission of Canada calls to action.' Published 2015 Catalogue Number / IR4-8/2015E-PDF. 'Aboriginal peoples Residential Schools'.
22. 'Bringing Them Home': The 'Stolen Children' report (1997). Report of the National Inquiry into the Separation of Aboriginal and Torres Strait Islander Children from their families. Australian Human Rights Commission.
23. 'Federal Indian Boarding School Initiative Investigative Report'. May 2022. Assistant Secretary – Indian Affairs, Brian Newland, submission to United States Department of the Interior Secretary, The Honorable Deb Harland, April 1, 2022.

24. 'Whanaketia ki te tihi o Maungarongo' – Through pain and trauma, from darkness to light.' Presented to the Governor General by the Royal Commission of the Inquiry into historical abuse in State Care and the Care of Faith based institutions. July 2024
25. 'One Thousand Children' *Wikipedia*
26. THE SPINOFF. 'Our stolen generation: a slow genocide' Aaron Smale, ATEA November 17, 2017
27. 'The Impact of the American Doctrine of Discovery on Native Lands in Australia, Canada, and New Zealand. (2011) Blake A Watson. University of Dayton, Law Faculty Publications School of Law. 2011
28. A Brief Account of the Destruction of the Indies by Bartolome De Las Casas. First published, 1552 printed by Sebastian Trugillo at the port of Seville, Spain. The Project Gutenberg Ebook (giving access at no cost under the Project Gutenberg Licence). The original archaic spelling and punctuation has been retained.
29. Tecumseh. A life. Author, Dr John Sugden. First Published in hardcover i1997 by Henry Holt and Company. First Owl Books Edition 1999. First ebook edition June 2013.
30. 'Hitlers American Model' The United States and the Making of Nazi Race Law. James Q Whitman. With new preface by the author. Princeton University Press, Princeton and Oxford 2018.
31. 'The Falling Sky' WORDS OF A YANOMAMI SHAMAN. David Kopenawa, Bruce Albert. Translated by Nicholas Elliot and Alison Dundy. The Belnap Press of Harvard University Press, Cambridge, Massachusetts, London, England. 2013
32. Ailton Krenak. 'Ideas to postpone the end of the World'. First Published in English 2020, House of Anansi Press Ltd, Canada.
33. The Counterstrike: Brazilian Congress moves to block Lula's environmental agenda. Source: Mongabay Environmental News. By Andre Schroder, 1 June 2023
34. The Incredible Human Journey. The story of how we colonised the Planet. Alice Roberts. First published in Great Britain 2010. Bloomsbury Publishing
35. The Invaders: How Humans and their Dogs Drove Neanderthals to Extinction. Pat Shipman. Published 2015 The Belknap Press Harvard University Press Cambridge, Massachusetts London England

36. Sapiens: A Brief History of Humankind. Yuval Noah Harari. First Published 2011 in Israel. Then September 4 2014, Random House
37. Earth system impacts of the European arrival and Great Dying in the Americas after 1492: Quaternary Science Review: vol 207, 1st March 2019
38. 'The Godfather'. Mario Puzo. New York, G.P. Putnam's Sons, 1969
39. 'The Spanish Requirement (Requiromento) of 1513' by Mark Cartwright.Published, WHE 18 August 2022
40. Library of Congress, U.S. Reports: Johnson v McIntosh, 21 U.S. (8 Wheat.) 543 (1823) Marshall John (Judge) Supreme Court of United States (Author)
41. 'Unsettling Truths' by Mark Charles and Soong-Chan Rah. ISBN 10: 0830845259 ISBN:13 9780830845255. Publisher: Inter-Varsity Press, US, 2019
42. 'The LAND is NOT EMPTY, following Jesus in Dismantling of the Doctrine of Discovery' by Sarah Augustine. Published 2021 Herald Press PO Box 866, Harrisonburg, Virginia 22803. 800-245-7894 www.HeraldPress.com.
43. 'Pagans in the Promised Land' by Steven T. Newcomb. Fulcrum Publishing 2008
44. Nazi Germany's Race Laws, The United States, and American Indians. Robert J Miller: Journals at St John's Law Scholarship Repository, St, Johns Law Review, Volume 94, 2020, Number 3
45. 'Why we can't wait', Martin Luther King Jr: Published by Penguin Books 1963.
46. 'Hitlers OstKrieg and the Indian Wars. Comparing Genocide and Conquest.' Edward B Westerman. Published 2016. The Kerr Foundation.
47. 'Hitlers American Model' The United States and the Making of Nazi Race Law. James Q Whitman. With new preface by the author. Princeton University Press, Princeton and Oxford 2018.
48. 'A Brief Account of the Destruction of the Indies' by Bartolome De Las Casas. First published,1552 printed by, Sebastian Trugillo at the port of Seville, Spain. The Project Gutenberg Ebook (giving access at no cost under the Project Gutenberg Licence). The original archaic spelling and punctuation has been retained.
49. The Failure of Australia's Attempt to Create an Indigenous Voice: The New Yorker: Naamah Zhou / October 19, 2023

This book is printed on paper from sustainable sources managed under the Forest Stewardship Council (FSC) scheme.

It has been printed in the UK to reduce transportation miles and their impact upon the environment.

For every new title that Troubador publishes, we plant a tree to offset CO_2, partnering with the More Trees scheme.

For more about how Troubador offsets its environmental impact, see www.troubador.co.uk/sustainability-and-community